The Warlord of Thach Hanh
By
Michael R. Conroy

The Warlord of Thach Hanh
First Edition

Published by:
Biographical Publishing Company
95 Sycamore Drive
Prospect, CT 06712-1493
Phone: 203-758-3661
Fax: 253-793-2618
e-mail: biopub@aol.com

Publisher's Cataloging-in-Publication Data

Conroy, Michael R.
The Warlord of Thach Hanh / by Michael R. Conroy.
1st ed.
p. cm.
ISBN 9781736901984
1. Title. 2. Fiction. 3. Vietnam. 4. War. 5. Marines
Dewey Decimal Classification: 813 American Fiction
BISAC Subjects:
  FIC032000   FICTION / War & Military
  HIS027070   HISTORY / Wars & Conflicts / Vietnam War

DEDICATION

This work is dedicated to Gwynne Thomas of Oklahoma City. The best friend any person could ever have, she has been a constant source of support and continuing encouragement. Without her this book would never have evolved from the manuscript stage. Thank you, Gwynne.

And to the men I fought alongside in the 1st Battalion, 9th Marine Regiment and the 1st Battalion, 3rd Marine Regiment, Oooo Rah! you unforgettable heroes, every single one of you!!!!?

PROLOGUE
THACH HANH, REPUBLIC OF SOUTH VIETNAM 1200 HOURS, MARCH 30, 1972

Steve Kowalski, code name Viking Six, stood at the flimsy railing of a tired, rusting railroad bridge spanning the Thach Hanh River on the western edge of Quang Tri City. The bridge had not borne rail traffic in more than a decade. Yet it remained serviceable in spite of an obvious lack of maintenance, a tribute to its French designers.

Nicknamed "The Viking" because of his blue eyes, almost platinum-blond hair, and frame like a mythical Norse god, Steve looked down at the gravy-colored waters, estimating the surface speed of the river by observing the ugly body of a bloated rat floating past the bridge. He hated rats. It didn't bother him to see a dead one. He shuddered at the thought of some locals eating the nasty things. Vietnam had proved to be a daily learning experience, even for a two-tour veteran. Steve had recently seen what he mistakenly took to be a Komodo dragon in a flooded rice paddy. He'd aimed his M-16 at the beast only to have the muzzle of his rifle pushed upwards with a shout.

"Don't!" Lan, one of the villagers, had cried. "It's a monitor lizard. They eat the rice rats. Without them, we would have no crop."

There were dangers other than from a six-foot-long, two-foot-high second cousin to a dinosaur. The river was particularly dangerous, with monsoon runoffs from the mountains to the west rushing toward the gulf. Steve was contemplating diving twenty feet or so into the polluted river. Knowing the silty runoff from the mountain jungles and nearby rice paddies was laden with feces of all kinds, including human "night soil" used as fertilizer, would not deter him from the performance of his duties.

"Pig shit, buffalo crap, and human turds," he muttered. "I may as well be diving straight into a sewage lagoon." Fortunately, my shot card is up to date for every disease known to man, he thought. Like most Marines who served in Vietnam, he'd been inoculated for typhoid, cholera, and diseases he'd never heard of. He trusted that the Navy doctors had covered all the possibilities. It didn't really make any difference. He had to go into the water to check the piers and to clear them of any breach in the barbed wire surrounding them or of explosive devices enemy sappers might have attached to them during the night.

He and a SEAL team diver had wrapped the piers in protective razor wire during the previous dry season when the river was at its lowest level. Erecting the bell-shaped obstacles had resulted in numerous cuts, each of which had become infected. Even with immediate treatment, it was almost three months before all those cuts were well again. Even shallow scratches from sharp grasses often became infectious in Vietnam.

This is probably as bad as Shit River in Olongapo, Steve thought as he adjusted his goggles, considering the diseases he would be exposed to in the festering muck below. It was a commonly accepted fact throughout the 7th Fleet and the Third Marine Division that anyone falling into that terribly polluted Philippine river would have to submit to hospitalization and dozens of shots and tests, not only for typhoid and cholera, but for plague, and worse, if there is such a disease.

Resolved once again to the odious daily task under extreme conditions, the Marine took a deep breath. Smells like pure shit, he thought. But at least the air doesn't have solid particles floating around in it. Poised to enter the river feet first with a firm grip on his face mask and mouthpiece, the experienced combat veteran heard the unmistakable sounds of artillery being fired in the near distance.

The Marine hesitated as four sharp reports rolled across the nearby rice paddies. Most likely one-oh-fives, Steve thought. Lord knows I have heard them often enough to know. An image of an artillery crew formed in his mind.

One man was calling out six-digit map coordinates, the location of the target. Another was turning wheels to move the barrel left or right and to its proper elevation. A crew member was passing a thirty-pound shell to the loader who rammed it home, worked his mechanism to seat the round, and stood back with his hands in the air, calling, "Clear!"

The gun commander called "Fire!"

The gunner yanked the lanyard. The piece boomed and recoiled, setting the entire procedure into motion again. Steve was glad he wasn't in the boring assed artillery, even if they didn't have to swim in rivers stewed thick with shit.

Thunder seemed to drum across the shallow rice paddies and brackish backwater marshes between Ai Tu, the ARVN division's headquarters to the north, and Quang Tri City to the bridge's immediate east. It's a routine fire mission, Steve thought, nothing to be alarmed about. Nothing of consequence to me. Our gooks firing at their gooks, he thought, was a reflection of his attitude toward the Vietnamese Army and its poorly trained, generally undisciplined soldiers and even worse leadership.

Those thoughts had hardly been formed before being blown away as completely as the rundown old ice house only three blocks to the east. Sheet metal cladding was ripped from the building's structural steel framing by the exploding shells. Twisted, torn, and bent pieces of the thin-gauge metal were tossed about by a force far greater than the strongest tornado. One rusty sheet wrapped itself around an electric utility pole like a cape around a neck. Another screeched and clattered down the asphalt street, balling up and bouncing along like a West Texas tumbleweed.

Three more shells impacting almost simultaneously marched in a ragged line toward Steve. The artillery rounds exploded in a cloud of fire and smoke, spraying deadly showers of shrapnel and chunks of debris in every direction, causing immediate catastrophic damage among Quang Tri's refugee-swollen, squalid, rabbit-warren residential district. The poor homes of cinder blocks and fading red clay tiles and sheet metal roofing blew apart like a flimsy house of cards in a hurricane.

The city was being turned to rubble. Concrete buildings collapsed both from direct hits and blast concussions from near misses. The ruins spilled over into the crowded streets. A choking haze of dust and debris seemed suspended in the air like a heavy fog.

"Son of a bitch!" Steve exclaimed. Surprised rather than shocked, he tried to move like a sprinter coming out of his blocks at the sound of the starter's pistol, but his leaden feet seemed rooted to the sticky asphalt surface of the bridge. He was certain the bridge was the intended target of the shelling and the next salvo of rounds would blow it apart with him still standing stupidly in the middle of it.

Steve's mind was busy processing information. From the blast damage, he had correctly calculated the impacting shells to be from a 105mm cannon. He knew the maximum range of that gun to be about seven miles. That would put them south of Ai Tu, well into South Vietnam. He had not counted the seconds between hearing the guns fire and seeing the rounds explode. Doing so would have provided an estimated range. He knew, however, that the guns were much closer than seven miles away. Two at the most, he estimated.

The city was already in chaos. Shrill voices cried out. "CuToiVoi! Bac Si!" People were calling for doctors. As pitiful as their pleas were, Steve didn't respond to them. He did not rush to aid or rescue them, thinking, I'm not a doctor. I can't help them. The Marine was a man with a different calling. He was a U.S. Marine with an M-16 rifle usually slung over his left shoulder and a K-bar fighting knife strapped to his right leg. You could almost see Death riding on his other shoulder, gleefully shouting demands into his ear—demands for his own death perhaps, but for others first, as Death will not be denied its toll, not even for the brightest and bravest among us. Steve had learned this lesson the hard way during his first eye-opening, growing-up tour of combat duty.

He had never dwelled on the thoughts of death, although the bringer was certainly never far away in Vietnam. He was swinging his sharp scythe quite close to Steve at the moment. There was no time for the Marine to think about it. That would come later. Now was the time for action. Steve's assignment was to dispense death, to defend the Thach Hahn Bridge, the northernmost intact rail bridge in South Vietnam, and therefore, one of the most important. The rail line could deliver tanks, artillery, and troops in significant numbers to the DMZ quickly and more efficiently than by other means. It had to be held.

Four more echoing booms were followed quickly by explosions to the southeast, closer than before yet still among the clamor and shrieks of the confused, scared civilians who were racing from their houses and home-made bomb shelters. A U.S. Army MP at the east end of the bridge stood there with his mouth agape. Shock and surprise had rooted his feet to the roadbed too, and he was closer to the impacting rounds than Steve.

The narrow bridge had not been designed or intended to support foot or vehicular traffic. In spite of Quang Tri being South Vietnam's third largest city and an important port for both export and import, trains had not run this far north for over a dozen years. The port city was critical to the war effort. Traffic moving into the city or outboard toward Ai Tu or Quang Tri Combat Base as well as Cam Lo was controlled by an Army MP stationed at each end of the bridge. The narrow bridge allowed traffic to pass in only one direction at a time. There was no need to prioritize military traffic. There wasn't much else.

At the time of the first explosion, traffic had been moving east into the city. A line of trucks waiting to cross the bridge to the west idled on the north side of the road as vehicles trapped on the bridge rushed toward the city, there being nowhere else for them to go.

The MP at the west end of the bridge held up traffic there so the vehicles trying to get out of Quang Tri could leave. Drivers at that end of the bridge refused the role of sitting ducks waiting to enter the city that was being shelled. In the narrow confines of the approach, drivers began to maneuver to turn their trucks around. They backed them up a few inches, cut their wheels sharply, and angled a foot forward at a time. The drivers' shouts were punctuated by curses, honking horns, and bent fenders. In short, complete chaos.

As soon as they were able, drivers who had cleared the hairball of the traffic snarl streaked back toward Quang Tri Combat Base as if they were cats with their tails on fire heading for water. Their only defense was speed. In the meantime, led by a Jeep with a driver and his passenger, the traffic moving out of the city was cleared to proceed to the west. However, traffic at the west end of the bridge was blocked by the tangle of vehicles trying to turn around on the narrow crushed gravel road.

The younger of the two men in the Jeep was driving. He appeared to be tall and lean. His features were dark. His face was all sharp angles, giving him a hard appearance. The older man was a pugnacious-looking gray-haired fellow who appeared to be a little on the short side, obvious even when he was sitting down. But he had a look in his eyes that told you he'd been around the bend and then some.

A salvo of artillery rounds struck two transport trucks near the west end of the bridge. Spectacular explosions resulting from direct hits effectively blocked traffic on the bridge behind the burning trucks. Flames devoured their cargo, green canvas coverings, foam-padded seats, fuels, and lubricants. They ate at the paint. They licked and buckled the metal. The tires and a driver fixed in place by the fiery cauldron filled the air with distinctive odors.

From his vantage point, Steve had witnessed the trucks exploding. He hoped the driver had been instantly and mercifully killed by the artillery rather than suffer the agony of burning to death. Already, his brain would have been cooked, his blood boiling, and his flesh blackened. His tendons contorted his body into what the Marines called a "crispy critter" when referring to enemy soldiers who had been killed in a similar manner, or by napalm, which was most often the case.

The lanky driver of the Jeep with yellow Marine Corps markings on its fender hit the brakes hard as the trucks in front of him exploded. As a ball of flames engulfed the trucks, the Jeep driver assessed the possibility of squeezing the smaller vehicle past the burning vehicles. There was no chance of his moving forward. The driver turned to look over his shoulder. A cargo truck was tight on his bumper, a six by completely blocking him and obstructing his view. The Jeep was trapped at the west end of the bridge.

A man in a black diving suit ran up to the Jeep. As he approached, Steve wondered if the older man might have some sort of complex about being short in stature. It was something he had observed more than once during his brief Marine Corps career. General Krulak was famous for it. This would be a complication he didn't need but was prepared to deal with.

Neither of the men wore stripes on their sleeves the way the Army wore them or insignia of rank on his collar in the manner Marines display theirs on utility uniforms. Both were wearing new, starched, and ironed tiger-stripe field uniforms. Their combat boots had been spit-shined. You didn't often see that in I Corp. Fucking newbies, Steve thought, just off the ship.

"What do you fellas do?" he asked with a degree of authority and expectation in his voice. Steve had realized how his deep voice added to his in-charge demeanor. The men looked at one another almost stupidly, perhaps stunned by the shelling and surprised by his question.

"What's your MOS?" Steve asked impatiently, noting the heavy-duty communications equipment built into their Jeep.

"We, uh, we're administrative," the older man answered. He was calm. He didn't appear to have been frightened by the artillery or the burning trucks, which were close enough to be giving off toasty warmth. Steve was impressed by the man's composure. He thought perhaps he was one of the last dinosaurs left over from World War Two and perhaps Korea.

"Oh, crap," Steve moaned aloud. "I need riflemen."

The driver reached behind his seat, flipping back the corner of a rubberized tarp, revealing two M-16 rifles, a shotgun, and a case each of Claymore mines and fragmentation grenades. A couple of well-armed and probably scared to death clerks, Steve thought, although they didn't appear to be frightened or unnerved. He noticed they also carried .45-caliber pistols on their hips.

Steve was sure they wouldn't be able to hit a standing elephant from three feet away with any of the weapons. Be more likely to hit him with a thrown typewriter, he thought. Steve held his tongue and hoped for the best. Sometimes that's all you could do.

"Hey, you!" Steve called to the Army MP, who was standing there gawking at the burning vehicles near the end of the bridge. The sergeant turned. There was a big question mark on his face.

"Yeah, you, numbnuts. Get over here!"

It was not Steve's rank that got the man moving, as in his diving uniform there was no rank insignia for anyone to see. As a matter of fact, the sergeant outranked Steve. It was the Marine's confident manner and his authoritative bearing and tone of voice, the fact that he had unhesitatingly taken charge of the situation, that got the MP moving.

Steve was keenly aware of the rank differential. By God, this is my fucking bridge and I'm not going to turn its defense over to anyone until I have to, he thought, knowing if anyone questioned him or his authority, there were several people on the bridge who outranked him and were likely to take over command of the combined forces present. That included both MPs who had never been a factor in planning the defense of the bridge, possibly a driver or two, and even one or both of the clerks. He decided he would remain in charge until properly relieved.

"You're in charge of this end of the bridge," Steve told the MP. "These two clerks are yours. I'll send you some more help when I can."

In the distance over the sergeant's shoulder and through the shimmering heat waves of the burning trucks coming atop what was more of a swell in the ground than a hill were what Steve quickly identified as Russian T-72 tanks, a main battle tank probably manufactured in China.

"Holy shit!" he exclaimed, causing the other Americans to turn and follow his stare.

Infantrymen generally have a love/hate relationship with tanks. Those steel monsters can devastate an unsupported infantry company. As a former anti-tank assault man while waiting on his security clearance and assignment to an intelligence unit to be approved, Steve had been trained to knock out tanks with the 3.5-inch rocket launcher, a cumbersome but effective weapon, an evolution of the World War II bazookas. The training had included studying enemy tanks and their known vulnerabilities as well as learning to judge speeds, ranges, and angles of attack. A soldier has to have a giant set of balls to get close enough to strike the tank at one of its vulnerable points and then stand up exposed long enough to calmly aim and shoot the shoulder-fired weapon. Steve hadn't particularly cared for that assignment.

The rocket launcher, now out of service, had been replaced by the LAAW, or Light Anti-tank Assault Weapon. The LAAW was totally ineffective against armor. The key to that is the first word of light anti-tank assault weapon. There aren't any light tanks. Machine guns and rifle fire are just about as effective against a tank as firing a cap pistol at it. A mine can knock out a tank if you lay it where the tank will roll over it. The dense local population and surrounding rice paddies had prevented Steve from laying a minefield defense.

Mortars can be effective if they score a direct hit on the lightly armored top of the vehicle, a damned difficult task. On the battlefield, armor is the primary target of enemy tanks and artillery, naval gunfire when it can reach you, ground support troops with an assortment of anti-tank weapons, and worst of all, air strikes.

As an infantryman, you love your tanks. They are your mobile artillery support. From time to time, you can ride on top of them. You can strap some of your heavy gear to them. You can get behind them when machine guns or small arms are being fired your way. Tanks are a terrifying force multiplier.

The Marine Corps doesn't have a lot of tanks. The Defense Department supply system habitually places the Marine Corps at the end of the list for improvements to existing models, to up-guns, to improved communications, and to things such as optics. And, of course, to the latest models off the R&D and production lines. Even without those upgrades, the tanks were a formidable weapon. Steve didn't have any tanks to throw at the enemy.

Sure, the Corps had tanks in Vietnam. However, the mountain jungles in I Corp, where Marines conducted most of their operations, were not a favorable tank environment. Steve's experience was that Marine Corps tanks were being used primarily as rapid mobile artillery support for defense of the permanent bases.

Not all tracked vehicles are tanks. Not all tanks were the same. The stereotypical tank is a huge steel beast with shoulder-high treads, a swiveling turret, at least a 90mm cannon, and machine guns firing from inside and atop the turret. Generally, the fuel-guzzling, diesel-smoking monster carries a crew of five. In some tanks the commander has a hatch he can poke his head through, providing him better overall vision than the small viewing ports. The topside machine gun, usually a fifty-caliber weapon, was manned by the tank commander, who wears a helmet and mouthpiece so he can communicate with his crew and all tank commanders on a common radio frequency from that position. A long whip antenna rises from the rear of the turret, leaning like a wind-blown sprig.

Steve recalled that in Vietnam, a tank sometimes served as an outpost. He remembered seeing one parked rather permanently on Highway One between Dong Ha and the DMZ. It overlooked rice paddies on both sides of the road. Its turret was pointed north toward the DMZ and a village in the near distance. Two of the tank's most vulnerable points are its treads and its engine. Engine emissions pass through grates at the rear of the tank. The one he remembered had been sandbagged to the rear and both sides to above the top of the exhaust grates and treads.

A tank at Quang Tri Combat Base had been backed into a sloped berm. It was covered with runway matting and sandbags, with only the barrel and hatch being uncovered. The turret was fixed with its main gun pointing toward North Vietnam, only a few miles away. But that tank could quickly emerge from its berm.

An astonishing amount of information can pass through one's mind at critical moments when quick decisions and actions are required. It took no conscious effort for the information on tanks to come to Steve's mind. He quickly realized that the tanks at Dong Ha and Quang Tri Combat Base would not have the range to engage the enemy tanks bearing down on his position with their turrets closed for combat.

"Those tanks have been upgunned from 90 mm to fire one, oh, five rounds," he noted. "Provides them longer range and more firepower."

The Marines in the Jeep shared eyebrow-raised glances. Steve, who had excellent peripheral vision, caught the looks out of the corner of his eye. He didn't have time to give the exchange of expressions any thought. The enemy tanks were clanking and creaking ominously toward the bridge, firing as they came. Flames flickered in blue tongues as excess gases were burned off. Rooster tails of yellow dust spread out behind the tanks, obscuring whatever ground forces might be coordinating an attack with the armored force. That would require a different type of defensive response.

Steve counted four tanks on the horizon, the source of the four round salvos slamming into Quang Tri City. At twenty miles an hour they would reach the bridge in ten minutes. That wasn't much time to organize a defense.

"Give me that radio!" Steve shouted urgently to the graying clerk. At the same time he was pulling an acetate-covered waterproof map from his dive suit's thigh pocket. He knew the area around the bridge quite well. He had been preparing for months to defend the bridge while hoping he would never have to do so.

Steve had conducted patrols in every direction from the bridge. He had learned the terrain by marching over it. The features and estimated distances were fixed clearly in his mind. Steve oriented the map quickly. He wrote the map coordinates of the tanks and their direction of travel on his underwater slate, estimating the speed of their advance. Due to his training and experience, it all came smoothly, automatically.

Steve quickly dialed the radio frequency he wanted. He keyed the radio handset. Again with raised eyebrows, the clerks seemed surprised that the young Marine seemed to know exactly what he was doing. Steve did not notice the silent communication that passed between the clerks. He spoke into the hand set.

"Sea Dragon, Sea Dragon, this is Bushmaster CAP Six, over."

The clerks knew Sea Dragon to be the call sign of a naval task force off the coast. The clerks took note of Steve's call sign, CAP Six. They knew CAP to be an acronym for Combined Action Platoon. The six always designated the commanding officer of a unit. Platoons being commanded by twenty-two-year-old junior lieutenants, they assumed Steve to be a second lieutenant fresh out of OCS and The Basic School for Marine officers. His command presence, however, seemed to be a bit superior to most inexperienced newly commissioned officers.

The Navy's radio operator who responded sounded bored to Steve. "Fire mission!" the Marine announced with urgent emphasis in order to gain the man's full attention. "Enemy tanks at one, zero, seven, nine, six, two. Moving south at twenty to twenty-five miles per hour. Priority one. I am under attack, over."

"Wait one." The clerks and the MP could hear the response.

"Wait one?" Steve said to anyone, to everyone, perhaps to the Gods of War. "What the hell is he doing, finishing a poker hand?"

The clerks were out of the Jeep, unloading the weapons and ammunition. That bit of initiative didn't go unnoticed by Steve. The tanks fired again.

"They're firing at us, at what to them must look like the thin edge of a ribbon across their beam," Steve said to the clerks, thinking out loud. "They're maneuvering so as to fire down the long axis of the bridge, making us a much easier target for them to hit. We're going to stop them," he said firmly, his tone and manner full of resolve.

The clerks nodded affirmatively as if those four tanks didn't concern them at all. In spite of sounding fearlessly confident, Steve didn't explain how he planned to stop four main battle tanks with a couple of M-16 rifles and a trio of .45 pistols.

The sky was suddenly filled with a noise something like a jet engine roaring low overhead melded with that of a rushing, rattling freight train. Steve knew the sound well. The clerks ducked instinctively but watched with Steve as the naval barrage struck, throwing up geysers of black smoke and cloudy balls of boiling fire yellow on the outside with red and orange surrounding the explosions' hot core. The exploding rounds threw dirt and large rocks over one hundred feet into the air and made large craters in the ground but narrowly missed the tanks. Steve depressed the radio hand set as he watched the approaching armor grow larger in appearance and spread out now that they were under fire.

"Well trained," Steve commented as he calculated distances and rates of speed. "Like shooting ducks," he said as much to himself as to anyone else who might be listening. "We'll have to shoot where we expect them to be, not where they were or are now.

"Sea Dragon, Sea Dragon, down fifty, left twenty-five. Fire for effect, over." Steve paused for a moment and depressed the radio's send button again. He didn't bother with further proper radio protocol. "You guys gimme all you got, a broadside or whatever you call it."

That seemed to amuse the clerks who couldn't suppress small chuckles.

"I've always wanted to say that for real. I watched a lot of pirate movies as a kid," Steve explained.

The air rattled and whooshed in almost rippling waves as naval shells of various calibers passed overhead. Sea Dragon had roared and spit her flames. The sky was filled with the familiar shuffling sound of artillery shells passing overhead. Those shells were the size and weight of a small Volkswagen.

"That's some heavy shit," Steve said in awe as the entire area around the tanks erupted with one huge geyser of exploding anti-tank round after another, obscuring the immediate results. Air bursts followed the HEAT rounds. The Navy gunners knew what they were doing. All Russian tanks were equipped with vulnerable exterior fuel tanks strapped behind their turrets. Air bursts with thousands of lava hot barbs of jagged steel rained down with tremendous force, exploding the fuel or at least setting it on fire, both of which proved fatal to the tanks. Air bursts were also extremely effective against ground troops in the open.

One of the tanks took a direct hit from a HEAT round. The armored vehicle exploded spectacularly. The tanks were enveloped by eruptions as heavy armor-piercing shells smashed into them and the ground around them. For a moment it was almost like watching a violent sun flare. Adding to it was a secondary explosion as one of the tank's ammunition and fuel erupted. One after another, the tanks were exploding from the inside like popcorn, with much the same result. Although he watched the enemy destruction in awe, Steve was aware of the horror of it.

Another tank exploded. Yellow tongues of fire licked at the blue sky as if to devour a cooling cloud. Smoking shrapnel created curly-cue ribbons of coiling white smoke tendrils reaching out in every direction like Medusa's head full of writhing snakes.

"Poor bastards," Steve muttered, thinking of the tanks' crew members. "You couldn't get me in one of those sardine cans for any number of stripes or bars." He keyed the hand set once more.

"Sea Dragon, Sea Dragon, this is Bushmaster, over."

"Sea Dragon. Send your traffic over."

"On time, on target, Navy. Splash four NVA tanks. Thank you so much. Out."

Steve handed the radio set back to the clerk, asking, "You know how to call in artillery, pop?"

"I believe I do." The older man was impressed. He knew Marine Corps officer candidates were taught to direct all forms of supporting fire as part of their basic school education. Levelheadedness and focus under duress were intangibles that simply could not be taught. The young Marine was performing flawlessly. The older man was anxious to see what he would do next.

Steve was satisfied with the understated confidence he read in the older man's reply. He handed his map over. "You fire at anything else unfriendly that moves out there. Call Whiskey Battery at two, three, five point two."

Steve pulled a smaller radio, a PRC-25, and its fiberglass back pack from the rear seat of the Jeep. "You guys belong to the sergeant," he told the clerks, handing the younger man the backpack. He turned and shouted to the driver of the truck just behind the Jeep. "Pass the word back. You fellas, give me some room here!"

Steve got behind the wheel of the Jeep. The vehicle's radio was major. The Marine just realized he had commandeered some sort of command vehicle. He examined the Jeep and its markings closely.

"I could probably talk to D.C. or at least Dallas on this thing," he said. "Maybe even send up a red rocket transmission."

He looked to the driver, not registering how much he had shocked the clerks. A red rocket transmission would only be used in case of a truly war-changing event, something that might start World War Three, for example. No one below the rank of full colonel, and not even all of them, should have access to it or even knowledge of it.

"You two must work for some heavy brass," Steve said.

The taller Marine looked to his older companion. Steve noticed he seemed to be doing that a lot. Something almost telepathic passed between them. Turning toward Steve, he answered, "Yeah, we do."

"Well, he's not here right now, but I am, so your asses belong to me. Don't forget, you're basically Marine riflemen, the most deadly element on the battlefield." Steve paused a moment to gather his thoughts. His tone was more conversational when he resumed.

"Look, guys, Quang Tri's always been a major political target for the North Vietnamese. They wouldn't attack it with just four tanks. These have to be their scouts. It looks to me like they'll be coming across the 'D' in a major way any minute, sort of like the Germans did at the Battle of the Bulge. They'll take the city if they can and destroy it if they can't.

"I have a trained CAP unit, the equivalent of a company here I'd put up against any company in the South Vietnamese Army. Our primary mission is to hold this bridge and halt an advance over it until some help arrives. Do your best for me, and I'll do all I can for you."

Steve didn't need or expect a response. He put the Jeep in gear and spent a few frustrating moments trying to find space to maneuver the vehicle out of its boxed-in position. Finally, driving in reverse, barely squeezing past two trucks with only a minor exchange of paint, he came to a point where he could go no further. The trucks behind the Jeep were too logjammed to give him room to pass. Steve gave up on the Jeep and began walking down the length of the bridge.

He looked back to where the enemy tanks were burning. "I wonder if they'll paint four little tanks on the side of their ship," he muttered, thankful for the naval gunnery he might have to depend upon again. He didn't really have much time to think about such things.

Steve was blessed with unusual mental capabilities. With no training and little effort, his mind worked like a kitchen range. His focus was like a main course cooking in the oven. Adjuncts to the most pressing issue were heating and simmering in his mind like the four top burners of a range. They would all come together at the proper time as a complete unit. The immediate problem was getting the trucks, which would be targets as well as ranging aids, off the bridge.

In addition to the Jeep, four six-by-six trucks had been caught on the bridge. One was full of Marine riflemen who'd unassed the vehicle quickly. The squad had taken up firing positions along the north side of the bridge. That was good. Steve knew they were going to need that level of training and discipline if the enemy had crossed the DMZ and was attacking in force. Steve walked past the reinforced squad, knowing they were also going to need the special fighting spirit, that Esprit De Corp., which helps make Marines special in so many ways, in the long hours to come if his perception of events was anywhere close to being correct.

"Who is in charge here?" he asked.

A tall, black Marine stood. He was as tall as Steve, but he was broad-shouldered with a narrow waist Kowalski couldn't aspire to achieve. Tight end, Steve thought.

"Corporal Obasi Holt, sir," he answered. Steve didn't bother to correct the assumption of his rank.

"Well, corporal. We're in a bit of a tight spot here. There's nowhere for you to go. I'd like to incorporate your men into my CAP unit defense."

"Yes, sir."

"What have you got?"

"A basic thirteen-man rifle squad, grenadier, four-man 80mm mortar crew, machine gun team... I guess that's it. No radioman, scout, or corpsman, twenty men total, sir."

"Get me a status report on your weapons, ammunition, and supplies," Steve instructed before his attention was needed elsewhere. At the east end of the bridge, the MP was being harassed by a mob of gabbling Vietnamese civilians, refugees now escaping in the other direction, another problem for Steve to solve. As he approached, the scout was already evaluating the problem.

The MP could not understand the Vietnamese. The sergeant simply did not know what to do except to yell at them louder, which only elicited the same response from the Vietnamese, continually escalating everyone's level of anger and frustration. However, he was doing the right thing by keeping people off the bridge.

"Sergeant!" Steve called harshly. "There could be sappers and other Viet Cong agents and infiltrators among those keening women and children. Don't let anyone on this bridge. Shoot them if you have to."

Steve had noticed a quartet of drivers gathered around a coffee pot. He wondered where that had come from. "You men!" he shouted, waving to get their attention. "You're infantry now. You're attached to this sergeant. Grab your weapons and get on line behind him."

Steve gave further instructions to the MP. While those orders were being carried out, Steve climbed up into the back of the nearest truck. To his delight, he found the bed of the truck filled with cases of C-rations and five gallon cans of both water and diesel fuel. If they were to be engaged at the bridge for any length of time, all those supplies and more would be needed.

The MP sergeant and his fire team of drivers had moved the line of angry civilians back far enough to allow the truck to be backed up and steered onto the dirt road paralleling the river.

"Sergeant!" Steve called. "Get the driver of this vehicle up here!"

One of the Marines stepped forward, a sandy-haired, hazel-eyed kid In baggy utilities and boots that had never trod a jungle trail.

"Pull this truck up next to that pink concrete block building," Steve ordered, pointing to a popular local restaurant with a glass front facing the bridge. As the driver climbed into the cab, Steve walked down to the building, gathering a working party of nervous villagers as he went. They were residents of Thach Hahn, not refugees from Quang Tri City. Most of them were family members of his CAP unit personnel.

The truck was unloaded by now smiling Vietnamese who the Americans all knew were looking for any opportunity to steal whatever they could. The unloaded truck was driven back up the dirt road to the bridge where it was positioned across the narrow street. The fuel was drained before the squad of Marine riflemen pushed and rocked the heavy vehicle until it tipped over on its side. Glass shattered. Steel bent. The truck leaked oil and transmission fluid. The MP and the drivers took up defensive positions behind it.

The enemy tanks were still burning with black, oily smoke marking where the steel beasts had died. At that end of the bridge, the American trucks had burned more quickly. The tires, however, burned much longer, filling the air with noxious fumes and floating strings of black soot that settled on every surface. A breeze carried the mixed smells of combat. Among them was the smell of death, of what the Marines rather callously called "crispy critters." Only this time they were American soldiers.

In spite of losing two trucks and their drivers, Steve thought things were shaping up nicely. Two trucks for four tanks was a positive combat trade-off any commander would take. The situation got even better when Steve climbed into the back of the third truck. It was loaded with LAAWs, Claymore and other mines, explosives, rolls of detonation cord, and boxes of blasting caps and fuses. It was a shipment intended for the engineers or perhaps for the Seabees. Plus a couple of cases of beer, one of soda pops, and some Navy five-in-one rations. Steve had the driver back the truck down the road to where the food had been unloaded and stored. That load was currently being guarded by one of the squad members.

The second truck was loaded with materials for the combat base's primary medical facility. The medical supplies were delivered to Doctor Quoc, who lived in a modest but well-maintained cinder block home at the edge of the hamlet southeast of the bridge. The truck that had been transporting the squad was also hauling a dozen crates of ball ammunition and more grenades. Steve had enough of everything to wage a small war, which was exactly what he planned to do.

Once unloaded, this truck was tipped over to block the road south of the village. The real threat was from the north and the west. Steve had no option but to send a fire team from the local defense force to the south end of the hamlet to guard their rear.

Steve planned to direct the coming battle from the bridge, defending it and the squalid southern portion of Thach Hanh. He would fight from there for the more prosperous half of the hamlet with the hope of assistance from the nearby South Vietnamese Army. The bridge was not only the enemy target but the high point of elevation throughout the rectangular-shaped hamlet.

The Marines did not have the men or weapons to mount a prolonged defensive presence in all parts of the village. He ordered another truck to be turned over at the junction of the road to Quang Tri and the road leading down to the north end of the hamlet. The remaining truck and the Jeep were parked out of sight behind the restaurant. They would be needed to haul the wounded, ammunition, and rations during the coming battle. Steve gave no thought to it being used to escape, perhaps to the south.

CHAPTER ONE
QUANG TRI COMBAT BASE
1969

"Jesus Christ, Tsoi, it's a hundred and seventeen fucking degrees in this tent!"' Steve uttered, rolling a cold can of sweating beer across his forehead. His cursing wasn't a surprise to his Chinese-American friend, just a bit unusual for the young Texan who was only a shade from being what the Corps called a "Choirboy."

"Thank God the worst part of the summer is behind us," the San Francisco native responded wryly. He drained the beer in his hand, dramatically throwing his head back as he drank half a beer all at once. Learning to do that had taken some practice. He slammed the can down on a wooden desktop and belched loudly. His mother would have been shocked by his crassness.

"The heat wasn't the worst part of the summer," the tall shirtless Texan told his friend.

"Yeah, I'm sorry I missed that little dance."

"No, you're not Steve. It was a pretty bad one."

Steve's left eyebrow raised in an almost perfect parabolic arc. Such a comment was completely out of character for his gung ho buddy. Steve grinned at the raised eyebrow look. Tommy Tsoi's facial expressions and head tilts were as expressive as Steve's favorite dog, an intelligent Border Collie.

Tommy had heard the stories and the building legend about what would become known as the summer battle for Dong Ha. Most accounts had the engagement beginning with the Marines being attacked along the Cua Viet River. The "Magnificent Bastards" had been in a real donnybrook, a satisfying close quarter's slugfest the American commanders had been hoping for.

The large-scale battle had actually begun hours earlier. Lance Corporal Steve Kowalski, an S-2 scout from Headquarters and Service Company, was leading patrols from Bravo Company of the First Battalion, 3rd Marine Regiment at the time. G-2 (division intelligence) had received information that a revanchist 2nd NVA Division was moving back into the Third Marine Division's TAOR (Tactical Area of Responsibility) after being brought to the point of combat- ineffectiveness by the blazing rifles of the Marines at Jones Creek during the summer offensive of the previous year.

The defeated and demoralized enemy division had retreated north across the DMZ. The Marines, reluctant to break contact, harassed and pressured the enemy units to within five hundred meters of the border before breaking contact. Back in North Vietnam, the battered division recruited, trained, resupplied, and was re-equipped with new top-of-the-line weapons. The 2nd NVA Division returned to South Vietnam, infiltrating in small units down the Ho Chi Minh

Trail inside Laos to rejoin, reorganize, and conduct training missions and combat operations in Northern I Corp, becoming more effective due to the harsh lessons learned and corrective actions taken after the previous summer battles by their highly skilled veteran battlefield commanders.

Intelligence information is evaluated and rated from A to F based upon the reliability of the source and from 1 to 6 based upon the plausibility and probability of the information. A B-4 report stating the 2nd NVA Division had buried ammunition and weapons in a graveyard at Bong Sai was forwarded to the Third Marine Regiment for action. The regimental commander sent the order for action to his First Battalion,[1] the most rested of his three rifle battalions. That commander tasked Bravo Company with the mission of securing the village and denying the weapons to the enemy either by capturing and removing them or by destroying them in place.

Captain William McKenzie, "Mac," of course, assigned one of his nine thirteen-man squads to the mission. The squad leader assigned the task was a pink-faced 22-year-old farm boy from Wisconsin, an E-5 sergeant promoted by attrition, not making waves and by surviving his first six months of combat duty. Terry Miller, with his blocky, soft frame, apple-pie manners, and looks with a general "aw shucks" demeanor, was cut from a different bolt of cloth than the Sgt. Rock of Easy Company comic book non-com this generation of Marines had grown up reading as ten-year-olds.

Sergeant Miller though, had a Marine mentality. He knew how to get a job done. He received his patrol assignment without comment. He warned his fire teams and attached personnel to be prepared for movement to action on his command. His fire team leaders knew what to do. With the scout making suggestions and recommendations, a patrol route with check points was laid out. Thrust points used for calling in artillery and air support were established. The squad members quickly performed dozens of tasks required of small units prior to undertaking a combat patrol.

A reinforced combat patrol, Sgt. Miller's squad was made up of himself and three four-man fire teams. At full strength, with no one sick, on leave, on R&R or yet to be replaced due to combat losses, the squad was beefed up with the attachment of the scout, who was essentially the patrol leader; a three-man M-60 machine gun team; a Vietnamese Kit Carson Scout; a Navy hospital corpsman; a radio operator; and a grenadier who was armed with an M-79 grenade launcher called a "blooker" because of the distinctive sound the weapon made when fired. The short-barreled weapon, which broke down and loaded like a single-bore shotgun, fired a single 40mm rifle grenade. With a range of 900 yards and a tight but deadly kill zone, the weapon was a favorite among the Marines.

Twenty-one young men armed to the teeth, so to speak, with pistols, rifles, bayonets, grenades, and shoulder-fired LAAWs were hard and lean, their faces and arms tanned and leathered by the harsh Vietnamese sun. Two were FANUGIs, "Fucking New Guys," who would have to earn their place among the more seasoned veterans who were survivors of daily patrols and numerous encounters with the enemy, generally in small unit engagements. Over half of them had been awarded Purple Hearts for wounds suffered in combat. Four had earned Bronze Star Medals for valor. One of them had been recommended for a Silver Star that had not been awarded. There were mixed feelings about medals and awards among these young men. Some resented the "looseness" with which the Army seemed to award medals. Others were jealous of anyone who earned them. A handful took pride in how difficult it was to earn medals in the Marine Corps.

The patrol was made up of one Vietnamese, one American, three Mexican-Americans, eleven Afro-Americans, and five Caucasians. The Marines were from San Jose; Houston; "Chi-town, baby"; Motown; Pennsylvania, Wisconsin, Oklahoma, and Texas, all over the United States. There was a mixture of socio--economic backgrounds as well as accents and political leanings.

At eighteen, "Baby D.W." Johnson was the youngest of the lot. D.W., a blue-eyed blond with the face of an innocent ten-year-old, always wore his flak jacket fully zipped. In every village, he was the first to make friends with a child and adopt a puppy.

At twenty-three, Steve was the "old man" of the patrol, older even than the squad's butter bar second lieutenant platoon commander. Steve motioned for the radio operator to join him on the friendly side of the razor wire perimeter surrounding Bravo Company's position. The razor wire was barbed wire's mean cousin. Looking back to catch a nod from Sergeant Miller, the scout keyed the handset to transmit.

"Bravo six, Bravo Sierra Two, over."

"Bravo six. Send your traffic. Over." The radioman at his desk in the company headquarters sounded typically bored by the routine exchange. Seldom sent into the field, the radioman was like a spectator who attended a stock car race only for the wrecks.

"Candy Tuft, Bravo Sierra Two. Super Guard Slugger, at bat," Steve announced, advising the battalion headquarters that the reinforced squad was departing the base perimeter. The scout led his patrol on a winding path through the minefield, all his senses already fully alert. Rifles were locked and loaded, safeties off, and pointed outboard. Every man was ready for action that could come at any moment. The scout put a distance of thirty yards between himself and the main body of the patrol.

Sergeant Miller split a fire team, using it as flankers, two men to the left and two to the right. The machine gunners would watch the rear.

Typically, the patrol turned into a long, hot march in the sun. The young men sweated, attracting insects that stung and bit as hard as the largest, meanest Texas horsefly ever born. The Marines did not relax their vigil for a moment. Nerves frayed more with each step the Marines took. The patrol was operating in a free-fire zone, Indian County, as they called it. The inhabitants had been relocated, often by force, to create an area where any person they spotted was considered an enemy soldier. Anything moving inside that zone would immediately draw fire from the combat-eager Marines.

Avoiding paths, trails, and roads as they might be mined or a site for ambushes, the patrol marched in route step through three thousand meters of knee-high grass that had been sucked dry and burned brown and course by the harsh summer sun. Kowalski signaled the flankers forward to approach the back side of a small knoll, which was the first checkpoint. The patrol moved warily rather than cautiously. There was no attempt at stealth on this patrol.

The Marines all knew their base camp was under constant observation. The enemy knew right where they were. This was a combat patrol. The intent was to draw out a numerically larger enemy force that could be defeated by the superior firepower of American supporting weapons. An artillery battery was on standby. Provided a copy of the patrol route, the artillery officers had pre-selected the range of specific locations along the route. Two Marine F-4 Phantoms sat on a hot pad at the Da Nang airfield. Even naval gunfire was on standby.

After having disappeared into the brush, the flankers revealed themselves at the top of the knoll, signaling that the immediate vicinity was clear. Once they gained the knoll, the patrol spread out to form a perimeter just below the crest.

"Drop your gear. Take five," Sergeant Miller called. The squad performed a well-practiced drill with half the men alertly watching in all directions while the other half drank from their canteens, poured water over their heads, and lit up cigarettes. Instead of shrugging out of their packs for five minutes, the Marines sat back, leaning against them. There was little talking during the break. Kowalski signaled for the radioman, a husky kid with a top knot of tight sandy curls who looked to be about sixteen. The scout called in a routine situation report.

"Candy Tuft Bravo Six, this is Candy Tuft Bravo Sierra Two, over."

"Six, over," the company commander responded. He was always close to the radio when he had a unit out on patrol.

"Check point one, over."

"Acknowledge, out."

Everyone with the need to know had the coordinates of checkpoint one and could pinpoint the patrol's location. Distances and times were noted.

Too soon to suit the Marines, the patrol was on its feet and moving again, a different fire team on the point and another new one on the flanks. This rotation kept the point fresh and equalized all the aspects of the patrol's marching order. The patrol would soon be moving out of the tall grass and into the scattered scrub brush fringe of the jungle. The 1500-meter route to checkpoint two, a trail intersection and potential ambush point, was routinely and quickly covered. Every nerve was on edge. Even "routine" patrols in Northern I Corp were stressful, nerve-taxing, adrenalin-pumping hours of vigilance and boredom with a heightened level of awareness.

Checkpoint two was called in during another five-minute break. Sweat was dripping down faces and arms. Backs were wet from perspiration. Sergeant Miller moved among the men, reminding each of them to take his salt tablets. There was little other talking during the break. The jungle was closing in on the patrol; its smell, its darkness, its mystery, and most of all, its danger. The level of danger would increase with each step taken deeper into it.

Moving on again with only a few moans and groans, the patrol moved toward checkpoint three, a village called Bong Sai. Officially, the village was abandoned, being in the free fire zone. However, it was almost impossible to keep farmers who had century-old family roots in the village from returning to harvest volunteer crops and native growth. Removing them was a continuing and dangerous task.

The North Vietnamese often used such villages as rendezvous and staging points for their operations. Sometimes they dug in hard with elaborate complexes of bunkers and connecting tunnels. They would dig in to stay and fight with great determination and quite often more skill than most newsmen and Americans at home would ever give them credit for.

You could never relax your vigil on one of those patrols. You could walk through those villages half a dozen times without incident only to find yourself in a pitched battle against a fortified location the next. Steve knew the patrol might be walking into the waiting guns of a larger enemy force. Troops on the move tend to bunch up, making them better targets for every type of weapon. At Steve's hand signal, the patrol fanned out, increasing the distance from man to man in every direction.

Spotting a clearing ahead, the scout held up his right hand, halting the patrol in place. Screened by thick undergrowth, Steve crept forward on his belly to observe the village and its surrounding terrain in all directions, searching slowly and carefully through trained eyes. He heard no noise. He saw no movement. There appeared to be no activity in the village or along the nearby creek. There wasn't supposed to be.

The village, though small, had a sizeable graveyard nearby. Generations after generation of ancestors are buried in those mounded graves, Steve thought, continuing his visual reconnaissance. The long axis of the village was generally parallel to the creek, a continuous source of water that ran from the mountain jungles in the west toward the South China Sea to the east. That water source was certain to attract North Vietnamese troops somewhere along its route. Although it was a reliable source of water, the creek would be at its most shallow level during the end of the hot summer season. The creek was located on the south side of the village. The scout was concerned about the thick tree line north of the village. There were dark shadows there that could conceal a considerable enemy force. And it was within the effective combat range of most military rifles, certainly the SKS and AK-47s favored by the enemy.

Sergeant Miller had crept forward to a position next to the scout. "See anything?" he asked quietly.

"Nah, nothing."

"You got a feeling, a premonition or something?"

"No, just being careful." Steve paused a moment and pointed, "There could be a shitload of gooks in that tree line. We've got to cross the opening and the creek. It may as well be here as anywhere else."

"You want to recon by fire?" That meant firing blindly into an area where the enemy was likely to be in hopes of getting a revealing response, perhaps of springing an ambush early.

"I don't think so. If they're in there and we start shooting them up, they're going to come boiling out of there like pissed off red ants. Could be an entire division in there."

"A squad of Marines against a gook division. Ought to be a pretty even fight."

The Marines laughed. "For like ten minutes," Steve remarked soberly.

"Let's put some arty in there, Ski," the sergeant suggested.

"My thinking exactly. I'll call it in." The scout signaled for the radio operator who came forward in a crouch and handed Steve the hand set.

"Whiskey Twelve, Whiskey Twelve, this is Candy Tuft Bravo Sierra Two, over."

"Whiskey Twelve, wait one," came the prompt response. There was a brief period of static-filled background noise as the artillery battery radio operator copied incoming transmissions and assigned fire mission requests to various gun crews.

"Bravo Sierra Two, Whiskey Twelve. Send your traffic over."

"Fire mission, HEAT, no spotter rounds, battery two, can observe and adjust fire. Safety facto medium close. Grid two, six, zero, six, eight, three, over."

"State your priority, over."

The scout looked to the sergeant. Neither of them wanted to move into the graveyard without first firing up that tree line, but the priority for this type of request was low as the squad was not under fire and no enemy presence had been observed. They both know the radio operator would not have asked for a priority if they had gun crews immediately available. The scout shrugged. "Priority Charlie," he reported. "No enemy activity."

"Sorry, Bravo two. We are currently in support of engaged units and cannot assist you at this time."

"Thank you much. Out," the scout replied as he turned toward the squad leader. "Gird the Loins. Summon the Blood."

"There you go, talking a completely different language than the rest of us again."

Steve was used to being teased about his Texas accent, his western twang, and dropped sounds. "That's Shakespeare, from Henry the Eighth, I think."

Shaking his head a bit in puzzlement, a bit in wonderment, the sergeant rolled over and waved the squad forward. In fire team rushes, with two teams providing cover while one team moved forward, the patrol crossed the opening and the creek without incident. The scout led them into the village, searching all around for recent signs of enemy activity, glancing from time to time toward the bothersome tree line.

Bong Sai was a poor rural village, more of a hamlet actually, though there was no real definition of what qualified as a hamlet and what qualified as a village. The homes were all crude thatch huts with little effort at design or decorations. The dirt floors had been swept often and pounded hard by life.

The framing was of mature bamboo, six to eight inches in diameter. The walls and roof sections were made of tightly woven thatch mats. There were no door or window frames, just openings. It was all tied together with coconut hemp rope.

There were no scrawny chickens clucking and scratching at the earth. No barking dogs had run out to challenge or greet the visitors. There were no pigs or water buffalo, only the faint odor of their past presence. Ashes in the cooking pits were scattered and cold. The patrol worked their way through the village, relaxing a bit as they approached the graveyard.

The Vietnamese bury their dead without embalming them. The bodies are sometimes folded into large pots which are sealed so nature can take its course. Others are placed in simple wood coffins. They are buried in round, mounded graves marked by thin concrete gravestone slabs, rather tall and slender with rounded tops. They are about three feet tall, eight inches wide, and only two inches thick with no steel reinforcing. Because of the general reluctance of most U.S. personnel to desecrate a grave, the North Vietnamese soldiers routinely used them as places to cache their weapons and equipment. The NVA and Viet Cong were not restricted by rules of conduct or engagement or by mores. A stomach-turning stench of decaying bodies enveloped the Marines and assaulted their nostrils before they spotted the disturbed graves. One of the machine gunners turned aside and heaved.

"Get down!" the scout shouted over his shoulder as he dove to the ground, rolled to his right, and came to rest in a prone firing position with his rifle pointing north. In that blink of an eye, the war gnashed its bloody teeth in the direction of the Marines.

Steve had heard a volley of light 60mm mortars leaving their tubes with an echoing Kathunk! Kathunk! Kathunk! He knew right away that those weapons with a range of 2,000 meters were located just inside the tree line that had concerned him. Wham! Wham! Wham! The earth seemed to shudder as the well-aimed mortar shells exploded all around the Marines. Debris rained down through thick columns of pungent red earth and cordite-laced smoke. Shouts of surprise and anguish filled the air as wounded Marines called out in pain or called "Corpsman up!" for a wounded buddy.

While the surprised Marines hugged the earth, Steve Bartold, Navy Hospital Corpsman Third Class, scrambled from man to man, inspecting and evaluating wounds, slapping on pressure bandages to stop bleeding, injecting morphine when warranted, and offering words of comfort to PFC Tyrell Jones, an eighteen-year-old rifleman who would obviously die soon of his severe wounds. There was no chaplain, no person at all who could provide real comfort in the Marine's final moments. Every man in the small, outnumbered unit was in a desperate struggle for survival.

Jones, a fit, lean man who did not have the body bulk that accompanies maturity or the mass of a weightlifter, had suffered traumatic wounds to his chest, stomach, and groin, with lesser wounds to his head and limbs. The corpsman administered morphine to ease his pain and passing. The drug also served to prevent his shrieks of pain from demoralizing other squad members. There was no time for PFC Jones. With Jones quieted and bleeding out, Bartold moved to the next wounded man. PFC Jones died in a drugged haze essentially alone.

On the west flank, against the skyline of a nearby small rise, NVA soldiers began a ground assault. They were armed with light infantry weapons—SKS single-shot rifles, AK-47 semi-automatic assault rifles, grenades, and light machine guns.

"Contact left!" Kowalski called as the enemy machine guns opened up, kicking up a row of puffs in the dirt and chipping bits of concrete off the headstones as they came to bear on target. Marines scuttled behind the protection of grave markers and earth mounds, forgetting about the smells coming from the freshly disturbed graves. They brought their rifles around to return fire against the advancing enemy platoon. Shot through the head, another Marine died quickly and silently, reduced suddenly to battlefield litter. Another, riddled with chest and gut wounds, cried out for his mother as his life's fluids slipped through his fingers. His bowels loosed as the corpsman reached him. Bartold took a bullet in the thigh doing so and was prevented from administering a merciful shot of morphine to the mortally wounded man.

Sergeant Miller was frantically calling Whiskey Battery for artillery support. Apprised of the squad's perilous circumstances, the officers in the Fire Direction Control Center made Miller's fire mission their top priority, firing round after round of anti-personnel shells from every gun in the battery at targets to the north and west of the beleaguered squad.

The air-bursting artillery was exploding close by. Noses bled from the concussions of exploding artillery shells. Ears rang. Enemy soldiers simply disappeared in a mist of blood due to a direct hit on their position. Two helicopter gunships loaded with Zuni rockets were tasked with flying support, arriving immediately once the artillery barrage was lifted. In spite of the artillery, the enemy continued to engage the Marines, killing three more of the squad members during the fifteen-minute barrage.

The Marines had responded fiercely. Even the wounded, who were sometimes wounded again, kept the numerically superior enemy force from mounting an effective assault aimed at overrunning them. Every rational man on that battlefield was scared. Every heart was racing and pumping. It seemed to be pure adrenaline and courage rather than blood. There was no panic or feeling of being doomed. The Marines maintained their discipline and fire control, shooting at selected targets and not at shadows or noises. The machine gunner fired his M-60 in controlled four- and five-round bursts. Terry Miller had trained his squad well.

With M-16s pressed tightly into their shoulders, the Marines searched for targets. They had all qualified on the tough Marine Corps rifle ranges. Steve shot two NVA soldiers who were advancing on the left flank. When they went down, the scout rolled and rose up to aim at charging infantrymen to the north. A mortar round exploded nearby. Steve felt a strong, almost electric jolt, accompanied by the slamming of a mallet striking him in both legs and the left shoulder. His wounds, although requiring medical treatment and brief hospitalization, were, under the circumstances, largely ignorable for the duration of the battle. He continued firing at the enemy.

Faintly, the sounds of approaching helicopters beating through the air came to the ears of the soldiers on both sides of the engagement. The guns ceased firing for a moment in anticipation of this new element being added to the fray the enemy weapons now pointed skyward. The North Vietnamese hoped for a lightly armed UHIE medevac chopper that would have to slow and flare in order to make a landing so the wounded could be loaded. In spite of its door guns, the medevac choppers were vulnerable targets during this type of operation.

The Marines, however, knew the Cobra gunships they had called for were already rolling in for their first attack run. The sleek little helicopter was basically a jet-powered gun platform. There were a variety of options available so far as to how the Cobra's weapons points were rigged. These Cobras packed ZunI rocket pods at the hard points on their stubby wing pylons. Each of them was armed with 20mm M-179 swiveling Gatling guns firing at a rate of 760 rounds per minute from a gun pod beneath the nose. Although the Cobras were lightly armored, they had slim head-on profiles that made them difficult targets to hit. The deadly gunship had a wing span of only ten feet, although she was fourteen feet high with the pilot seat above and behind the gunner.

The pilots of the highly maneuverable aircraft got clearance for hot gun runs. The first aircraft rolled in, its 1,400-horsepower engine pushing it along at 165 miles per hour. The gunner lined his sights up and began firing 2.75-inch Zuni rockets into the long axis of the tree line. He had four pods of rockets, a pair slung from each hard point. Each of the pods contained 19 rockets. Flames shot from the back of the pods as the rockets were ignited and launched independently. Smoke trailed the three-foot-long rockets to their targets. The rocket warheads were similar to the LAAW. However, they were considerably more effective.

The flight leader had set his run up from south to north. The attack helicopter was over and then past the target before the enemy could respond with any degree of effectiveness. He was barely clear when his wingman began his run from east to west. For good measure, after firing their rockets from stand-off position, the pilots hosed the enemy locations down with gunfire in passing. Shell casings rained down on the Marines. The Cobra's guns could easily take out a tank or cut a bloody swath through an infantry unit.

The first gunship had made a loop back to the west so his second run would be similar to the second gun attack but from the opposite direction. He came in at a different elevation, slightly higher and a bit to the north. The second Cobra pilot made his loop to the south. He came back into the attack from the southwest, flying to the northeast so as to cover a greater area of the target zone and avoid the same flight path as that of his wingman. An explosion indicated that his bullets had hit something besides soft flesh, perhaps a fuel tank or stored ammunition.

The enemy broke contact and fled, many of them being slammed to the ground by the impact of heavy bullets from the Cobras' Gatling guns. The pilots adjusted their flight paths so as to be on track of the fleeing soldiers. Their rockets killed some and scattered the remainder, destroying the enemy's unit cohesiveness, a critical element on the battlefield.

A larger infantry unit would have exploited the situation, attacking into the tree line or west to mop up the scattered NVA infantry. But the decimated squad simply lacked the numbers for such an action. The Marines were still taking sporadic rifle fire from the more stalwart enemy troops who remained in the tree line.

The Cobras had performed magnificently. They had broken up the enemy attack. The helicopters pulled out with half their ammunition on board, having already been assigned another mission. Two F-4 Phantom fighter/bombers had also been assigned to support the squad. While yet another Marine died on the ground, a call from the fixed wing pilots announced that the "fast-movers" were zero five minutes out, an eternity on the battlefield.

The Marine riflemen continued to search for and fire upon enemy targets. Kowalski gave no thought to the fact that he might die. His focus was automatically centered on the situation, on destroying the enemy with all the resources available. Pausing to change ammunition clips and to allow the barrel of his rifle to cool, Steve took a quick drink from his canteen. The warm water tasted metallic. It had another taste that came from the Halizone tablets he'd dropped into the canteen to kill bacteria and germs.

A heavy pounding from across the battlefield was significantly louder than the rifle fire and mortars. "Dinks have a fucking anti-aircraft gun over there," he hollered.

The enemy soldiers who had not fled were reacting to the biggest threat. Perhaps an experienced commander had ordered them to hold their fire in anticipation of the arrival of air support which was a more lucrative target.

"Man, we in some deep shit." The voice was rich and thick, with a southern-laced, somewhat backwoods accent. It was Bear, a huge black Marine with thick, hard muscles. Bear was from rural Alabama where he grew up on a cotton farm, part of what had once been a plantation worked by his ancestors as slaves.

"You suppose they're bear huntin'," another Marine asked loudly.

"Sometimes you git da bear. Sometimes da bear gits you. Most times they come home with a little rabbit like you," laughed the black Marine. Bear rose and fired a long burst from his M-16 into the trees.

"Get some, Bear!" Kowalski called out, using a common expression of encouragement and appreciation among the Marines.

Quite unexpectedly, a massive explosion ripped through the air as one of the departing Cobras exploded, boiling with smoke and hungry red and orange flames. Parts of the helicopter spun off as the gunship nosed to the ground. Two more Marines were lost.

Encouraged by the turn of events, the enemy forces began to reorganize and come back into the attack. The battle continued with renewed intensity. A forward air controller sent the surviving Cobra on to its next mission. He set up the fixed-wing aircraft for strikes against the enemy forces, warning them of the enemy anti-aircraft gun, which was now their primary target. Instead of coming in one behind the other, the F-4s attacked the target in a dangerous maneuver, one from the north and the other from the south, at a slightly higher altitude and only twenty feet apart, wing tip to wing tip.

Their jet engines howled, their cannons quiet, and the F-4s shrieked in, each releasing four silver canisters that tumbled end over end, flashing in the sunlight like diamonds falling from the sky. Antiaircraft and heavy machine gun bullets danced on the wings of one of the attacking aircraft and then chased after him as the unstoppable canisters tumbled to earth.

With astonishing accuracy, the canisters struck and continued to tumble, bouncing along the ground, creating long lines of breath-taking oxygen-robbing balls of fire that enveloped the tree line. Everything within a box fifty meters wide and two hundred meters long was on fire. Secondary explosions were heard, one following another as the hellish napalm burned among the enemy personnel, their weapons, and ammunition.

"Get some, air wing." A relief-filled comment full of awe.

"Makin' crispy critters," said another Marine.

"Poor bastards," observed Kowalski, glad he did not have to fight their side of the war. He glanced up at an F-4 as it streaked by in another low-altitude gun run. Steve noticed the white star in a blue circle with red, white, and blue bars to each side, a U.S. symbol. The number 106 was painted on the nose. NF-6 was painted above the large blue lettering spelling out NAVY. Along the top of the fuselage was the name of the pilot's ship, the U.S.S. Midway.

The Marines had hardly realized it as absorbed as they were in the napalm attack and follow-up strafing runs, but the NVA infantry opposing them had disengaged and for all purposes disappeared, dragging many of their dead and wounded with them.

"Quit gawking. You're not a bunch of fucking tourists," Sergeant Miller shouted at his handful of remaining squad members. "A troop of Girl Scouts throwing cookies could overrun this position. Gather the weapons and redistribute your ammunition. Improve your positions and prepare to defend against another ground assault."

While the squad was taking care of the wounded and gathering ammunition, some of which was recovered from the Marines who had been killed, Steve moved from one grave to another, finding that many of the mounds had been dug into. There was clear evidence the NVA had uncovered dozens of crates of weapons and ammunition. Steve found two crates still containing new SKS rifles wrapped in cosmoline and waxed paper. "Trophy weapons, guys!" he called out.

With the proper tags, those weapons could be taken home when a Marine's tour of duty was completed. The SKS is an excellent deer rifle. The men would be glad to get one. There were enough weapons for each of the surviving patrol members to claim one as well as for the headquarters command, thereby assuring the approving paperwork would be filed properly. Since the war trophy process began in the intelligence section, Steve would make certain the Cobra and F-4 pilots would get a weapon and that several would be sent to the supporting artillery battery.

While Steve was working among the graves, Sergeant Miller had requested emergency evacuation of fourteen men who had been wounded, seven patrol members who had been killed, and the crew members of the helicopter that had been shot down.

One of the Marines had his arm around a squadmate, consoling him over the loss of his best buddy. Another man with a wound tag around his neck was holding a bloody pressure bandage to his chest. His facial expressions revealed that he was still dazed, perhaps even in shock. One of the men who had not been wounded was taking photographs of the enemy dead.

Sergeant Miller approached the scout with news. "The dinks bugged out toward Dai Do. There are reports of major fighting all up and down the Cua Viet River. Seems like most of the Second NVA Division and the Third Marine Division are involved."

"So, we got here after most of them had recovered their weapons and taken off."

"A couple of hours earlier, and we'd have really been in the grinder."

"Marine sausage."

"The best kind."

"All bone, gristle, and bullshit."

While the battle against the 2nd NVA Division raged throughout I Corp, Sergeant Miller's squad, which had been rendered combat ineffective, was retired from the field. Due to his wounds, Steve spent five emotionally agonizing days confined to the Naval Support Activity Hospital, Da Nang, near the area called China Beach. While his wounds were mildly painful, the agony came from his self-induced restlessness and frustration over being out of action during the heavy fighting in which hundreds of Marines and thousands of NVA soldiers were being killed and wounded. It was part of virtually an entire generation of young men the North Vietnamese lost during the long war.

Steve, who was normally prone to teasing and flirting with the nurses or to get cards and chess tournaments started, became a fixture in the communications center, monitoring situation reports coming in from the field. The hospital was soon swamped with wounded of every kind, including POWs. Every medical specialist was involved in bloody emergency trauma surgery. Steve and other walking wounded from all services lent a hand where they could, moving stretchers and beds, carrying bandages and bedpans, sitting with the more seriously wounded, writing letters for those who couldn't write their own, but always asking questions, finding out what was going on, how the First Battalion was doing, seeking out friends and acquaintances, and sometimes choking back tears at the news of a friend's death.

By the time Steve was discharged from the hospital, the summer battle for Dong Ha was largely over. He returned for duty to a very somber, hauntingly thinned-out battalion. There was a full complement of headquarters command and staff support personnel present, clerks, cooks, drivers, and communicators, but the rank-and-file warriors, the machine gunners, mortarmen, radio operators, and the Marines of pure combat arms were few and far between. The prevailing uniform of those Steve did see was green camouflage utilities and white bandages.

Stepping into the headquarters tent, Steve stood before the desk of the chief administrative clerk, Gunnery Sergeant John Biggers. All the clerks were busy typing away or shuffling papers. Steve had never seen the Hide and Skaters so busy. He knew they were cranking out unit diary entries, death notices, recommendations for awards and promotions, combat after-action reports, and other papers and forms only the administrators knew had to be filled out.

The Gunny barely looked up from his tasks, his desk being covered with small piles of various forms and record books, each page requiring his approval and initials plus an officer's signature. Steve knew he would have to write the intelligence summary for the S-2 officer to sign.

There are all kinds of Marines, Steve thought. Himself an oddity among the Headquarters and Support Company (H&S=Hide and Skate), the scout knew the clerks, cooks, supply, and logistics staff often considered the intelligence scouts to be prima donnas. Still, the scouts were the only headquarters section whose personnel spent the majority of their time in the field with a rifle in their hands.

"Kowalski, right?" The Gunny asked gruffly as if he didn't know.

"Yeah, back from the hospital." Steve handed his return-to-duty order over to the chief clerk. It went on top of a stack of similar documents—an impressive stack. Each of the documents represented a wounded Marine who was being returned to combat duty. The clerks would be busy typing their Purple Heart awards.

"Go on back," Gunny Biggers said with a head nod. "The major will see you."

With a shrug, Steve shouldered his safed weapon and walked through the tent past rough wood desks painted dark forest green where the clerks were bustling about, four of them, all busy for a change. He stopped and, lacking a door to knock on, cleared his throat while standing at attention centered on that part of the tent that had been partitioned off for the battalion commander, Lt. Col. James Blackburn.

But it wasn't Colonel Blackburn who looked up from signing papers. It was Major Small, who a week ago had been a captain and Steve's S-2 officer. A smile crept across the major's weary face.

"Lance Corporal Kowalski reporting as ordered, sir!" Steve boomed.

"Drag up a chair, Kowalski. It's good to have you back."

"Good to be back, sir."

There was an awkward moment of silence. Although there was only a six-year age difference between the two men, the rank differential was uncomfortably large given how closely together the men worked.

"Place is a cluster fuck," the major admitted, knowing his S-2 scout to be above average in perception and intelligence. He also knew Kowalski held a top secret security clearance and an associate's degree from a Texas junior college.

"We kicked the 2nd NVA Division's butt. It will take at least two years for them to return to the field with the ability to conduct combat operations again. The Third Marine Division got hammered a bit too. The division is in good shape, but One Three will not be fully combat effective for another four to six months."

"Yes, sir," Steve responded, wondering where the discussion was going.

"With rotation attrition and combat losses, our rifle companies are down to about ninety effectives."

Steve knew a fully staffed, unreinforced rifle company roster was 204 men.

"About a third more are walking wounded like yourself who are returning from hospitals. They fill the roster but will be on light duty for up to ninety days."

"Yes, sir." That explained the four- to six-month time line.

"Division is sending out majors to temporarily command companies and captains to command platoons. Most of them will come from support staff. They may not have much combat experience in small unit tactics. It's a chance for them to gain command experience." The major paused to organize his thoughts. "Survivors, almost to a man, have been promoted, including you," he continued.

"Thank you, major."

"Don't thank me, Marine. You earned it."

"Yes sir."

"Along with a recommendation for the Bronze Star."

Steve didn't know what to say. Thank you hardly seemed appropriate.

"That's the good news," Major Small continued.

Steve waited to hear the bad news. The major was in the habit of pausing between passing along bits of information as if allowing his "audience" time to digest each snippet.

"We are shorthanded elsewhere. The two shop was the hardest hit."

The S-2 "shop" was made up of the S-2 officer, the intelligence assistant or chief scout, and eight field scouts, four Vietnamese Kit Carson Scouts, attached snipers and dogs with their handlers, and a translator. When asked what they did, the scouts often answered, "A scout's job is to know the lay of the land...and be able to lead you to her."

"We're sort of like the old cavalry scouts who came riding hell bent for leather back to the fort, three arrows in their back, hollering "Injuns!" Steve sometimes pointed out. The truth was that the job was stressful, demanding, and extremely dangerous.

"How hard were we hit, major?"

"Personius, McCool, Sanders, KIA. Middleton WIA and medivacked home. Dykus, Hoskins, and yourself WIA and returning to light duty. Sergeant Burton was wounded. We don't know how badly yet. Tsoi was on R&R."

"Damn, that's a one hundred percent casualty rating, sir."

"We are filing requests for replacements now. They'll filter in as they receive their orders. With the returning wounded coming in as their condition improves, we'll be fully operational before the rest of the battalion."

"Yes sir." Steve was aware of the redundancy of his responses but didn't know what else to say.

"For now everyone is stepping up and pulling double duty."

"I understand, sir." Steve really wanted to talk about the major's promotion and command position, curious as to his possible replacement as the S-2 officer.

"I will not be returning to the two shop. When we get a light colonel, I will become the battalion's executive officer."

"Congratulations, sir." This was good for Steve to know. He'd always gotten along well with Major Small, who, as a captain and his commanding officer, had given him excellent conduct and proficiency marks.

"Until we get a qualified intelligence officer, and that may be a while, you'll be the acting S-2."

Newly promoted to corporal, Steve was shocked to even be temporarily standing in for the captain, a position way above his pay grade.

CHAPTER TWO
QUANG TRI COMBAT BASE
REPUBLIC OF SOUTH VIETNAM

The evening's round of back alley bridge card games had just begun in the two shop. There were poker and craps games being played, but not nearly to the extent as portrayed in World War Two movies and popular fiction. They were only played for money. Back Alley was played for bragging rights. It was another war, another generation in so many ways. In a war zone everyone is on duty twenty-four seven; however, at the rear headquarters those not on an actual post took time to relax when they could, to listen to the radio, write letters, read, play a game, or have a drink and socialize with friends.

Steve was a fierce competitor at every game he played, from football to chess. Although he hated to lose, he was a good sport who was frequently sought out by someone looking for a partner or building a team. Steve's regular card game partner was Second Lieutenant David Reuthling, a tall, dark-featured graduate of Notre Dame. The former basketball star was Bravo Company's forward observer for artillery. David was a recent graduate of the artillery officer's school at Fort Sill in Lawton, Oklahoma. In the field, he shared a "hootch" made from two shelter halves with Steve.

Second Lieutenant Kevin Cahallan, a rather unique individual from Franklin Square, New York, was one of the usual foursome. Extremely bright, Kevin had a keen sense of social obligations that extended globally. He was a former member of the Peace Corps who had worked in Pakistan before joining the Marine Corps.

Sandy Hunt, the somewhat clumsy and inept son of a serving Marine Corps general, was Kevin's partner. The young platoon commander was being given the opportunity to grow into his bars by his more experienced platoon sergeant and his company commander.

Hoskins was leading a night patrol around the base perimeter. Tommy Tsoi was writing a letter to his girlfriend, Janet. Dykus was on radio watch.

"Another beer?" Dave asked generally as he stretched a hairy, lanky arm out to the cooler.

"I'm good," Steve said.

"Sure." Sandy reached out for his beer.

"As long as it's cold and alcoholic," Kevin replied.

In the rear area, each Marine was rationed to two free canned drinks per day, either soda pops or beer. Anything over that cost the Marines ten cents per can. The Marines in the rear drank a lot of beer whenever they got the chance. Sandy was writing a book his friends were sure would become a best seller with the title Vietnam: In the Mud, the Blood, and the Beer.

"Eight spades," bid Dave. It was a strong bid with only thirteen tricks per hand. Dave was an aggressive player who routinely got set as a result.

"You're set, mother fucker,"from Sandy, who was keeping score. Sandy was making an effort to toughen up, at times mistakenly using some crudeness to enhance that image.

Dave led with aces in diamonds and hearts, followed by the high joker, low joker, and the ace of spades. Kevin picked up the off-suit lead in clubs, but Steve trumped his second club lead with a seven of spades, losing to a king-high heart from Sandy's hand on the next play.

Sandy took tricks with a king of diamonds and the king of spades, a poor lead with the highest trump card out. A low spade lead was taken by Kevin, who followed with the ten, which Steve took with the jack. Dave took the last trick with the remaining high spade.

Dave leaned back, grinning as he and Steve won the hand eight to five. Kevin began shuffling the deck for another hand. The company runner, the youngest and smallest Marine in the battalion, burst into the tent breathing hard after running from tent to tent with an announcement.

"We've got a notice of movement to action. Officer's call in five minutes," he gasped.

And then, without answering questions being fired at him, the runner was off on his way to another tent. The Marines flew into action, cards and letters forgotten. Steve rushed to check with PFC Dykus. Since he was on the radio, he would know exactly what was going on.

"What's up, Bill?" Steve asked.

"Charlie Company's getting hit out in the boonies. No big deal yet."

That puzzled Steve. "Something's up. We got an officer's call and notice of movement to action. What is Charlie's location?"

Dykus read off the map coordinates. Steve checked them against his supply of maps. He looked at the situation map and made several notes. With those in hand, he made his way to the headquarters tent, which was quickly becoming crowded with the battalion's officers and section heads that were required to attend the officer's call. Charlie Company was in the field and Delta Company was on perimeter duty. As a result the assembly was only half a battalion's worth of officers.

The new battalion commander had only arrived three days ago. He'd been in constant meetings with regimental, division, corps, and Vietnamese staff. He'd yet to meet most of his own staff, and now it appeared he was to lead them into combat. Steve was probably not the only one to wonder if the colonel was overreacting to the contact. Each of them was curious to some extent about the new commander. They all wanted a real tiger, a Chesty Puller, a fighting Marine who had real concerns not just for his mission and his own career but for the

Marines he commanded as well.

The only word on the colonel so far was that he looked like a Marine and talked like a Marine. "So, he talks the talk, but the question is, can he walk the walk?" Dykus had asked.

Lieutenant Colonel Greenwood was sallow and lean. He appeared to be too old for his rank and command. He had a pronounced Adams apple that appeared to bob up and down as he talked so much you couldn't help but watch it. The immediate perception was that the colonel was a career pencil pusher who was getting his six-month combat command ticket punched so he could retire at full colonel's pay. That could mean trouble for a battalion. Fortunately, that didn't happen often in the Marine Corps.

The thin, gray-haired colonel stood and cleared his throat to quiet the murmurs in the room. "Gentlemen, we have a situation," he announced. The commander was slapping his left palm with a bullet-tipped swagger stick held in his right hand. A bit of posturing perhaps, thought many in the tent.

"Charlie Company, while conducting a routine combat operation in the vicinity of Antennae Valley, came under fire from well-coordinated artillery-supported infantry shortly after establishing their night defensive positions. Casualties were light; however, the listening posts have reported significant movement from all quarters. It appears the NVA is attempting to surround and overrun the company. Of course, we will not allow that to happen. I'll hear from operations first."

Major McDougal, a shirt-sleeved officer with combat weariness ringing his eyes, stood. "Yes sir. Our rifle companies are currently operating at sixty percent of our authorized organizational strength. Of that force, approximately forty percent of the men have less than three months in country and have had no significant combat experience.

"Delta Company will not be available until they are replaced on the perimeter, two days at the very least. Alpha and Bravo companies are combat-ready and available. A light provisional rifle company can be assembled from our cooks, clerks, and other support personnel." The major sat.

"Leave Delta Company in place, major. Assemble that provisional rifle company under your command. Strip headquarters staff to a skeleton. I want everyone who is able to carry a rifle in the field."

"Yes sir."

"Supply?"

"Major Demming, colonel," the supply officer responded as he stood like a jack in the box. He was a bookish-looking man whose thick glasses gave him an unfortunate nickname "Fish eyes." "We have sufficient supplies of ammunition, rations, and other necessities to sustain four rifle companies in combat for four days. We will daily requisition depleted amounts in order to maintain that level of supply. There are no divisional shortages. There are no major operations underway. At the moment, we will have the top priority throughout the division for land and air support efforts."

"Make seven days our new SOP major. I don't want any of my Marines to ever be low on bullets, beans, or band-aids. Do you understand that, major ?"

"Yes, sir," the chastised supply officer answered, already thinking of requesting a transfer.

"And major, once we have a secure LZ, I want you on site, coordinating all flights in and out. Give your assistant some back-up experience. I want the rank and file to see the command staff of this battalion in the field with them. It's good for morale."

"Yes sir."

"Where's my two?"

Steve stood. "Corporal Kowalski, sir."

The colonel seemed startled. "You are my senior intelligence staffer, the S-2 officer?"

"Yes sir."

"Well, let's get on with it, son."

Without a show of nervousness or hesitation, Steve began the briefing he had been going over in his mind. "Charlie Company is located at zero, six, eight on map 5312 dash three. If you need any maps, I have a supply of them on hand at the two shop.

"Historically operating in the immediate vicinity has been the 88th NVA Artillery Regiment supplied with 100mm rockets, 75mm pack howitzers, 57mm anti-aircraft guns, 60 and 82mm mortars, and RPG-7s. This area is also the home base of the 66th NVA Sapper Battalion. They primarily act in support of the 6th VC Infantry Regiment and units infiltrating from the Ho Chi Minh Trail.

"I have established BLACK HORSE as the number brevity code as of 2400 hours this evening. Thrust points are as follows: states at zero five, eighty-six; presidents at zero seven, ninety-two; and colors at zero six, ninety-eight."

The officers were copying this important information in the notebooks they all carried. The number brevity code was always two five-letter words with no letters being repeated. The letters were used in code, with B representing one and continuing consecutively with E representing zero. Thrust points were intersecting grid coordinates used to avoid sending locations in the clear. Any state, any president, and any color were used. In that manner, a call relaying from Grant up two, right three, or from Texas, down three, right five, and from Blue, up five, right four, would all be at the same location on the map. The next man who called in using this system might use from Roosevelt, from Oklahoma, and from Green, and the coordinates would remain the same. The potential mixtures were a very large number, a difficult code to break, and one that changed at any time but at least frequently. The next set might be from animals, from cities, from planets, or anything else of common knowledge you might think of.

"Alright, gentlemen," the colonel interrupted. "We all know we need to relieve Charlie Company. The NVA may attack them at dawn or even before. We've got to be in a position before they launch their attack in order to relieve those Marines. It is not feasible to land helicopters in the dark without a prepared and marked landing zone that becomes an aiming beacon for that enemy artillery unit. This means a night march to get us in position to reinforce Charlie Company."

There was a collective sucking in of breath. A night march would be dangerous and scary indeed. The enemy generally owned the night.

"I grant you this is a hazardous undertaking fraught with the potential for failure. It is also bold, and I would think unexpected...Kowalski, are you up to leading us on a night march?"

"Yes, sir," Steve didn't hesitate to affirm his commander.

"You have the training for this?"

"I do, colonel."

"And the experience?"

"I don't think any of us have enough of that, sir."

There was a scattering of nervous laughs.

"You got the balls for this, son?"

"Solid brass, colonel."

"You'll do, corporal." The colonel turned his attention to the entire assembly. "Gentlemen, we mount out in fifteen minutes. We'll ride in a truck convoy to Route Nine about six clicks south of Charlie Company's position. We'll depart the trucks there and immediately commence our overland approach. Strict noise discipline is of the utmost import during this movement.

"The order of march will be the scout element, Bravo Company, the command group, and Alpha Company. I will be with the command element. Major Small will be in command here. I'll see you gentlemen and your Marines on the road in fifteen minutes."

The colonel had managed to raise some eyebrows. The old man talked like he just might be a tiger. Not all of his staff officers were excited by the prospect of facing close combat; however, all of them who came under small arms fire would be awarded a combat action ribbon equivalent to the Army's combat infantryman's badge which could be important to one's career.

The Marines filled their plastic canteens from lister bags scattered throughout the tent camp. They wiped down and checked the actions of their weapons. Magazines and bandoliers were filled with ammunition. They strapped on web belts hung with first aid packets, bayonets, machetes, and magazine pouches. They hung grenades for various uses, explosive, smoke, and gas, from chest straps. Into their pockets they stuffed maps, strobe lights, rifle cleaning supplies, bug chow, Halizone and salt tablets, cigarettes and lighters, photos and a letter, even bottles of Tabasco sauce. Within moments, the Marines had screwed their helmets on and were prepared for war.

Twelve six-by-troop carriers were quickly loaded with twenty Marines each. There would be no armed escorts. The canvas sides were rolled up for observation and to allow quick egress in case of ambush. Each of the Marines had been through numerous quick reaction drills and knew where to go and what to do in case of an ambush. During the ride, their sergeants went over those actions again. A part of Marine Corps training is to drill, drill, and drill again until the lessons have been learned to the point of becoming automatic.

"The more you sweat in peace, the less you bleed in war," was a Marine Corps axiom Steve Kowalski had wholeheartedly embraced. There was concern over the dangers the Marines faced from the moment they boarded the transport trucks. Armed convoys were frequently ambushed along the roads in Northern I Corp. Those roads were often mined. Circumstances and the situation dictated the high-speed race in spite of the possibility of ambushes, mines, and even accidents under blackout conditions. For an hour the keyed-up Marines jostled and bounced, feeling every bump and dip in the crushed gravel road, expecting disaster to strike at any moment.

Steve heard the grumbles. "Fifteen minutes by helicopter... dangerous night march... unnecessary..."

He had formed his own opinion, judiciously keeping it to himself. The enemy was undoubtedly expecting a heliborne assault soon after dawn. Their anti-aircraft weapons would be positioned to present a formidable defense against helicopters and even supporting fighter jets. Their ground forces would be prepared to melt into the jungle if the numbers were overwhelmingly against them. The colonel's tactics would surprise the enemy, providing an opportunity for the battalion and its new commander to score a decisive victory.

The trucks finally pulled over and stopped, engines running. There were no intersecting roads or trails, no huts or villages close by. The relatively flat terrain was covered with thick, knee-high fibrous grasses. Stepping into it, Steve knew he would feel exposed. Nearby hills with thick green foliage overlooked their position. That was where the patrol was heading. Steve's nerves were tingling with anticipation.

Platoon commanders and squad leaders counted heads and signaled their readiness to move out. The order to assume marching was passed quickly up and down the line. Show time, Steve thought. Using hand and arms signals, the scout led the battalion out on a compass heading of 270 degrees true north, trying to remember every lesson of his orienteering course as well as the scouting and patrolling classes he'd attended. The scout element advanced in a diamond formation with Steve on the point, Hoskins on his left flank, and Tsoi on his right. Dykus, in the rear, had the difficult job of maintaining both distance between and contact with the scout and the main body. Kowalski, though, was comfortable with his team. They had all repeatedly proven themselves in combat situations.

The job he had given Dykus was difficult enough on daytime patrols when the jungle could suddenly swallow an entire seventy-two-man platoon in only a few steps and with radios, but a night march under silenced conditions and with added stress factors required particular diligence. Dykus usually carried a radio to facilitate communications between the lead element and the unit they were working for. On this mission he had no radio and his hand and arm signals could not be seen.

Peering into the darkness, his rifle cradled in his arm for quick response, the oft-referred-to compass in his right hand, Steve stepped off into a night of gut-wrenching activity. Everything in Vietnam was the enemy. The people, the terrain, especially the jungle, the insects and animals, and the noise soldiers made on the move. Looking over his shoulder, Steve saw the patrol bunching up. It was only natural in the face of imminent danger to seek your own, to bolster your courage by their presence, to calm your nerves.

Bunching up though was dangerous. A grenade would kill more than properly spaced men that way. An artillery or mortar shell could devastate a platoon of men if they were tightly grouped near the impact zone. Emphatically signaling for the men to spread out, Steve could get no response. The men could not see him. The chief scout held the patrol up with a quick flash from his red lens pencil flashlight. He ran back to Dykus and whispered instructions into his ear. Not waiting to see his instructions carried out, Steve hurried back to the point position. Dykus dropped back, tactfully reminding the company and platoon commanders, captains and lieutenants, to have their men maintain a proper distance.

Back on point, Steve moved forward, searching for a small wash draining from a creek running northeast. When they reached the creek, the patrol would change directions to throw off any watchers or searchers responding to a report of their presence. Five hundred meters into the patrol the foliage began to change. Widely scattered green elephant grass grew in high bunches. Steve examined one of them. The grass was unsupported by anything other than a single stalk. The leaves were thin and thick, growing close to the stalk. It had no thorns. However, the stalk and undersides of the leaves were covered with hair-fine threads that clung to his hand. They left a long-lasting burning sensation like stinging nettles. Another enemy to be avoided. Through Dykus, Steve warned the patrol to avoid the plants.

The brush didn't grow steadily higher at a given angle or thicker by graduation. The Marines came suddenly upon a brush thicket, a wall separating the two types of foliage virtually hidden by the darkness. Beyond this thick stand of brush was a tree line standing like soldiers guarding their headquarters. Steve knew this growth of trees would be more like a dense forest than a jungle.

The thicket was a mixture of a wide variety of foliage. This place is a botanist's wet dream, Steve thought. Before his arrival in the jungles of Vietnam, Steve had no idea of the remarkable diversity of plant life there was in the world. The trees before him were thin and tall without branches until near the crest, where the tree branches out into a thin umbrella of small leaves. Those trees would provide little shade, but that was not their purpose in life.

Among the trees were patches of low brush, each growth perhaps two feet in diameter. Among them were thickets of broad leaf plants with sharp points reminding the scout of mother-in-law's tongue. Steve recognized these as dry land plants that thrived in sunlight. The ground was hard but not sandy like a desert.

Have we missed the wash? Steve wondered. If there is a creek or stream, it will be along that tree line, he decided. Steve called the patrol to a halt by throwing his right arm up. The Marines behind him squatted down among the foliage, poised to move. Only their shoulders and helmets were above the tall grass. The men had begun to sweat and itch. A break was welcome. Steve pulled a plastic shelter half over his head. He pulled out his map and a small pencil light. He studied the map, searching for the wash and the creek and verifying its location. The wash must be dried up, Steve concluded. The creek has to be along that tree line.

The scout signaled the patrol to move out toward the tree line. The foliage changed again, giving way to green grasses and thick brush with broad green leaves, an indication of the nearby presence of a water source. Steve found the creek. The banks were only a foot high. It was, however, broad and shallow like many rivers on the Great Plains of America.

The water ran smoothly over a bed of time-polished rocks. Steve thought the enemy might have a watering point or a base camp on the creek's banks. Walking down the center of the creek would be the easiest route to take; however, there was too much danger that doing so would expose the patrol. And there would undoubtedly be too much loud splashing, even slipping and falling with loud splashes.

The scout sent flankers out to both sides of the creek. Although Steve would theoretically be on point, the flankers would be ahead of him so they could warn the patrol if the enemy was spotted. Following the chief scout's suggestion, the patrol members split up, half to the left and half to the right. They covered their faces with mud from the creek. They settled into the shallow water, hugging the banks on their stomachs in the classic infantry crawl. Using his rifle as a guide, holding it in his right hand up out of the water along the bank, Steve knew he could bring his weapon into a firing position quickly.

At the same time, he realized the left-handers forced to hold their rifles in their right hands would have some difficulty bringing their weapons into action. The same was true of the right-handers on the left bank. It was a small thing involving only four left-handers who traded places with right-handers on the opposite bank. Still, it emphasized Steve's attention to details and made a difference of eight rifles that could get into action more quickly, and speed was often a lifesaver on the battlefield.

On his stomach in the water, Steve pulled hands full of grass to loop over his helmet. He knew the small creek was moving tons of fertile soil from the mountains to the lowland rice paddies. He tried not to think about the leeches that would be attaching themselves to his body, bloating themselves on his blood. Slowly and quietly, the patrol crawled along the creek bed. Every man was critically aware of the need to maintain strict noise discipline.

Gradually, the creek narrowed and deepened. The banks became higher. The water moved faster. Foliage grew taller, arching out over the banks, helping to conceal the Marines. The deeper water cooled the soaked Marines. Steve began searching for a place to leave the creek. That location presented itself where the creek widened into a pool where the grass-covered banks were shallow. Palms grew down to the water's edge. Steve knew that would mean cultivation, possibly with civilians in the immediate vicinity. Their presence could complicate the mission. The flankers, however, had given no warnings.

Steve had the patrol stop in place. He crept forward to a large palm tree. A one hundred-foot length of quarter-inch nylon rope hung at his hip. A small metal ring was fixed to one end of the rope. The scout wrapped the rope around the palm, pulling the opposite end through the ring. It was more secure than a knot and quicker to undo. Steve walked back to the creek. At the end of the rope, he tied ten knots a foot apart. They would provide solid grips for the waterlogged men to use as they pulled themselves out of the water without slipping and splashing or floundering and making noise.

Exploring the creek was completely successful. The patrol moved into the thicker jungle mountain terrain they could not avoid passing through to reach Charlie Company. With every step they took and every foot they moved closer to Charlie Company's location, the danger of being discovered increased. There was no doubt that the enemy was there, but exactly where? How tired and alert are they? Steve wondered. How are they deployed? Which way are they facing? Do they have guards and listening posts established? Do they have night vision goggles? Have they placed ambush units on the likely approach routes?

The scout scanned left to right and forward, his eyes sweeping like radar working from the horizon. In and then back out every few paces. He stopped to look and listen every one hundred paces, watching for the twinkling of a campfire or the glow of a cigarette. He listened for the hum or squawk of a radio, for coughs, snores, the shuffling of feet, or the click of metal on metal. Steve had also learned that he could sometimes smell the enemy. He sniffed the air for body odors, the smell of oil and gasoline, even the smell of their food, especially the pungent spicy sauces they used on everything. A non-smoker, Steve had a keen nose for cigarette smoke.

The use of all his senses came automatically after years of training and months of leading patrols in combat. There was also an element of survival instinct involved. Moving on, Steve felt as if he were leading a platoon of elephants with the noises he heard the Marine behind him making. A canteen clanked against a bayonet. Untapped dog tags tinkled against one another. A man coughed. Another stumbled and swore. You loud sumbitches are going to get me killed, Steve thought.

With every sound, the scout stopped to listen for whispered commands or the click of a rifle's safety. There were no threatening noises among the buzzing of insects, the mating calls of lizards, and the squeak and scurry of a mouse. All Steve heard were the natural sounds of the jungle. A nerve-sapping hour and a half after unloading from the trucks, the patrol reached checkpoint one. They had only traveled a bit over a thousand meters. There were five more clicks to go and only three hours to get in place before daylight. They would have to move faster, at the sacrifice of some security, of course. Steve motioned for the scout element to converge on his position.

"We've got to pick up the pace," he told them in a muted voice. "I want the flankers to close in a bit. Tsoi, you take the point. If you are challenged, start speaking harsh Chinese. Throw the challenge right back at them. Hoskins and I will scout well forward and move you up in five hundred-meter increments at twenty-minute intervals. Pass the word back to the colonel."

Steve handed his rifle to Dykus and unshucked his pack. He stripped down to his jungle utilities, giving up his grenades, canteens, and ammunition, down to nothing but a black carbon bayonet gripped in his right hand. Hoskins followed suit, a large lump in his throat.

"Oohrah!" Steve growled softly. It was a Marine thing. The scouts melted quickly into the jungle. Moving silently from deep shadow to deep shadow, all their senses quivering, the scouts covered and cleared the next five hundred meters in the allotted twenty minutes. The main body would now begin moving forward.

Checkpoints two and three were cleared and reached quickly. Approaching checkpoint four, Hoskins gave Steve the signal for Stop! Look! Listen! The senior scout froze in his tracks. He peered into the darkness. He observed nothing to alarm him. He concentrated on listening but heard nothing. Hoskins pointed to his nose, but Steve could smell nothing but the rather fetid smells of the jungle.

Steve trusted that Hoskins had smelled something. He might be near a camp where he could smell the nguoc mam, a fermented fish sauce the enemy would have mixed with their rice. He might be near a slit trench where the enemy had relieved themselves. Or he might be close enough to smell their sweating bodies.

Steve knew he would have to trust Hoskins and follow his lead at that point. The Michigan Marine motioned for a hammer and anvil style approach. Moving in silently, trying to control his breathing and hammering heart, Steve closed in on the other Marine's forward flank. Then Steve spotted movement. It was there, and then it was gone. What was it? Could it have been an animal, a large insect, or was it a man? The Marine froze again. There has to be two men. He crouched down, waiting for a shout of alarm or the hissed whisper from the guard who had spotted him. He made out the silhouette of a man.

There was a rifle in his hands. He wore a pith helmet. His back was turned to the Marine. Steve crept to within ten feet of the NVA soldier without being detected. But he could not locate the second guard. A decision had to be made. This was not the time or place for the parade ground spit and polish part of being a Marine. It was time for the down-and-dirty basics of being a trained killer.

Like a pouncing cat, Steve sprang forward, his left forearm slipping under the guard's chin and pulling him backwards. Simultaneously, Steve slammed his knee into the man's back with all the force he could muster as he drove his bayonet into his kidney, ripping outward and cutting through organ and flesh. It was, as taught and intended, a vicious attack designed to be quick and deadly.

The dying man quivered in Steve's arms. The scout let him down gently, not out of respect for a slain warrior but to minimize any noise he might make. Steve moved toward where he had last seen Hoskins in case he needed help. That Marine didn't need Steve's assistance. He had located the other NVA guard at the listening post. He'd been sleeping nearby. He never woke up.

The scouts returned to the patrol to retrieve their weapons and gear. Steve took a long drink of water and used a full canteen to wash some of the blood from his hands and bayonet. Then, rather than working forward, the scouts had to work the flanks, silently taking out two more listening posts to clear the path for the rifle companies to advance. Unaffected to a large extent in the short term by his actions, the long-term effects of such violent hand-to-hand actions would cause many men to experience serious post-traumatic stress problems.

It seemed a miracle, but the entire unit arrived at their assault point undetected. With the listening posts eliminated, the relief force could now move through the enemy lines under stealth. They would remain in place and rest briefly before doing so. The colonel held an officer's call to issue his revised orders for the attack in relief of Charlie Company.

"At 0600 Charlie Company will throw green smoke grenades just outside of their perimeter. That is the signal for the relief force to begin fighting its way through the enemy and enter the defensive lines and, in time, expand and improve the perimeter with the goal of conducting search and destroy patrols from that location. Stand down at fifty percent until 0530. Have your men ready to respond without additional orders when those green smoke grenades pop. Maintain tight noise discipline until then."

The Marines were alert and poised for the attack when the green smoke grenades were tossed out. The Vietnamese, unaware of the relief force's presence, were not. With rifles firing on full automatic, grenades being tossed to the left and to the right, bayonets slamming into fragile chests, and rifle butts smashing into blood-pulped faces, the Marines quickly forced a wedge in the enemy lines.

No Marines were lost in the attack, although several received relatively minor wounds. The relief forces took up positions along the existing perimeter and began firing toward the NVA forces. Although they had been totally surprised, the enemy recovered and responded quickly. The Marines were soon being pounded by heavy artillery. The sounds of "Incoming!" being shouted seemed a bit superfluous as the enemy rounds exploded within the Marines' perimeter.

As the first round impacted, the Marines scurried for cover. The new arrivals had not even begun to dig fighting holes. Steve ducked behind a Jeep. He watched in awe as an exploding artillery round flipped another Jeep over in the air as if it were a mere plastic toy. To Steve, it looked like a scene straight out of a war movie. It was almost unreal, as if he were watching that movie in 3-D.

Charlie Company had established its headquarters in the basement of the ruins of a shelled-out pagoda. The roof beams had collapsed due to the explosions and resultant fires. Only a corner of the temple's walls still stood. Steve decided it was a better place to be than behind the Jeep the Vietnamese appeared to be targeting. He raced across the impact zone and slid down the rough wood steps of the basement, his butt bouncing painfully on each step. The assembled staff looked up with startled expressions on their faces. "They're shooting big bullets up there," Steve commented wryly.

Once his eyes adjusted to the dim lighting in the basement, Steve noticed the corpse of a Vietnamese soldier that had been shoved into a corner. His had not been a recent death. Still, he was more rotten than mummified. Six months previously, Steve might have lost his lunch at the sight. Now he simply accepted the putrid smell as a part of combat, a smell that would always take him back to Vietnam.

Unrelated to the corpse, Steve was shaking and weak in the knees. He was living a nightmare, not a war movie. He had just killed three men with a bayonet. Per his training, the attacks were vicious, with no quarter given and none taken. This wasn't a gentleman's chivalrous war like the fliers of World War One had fought. Steve had not given any of the enemy soldiers a chance to fight back. He struck like the Recon motto: Swiftly, Silently, Deadly.

Steve needed a moment to regain his composure. This was surreal, more like a movie than the real thing sometimes, the overhead light fixture shaking with the artillery whistling overhead and exploding nearby. And there was a rank differential. Even the clerks outranked Steve, but he was the man with the responsibility for making life-and-death decisions for others.

Steve realized that he was changing in a number of ways. He wasn't sure if he liked what he was becoming. Physically, he was down from a hard, muscular 210 pounds to a lean 178. There had not been much fat for him to lose. He'd been an athletic Marine in excellent condition when he arrived in Vietnam. It wasn't the physical condition that gave him cause for concern. The killing no longer seemed to bother him. He was not a robot. He had not become a thoughtless killing machine or a psycho who enjoyed the war. He simply coped by becoming numb to it all.

Steve's father had fought in the "war to end all wars," which the Allies had won. Why then has war come upon my generation, he wondered. Steve often pondered such questions as why am I here?

Mixed with thoughts such as I could have been in college. How do so many others my age know what they want to be and do with their lives at such an early age? I could have taken a job and avoided the draft and run away to Canada as many have. But not me. NOOO, I have to go and join the fucking, groundpounding, brute-brawling Marine Corps.

At the induction center, I passed everyone's test. All the service recruiters had wanted me. I could be doing something more with airplanes than jumping out of them every chance I get. I could have joined the Navy and been stationed at Pearl Harbor maybe. Live on the beach chasing girls in bikinis; have a girl in every port.

My black book is full. I could have avoided military service by getting married. I dated at least a dozen beauties who'd marry me in a quick minute, but there isn't a whole brain among the lot of them. Annette, "Annie and her 45s," we called her, my Dallas Texans cheerleader, is going to make someone a nice trophy wife. I will never climb those midnight mountains again. Suzie had gone to Hollywood and was screwing her way into bit-part B-movie roles. Hot little Cindy had married the nephew of the lieutenant governor. Steve wondered if he knew "My Cin" still wrote her Marine.

More than any of them Steve wondered about "carrot top," the woman who had kept him tongue-tied and made him feel as clumsy as some country bumpkin on a date with a world-class movie star. But he didn't have long to think about home and life's different paths in the midst of a raging battle.

Throughout the night a squad of Marines that had become separated from the main body called in situation reports of their desperate struggle against a numerically superior enemy force. A helicopter assault was scheduled to provide relief and extract the squad from the dangerous situation. Steve heard the radioman announce, "Choppers inbound."

Bravo Company was ready. Steve left the basement to join his company. Near the staging point, seven Marines who would be forever young in the memories of family and friends lay in a row, covered by their ponchos, waiting for transfer to the mortuary in Da Nang. Steve watched the "Sea Knight" as it flared, descending, its howling jet engine and rotors shooting stinging blasts of dirt, wood chips, and pebbles in every direction. A corner of a poncho caught some air and peeled loose, flapping wildly in the rotor-produced wind storm.

Sergeant Miller, his young face pale and waxen, slightly bluish already, was revealed by the loose poncho. As he passed, Steve wondered what purpose Miller's death had served. He wondered where Terry was now and what he was now, besides rotting flesh. Steve did not have time to dwell on the questions. He ran up the ramp of the helicopter which was taking sporadic small arms fire. The pilot and crew were anxious to get in the air and put some distance between their craft and those guns.

The doorgunner responded to the enemy's rifle fire, opening up with his M-60 machine gun . The ramp was closing as the heavily loaded aircraft moved forward, nose down to pick up speed. They lifted off, rising almost magically. The pilot circled the landing zone while other helicopters landed, loaded, and joined the formation. The door gunner stopped firing. They had quickly flown out of the range of enemy guns. Steve watched as the assistant gunner smoothly changed barrels, cleaned the gun, and fed a new belt of linked ammunition into the machine gun. Using his foot, he swept the links from the expended ammunition out of the door.

The flight was noisy, cool, and brief. Steve felt a falling-away sensation as the helicopter began a rapid descent. The machine gunner was hammering away again. Steve couldn't see what he was shooting at. The crew chief gestured and hollered over the howling of the jet engine. "Lock and load!"

Every Marine aboard that aircraft knew they were challenging death again. Steve thought about it briefly as he jammed a magazine home and pulled the chambering lever back. Releasing it, he clicked the safety to the off position, and the selector switched to automatic. The hydraulic ramp began to whine and lower. A blast of light and cold air rushed in. The chopper touched down. The Marines raced off, under fire, once again born to battle from the womb of a helicopter.

An officer from Charlie Company was directing troops to positions around the small knolls with a slight saddle running between them. The knolls were the predominant terrain feature of the immediate vicinity. They sat atop a hill with a medium-grade climb six hundred feet above the surrounding terrain. A stream meandered through the valley, disappearing in a copse of some size before appearing again to the east. It was a good defensive position. Had it not been, a squad could not have held it throughout the night.

The intensity of the battle that had taken place there was quite evident. Small cardboard boxes that had once held rifle ball ammunition littered the ground like fallen leaves. The Marines would have used the ammunition in their magazines before pulling individual bullets out of the boxes and loading them into the 19-round magazines.

The plastic wrapping of field dressings had been blown and scattered by the wind and the helicopter. One of them hung up on a brush where it played in the breeze. Bloody clothing had been cut off the wounded men and laid where it had been tossed in the frantic attempt to save lives. Empty tin cans and other debris from C-rations littered the ground. This site would continue to be a killing ground as insects and a chain of predators were attracted to the battlefield refuse.

Steve dropped into a fighting hole that had been dug next to a tree now denuded of leaves by exploding mortar and artillery. It was a large old fighting hole probably dug by the North Vietnamese for a crew-served weapon. There was no parapet, no shelf dug into a wall for ammunition, rations, and no grenade sump, things the Marine would improve on if he stayed there overnight.

Steve Bartold dropped into the hole beside the scout who was leaning back against the earth wall as he caught his breath. "I was just thinking," the scout said, "that I should have joined the Navy."

That got a smile out of the Navy corpsman and a snappy retort. "Yeah, then you could run around with a bunch of crazy-assed Marines, unarmed, while the dinks take target practice at you."

"You've made a point."

The corpsman shrugged out of his bulky pack. Shots were being exchanged around the perimeter but not at a sustained rate. "How long do you think they'll leave us out here?' he inquired.

"Who knows? I'm just a Marine. Mine is not to reason why. Mine is but to do and die."

"I thought you were the intelligence officer of this outfit."

"Acting. Only acting."

"So you are just pretending to be the S-2 officer?"

"Something like that."

The sounds and echoes of firing weapons increased. An entire barrage of mortars rolled across the hill. KAWHAM! KAWHAM!! KAHWAM!!! They exploded all around the Marines, getting louder as they got closer. Men who had been caught in the open raced for cover. Not all of them made it.

"Corpsman up!" called a wounded Marine.

Bartold grabbed his first aid kit and was off, racing through the deadly impact zone to save the life of a wounded Marine and at the same time risking his own. He referred to it as making house calls. A few months in the past, as Steve had opened a letter from home, a photo fell to the ground, landing face up. Bartold picked it up, examining it before handing it over to the Marine. It was Connie, her long blond hair done up with a spray of small white flowers over one ear. It was her high school prom photo.

"Who's the babe?"

"My sister."

"Nah, your sister'd be double ugly to a bulldog."

"Chases cars, bays at the moon, buries bones in the backyard," Dykus added.

Kowalski had hooked the corpsman and his sister up. They were now exchanging letters regularly. Steve knew his little sister could do a lot worse than a corpsman who aspired to become an emergency trauma physician.

Steve tried to shrink up under his helmet and wait out the mortar attack. But he had to stay alert as ground troops often move into assault positions under cover of artillery and mortar barrages. At least one enemy gunner had established a pattern, Fire! One click of ranging, Fire! Another click...

The effect was that his mortars were "walking" across the hill, impacting roughly every five meters. Without even thinking about it, Steve raced a few yards down the hill to his left. The former football player reached into a fighting hole and physically yanked his surprised ninety-five-pound Vietnamese Kit Carson Scout out of his position of relative safety, dragging the ineffectively protesting man away. A mortar exploded nearby. The blast created a massive pressure wave in Steve's head. All he could hear afterwards was ringing. He was enveloped in smoke and lung-irritating dirt that gave him a rasping cough. He tried to push himself off the ground, but his left arm wouldn't work.

He saw the problem. Blood was pumping out of his left bicep with every heartbeat, and it seemed his heart was beating wildly. Another round exploded nearby, but with a muted sound. This one had impacted Bui Vau Tham's fighting hole. The wide-eyed Vietnamese began yelling, "Bac Si! Bac Si! Cu Toi Voi!" the equivalent to Corpsman up!

Bartold was at his side before the dazed Marine quite realized what had happened. He and Bui dragged Steve back to his fighting hole. The corpsman ripped the sleeve off the scout's uniform. A jagged hole in Steve's left bicep was bleeding strongly. "It looks worse than it actually is," Bartold said as he wrapped a medically treated field bandage around his friend's arm. The corpsman raised the wounded arm, bringing a grimace to the Marine's face. There were several small shrapnel wounds to Kowalski's forearm, his left hand, and his fingers. The fingers were intact but bleeding.

"They'll wait," Bartold said as if such wounds were an everyday inconsequential matter. He looked into Steve's eyes. "Mild shock and concussion, but you're functional. No medevac ticket for you, Marine."

Kowalski didn't hear a word the corpsman said over the ringing in his ears. There were multiple calls for a corpsman from every quarter. Bartold raced off to make another of his house calls. He hadn't even given his buddy a shot of morphine. Oddly, the Marine wasn't in a great deal of pain. He was more concerned about his hearing than his wounds. He grabbed his rifle and pointed it down the hill.

The forward artillery observer, Steve's tentmate in the field, and his radio operator raced off to the left flank to provide them a better view of suspected enemy positions several thousand meters away. Steve expected artillery counter-battery fires to be on target within minutes. However, a sniper shot to Dave's head ended Steve's hope for immediate relief from the enemy guns.

The mortar barrage was moving back Steve's way. Like an animal fleeing a forest fire, a wounded Marine, glassy-eyed with fear, was running and stumbling his way as if he were leading or being chased by the mortars. Steve reached out and made a one-handed shoestring tackle, dragging the rifleman into his fighting hole. Bartold, who had witnessed the event, slid into the hole and began locating and treating the man's wounds.

"We've got an aid station and evacuation point established on the back side of the ridge. They aren't under fire there," the Corpsman told the scout. Then he realized that Kowalski couldn't hear a thing he was saying. He mouthed his words distinctly so the scout could read his lips. Kowalski watched as the corpsman bandaged the wounded man and administered a shot of morphine. "Can you get him over there?" the corpsman shouted.

The scout crawled out of the fighting hole, lifted the wounded Marine in a fireman's carry, and stumbled across the rough terrain to the collection point. There were dozens of bandaged Marines and others who were still waiting to be treated. Steve laid the wounded man next to another who was wearing bloody bandages and wound tags.

Steve really didn't want to go back to the side of the hill where the company was taking a pounding. He was wounded. None would have found fault with him if he sat right there and waited to be medivacked. Company officers were moving men from this side of the perimeter to the other, which was under attack, replacing the men who had been killed and wounded. Walking wounded were now manning the perimeter on this side of the hill.

Steve fought back a taste of sour oranges burning his throat, the taste of fear maybe? Rather than join the walking wounded who were guarding the backside in case of an assault there, he ran through a mortar barrage back to his fighting hole. Bartold had turned it into a forward aid station. The barrage was suddenly lifted. But for the constant ringing in Kowalski's ears, the hillside was eerily silent.

Enemy troops boiled out of a tree line about eight hundred meters away, firing their rifles, machine guns, and rocket-propelled grenades as they advanced. Marine riflemen responded. The NVA forces had exposed themselves at a range beyond the most effective for their weapons. It was almost perfect, however, for the machine guns. The M-60 machine guns hammered away, cutting a swath through the enemy ranks. In spite of their losses, the brave little fuckers kept coming, losing more of their comrades as they charged into the most advantageous combat range of the Marine weapons. Among them, at some unseen signal, a dozen enemy soldiers stopped, kneeled, and raised their rocket-propelled grenade launchers to their shoulders. Marine crew-served weapons were their targets.

Steve took up a rifleman's classic sitting position next to the fighting hole, wedged against a nearby tree stump. He was behind the main and even the secondary perimeter lines of defense where the men were putting out unaimed general defensive fire as they tried to gain fire superiority. Steve enjoyed the luxury of selecting his targets, aiming at them individually and seeing where his rounds were going. The distance was still slightly beyond the most effective rage of an M-16, but by constantly adjusting his aim, Steve and other similar-minded marksmen were touching the NVA up. It did not even come into his mind that he was killing someone's son or father, brother or husband, that he was ending a whole chain of hopes and dreams for another family. On the lines, the Marines tried rolling grenades downhill. That proved ineffective due to distance. The gooks would have to get closer for the grenades to do any damage. The enemy ground assault bogged down due to their losses, but there were now pockets of enemy soldiers within five hundred feet of the Marine lines, and they were continuing the battle.

Kevin Cahallan wore a towel wedged between the fiberglass liner and his steel helmet to cover the back of his neck, something like the kepis worn by the French Foreign Legion or the turban of Lawrence of Arabia. As a result, the Marines had begun calling him Larry of I Corp. The white towel kept the sun off his neck but made him a target. It stood out against the green environment. Kevin stood to direct his platoon as the Marines reorganized their positions. A bullet smacked into the base of his throat, exiting through the medulla and ending the promise of the young leader's life. Steve would never play Back Alley Bridge again without seeing the ghosts of David and Kevin at the table. In a short time, he gave the game up altogether.

Sandy, the general's son, perhaps more scared than Steve, maybe just smarter, crawled from position to position, reorganizing his platoon, personally distributing ammunition and supplies left behind by the dead and wounded who had been evacuated. His runner and radio operator were both down and out of the fight. His actions and demeanor were reassuring and helped bolster the confidence and fighting spirit of his platoon. It was a sign that he was growing into a fine battle-tested leader.

A thin streak of black smoke in the sky to the north revealed the presence of a flight of F-4 Phantoms arriving on station. Steve didn't know who was directing them now that Dave was out of the fight. He was too busy to question it. The enemy had continued to advance. Steve was no longer selecting individual targets. He was putting a few rounds as close as possible to anything that moved in the general direction of the enemy soldiers, forcing them to keep their heads down. Others were doing the same.

Most of the Marines, however, were watching the air wing put on a show, bombing the crap out of the jungle if not the enemy. They may not have hit a thing, but the NVA guns were silenced. With that, except for Steve, the Marines could hear pitiful moans and calls for a corpsman. Steve spotted movement in the brush to his front right quarter. He could tell it was a Marine. He laid his rifle down and crawled toward the wounded man.

He found Staff Sergeant Donaldson crying for help. His right shoulder was a bloody, ruined mess. He would obviously lose a shredded arm. "Morphine!" he cried. Steve was not a corpsman. He didn't carry morphine or other painkillers. All he could do was roll the large man onto a poncho and gesture for another Marine to help him drag the severely wounded man toward the aid station.

"Put me down, damn you! Let me die!" the sergeant shouted at his rescuers every step of the way. Many years later, Steve sometimes heard Sergeant Donaldson cursing him in his nightmares. They were only part of the way up the hill when Steve was slammed violently to the ground. He didn't know who had helped drag the sergeant off while he lay there, shot through the right leg. The searing pain was agonizing. A corpsman he didn't know bandaged his wound. While a makeshift splint was being applied, the rifles began cracking again.

The enemy had somehow snuck closer to the nervous, watchful Marines. Their renewed ground assault came from only three hundred feet away, but that was quite an effective combat range for the Marine riflemen and their weapons. However, it certainly wasn't a one-sided engagement.

Steve didn't see Sandy Hunt die. He only learned of his and other deaths later. He crawled back to where he had lost his rifle when he'd been hit. The scout couldn't stand or assume a proper firing position. He lay prone, hurt and bleeding from multiple wounds. He fired the rifle without aiming. The NVA soldiers pressed their advance, firing their rifles effectively from the hip. Those who fell shot were being replaced on a broad front. Small arms fire was impacting all around Steve. He rolled and fired, rolled back and fired another burst, and changed his position by crawling on his belly up the slope.

The Marines were being overrun. Their rifles were being fired on full automatic to keep the enemy at bay. Supplies were getting short. Steve couldn't remember where he had left his bandolier of ammunition. He had radio and other sensitive code information in his pocket notebook. They were low-level security items, but still not the type of things you would want the enemy to have if you could prevent it. The non-smoker had nothing with which to burn the confidential information. He ripped the pages with the information on them out of the spiral-top notebook and chewed on the paper a couple of times before swallowing it.

His back against a fire-blackened boulder dotted with bullet strikes, Steve took up what he expected to be his last firing position, the place where he would most likely take his last breath. Oddly, he didn't think of his mother, his family, or Mary Ann. He was not having any thoughts of his death or the afterlife. He wasn't passing out. He was actually quite clear-minded and focused. Later, he could not even remember being scared. He had given no thought to being resigned to his fate. His focus was on duty and on destroying as many of the enemies as possible.

Steve began humming The Marine Hymn. He was firing his rifle on semi-automatic to conserve ammunition. The images of the enemy soldiers seemed to fade in and out of his vision. In the meantime, Marines from the back side of the perimeter, most of them walking wounded, came on line and helped force the enemy back.

Steve did finally pass out due to shock and loss of blood. He spent the night in a morphine-induced haze, shivering under a poncho. The blood he had lost was not being replaced. He had been wounded five times, none of them individually life-threatening. That was coming from the combination of shock and loss of blood. While none of his wounds were immediately crippling, he would suffer from traumatic arthritis at an early age.

Steve was medivacked the following morning. Unaccompanied by a scout, a patrol from Bravo Company went into the valley at midday. Gary Maxwell, a corporal from Oklahoma City who was leading the patrol, along with Steve Bartold, the duty corpsman, was killed in an ambush. Steve would always suffer from feelings of guilt for not being on that last patrol. He passed up the opportunity to be medivacked home and requested to return to his unit on light duty status until his leg was out of the walking cast the doctors had put on him. This is how he became The Warlord of Thach Hanh.

CHAPTER THREE
DALLAS, TEXAS

It took just over five minutes for Mary Cox to drive her new candy apple red Corvette from her family's fashionable home in Bunker Hill, an affluent suburb of Dallas, to her art gallery. The New Louvre was on the south side service road of Interstate Twenty, a major east-west artery of the city.

Mary thought of her boyfriend, Steve, a Marine who would think it to be a perfect day for driving with the top down. The wind would be in his face, blowing his blond hair, the sun bronzing his muscular body. But not Mary. She kept the convertible top in place. She arrived at work perfectly poised and coifed. She would return home at the end of the day the same way. Mary had always been impeccably groomed in stark contrast with her free-spirited artist mother, who was prone to show up for work wearing a Mumu, her long hair tangled and wind-blown. Around her neck would be large bangles and beads, perhaps stones and wood chips of interesting shapes. She habitually wore gaudy cheap sandals and loose flowing gowns. In direct contrast to her daughter, she obviously dressed for comfort and not style.

Externally, the older Mary Cox was more of a fit for the popular image of what an artist should look and be like, the carefree spirit with talent but little else, than her daughter, who was equally talented in her own way. Mary Cox, however, was more than a starving artist of the sixties. She was quite a successful businesswoman.

The New Louvre was more than an art gallery featuring the works of mother and daughter. Half the gallery was devoted to teaching spaces. The lessons were not cheap. A realist, Mary knew her business thrived on largely unrealistic dreams and inflated egos. She knew she would teach no Rembrandts or Picassos. For the most part, she taught little old ladles who had nothing else to do with their time. A Saturday morning class was filled with golf and football widows. She taught latchkey kids whose parents used her as an after-school babysitting service. And she taught a small group of "Starving" artists who usually held other full-time occupations but who would one day give up tending bars and waiting tables to scratch out a living as an artist if only locally.

No matter how inept or untalented they might be, all Mary's students learned about colors, techniques, and art history. She made sure they learned at least some of the basics, even when they had no talent for the application. They could mix paints and prepare canvasses. Mary took them on field trips to art museums where she taught them about artists, their lives, and their works. Every one of her students came away with something positive from Mary's classes.

An important part of the business was selling canvasses, brushes, oils, and other equipment and supplies to the students and to the general public. While

Mary's job was primarily teaching each person what they would learn of the various mediums, of colors and composition, style, textures, and techniques, she was a highly skilled restorer of aged works of art. She was a wonderful portrait artist as well. Her daughter, also highly skilled, tended more toward the contemporary and abstract schools of art.

Of Greek descent, Mary was dark-haired with an olive complexion and was fleshy in her middle age. She loved to paint and laugh, to cook and eat. The true love of her life, a brawny freckle-faced, red-headed Irish construction worker, had perished in a work-related accident ten years earlier. Mary was not inclined to seek anything beyond friendship from any man after her husband's death. Their daughter, an only child, had been twelve when her father died. The girl grew up with a great sense of loss. Typically a daddy's girl, the teenager had no father figure in her life as her mother seldom dated and gave no thought to marriage or live-in relationships. The daughter grew up deeply immersed in the art world among the smells of paint and thinner. She went on every field trip with her mother's students, listened to every lecture, and participated in the classroom activities. A serious girl and a good student, Mary Cox grew up lonely. She had never fit in at school. All of her weekends and after-school time was spent in The New Louvre.

At thirteen, Mary was all legs and already as tall as her mother. She measured herself almost daily, afraid that at 5"-10" tall she was going to grow into some kind of freak. The first thing you notice about Mary Cox is her hair. It was not red or strawberry blond. It was actually a natural orange, leading, of course, to her being teased and called carrot top throughout her school career. The next were her amber cat's eyes. Her mouth seemed small, but on the whole she was a most exotic creature with a cameo profile.

By the time she was sixteen, Mary had a figure that drove boys and men to distraction and made all her female schoolmates jealous. The boys fantasized and talked, spreading locker room rumors about the teenage beauty. The girls also talked and spread vicious, untrue gossip. While her mother was loud and warm and quick to laugh, Mary was aloof, artsy, and strange. She did not encourage friendships, not even among the other school outcasts, the nerds and geeks. She was neither popular nor unpopular. Her life changed dramatically during her sixteenth year.

The nude figure is a basic art form, one all true artists must master. When you think of nudes in art, David and the Venus de Milo immediately come to mind. Seeing nude men and women posing for art classes was old hat for the teenager. The elder woman volunteered her daughter's services as a nude model. Neither of the women was hesitant, embarrassed, or overly anxious at the prospect. It was simply a business transaction and part of their world. An unusual element, however, had been added.

A true professional stylist had been hired for the benefit of a photographer who paid Mary a full model's fee of sixty dollars per hour. The stylist saw in Mary Ann an exquisite woman struggling to metamorphosis from the natural but unaware, untrained girl.

"My goodness!" the stylist had exclaimed upon being introduced to the high school sophomore as she reached out to run her fingers through Mary's curly orange shoulder-length hair. "We absolutely must do something with this unruly mop. Mary was not a girl to tear up or cry. The stylist saw a flash of fiery anger in the girl's eyes. The girl had spirit. She could do something special with a girl like that.

"Don't worry, sweetheart," she assured the girl, "I see a lot to work with here. In two hours, you will be absolutely stunning."

With that promise in her ears and on her mind, Mary allowed herself to be handled as a piece of property. Although she appeared to be somewhat confused or disoriented, Mary was paying careful attention to every comment and action. She disrobed completely as requested. The stylist walked around the nude girl, examining her with appraising eyes, making comments such as "pedicure... hot wax..." and "firm...round...heart-shaped buttocks" to her assistant.

"You could pass the pencil test," she told Mary, observing the girl's firm, up-tilted breasts.

What the hell is the pencil test? Mary wondered. The stylist discerned the question in Mary's expression. "That's where we place a pencil horizontally under your breast. If the pencil falls to the floor, you've passed the test." If not, you might want to consider a procedure. You won't work for us long if you don't pass the pencil test."

Mary was shaved, bathed, and massaged in scented oils. She was painted and taught, with the stylist selecting a foundation, blush, eye shadow, lipstick, and so on, with every selection taking advantage of Mary's natural coloring and facial features. Her hair was cut, shampooed, and styled. After it was all completed, Mary was turned to face a mirror. She was quite amazed. Never an ugly duckling, the fresh-faced, beautiful young school girl was now a breathtakingly gorgeous young woman, a true walking goddess.

"Honey," the stylist told her, as if this type of transformation was something she supervised on a daily basis. "You could turn the heads of the marble statues on the Vatican steps."

For six years now, Mary had not changed the styles that had caused such a sensation the first day she had worn them to school. However, there was a downside to the sudden changes in Mary's appearance. The new look attracted all manner of men, from boys who could barely stammer hello as they passed in the hall to silver-tongued gray-haired foxes who seemed to appear wherever she went.

Mary went out on dates now, a lot of them, but seldom with the same man or boy twice. Mary Ann Cox treated dating as a trip to the marriage market. She was searching for her one in a million man, a man who was strongly attracted to her physically but who admired and wanted her for more than her physical attributes.

In time, Mary became quite confident in her ability to "read" men. She turned down far more dating offers than she accepted. Mary worked and studied long hours to help make The New Louvre a success in part to prove that she was not dependent upon any man. She was in demand as an artist's model but carefully selected the venues where she posed.

One of the tradeoffs for being allowed to exhibit her works at some of the larger, more affluent galleries where she could get more for them than at her own gallery was to commit to a block of sales representative time. It was the only way for many artists as well as galleries to realize a profit. It offered an opportunity for the representative to steer potential clients to their own work.

In 1966, the twenty-year-old artist was spending four hours each evening at the Lucind Gallery in fashionable Westbury Square near the Southern Methodist University campus. The gallery was at the back of the European-style shopping locale. Westbury Square was not a mall or a shopping center. At the time, Westbury Square was more of an event.

The Lucind Gallery faced a large brick plaza with an elaborate fountain as its centerpiece. Lovers and teenagers on dates found it an enchanting setting. Night by night, the beautiful young artist watched the couples stroll by hand in hand, stars in their eyes, dreams in their thoughts. Mary no longer thought of herself as being lonely. She was simply a woman biding her time. The gallery was not often busy. The owners considered it to be a pure art gallery. Lessons and equipment and supplies were not part of the business. Prices were inflated because of the gallery's location, not because of the work exhibited. There were not many browsers and even fewer sales. Mary wondered how the gallery stayed in business. She always brought a book to work to help her pass the time.

She looked up briefly from her reading as a young man passed the large front window. He was slowly eyeing the featured paintings in the window. Mary went back to her reading. The man did not fit the buying customer profile she had fixed in her mind: professional, affluent, middle-aged, married, who bought paintings at the upscale gallery. A page later, the bell over the door tinkled.

Mary looked up, closing her book. The young man she'd noticed at the window had come in for a closer look at the paintings. A browser, not a buyer, Mary was sure. The man would do nothing but waste her time, or perhaps provide an interesting diversion. She let him walk around, keeping one eye on him and the other on her book, more or less.

There were always wolves on the prowl that spotted her through the window and came in to chat her up rather than to purchase a work of art. Mary could usually spot them right away, viewing the paintings but sneaking sideways glances at her before making their approach and feeding her some worn-out old line.

Solid guy, Mary thought, herself giving the man some of her own sideways glances. He was tall, broad-shouldered, and heavy in the chest. Mary noticed that his nose had been broken. Although it had not been set well, it didn't detract from his looks. There were a couple of small cut scars on his face. Although he tried to hide it, he limped slightly. A jock, most likely a football player or something like that, she thought, and then her interest became real. Could he be a Dallas Cowboy? "Whatever he was, he could undoubtedly find a way soon to tell her of his important position and his money.

Mary's memories of high school athletes were not good. But this guy had her attention. Maybe it was because he was ignoring her. She studied his appearance. He seemed to be particularly well-groomed. There was no hint of a five o'clock shadow even this late in the evening. His posture was good in spite of the limp. His hair was cut in a short flat top. It suited him. He seemed comfortable in an off-the-rack sports jacket and dark trousers. His socks matched. They didn't always. His belt and shoes were both black. That didn't always happen either. Most men didn't seem to have much fashion sense. His shoes were highly polished, almost like glass had been poured over them. That was no shoe-stand or brush shine. His large hands were clean, the nails trimmed but not manicured. He wore no rings. There was no pale telltale skin sign of his having taken one off. Mary had learned to look for that.

He might have some money after all, Mary decided. He could be a rookie Ranger or Spur looking to spend his bonus money to decorate his waste-of-money look-at-me mansion. He hadn't sneaked a peek at her yet. That was somehow unsettling. Didn't he find her attractive? Mary laid the book down. She had lost interest in it a few moments after the man walked into the gallery. She patted her hair in place and approached the man from behind. He didn't hear her. He was totally absorbed in a painting, a large canvas with a black lacquered frame that cost as much as most of the paintings she and her mother sold in The New Louvre. His nose was right up to the painting. What was he doing?

"May I help you, sir?"

The man didn't appear to be startled by her sudden appearance. There was no long-drawn-out double entendre of lustful wolfish leer. "Well, perhaps," he responded, smiling. Perfect rows of white teeth. There was a hint of mint on his breath. "I was looking at the palate knife technique. Are you the artist?"

"N..no," Mary stammered a bit. This guy actually knows something about art, she thought. "That is one of Carol Orr's works."

"Never heard of her," he replied as if to dismiss her.

Mary bit back the impulse to ask him who he <u>had</u> heard of. "She's building a good reputation for herself locally. That painting will increase in value in the near future."

"Do you have any more of her work?"

"Of course," Mary answered, turning and leading the best-looking man she'd seen in a long time, maybe even forever, to the back of the gallery. She couldn't see the expression of appreciation as he observed the way her hips swayed and the way her skirt clung tightly to her ass as she led him to the Orr collection. She turned and gestured to the painting on the back wall.

The young man examined the works up close, then stepped back to look at them. He stepped to the side to observe them not only from a different angle but in a different light. They were all smaller and less expensive than the first canvas he had scrutinized.

"I'll be closing in a few moments, sir," Mary announced, sure there was no sale here.

"These are good, but not as good as the one in the front window."

Steve was right, of course. Although there were many expensive paintings on display throughout the gallery, the Orr in the window was the marquise draw for the gallery.

"How much is it?"

Too much if you have to ask, Mary thought immediately. "Three thousand," she answered, using her judgment to quote the lowest acceptable sales price for that particular painting.

"I'd love to have it, but that's a bit rich for me," Steve admitted. "What about the hunting owl?"

"Seven fifty," Mary responded eagerly. Maybe she would make a sale after all tonight. The man pulled out his wallet and began counting his fifties and twenties. Mary smiled, thinking of how she would spend her commission.

The man stopped counting and looked up at her. "You wouldn't happen to have a lay-way plan, would you?" he asked hopefully.

"Yes, as a matter of fact, we do," Mary answered, already spending her ten percent of the smaller sale, although she would not collect her commission on the layaway sale until after the last payment was made. Mary pulled the painting from the wall. Steve again admired her from that view point, but his attention was drawn back to the painting.

Long and narrow, against a red background with a leafless tree n the foreground, a full moon shone in the scene of a mouse in the grass looking toward the sky where a barn owl was flying with its wings fully spread. His head was turned toward the mouse that could easily be missed at first glance. Steve could almost hear the scurrying sound the mouse would have made that attracted the owl's attention. It was an unusual, very commercial piece, not the sort of work usually found in upscale galleries. It said something about the artist that portraits and landscapes cannot tell you. Steve appreciated that aspect of the work. It made him want to talk to the artist.

Just as they reached Mary's desk at the front of the shop. Rusty, the manager and leasing agent for Westbury Properties, who was making her nightly rounds, poked her head into the gallery, knocking over a walking cane someone had left near the door.

"Hello, Mary," she chirped, and then turned to the customer, picking up the cane and handing it to him. "Here, Steve. You'll probably need this later on. Your mother called and said to tell you not to push things so hard."

And then Rusty was gone, continuing her nightly ritual. The man who was now holding the cane seemed somewhat embarrassed. Push what? Mary wondered. "How do you know Rusty?" she asked.

"My office is next to hers."

Mary knew the Westbury Square offices were high-rent properties. There was a psychiatrist, a couple of lawyers, an optometrist, and an advertising firm, a real estate company and an architect up there. The architect, Mary recalled. His office is next to Rusty's.

"You work for the architect!" she blurted, pleased at having solved the small puzzle. The guy didn't look like an architect.

"Well, sort of," he answered.

"Sort of?"

Steve liked the dubious expression on the lovely girl's face. "I am the architect... sort of."

Mary was not a woman to be teased. "Well. Mr. Sort of, it's past my closing time, and..."

"Do you not want to sell me the piece?" he interrupted.

"Of course I do," she snapped a bit more sharply than intended.

"Alright, then. Is there any wiggle room in the price of the window piece?"

Mary did not want to lose the sale. "Actually, there is," she admitted. "I can reduce it to twenty-five hundred if you want both pieces right now.'

"You sound like a used car salesman."

"I take umbrage at that, sir!" Mary snapped.

"Sorry, I didn't mean it that way. Unfortunately, that's still a bit more than I'm prepared to pay.

Another one getting away, Mary thought. On impulse, without a reason other than the fact that the man actually seemed to like and appreciate the piece, Mary decided to forego her commission on his purchases. "The least I can let it go for is twenty-two hundred," she told him. "But only if you take both of them right now, and don't tell anyone what I sold them to you for."

That will tax me pretty well right now," he admitted..."but, done deal," he announced as Mary crossed the room to lock the door. "On one condition."

"And what's that?" She asked warily, sure of what this guy wanted for his money and just as sure of what he wasn't going to get at any price.

"Have dinner with me."

"It's late. It's ten-thirty," Mary protested.

"I know a place where we can get a good burger."

A good burger! The guy was incredibly simple and unsophisticated. Mary was used to being offered caviar and champagne, even diamonds and furs. Still, his offer was somewhat refreshing. And he had yet to tell her about himself. "Well, I could eat a bite," Mary admitted. "It's been a long day."

"Good. Let's get this business out of the way."

Within fifteen minutes, the forms had been filled out, the cash and credit card receipt tucked away, and sold tags were placed on the pieces. All the while Mary wondered why an architect with an office in the high-rent district couldn't afford a relatively minor piece of art.

Steve steered her left as they exited the gallery. Rumpleheimer's lights were still on. Chairs were being turned up on the tabletops. The last of the customers were paying their bills. Steve limped slightly and leaned into the cane as he walked, but he wasn't making a show of it. He wasn't begging for sympathy, pity, or even attention.

"So, Steve Kowalski, your father's the architect, right?"

Steve laughed. "My dad couldn't draw a straight line if his life depended on it."

"Really?"

"Yeah. My dad's a cop. He spent most of his life in uniform as a patrol officer. He spent a couple of years as a detective after that, got his half-pay pension, and moved out here for the weather and the lifestyle. He opened up his own business, Ace Detective Agency. He handles security for the square."

"I know your father," Mary squealed. "At least I think I do. Big guy. It looks like he could fight a bear with a switch and win. Don Kowalski, right?"

"That's him."

Without realizing it, the couple had walked all the way down the side of the square. Steve began leading Mary up the steps leading to The Colony Club, an upscale members-only club and restaurant. A heavy wood door opened, and a host in formal wear greeted them.

"Good evening, Mr. Kowalski. Miss."

There was still no pretense here. Steve did not call the host by his first name or ask for his usual table. Seated, Mary hissed, "Hamburgers, huh?"

"Membership comes with my office rental."

There was too long an uncomfortable period of silence as they studied menus and finally ordered. Mary was somewhat taken aback by the prices. "You could get twenty hamburgers with fries and cokes for that," she said in a scolding manner after Steve had placed his order.

"Don't get the idea that I'm rich. We won't eat here very often."

"That's quite presumptuous of you. Who's to say we'll eat anywhere together again? This is not a date."

"What is it then?"

That question puzzled and silenced Mary for a moment. This guy was playing her. She knew it. She just wasn't sure how. He was good-looking if you went for the rugged type. Unfortunately, she did. He had clear, expressive, twinkling eyes, the dangerous kind girls fall in love with easily. Intelligence was behind them. She found that attractive. His short hair appeared to be a golden blonde, but there wasn't enough of it to really tell.

There was a thin diagonal slash running through his left eyebrow, like a row plowed through a green field. A second small scar under his lip near the right corner of his mouth and another thicker scar splitting his chin added to the rugged image without detracting from his good looks.

"Do I pass muster?" he asked.

The gall of him!, she thought. He was actually amused that she was obviously studying him. "I want to be able to give a good description to the police," she quipped.

His laughter was deep and genuine. She liked his smile. But again, they grew awkwardly silent. Mary was not used to this. Men usually bragged endlessly to her about themselves, their influence, and their accomplishments. This one surely wasn't shy. He hadn't wasted any time asking her out.

"I.." They broke the silence simultaneously. Mary gestured for Steve to continue.

"I really don't know what we're doing here."

Mary's response shocked Steve. "It's a mating ritual. All dating is nothing more than a mating ritual."

Steve didn't know how to respond to that. Mary laughed at the expression on his face. "I'm not trying to seduce you," she said. "I don't need a husband or a mate. I'm simply a realist."

"So it is a date," Steve said. Mary was amused. The night grew late as the couple came to know one another.

"Live with my mother..."

"In a one-bedroom apartment."

"An only child,"

"Six brothers: Robert, John, Tim, Joe, Rusty, and Terry. And four sisters: Linda, Connie, Susan, and Elaine."

"Samuels High School, Class of '65." That would make her two years younger than Steve.

"Bryan Adams. Class of '63."

"Art club."

"Speech, drama, student government, football, baseball, basketball, track, and boxing." That explained the nose and the scars.

"Greek and Irish."

"Irish and Polish."

"Warm, cozy evening in front of a fireplace."

"Night driving with the top down."

"Blue."

"Red."

"Chicken."

"Steak and potatoes."

Long after the meal was over, a discreet waiter who had seen all the other guests out presented the bill, which Steve signed.

"Good Lord! Look at the time!" Steve exclaimed as his eyes fell on the clock. "Its almost three A.M. Your mother will be frantic."

Mary laughed. "She's more likely hoping I have found Mr. Right and am currently screwing him cross-eyed."

That provided an opening for a ribald comment or suggestion that Steve did not make, which led Mary to place him even higher on her short list of nice guys. Nice guys did not finish last with Mary Cox, and this one seemed genuinely nice.

Yawning, the couple left the club and walked leisurely, hand in hand, to the parking lot where Mary's car was the only vehicle remaining. In spite of the late hour, neither of them wanted the night to end. Mary leaned with her back against the car door, preventing Steve from opening it for her.

"How did you hurt your leg?" She finally felt comfortable enough with Steve to ask.

"Not my leg, my back," he answered, and then seemed lost in thought or memories for a moment.

"Okay, so how did you hurt your back?"

"A bad parachute jump. I broke something at L-5 and damaged some nerves. It's taking a long time for me to recover."

"Is it painful?"

"Very."

Mary was pleased with the honest answer when what she expected was the usual line of macho bullshit. "How do you get to be a 'sort of' architect?"

A smile then. "I worked for an architect when I was fourteen, running his blueprints and so on, but listening and learning. He put me on a drawing board doing reversals and taught me how to letter properly. Being an architect has always been a dream of mine. I earned my associate's degree in architectural technology at Plano Junior College. I have about six months to recuperate from the injury. Instead of lying around doing nothing, I opened up an architectural firm. I pay a retired architect to check over my drawings and use his A.I.A. stamp to make everything proper. Someday, in about five, maybe six years, I'll finish college and be a real full-fledged architect. In the meantime, I study and practice drafting and design, and my lettering, every chance I get."

"And what happens in six months?"

"I pass a physical and return to full duty."

"As what, where?"

"I'm an active duty U.S. Marine currently on convalescent leave. I'll go where the Corps sends me, probably back to Vietnam."

That shocked Mary, who was about as removed from the war as a U.S. citizen could be. She had no opinions about the war. She didn't follow the news of Vietnam. She had no family involved in the war and no friends that she was aware of. She had never given thought to former classmates who might be serving in Vietnam. With almost a prayer in her heart, Mary had to ask, "You're not one of those girls" in every port, love 'em and leave 'em kind of guys, are you Steve?"

"I have been," he admitted without hesitation. "But that's only because I haven't found the right girl in any of them yet."

His statement left Mary confused and at a loss for what to think, say, or do. She wanted to see if there could be something between her and this man. She rose on her toes and put her lips to Steve's ear, whispering, "It's late. HO five, seven, five, nine, six. Call me."

She turned without a kiss or a hug and climbed into the car. Steve stood silent, watching. He didn't want this intriguing woman to go. The car started. The electric window was lowered several inches. Mary called out. "Goodnight, Stephen," as she pulled away. What Steve did not hear was the comment Mary made to herself as she pulled away. "Heloooo, Mr. Right."

With his return to duty, most likely in Vietnam, pending, the couple's relationship moved forward quickly. There was a certain urgency yet to build some depth to their relationship. By the time Steve received his orders, he and Mary had achieved a mature commitment to one another but without an engagement. They were both psychologically holding their breath until time brought them back together.

Steve had been in Vietnam for six months, writing whenever he could; however, after receiving no letters from him for three weeks, Mary began to worry. She maintained her silence and her routine, praying and hoping to receive a letter soon. She was operating on automatic after having dreamed that Steve had been killed in combat. Was it a premonition? She wondered. Do we have one of those eerie, almost unbelievable psychic connections? What will I do if I lose Steve? How will I carry on? How will my life and my plans for the future change?

Like a horse that knows its way to the barn with little guidance, Mary's car almost seemed to drive itself along the daily route from her home to the gallery. Mary opened the front door, not really wanting to be there for the first time in her life. She immediately spotted a letter, white, against the green carpet that had been slipped through the mall slot. Instead of a postage stamp, the word free had been written in the top right-hand corner of the envelope. The triangular logo of the Third Marine Division was printed on the top left corner. Steve! She knew immediately. Mary ripped the envelope open quickly, unfolding the too brief letter. She could feel her heart hammering away inside her chest like a pinball bouncing madly off rubber bumpers.

My dearest Mary:

I have received your letters, with the last of them dated August.

It is always wonderful to hear from you. I wish I was there with you, but I need to be here for now.

Forgive my lack of communications of late. We were out on an operation. I took a very slight, very minor hit and was in a hospital for a bit.

A tear slid down Mary's cheek at the thought of Steve being wounded. She imagined she could feel his pain.

Believe me, the wounds were minor.

Wounds, as in plural?

You will note the new rank on my return address. The promotion means a little more money each month. Enough, I hope, for you to meet me in Hawaii in late October when I plan to take a week's R&R.

I also have a new job. Being the chief scout for an infantry battalion is interesting and challenging. It involves a lot of paperwork, though. We should return to operational status soon. I will be in the field then. I won't be able to write as often as when we are in the rear, but don't worry about me.

I have lost some weight, but everyone does over here. I had a small photograph of you laminated so I could carry it in my pocket always, in the middle of the monsoon, or neck deep in a river we have to cross.

I think of you every day, Mary. I read and study when I get a chance. Unfortunately, that is not often. But I've got to keep the dream alive.

Do you talk to my family much? My sisters ask about you in every letter they write. They want a wedding. I have not told them anything. about Hawaii. Have you?

Tell your mother hello for me. Please write as often as you can. I
miss you.
    Love,
    Steve

October is such a long time away, Mary thought as she crushed the letter to her breast. They would only have a week, but a honeymoon in Hawaii was beyond anything she had ever dreamed of. Keeping the secret from both families was difficult. Steve had only brought it up three months after arriving in Vietnam. A wedding gown was in lay-away, more to keep it out of sight than for financial reasons. Steve's dress blues were hanging in Mary's hall closet. In an attempt to save money for their honeymoon, Mary was working longer hours and painting "popular" commercial art rather than "good" art pieces.

"I miss you terribly," Mary moaned. It was an admission she had not allowed herself to make in the past. She had been so certain she would never need a man the way other women seemed to need them, not in a dependent way. Why Steve? She often wondered. Steve Kowalski was good-looking for sure, but he was not the most handsome man she knew. He was not the toughest or smartest, and he certainly was not the richest. So, why him?

Perhaps she finally decided; it is because Steve is the most pure man I know. Oh, he is a man, alright. He curses now and then and farts once in a while, belches boomers for amusement, picks his nose, and scratches his ass in public. He doesn't go to church very often. On the other hand, he doesn't drink or smoke. He would never hit me or abuse me verbally. He's very smart, smarter even than he knows. He's really a diamond in the rough, a man a woman can teach and polish and turn into a fine human being.

More than anything else, Mary knew beyond a shadow of a doubt that Steve absolutely idolized her. More than that, he enjoyed her company and respected her. He accepted her as she was, for all that she was, and in spite of all that she wasn't. Mary failed to understand that she was not reciprocating those feelings and values with her plans to change Steve.

In many ways, Steve had been so shy it almost seemed to be an act. Mary recalled when she had first mentioned the word love to him. It came about because of her three pampered dogs. She had boiled a chicken and was stripping the meat off the bones for each of them daily.

"Why don't you just feed those hounds regular dog food?" Steve had asked as she was preparing the chicken.

"Love me, love my dogs," she said in way of a teasing ultimatum. Steve, withered by the look she had given him, retired to the living room, where he sat next to her mother. The older woman had known right away what was happening between the young couple. From the beginning, she had advised and counseled both of them, promoting the relationship every chance she got. She had heard the exchange in the kitchen.

"Those dogs are a cross you'll have to learn to bear if you want Mary Ann," she admitted to Steve after patting him affectionately on the knee and retiring to her bedroom to give the young people some space. With her dogs eating, Mary joined Steve, sitting next to him on the couch.

"Mary," Steve said in as stern a voice as she had ever heard him use, "We need to talk."

Mary was ready. What she had said was not simply an offhanded remark.

"I don't know where to start."

Mary waited in patient silence as Steve searched mentally for that starting point. He was such a little boy in some ways, she thought, like I am his first girlfriend, and he has little confidence.

"I've never had any problems talking to or getting women," he began.

Mary knew that was something of an understatement. Steve's own sister called him "Don Juan el Romeo de la Casanova" and told Mary he was called the "double lip lock champion" of his high school. His friends she had met had told her about the girls in Steve's past, Linda, Annette, and Cayla, the twirler, cheerleader, and actress, and others as well.

"We talk and laugh and go out and do things, you know," Steve began. "Some things I wouldn't want my mother to see."

Like what? Mary wondered as she nodded yes.

"But you drive me crazy," Steve told her, his voice getting higher. Mary was pleased so far.

"You know how beautiful you are. At least a hundred guys have told you. I just don't know what to say or do when I'm around you. I get frustrated and go completely stupid."

Now Steve was not looking at her. She had seen but never understood his frustration or evident lack of confidence where she was concerned.

"I feel... I don't know... I feel awkward and inadequate around you." Steve took a deep breath. "What did you mean when you said, 'Love me, love my dogs?'"

Mary was much more confident than Steve. "I thought I was very clear, Stephen. If you expect to love me, and for me to love you back, you have to love me completely with no questions or reservations."

"That's just it, Mary. I don't care if you have dogs or spiders or snakes or whatever, as long as I can be with you."

"Are you saying you love me, Stephen?"

"Yes, I am, Mary. I love you."

Steve returned home that evening in something of a daze. He'd told a woman he loved her, and he'd meant it. He hadn't told her he loved her because that was what she wanted to hear in order to get her to sleep with him. He hadn't told her because it was time in the development of their relationship. Steve didn't know where to go from there. He let Mary take the lead. Fortunately, she was in no real hurry for him to put a ring on her finger. The time for Steve's return to duty came too quickly now that he was so deeply involved with Mary.

"Okay, that's the last of them," Steve announced as he patted down the strapping tape on a box of supplies. The walls of his office were bare. The equipment and furnishings were gone. The carpet had signs still of where his desk and filing cabinets had been the day before.

Mary laid a hand on his shoulder. "There'll be another office someday. Stephen Kowalski, A.I.A., Architects and Engineers."

"It's a dream I won't let go of."

"I'll be there to help your dreams come true, Steve."

"You already have, you know."

Mary's brow wrinkled. "How so?"

"There are a lot of different dreams. Knocking in the winning run in a big game. Getting a great job with a shitload of money. And loving the world's most beautiful woman."

He may be a bit shy and he may lack confidence where I'm concerned, Mary thought, but he does have his moments. There had been days during the last six weeks when those moments shone brightly. There was the trip to Sylvan Beach on Galveston Island. A night spent walking and talking after a party at his parents' house. And a night she knew he had almost proposed after dinner at an Allan's Landing club.

Steve was a man who could design the most fabulous structures but couldn't hammer a nail straight to save his soul or his thumb. He was not the least bit mechanical and knew nothing of electricity or plumbing. He was smarter than any geek or nerd Mary had ever known. He would read anything he could get his hands on. He had a mind like a sponge when it came to subjects that interested him. Mary was determined to help him expand his interests as well as to learn how to focus them.

She knew Steve Kowalski could charm the pants off any woman he chose. Mary had heard it about him, and she'd seen it in him. She saw the way women related to him. She'd already pulled one cute little news reporter doing an article on Vietnam aside and told her, "You make one more move on Steve Kowalski, and I will not only snatch you baldheaded, I will scratch both your eyes out in the process."

One buxom Navy nurse had been warned emphatically, "That's MY Marine!"

Mary knew it was the innocent aw shucks little boy in a grown man's body that appealed to so many women. Steve Kowalski would lose that innocence during his second tour of combat duty in Vietnam.

CHAPTER FOUR
QUANG TRI COMBAT BASE

Although events were moving a bit fast for Corporal Kowalski's comfort, he stepped up and took over the S-2 section with an outward appearance of confidence. Steve investigated every aspect of a battalion intelligence officer's duties and responsibilities. He molded his actions accordingly without becoming a rule-book martinet. Captain Small was his role model.

The S-2 shop was located in one enormous, heavy green canvas general-purpose tent designed to house forty men. The front half of the tent served as the S-2 office. In it were two wooden desks. A standard typewriter sat atop one of them. A pigeonhole map case full of rolled military maps took up most of one wall. A map taped to a rough plywood panel and covered by an acetate overlay rested on an easel like a painting on display.

The overlay was marked with various symbols designating the type and location of friendly units operating in I Corp, noted in blue grease pencil. The last reported position of known enemy units was indicated by red symbols. Steve knew there were more enemy units in the field than were indicated on the map. The current location of many identified units operating in I Corp was largely unknown due to their frequent moves and lack of fixed bases. By comparing his map to similar intelligence devices maintained by other Marine and Army S-2 offices, Steve was able to update and note additional information on the enemy presence throughout I Corp.

A field radio strapped to a sturdy backpack sat squawking like a chattering bird in a corner. The radio in the intelligence office was never turned off. Someone always had to monitor the battalion's radio traffic. In the living quarters of the tent, four cots with folded blankets made the tent appear to be luxuriously spacious. Ammunition crates stacked atop one another served as chairs, tables, and dressers. A red film of dust covered every surface.

A box of grenades sat atop one of the tables. Another box served for dining and card playing. A peanut butter candle had been placed in the center of the table. The amber peanut oil had dried and caked like a tin of old shoe polish that had been left open. A miniature jungle of mold had grown in the lid. C-ration cans cut to serve as C-4 stoves were in evidence. Every man made his own. Loose bullets, boxes of ammunition, twenty bullet boxes in bandoliers, and magazines loaded with bullets were scattered everywhere. By Marine Corps standards, the tent was a mess. Steve would take care of that as a lower priority but an important one.

There were plastic canteens, field dressings, bottles of "bug juice," various cans of ration meals, cans of WD-40, cleaning rods, and machetes strewn about the tables. A table next to Jim Hoskin's cot was littered with letters from his large family. Jim wrote them individually. His ever-present Michigan football banner was attached to a wire above his cot.

Bill Dykus, who was somewhat mysterious, was the only hard-drinker in the intelligence section. There was always a fifth of liquor on his table. Although he often drank to excess, Bill was not an alcoholic. Steve was sure it was only a matter of time. He wondered what he could do about Bill's drinking.

Taped to one of the ammunition boxes was Bill's short-timer's calendar, the suggestive outline of a nude woman, a Playboy centerfold. Her silhouette was separated into puzzle-like segments numbered from one to one hundred, with the one being that segment of the puzzle covering her mons. With one hundred days of his thirteen-month tour of duty remaining to be served, the short-timer blocked out a section daily until finally, on day one, he rotated stateside to the "land of round-eyed women." Bill would never fill in square one.

"Chink" Tsoi's space was meticulously organized. On his desk was a portrait photo of a beautiful exotic Oriental woman, his Chinese-American fiancee from Seattle. Kowalski had met Janet. Her intelligence had impressed him as much as her beauty. "She's way too good for you. Chink," Steve teased his buddy.

Kowalski's personal space was as individual as everyone else's. Books dominated his desktop. He read everything from paperback novels to college texts, including a very large, thick, expensive volume of the Architectural Graphics Standard, a work Chink often borrowed. There was a small stack of letters from his family and a larger group from Mary, the beautiful redhead in the framed photograph on the table.

The personal belongings of the men who had been killed or wounded seriously enough to be medivacked home had to be inspected, inventoried, and packed for sending to the next of kin. The inspection was personal and often quite revealing. While packing a man's belongings, Steve removed all condoms. Likewise, he removed photos of prostitutes or of a romantic nature. There was a surprising amount of them. No sense in allowing someone's wife or mother to see such things.

Weapons and field gear were turned in for cleaning and reissue. Properly tagged trophy items were mailed home. Bayonets, pistols, and NVA grenades were set aside. All forms of ammunition and explosives were removed.

With this priority task completed, including burning the photos that could not be sent home; the condition of the tent had to be improved. The corporal created a pool and hired a Vietnamese "mama-san" to do the cleaning, laundry, and cooking for the intelligence section. Although they paid the woman a pittance, it was far more than she could make in the rice fields where she had spent most of her life and would probably remain until quite near the day she died.

"Mama Ruthie" was a small woman, about five foot zero inches tall. She wore her course gray hair in a tight bun. Any time she stepped outside, Ruthie put on her conical straw hat, fixing it in place with a bright red ribbon which she tied under her chin. Like most of the other mamasans, Ruthie never wore anything but the plainest type of sandals, baggy black shiny trousers, and a dingy, wrinkled once white blouse with sleeves that reached her wrists. Cross-hatched with wrinkles on every exposed part of her body, face, hands, neck, and feet, one of the men remarked that Ruthie's skin reminded him of the parched dry earth of West Texas.

The scouts fashioned a sash for Ruthie, proclaiming her "Miss Texas, 1848." The Miss World contest was being conducted at the time. Soon almost every old crone at Quang Tri Combat Base was wearing a sash proclaiming her miss something or the other. In a few days the joke got old and the sashes became cleaning rags.

Although Ruthie worked in a machine-like fashion, nodded her head in affirmation of every instruction, and smiled widely through her bad teeth and lips stained red to black by betel, but she did not appear to speak or understand English. Steve was aware of the sensitivity of the intelligence office and the possibility that Ruthie reported everything she saw and heard to some V.C. intelligence officer. The only documents Ruthie would ever see were disinformation reports left out on purpose. There was never any indication that Ruthie had taken any of the papers or passed the information on.

The intelligence officer's duties were a mixed lot of the administration of a battalion's section, requiring record keeping, counseling, and oversight of the men assigned to the S-2 shop. Steve had to collect intelligence from a number of sources. He had to learn these things without training, instruction, or the assistance of a manual. He used the sources listed on documents that had been locked in the S-2 officer's desk. He called on other S-2 officers throughout the division and began developing his own network of resources.

New scouts had to be assigned. Experienced S-2 staff was not available. The replacements would have to be selected by other criteria. Training was a factor. The type of training required was largely a matter of having gained combat experience. It was called on-the-job training. The battalion's minimum requirement was six months in country.

It was not just a matter of training and combat experience, but of screening and evaluating the applicants on an individual basis. They would be granted a confidential on a need-to-know basis security clearance, but before they could change their official military occupational specialty the new scouts would have to pass a background check by the FBI in order to be granted the required security clearance. Steve already held a top secret clearance, one of the require-ments to hold the office of battalion intelligence officer. This was one of the requirements that could not be waived and had been an important factor in his being selected for the post.

There were a number of benefits that came with the posting. The intelligence officer was assigned an assistant, a Jeep, and a driver. He not only attended a daily briefing on the battalion level but was required to attend the daily briefing held at the Citadel in Quang Tri City. Unlike the Army troops, who were allowed liberty to go into cities during their time off, Marines assigned to Quang Tri Combat Base were not allowed liberty off the base. For Steve and his driver, the daily trips were something of an adventure, although a single Jeep traveling on Route Nine was a tempting target.

White crushed coral had been laid down over a packed red clay road that had existed for years. It had proven to be completely impassable during the monsoon season or after any heavy rain. American Seabees had quickly stabilized and improved Route Nine from Quang Tri City all the way to Khe Sahn. Rice paddies lined both sides of the highway for miles in both directions. Steve focused his attention on a group of half a dozen women working in the rice paddies. They gathered rice stalks in one hand and cut them with a very sharp, curved blade held in the other. The stalks were passed to the higher, dry dike where they were stacked.

"In Mexico, it's a sombrero. In Texas, it's a Stetson. Oklahomans favor a ball cap. Here it's a straw cone," Steve commented to the driver.

Thigh deep in the rice paddles, Steve could see the women all wore the same style of black pantaloons. There was not one woman who wore anything different from the waist down. One of them was wearing an almost white blouse. Three were dressed in brown blouses. One wore grey. Another woman wore a faded blue blouse. Steve wondered what that might mean. Was she just young and perhaps unconventional, perhaps a non-conformist, or did the color of the blouse she wore signal a simple message of some sort to an enemy watcher? None of the women rose up to look as the Jeep passed.

The driver came to a choke point, a railroad bridge over the Thach Hanh River, a wide, slow-moving greenish-gray sludge that originated sixty miles to the west among the high mountains and deep triple canopy jungles along the Laotian border. The only intact railroad bridge in I Corp bisected the village, which at home might have been called a sleepy or lazy suburb of Quang Tri City. Steve had time for a visual inspection of the hamlet.

Adjacent to the city, the refugee-swollen province capital, Thach Hanh was not a refuge for the wealthy that might desire a country home or place to escape the closeness and squalor of the city. The residents of the hamlet seldom took jobs in the city. Their children walked or rode bikes to Quang Tri's schools, to go to a hospital, to register for the mandatory census, and to trade what they could for necessary goods clothing, candles, and such things as cooking oil, which they could not do without. For the past several years, many of the women had been boarding a morning military bus going in the other direction, to Quang Tri Combat Base, where they did laundry or filled sandbags. The women received a penny in U.S. military payment currency for each sandbag they filled. It was hard work the American soldiers did not like to perform. An industrious woman could make a quarter an hour.

An enterprising woman with a mobile oven set up at the bridge every morning to bake baguets of French bread. Sales were brisk as the aroma, her best form of advertising, was hard to resist. Freshly baked bread was not an item on most of the passing soldiers' menu. A pair of bold, enticing schoolgirls bought Coca-Colas for a quarter a can. They paid a dollar for a fifty-pound block of ice at the nearby ice house. They sold cans of soda pop to the passing soldiers for a dollar a can. Even with soda pops for a dime per can at the base, there was a demand for the cold sodas even at the exorbitant price.

A local barber stayed busy with his scissors and hand trimmers. Long hair was not in favor among the men of Vietnam. Quang Tri's electric grid stopped several blocks short of the village. A small restaurant was located near the intersection of the railroad bridge and the village's long dirt main road that roughly paralleled the river. It was a favorite place for young people to gather after dark when work had ended and the military traffic had ceased rumbling past with its loads of rude, whistling, gesturing, kiss-blowing, hungry-eyed American soldiers.

An ornate Catholic Church built during the French colonial period was the real social center of the south end of the village. This was in spite of the vast majority of Vietnam's residents being practicing Buddhists. The church was staffed by both French and Vietnamese nuns. There was, however, no priest in residence. The closest Buddhist temple was in Quang Tri City.

By contrast, the social center of the north end of the village was the frequently visited whorehouse that had sprung up to serve what few American advisors were allowed into the city along with visiting journalists and other civilians. The majority of the clientele, however, were Vietnamese soldiers, South Vietnamese until the midnight curfew and V.C. and North Vietnamese soldiers afterwards.

A small bar, café and pool hall had been established near the house of prostitution. The older part of the village contrasted greatly with the poorer southern end. The homes there were constructed primarily of concrete blocks with sheet metal roofs. The north end of the village and the activities that took place there were a source of embarrassment to many. At the same time, they were topics of curiosity and guarded gossip among the schoolgirls, including Lan Thi Quoc, who was too shy to even bring herself to sell soda pops to the Americans who called out to her and made suggestive gestures or outright lewd propositions.

Lan's father was a doctor and one of Thach Hanh's most prominent citizens. Typical of most of the country, there was no hospital or post office in Thach Hanh. Neither was there a lawyer or social worker, welfare office, or police station. The village had no theater or drugstore. There was no supermarket or gasoline station, no convenience store. While there were no televisions or telephones, most homes had battery-operated radios and record players of some sort.

Close to the DMZ and adjacent to the coveted political prize of Quang Tri City, there was an abundance of danger in the riverside village. The South Vietnamese Army and the Quan Chanh, the military police, confiscated anything they wanted. Fortunately, Thach Hanh was too poor to often attract their attention. The Viet Cong came at night with their propaganda teams and tax collectors who followed the harvest, one of the reasons the farmers had little produce to sell. The more their fields produced, the heavier they were taxed. Roving recruiters also visited Thach Hanh periodically. Soldiers from the North Vietnamese Army came not only for the young men but for the young women to serve as nurses and "comfort girls" in their secure base camps and recreation areas.

Lan knew she was a target for all of them. She knew there was at least one Viet Cong agent residing in the village. The enemy knew too many small details about Thach Hanh and its residents for them not to have an inside source who kept his eyes and ears open and his mouth shut. Lan wasn't sure who it was. It was simply a fact of life, one the girl couldn't do anything about and therefore didn't spend a lot of time thinking about. There were other things on the young girl's mind.

Lan was keenly aware that she was noticed daily as she walked to school with her girlfriends. They were all similar in appearance. Each of them wore her long black hair straight with bangs cut just above her eyebrows. They wore black pantaloons under pastel-colored ao-dais that clung tightly to their small breasts and slender waists. Cut to the hip on both sides, the bottom of the over blouse swirled around their legs as the girls walked along in their platform heel sandals. Their pastel over blouses made them appear like a flock of passing butterflies every morning and afternoon. Though dressed in her oldest, faded, most drab ao-dai, Lan stood out like a monarch among the more common of her species. She was extremely beautiful, but perhaps she stood out due more to her bearing and attitude than anything else.

The river along the village where this beautiful young woman lived was lined with life. Shade trees had been planted along its banks. A perimeter line of fruit trees surrounded each home's plot. Beyond that were the irregular patterns of rice paddles and dikes.

Steve counted five sampans moving in the river. He counted thirty-seven small fishing vessels tied together in three rows at rest on the middle of the river, all of them on the south side of the bridge. The boats were no bigger than a large canoe. A walking path hardened by generations of bare feet ran the length of the river. The banks appeared to be almost vertical and were only four feet high. At irregular intervals, a set of concrete steps led down to the water.

The majority of the houses appeared to be of bamboo frames with thatch walls and gabled thatch roofs with an open porch at one end. This covered walkway was actually the entrance to the homes. Most had at least one palm tree in the yard. These beautiful thirty- to forty-foot-tall trees provided abundant coconuts and fiber for making rope to tie the house frames together and for numerous uses on the fishing boats.

Steve examined the part of the village that extended beyond the bridge to the north. That end of the village appeared to be more prosperous than the southern end. Though old, even more than a century In some cases, the buildings were a mixture of Vietnamese designs with both Chinese and French influences evident. The structures were of basic rectangular shapes. The walls and supporting columns, though crumbling and peeling, were of concrete. From one under construction, Steve could see the wood frame supporting the thatch roofs. There were arched door frames, French windows, tile or sheet metal roofs, and wooden doors on the more prosperous homes.

A crowd of children had gathered outside the restaurant. They watched as crates of a strange breed of pink pigs were unloaded. These pigs were donated by a U.S. agency who hoped they would be used to improve the local Vietnamese breed. But these pigs would not live long enough to be used in a breeding program. The children all had the same style of haircut: high in the back and sides for the boys, long and gathered in a ponytail for the girls. Most of the boys dressed in shorts and long-sleeve buttoned shirts.

The Marines passed over the rather long, narrow bridge into Quang Tri City, the third largest in South Vietnam. As a port city, it had thrived on rice exports, the historical economic base of the province, if not the entire country. The grain had been surpassed by the commerce of war soldiers and supplies. The South Vietnamese Navy had a presence in Quang Tri, as did the "Brown Navy" of the U.S. fleet. The city was heavily guarded by ARVN troops, including their Marines.

It was a bit unusual to be driving on paved roads and passing power poles and electric lines in Vietnam. Steve wondered about the source of their electric energy. It wasn't from dams and water-driven turbines. He assumed it to be from natural gas.

Along the unnamed street they were driving along was a commercial district with heavy foot traffic and busy shops. The houses they were passing at this point were a mixture of concrete and unpainted sheet metal roofs. The broad streets bore a heavy volume of bicycle traffic. There were American soldiers riding cyclos, with the small Vietnamese driver guiding and pedaling away from behind the wide single seat. There were signs that indicated American commercialism had reached Quang Tri.

RESTAURANT.

Steve had never been in a Vietnamese restaurant. He wondered what they served.

THE TWIST CLUB.

The twist was one of Steve's favorite dances. No doubt this was a hangout for G.I.s on liberty as well as for prowling prostitutes and enemy ears. Steve noted it as a potential intelligence source and problem area. They passed a rather drab-looking six-story motel similar to what he had seen in Tijuana, a hotbed hotel. The Lincoln was the tallest building in Quang Tri. The parking lot was full of motorized bicycles.

The cyclos were basically low-powered moped-style motorbikes. There were hundreds of them in the lot, but Steve focused on one. A woman was easing it out of the parking lot. A thin pastel lavender au-dai clung to her body. Her short hair was worn in a mass of curls, a style not seen outside of the major cities. To the young Marine, she was an exotic creature worthy of a long look in passing.

They drove past a two-story building with balconies cantilevering over the sidewalk. The structure was built of concrete, but it appeared less stable than any concrete structure Steve might have been involved in designing. He thought the columns were too slender for the weight they resisted and wondered how much rebar and wire mesh might be in them.

There were more signs in English for businesses that catered to the U.S. Army presence, SCIENTIFIC MASSAGE and STEAM BATH, for example. VICTORIA BAR. Salador Bar and restaurant. Wares were stacked in baskets on the sidewalks and streets in front of the business cases of protesting ducks, a pig, and barking dogs, baskets of rice, wilting vegetables, and fruit, bananas, pineapples, and local tropical fruit, Steve could not identify.

They passed a house with its porch turned into a market. Strings of sausages hung from hooks screwed into the ceiling. They were a dark reddish brown. The Vietnamese paid no attention to the flies that had been attracted by the feast. The busy insects seemed to coat the sausages. Stacks of strange fruit were displayed. Coconuts and a small variety of red bananas were being offered along with every kind of vegetable.

The center of the city proved to be more substantial. The streets were broad. Women in their flowing au-dais and sunglasses rode their motorized bicycles from shop to shop. The cyclo drivers were doing a brisk business. Most of them were older men either past military age or retired, at least exempted for some reason. But Steve noticed one of the men who seemed to be quite young, most certainly of military age. There was no discernible crippling feature that would prevent his serving in the military. He wore large wraparound sunglasses that made it difficult to get a look at his face. There was a license plate on each cyclo. Steve wrote down EK-6180. He would check it out later, noticing that the number 8 appeared to have been altered from the number 3.

At one stall, a young salesman was negotiating hard with three Americans in civilian clothes. The boy was about ten. Along the top row of one shelf were beautiful dolls with exaggerated figures covered by traditional Vietnamese garments, the colorful ao-dai. They were usually high-necked like Marine Corps dress blues. They hugged a woman's figure tightly all the way to the thighs. There was little left to wonder about when you saw a woman dressed in such a manner. There was a model dressed in gold, blue, yellow, pink, green, and red dresses.

Additionally, there were lacquered works of art and wood carvings for sale. Steve knew there were many items he could not see that would be of interest to him. At a later time, he might do some shopping along this street, where the profession of a number of young ladies walking along in ultra-miniskirts and high heels, swinging their purses, and posing as sexily as they could was obvious. A thin girl, her long hair dyed faintly red, in a camouflage pattern miniskirt called out to Steve.

"Hey, G.I. You go boom boom. Ten dollah MPC."

The girls shot them the finger as they passed without comment. A beggar blocked traffic on the sidewalk. His emaciated useless legs were twisted grotesquely behind him. He held his plastic jungle hat out to every passerby. As soon as money hit the hat, he scooped it up. Steve watched as the man handed the money to a child who disappeared into the crowd only to return a short time later.

"That man might be crippled, but he's not crazy," Steve told the driver. "He's not going to keep the money he collects on him and become an easy target for one of the many thugs on the street who look for such opportunities."

Another woman, heavily made up, was quite attractive in a purely Asian way. The girl standing next to her, however, was close to being downright ugly. She had one good feature. That was her magnificent chest. The Marines paid little more than passing attention to either of them.

The last bar on the strip was the Monaco. A senior Army enlisted man was walking past, checking out the girls in this supermarket of flesh. The wall of the bar appeared to be of painted galvanized sheet metal. Geometric shapes had been cut into the walls. The openings were framed with glossy black material. The girls on display were certainly a cut above those on the streets. A long-legged girl in mini-heels and a short fashionable print dress followed Steve's progress with soulful eyes.

Another who stood beside her had cut her hair in an attractive, stylish manner. She wore a gray belted one-piece suit that looked expensive. Steve watched as the soldier approached her. Several other women were seated at chairs so they could look out the window and call to men as they passed by.

Steve's first sight of the Citadel was not encouraging. The structure was over 500 years old. All around the perimeter was a stone wall only four feet tall. The stones were chipped and covered in mold and other forms of pollution. Inside was a maze of geometric shapes formed by more stone walls. Each set was higher than the last. An attacking enemy would be continually fighting uphill. If they overran one wall, the surviving defenders would retreat and reinforce another.

Holes for cannon muzzles were built into each wall. The period pieces were on display as if ready to be fired. At each level, the walls were not only higher but thicker. Above it all was a compound that had served as the local ruler's home and court. It was now home to the Vietnamese commander of I Corp, his staff, and their families. Atop the Mayan-like fortress at the peak of the mound was a thirty-foot flagpole. From it flew the flag of South Vietnam, three vertical orange stripes on a yellow field.

You saw all kinds of flags flying in Vietnam. Every river craft and most tanks had a U.S. flag on display. Individuals carried them in their packs. They flew over every permanent as well as temporary U.S. installation. There were some Confederate flags flown or sewn to packs or uniforms, a form of personal expression. A number of Texas flags. Not too many other state flags. The Muskogee (Indian) Nation flag was seen from time to time.

Korea, Australia, South Vietnam, and, of course, North Vietnam. The enemy flag was a terrific trophy and much more rare than the Japanese flags Marines coveted in World War II. Centered in the field of the enemy flag is a yellow five-pointed star. In the background, the top half is red, the bottom blue. As coveted as they were, the "owner" of an enemy flag often pinned them to the walls of the squad's bunker or displayed them in other ways. When the Marines found an NVA flag in a village or hamlet, they considered the entire village to be hostile.

Steve's personal captured flag was a little unusual. There is a yellow script in a half-circle arc around the star against the red field. At the point of the star is the word, Thi Dua. To the left, Dong Guy Dam, and to the right, Phu Giai Phong.

Steve made his way into the banquet hall which served as the briefing room. This was no Saigon five o'clock follies. I Corp personnel defended the northernmost border along the DMZ and a portion of the western border with

Laos. Few journalists attended these briefings. The representatives from each unit stood in turn, introducing themselves and relating anything of significance pertaining to their unit during the last twenty-four hours. Such things as changes of commanders were noted. A change in equipment, such as retiring the relatively unreliable long range 175mm guns to be replaced with the shorter range but more accurate 155s, was discussed. Information brought in by documents captured on patrols or discovered through interrogation of prisoners was shared.

Meticulously, Steve wrote down everything. He noted movements and enemy units on his map and related almost word for word the intelligence summary given by every man present at his later daily briefing for his battalion's officers. His actions impressed the battalion commander considerably.

After one of the briefings, Steve told his driver, "Go on past the ice house to Thach Hanh. Let's check on Le Kinh."

Le Kinh, a former NVA soldier, had surrendered to the South Vietnamese under a "Cheu-hoi" open arms amnesty program. Politically "re-educated," Le Kinh had been trained by U.S. Marines to serve as a "Kit Carson Scout." Given the rank and pay of a staff sergeant in the South Vietnamese Army, these scouts were assigned to a U.S. Marine rifle company where mistrust was sometimes proven in the field.

While serving with Bravo Company, Le Kinh had been wounded during the relief of Charlie Company. Upon his discharge from the hospital, the Marines gave him a month's medical leave with pay. Steve and his driver had delivered the wounded man to his home on the Thach Hanh River just outside of Quang Tri City.

Much to the surprise of the locals, they had crossed the bridge and turned south on the dirt road paralleling the river. Americans did not visit the south end of Thach Hanh. Le Kinh directed them several hundred feet deep into the village to a poor thatch and bamboo hut typical of the homes south of the bridge. The frame was of stout bamboo lashed together with coconut fiber cord. Steve had not known that bamboo grew to six and even eight inches in diameter before seeing it in Vietnam. The exterior walls were of layered grass and thatch. The roof was made of layered dry palm fronds. The interior walls were of tightly woven reed mats. The floor was hard-packed earth throughout. Cardboard and cans of c-rations formed a part of one end wall. C-rate and soda pop cans had been cut and flattened. They were attached to the cardboard in an overlaying fish scale pattern that would shed water. Steve immediately thought of asking his battalion to save their tin cans to help Le Kinh.

A curious crowd gathered as Steve helped Le Kinh from the Jeep. The scout's wife smiled shyly and welcomed the Americans with a small bow. Pink, their four-year-old daughter, was not the least bit shy. She reached out to the Marine with her arms held up. Steve scooped the child up, hugged her, kissed her on the forehead, and planted her on his hip. Doing so in such an unassuming and unhesitating manner won him more than one heart.

Pink is the English version of the girl's name. She was an extraordinarily beautiful child sprung from less than ordinary parents. She had a round face with dark, expressive eyes, shining white teeth, and short, dark gleaming hair cut with bangs and a style that hugged and framed her face.

Although Le Kinh had been treated by U.S. Navy doctors at the sprawling modern medical facility at Da Nang, the local doctor was summoned. He arrived shortly, accompanied by his daughter, Lan, who had been assisting her father since her twelfth birthday. At barely five feet tall, the Vietnamese beauty was fifteen inches shorter than the Marine. The girl with long black hair and an enticing slim figure made an immediate impression on the Marine, who thought she must have looked much like Pink as a child.

"I am Lan," the girl introduced herself in good English. "I am the doctor's daughter and assistant."

"Following in your father's footprint, so to speak."

Lan looked to Steve questioningly, not quite understanding him.

"You want to be a doctor?"

"I think I might become a nurse. What I really want is to become a doctor, to help people the way my father does," she said rather sadly.

Steve would learn that despite her keen intellect and the vast knowledge Lan had absorbed observing and assisting her father, there was little chance of her becoming a doctor, not in Vietnam.

While the doctor examined Le Kinh, the Marines passed out cigarettes to the adults and candy to the children. The fine, light hair on Steve's arms was a curiosity to the Vietnamese, who have practically no body hair and struggle to grow facial hair. Steve tolerated their picking and pulling at the blond hairs on his arms.

Seeing his patience with them, Lan asked. "You have children?" Her boldness caught the attention of all the Vietnamese. It was quite a forward thing for the girl to engage the American in conversation. But the locals did not know just how bold the girl had been, as Lan and her father were the only villagers who spoke English with any appreciable degree of fluency. Several others spoke some French and had assumed the Americans would speak it as well until he gave them blank looks and Lan offered an explanation. Lan had begun to translate his every question, comment, and answer.

"No, I have no children. I am not married."

Lan thought that to be a very good answer. She looked up from wrapping a bandage around Le Kinh's leg. The Marine was looking at her in an appraising but not lustful way. Her heart seemed to skip a beat and then drum faster. She could feel her face reddening and her temperature rising. This was a new feeling. What had the Americans done to her? Was this some magical power of Americans? she wondered. Vietnamese boys and men had followed Lan with their eyes constantly, but none had caused her to experience this reaction. What does it mean? she asked herself.

Le Kinh's wife retired to the kitchen and began cooking a meal. She spoke to Lan sharply.

"You will stay to eat?" Lan asked Steve, translating.

"Sure," he answered, his hot blue eyes branding her heart.

The village took Steve's presence as an opportunity to hold a celebration. Pots of glutinous rice were boiled. A squealing pig was chased through the village until it was finally caught and slaughtered. Parts of the pig found their way into the rice. Ducks were grilled. Exotic fruits Steve had never before tasted were abundant. The Marines tried each of them. Home-made beer was poured. There was chatter. There was laughter and music, which suddenly ceased when a trio of nuns arrived.

A young woman, not yet a full-fledged nun, had come with the elder, more severe nuns. The girl soon attached herself to the Marine, creating a puzzling spark of jealousy within Lan. The nun spoke Steve's language the same way she spoke Vietnamese, as if it had been learned as a second language with the accent retaining the influence of her native French. Still, there was a difference Lan didn't quite understand. She couldn't know the French nun had been taught by a British nanny to speak "The Queen's proper English."

The novitiate was a beautiful European woman with red chestnut-colored hair and blue eyes. She had the type of nose and other facial features no Oriental woman would ever achieve, except perhaps, under a surgeon's blade. But no surgeon could provide a shared history or identity. From out of nowhere, with no real reason, that bit of jealousy sparked like a bright flare in a midnight sky. Have I been so immediately attracted to this tall, blue-eyed man, or have I grown so used to being the center of attention that it wounds me when someone else is? Lan questioned. Self-criticism was a way of life in Vietnam.

The Vietnamese maiden had no real experience with men and little with boys her own age.

Every man in the village wanted her, but this one had cast her aside as if she were a mere child compared to the French nun. Lan had avoided Vietnamese men whenever possible, and before this man came to Thach Hanh she had never spoken to an American in spite of learning the language. She had played coy games with schoolboys but she felt she was beyond that now. Lan knew she would suffer a traditional arranged marriage and find her own happiness where she could. She must come into that marriage a virgin or she would be returned in shame to her family. There was no possibility of her having a relationship with the American. Lan huffed off to the kitchen, leaving the American to the French woman. She was expected to help in the meal preparations in the kitchen now that Le Kinh was bandaged.

Still, she wondered what had attracted him to the French woman. What can I do to make myself more attractive to him? she questioned as she chopped vegetables. I cannot change the shape or color of my eyes. I cannot grow a larger chest, although I am well-endowed by Vietnamese standards. Suddenly, the absurdity of her thoughts came to mind. The feeling of jealousy disappeared. Why do I care what this man thinks or does? I have just met him and will never see him again. Although he has awakened something within me, he is meaningless to my life. The novitiate can gain the man's attention, but she cannot have him any more than I can. There is no reason for my jealousy. Lan forced herself to concentrate on preparing the meal. Still, she could not help but overhear the conversation between the Marine and the nun.

"...from the north of France near the border with Luxembourg."

"Texas, inland from the Gulf of Mexico, a place called Dallas or Big D."

"...a textile merchant."

"My brother is in food commodities. Lives in the Rio Grande Valley. The land around there is quite fertile."

"So, you are farmers?"

"No, the farmers around my brother's place raise cattle and chickens and grow tomatoes, watermelon, all types of fruit and vegetables...even grapes for local wineries."

"Wine and cheese. It sounds something like home, but in Texas?"

Lan thought there was a touch of regret or maybe only longing for home in the girl's voice.

Le Kinh's wife was squatting before the small cooking stove in a corner of the kitchen. She spoke sharply to Lan. Responding to the older woman's instructions, Lan called out to Steve.

"You want beer?"

During his in-country orientation, Steve had learned the Vietnamese would always offer a visitor something, no matter how little they had. He had been taught that it was an insult to refuse what was offered. He also knew how the local beer was made.

Steve responded, "Tea, please."

In a short time, the meal was served in Vietnamese family fashion, with the men eating first, along with the nuns, who could not be expected to cook for them and serve their meals. Huge platters of food were placed in the center of the table, almost free-for-all to fill personal bowls following. Steve experienced new tastes, including nguoc mam, a strong, salty fermented fish sauce that no amount of brushing would eradicate easily. The meal was fiery with peppers and other sauces, but Steve had grown up on jalapenos and spicy TexMex dishes. He ate with a hearty appetite without making a pig of himself. He surprised them all with his dexterity in using wooden chopsticks.

The nun, sitting close enough but yet at a proper distance for a nun, asked, "Where did you learn to eat with chopsticks?"

"I did a tour in Japan, Okinawa, actually, before coming to Vietnam the first time. I learned there."

Lan watched as the American dipped his spring roll into the fiery sauce she had prepared. Politely, he did not take the best of what was offered. Neither did he eat fast, or obviously not all he could. Perhaps he is not such a barbarian after all, Lan thought.

During the meal Pink had climbed into the Marine's lap. He'd fed her delicate slivers of chicken and pork. She'd fallen asleep with her arms wrapped around his neck. The Marine held her there easily with one large hand until the dishes were cleared and beer was being served. Her amused mother took Pink to her bed.

Beer was served and passed around but the Marines did not drink any of it. The Vietnamese men grumbled, taking offense. Lan mentioned it to Steve.

"It is against my religion," he explained to Lan, who was busy trying to translate all the comments that were being made. Fortunately, religious beliefs were something the Vietnamese understood and respected. Steve had been counting on that.

"Are you Catholic?" the older nun asked.

"No, I'm not."

"You Buddha then, you drink," the barber insisted, surprising everyone with his use of English.

Lan did not like what she saw in the barber's face, some degree of malice, but why? Could it be jealousy? The Marine was quiet for a moment. He was obviously trying to think his way diplomatically around his refusal.

"No, not Catholic, not Buddhists; I'm a..a. Pedestrian! We do not smoke and do not drink."

"Ah, pedestrian. A very good but strict religion," the older nun said, nodding, a slight smile on her face as Lan translated. Lan had smiled as well. She did not like drunks, or more correctly, she did not like the way men became when they drank.

The barbarian knew a few words of Vietnamese, which he used after a brief but appropriate amount of time, shoving away from the table, thanking the doctor and Lan for their service, the hostess for their meal, and others generally for their friendship and hospitality. He shook hands all around, patted Le Kinh on the shoulder, and drove away in his Jeep. Life in the village returned to the mundane level of threat and danger with thin golden veins of hope.

The Marines drove past the village every day on their way to and from the Citadel. They frequently stopped for brief visits with the Kit Carson Scout. Having never been questioned about their activities or the length of their absences, the Marines often took the "scenic route" through the streets of Quang Tri to reach their official designation. Gary washed the Jeep in the river under the bridge, debriefing locals in the process. The Marines always stopped at the ice house before returning to Quang Tri Combat Base.

Steve had begun routinely stopping at his favorite restaurant just off the main road and the dirt road leading down into the south end of the village. Everyone soon knew him there. The small restaurant didn't seem to have a name. The pink building was hard to miss not just because of its color but with the design flare and substantial materials with which it had been constructed.

The waitresses soon knew Steve and Gary's favorite meals and drinks. Steve liked Pho with an extra portion of thinly sliced raw beef and a generous squeeze of lime. He preferred fresh pink lemonade colder and less sweet than the syrupy mixture favored by the Vietnamese.

The Marines's presence never failed to draw a crowd. The villagers came to see him for different reasons. Steve's pockets were always filled with hard candy. Like most Marines, he was a soft touch for the children. The elder Vietnamese enjoyed his cigarettes. They watched the Marine with all-seeing eyes. They weren't sure if the Marine liked Pho and lime drinks or the beautiful girls who took turns serving them.

Steve would swear it was the food, but with crossed fingers. Understanding that everything he did, every word he said, was being closely scrutinized, Steve made a point to regularly buy baguets of fresh French bread from the wrinkled crone to offset his attention to the young ladles. From time to time he bought fruit from another aged lady and a fish off one of the boats.

The restaurant was an excellent, seemingly innocent location to meet people and make friends. It was relatively secure, as vehicular traffic on the village road was extremely rare. There was a constant flow of military traffic on the nearby bridge. There were no bars or prostitutes south of the bridge where Steve spent most of his time. The only narcotic widely used was the betel nut chewed by so many of the women.

The restaurant was where Steve met with Sister Mai, the Vietnamese Catholic nun. Her church was at the south end of the village. Her young novitiate was a real head turner, rare except in the movies. The French woman spoke Vietnamese and English as well as her native tongue. Secretly, Steve thought she might regret actually taking her vows.

"That would be a waste of prime pussy," he told Gary irreverently.

Lan always seemed to be present with her crowd of classmates when Steve visited the restaurant. She was the only one among them who spoke more than a few words of English. Her presence as translator only seemed natural. Of course, she didn't translate everything the Marine said. He constantly flirted with her and teased her about being his girlfriend. Her coquettish retort was always the same.

"You say for me. I no say for you."

Steve continued his visits and study of the village. Instead of stopping at the restaurant one day, Gary drove the Jeep down the unnamed dirt road toward Le Kinh's home. Steve had noticed that no doorway faced directly into another. Likewise, due to Oriental superstitions, no doorway would open directly facing the street.

The village was larger than Steve had originally thought it to be. Six thousand Vietnamese lived in poor huts on twelve long streets paralleling the river. There was no industry and little commerce. The residents fetched or worked the family plots in the nearby rice paddies. Young children begged along the shoulders of Highway Nine.

Military traffic along the route was heavy. The bridge created a bottleneck. Convoys often sat for half an hour while the one-way traffic along the three hundred-foot-long bridge ran against them.

Half an hour was sufficient time for the high school girls to sell all their cold sodas. Steve and Gary didn't wait. They could always turn off and go down into the village that they were visiting with more frequency. They sometimes dined with the doctor, a man of strong political convictions. Doctor Quoc had been educated in France, a boon from his wealthy French grandfather. A staunch anti-communist, the doctor had returned to Vietnam to practice medicine at a hospital in Hanoi. When the French were defeated and the country was divided, Dr. Quoc was among the hundreds of thousands who had voted with their feet, fleeing to the south. With a pregnant wife, a small child, and little money, the doctor settled in Thach Hanh. He now practices his profession at a hospital in Quang Tri City. He usually offered his services for free in the village where he lived. Doing so was the currency that bought him and his family a certain degree of security.

Steve learned that by design there was no road leading to the Quoc home. One had to make their way on foot and bike path through a maze of paddy dikes and a seemingly solid wall of greenery to get to it. Lan aside, Steve enjoyed his conversations with the well-trained, intelligent doctor. The Marine learned more about the political climate and the realities of the war in Northern I Corp from the doctor than he did from the briefing at the Citadel.

During one of his visits Steve finished his lunch of fish and rice with the fiery nguoc mam generously applied. The Quocs had accepted him to the point where they no longer prepared special meals for him but fed him whatever they were having. Steve felt he would be lucky if the meal didn't give him heartburn or burn a hole in his stomach. Or worse, give him a severe case of the runs. It was a change from the standard C-ration diet but not a particularly good one. The saving grace was that Lan had served him and hovered nearby throughout the meal.

"Thank you, Lan. That was very good," he said in the Vietnamese he was quickly learning. The girl had proudly cooked the meal for him and had served it to him herself. The Vietnamese girl beamed a bright smile at the young American. She tried hard not to display pride at the Marine's compliment. Steve recognized her proper manners by local customs that meant she would not sit at the table with him during the meal. There was an attraction they were both aware of that grew stronger with each meeting in spite of neither of them saying or doing anything to advance that attraction or those feelings. There was a certain endearing yet mysterious native perspicacity to every movement the girl made, a sort of raw elegance, from preparing and serving a simple meal to riding her bike to and from school.

She was in almost every way, exotically different from any other women or girls Steve had ever known. She and Mary were opposites in almost every way. Perhaps that was at least a part of the attraction. Lan's complexion was beach sand brown. Her features were dark and delicate.

Steve was likewise completely different from Vietnamese men. His eyes were blue. His hair was blonde. Lan was particularly entranced by the large but well-proportioned man in spite of his barbarian ways. He didn't know to belch politely after meals or to pick his teeth at the table in Vietnamese fashion. But she had a rival of sorts, and it wasn't the girl ten thousand miles away.

The beautiful novitiate with the face of an angel was often in the restaurant during Steve's visits, noticeably more than in the past. Lan was usually there, always with a crowd of her friends. She watched with a certain amount of envy as the older, bolder girls, the ones who sold Coca-Cola to the soldiers, played an American radio and were taught dance steps by the Marines.

Eyes were always on the American, and therefore on Lan when she was near him, anticipating what he might do, good or bad. A Viet Cong cadre member, cautious mothers, and tongue-wagging gossips ready to repeat everything they saw or heard were all watching the Americans. The Viet Cong had made numerous attempts to cast the Marines's purposes in a bad light. But the Americans still did not drink beer. He always ordered the same thing, a glass of pink lemonade. He did not visit the brothel at the far north end of the village. These things were noticed by the Vietnamese who wondered just what they had in their midst.

"How do you arrange for a Jeep and driver every day?" the nun asked. She knew only high-ranking officers could do that, not young men like this one.

"I have to give an intelligence briefing at the Citadel every day," he answered without thinking that such information could bring him unwanted attention and even make him a target of enemy agents. A more experienced intelligence officer would probably not have made that mistake.

"So you stop by chance at the same time the beautiful schoolgirls are passing by each day," the nun teased.

"Purely by chance," the Marine assured her, his eyes twinkling mischievously, a look Lan took to mean something entirely different.

The routine was repeated daily for weeks until only a few of the villagers even noted the Marine's coming and going. And then one day the young French woman did not meet with the Marine. The older nun, however, did, once, briefly. Afterwards, the young woman seldom left the church grounds. She said nothing, but everyone knew the older nun had ended the visits. Lan was glad. The woman had obviously become too familiar with the Marines. Although it was sad in a way, it meant that Steve Kowalski had much more time for passing out hard candy to the children and more time for Lan. She was trying to work up the courage to ask him to teach her a dance.

It seemed to Lan that the American sought her out with his eyes, at least in any passing crowd. But he did not wave or call out to her. There was a longing there, but Lan could not be certain what it was. Was the man developing some true feelings for her? Was he only playing games with her, with her heart, with her mind? Was it only that he was lonely and so far from home? Was it simply a man's lustful nature?

Lan knew the Marine was a good man. He didn't visit the house of whores. She would have known. He did not seek drugs. He did not look at the other girls the way he looked at her, although that had begun to become a topic of conjecture and gossip. Was his interest in her just for sex? Did he see her as an easy conquest? What kind of girl, person, did he think she was? If he really wanted her properly, why did he not talk to the matchmaker? Or to her mother? Should she ask one of her girlfriends to talk to him for her? Lan decided against that as a possible source of terrible embarrassment.

Still, although Steve had never brought it up, Lan began to have thoughts of going to America, not only in order to escape the war and a life of unfulfilled dreams, but to a life that would be so much safer and to a place where her intelligence, willingness to make sacrifices, determination, and hard work would allow her to become whatever she wanted to make of herself, including becoming a doctor.

When Steve did not come for days, Lan lit a candle and three incense sticks for him at the family alter, a fact noticed by her mother. Lan prayed for Steve's well-being. She looked for him and his Jeep daily. She sat at the restaurant sipping lemonade at the times when he would usually be there, but he did not come. Everyone in the village knew what Lan's sad face meant and who she was waiting for.

When he finally returned after three long weeks, Steve did not speak of where he had been. There was a tired sadness about him, a distant look in his eyes. Lan wondered where he had been. What had he seen and done? She wanted to reach out to him, to hold his hand, to embrace and comfort him, but she could not.

It took a full day of human kindness and the laughter of children seeking candy in every pocket to put a genuine smile back on the Marine's face that finally came about in response to a hug from Pink. Le Kinh recovered from his wound and was returned to duty. Three days passed, and Le Kinh had not returned. During that time Steve had not been seen even passing on the bridge to his daily briefing. Lan feared that he was on a military operation. She waited and worried as three days became four... five... a week. Near tears with worry, Lan considered going to Le Kinh's wife for information, but that would openly announce her interest, and that simply would not do in Vietnamese society. Neither could she talk to her mother or even to her closest friend. She suffered her fears alone and in silence.

Lan, however, found the most unlikely of confidants in the French nun, whom she turned to out of desperation. After Lan's visit, the novitiate was joined by her mother superior.

"They call him 'Ha Shi Cau.' The Vietnamese simply cannot pronounce Corporal Kowalski, which becomes Ha Shi, the Vietnamese word for his rank, and Kow, which becomes cau, the Vietnamese word for candy. Ha Shi Cau, Corporal Candy, a barbarian to be sure, but such a barbarian as to set a young girl's heart aflutter and cause her to dream beyond herself, to hope beyond her own small village."

It was not necessarily what the young woman had said, but rather the wistful tone of her voice in saying it that caused the French girl to be invited to stay up throughout the night scrubbing wooden floors with a hand brush and harsh soap.

Another week passed before Le Kinh returned, his left arm in a bloody sling, but he was not driven home by Steve. A small crowd, including a somber Lan who was again assisting her father, gathered at the scout's house. Le Kinh told of the battle. Lan was anxious for news about Steve but could not ask. She listened intently.

"We flew in helicopters to a mountain called 'Mutter's Ridge.' It is full of sharp stones but with nowhere to hide. We dug holes in the rocky ground. Very hard work. More Marines came. The enemy fired his artillery. A helicopter is shot down. An air strike stops the artillery, but then mortars are hidden in a valley began firing from close by.

"The gunner fires his mortar, turns a knob one click, and fires another. They land ten meters apart all across the hill. Ha Shi Ca sees the mortar pattern. He leaves his hole to pull me out of mine. A round explodes right in the hole I just left. Ha Shi Cau has saved my life. But I was wounded. He dragged me to his hole. He bandaged me and left the hole to help others who had also been wounded. While pulling a wounded man to safety, he was felled by a mortar explosion."

Lan's breath caught in her throat. She looked away so no one could see the tears in her eyes. Le Kinh continued.

"There was blood from wounds in his chest and legs. If he is lucky, they will send him home. They do that with their seriously wounded."

Moving away and trying to hide her tears, Lan saw something no one else seemed to have noticed. A small portrait photo of the Marine had taken its place on the family alter as the last of Le Kinh's line to have died. Such an honor outside of one's family lineage had never been heard of before. There must have been much more to the story than Le Kinh was telling. Had Steve been killed? Lan trembled and forced herself not to weep openly until she had reached the privacy of her own special place.

Lan walked home, dragging an anchor for a heart. She did not want her mother to see her that way, to question or to guess why she was so upset. Lan spent the night huddled in a small ball at the base of a longan tree, muffling her sobs and repeatedly wiping away tears, which she could not stop. Upon returning home the following morning, crestfallen, tired, and red-eyed, Lan told her mother a believable lie.

"I thought the V.C. were coming, so I hid."

It took better than two months, but it was Has Shi Cau who came, not the V.C. This time the Jeep, followed by a snowballing crowd of excited children calling Corporal Candy's name, came down the village's narrow dirt road. There were three men in the Jeep that stopped in front of Le Kinh's hut. The driver stayed with the vehicle. A barrel-chested major and the limping corporal entered the thatch hut.

From her own home where she was listlessly studying mathematics, Lan heard the children shouting, "Ha Shi Cau! Ha Shi Cau! Has Shi Cau returned?"

And from the shrill voice of a child she recognized, "Ha Shi Cau! You souvenir me one cigarette!"

Lan dropped her books and shot from her chair, sending a tea cup and saucer flying. They shattered on impact with the hard-packed dirt floor. Lan didn't hear them.

"He lives," she said in a low whisper that did not escape her mother's ears as her daughter ran from the house and all the way to the home of Le Kinh. A crowd had gathered outside. Lan shoved and pushed, forcing herself to the front. The crowd gave way, knowing the doctor's daughter would be looking at the

American's wounds. Lan finally got to where she could see Steve. He was so pale and thin, and he was limping. Still recovering from wounds suffered while fighting for her country. Lan wanted to throw herself into his arms, but she knew she could not. That would never happen. Their two worlds would never come together harmoniously.

It was enough, though barely, for Lan to see Steve alive. He looked so somber. She knew he would laugh again in time if the war allowed him that time. Time would heal his wounds, and if fate meant for them to be together, it would happen. For now, he belonged to Thach Hanh again, and that was all that mattered.

CHAPTER FIVE
QUANG TRI COMBAT BASE

There wasn't much a man in a cast could do in combat. Steve Kowalski was deskbound once more. Again, the battalion had taken a beating. They'd been in one hell of a brawl, and the commanders at regiment and division levels knew it. An order for the battalion to stand down would hurt their pride and morale. Instead, they were assigned routine patrol operations within Quang Tri Province. They were designated the division reserve.

Steve knew his mother had been routinely notified of his being wounded. He had written to assure her that he was doing okay. He read a "be more careful and take care of yourself" letter from Mary Ann, but she seemed a little distant, a bit detached. He wondered if they had outgrown one another. Steve set that letter aside. He would have to give his answer some thought. He had put off something else he had to do. As their friend, he wrote Steve, Kevin, and Dave's families personal letters to add to the rather dry official Marine Corps death notification. In another letter, the gung ho Marine advised his seventeen-year-old brother to join the Navy or the Air Force. He realized the Marine Corps was not for everyone.

While recovering, Steve enjoyed hot meals, some of which were even delivered to his tent. Bored by the inactivity, the chief scout cleaned the office, read books, and filed the routine reports required and thought about the friends he had lost. He planned his immediate future...college on the G.I. Bill. He briefly considered Southern Methodist University but was sure he wouldn't fit in with the Highland Park highbrows. He decided to try for Rice in Houston but would probably have to settle for the University of Houston. In the meantime, he completed two correspondence courses from the University of California at Davis, something he didn't share with anyone.

It was hard to concentrate on anything in the heat of Vietnam. Northern Vietnam had two temperatures in September, hot and hotter. Still, it was an improvement over July. Steve had lost a few more pounds, but the full hot meals and forced inactivity were packing them back on. Kowalski was reading dull routine patrol reports from the previous day when a shadow fell across the desk. He looked up. Not just standing in but filling the entryway from top to bottom and side to side was just about the largest, blackest man Steve had ever seen. He held a rifle in one hand, a sea bag in the other. The silver railroad track captain's bars on his collar caught Steve's attention.

The scout stumbled rather awkwardly to attention as the man spoke. "Is this the two shop?"

"Yes, sir. Corporal Kowalski, acting S-2 officer, captain."

"At ease, corporal. I'm Captain Maxwell, and you are relieved."

"Thank you. So you're the new two."

And "the new two" became Captain Maxwell's name even beyond his tour of duty in Vietnam. The captain sat and conducted what the Corps calls a footlocker conversation. Rank was not a factor. It was a man to man. Marine to Marine, let your hair down and tell it like it really is skull session. These were learning and teaching opportunities for both men, with a certain amount of bonding thrown in for good measure.

The captain had already been given both the official and the commanding officer's BS version. Steve took the captain on a map tour of I Corp's terrain, not just the topo map he could read for himself, but real first-hand descriptions of the places he had been and what he had seen there. Steve pulled no punches as he told the captain what it was like to operate without proper orientation and support deep in the jungle with a three hundred-foot triple canopy overhead. They talked about operations in the salt marshes and the desert along the coast and along the waterways, each environment presenting a different set of challenges.

They discussed places: Khe Sahn, Cua Viet, Camo Lo, Dong Ha, Da Nang, and Quang Tri, as well as Camp Carroll, Con Thien, The Razorback, The Rockpile, and Mutter's Ridge. They were all locations that would become a permanent part of Marine Corps legend and history.

Steve talked about supplies, always too little and too late, and field packs, regulations versus reality in every phase of operations. The corporal explained what he knew of enemy units, their tactics, and their weapons. He enumerated those known to be operating in I Corp plus those identified across the DMZ and just inside the Laotian border.

They took a head break. When Steve returned, the "New Two" tossed him a blessedly cold beer. Drinking their way through a six-pack, the men discussed and evaluated every officer and senior non-com Steve knew and had worked with, as well as all the intelligence staff. They delved into politics and morale, racial issues, drug use, and alcoholism. At the end of four hours, Steve Kowalski knew the captain's father to be a Baptist minister and his mother a high school teacher. The captain had revealed that he was a graduate of Texas A&M, where he had played defensive tackle.

The men talked for hours. The captain was surprised by and impressed with the depth of knowledge exhibited by the corporal. He decided it was too early to make anything but a first impression, but this young man appeared to be someone he might consider recommending for the warrant officer program or even for OCS.

Finally, Steve admitted he couldn't think of anything else the captain needed to know. He waited for the new intelligence officer to ask questions. The captain stood and stretched. Steve wondered how in hell any ball carrier ever escaped him. The guy was not just big. He appeared to be rock hard and solid. The captain sat. The Marines had been talking for hours but they weren't done yet. They were on a roll.

"I understand you've been attending the daily intelligence briefing in Quang Tri City."

"Yes, sir."

"Ever learn anything of value to the battalion there?"

"Not of immeasurable import, no sir, but generally, there's no such thing as too much intelligence data."

"I understand that's turned into something of an ice run as well."

"We do drive right past the ice house on the way back."

"Ice is three dollars a block?"

"Yes, sir."

The captain laid five dollars MPC on the desk. "The two shop needs about three blocks a week. That cover my share?"

"Yes, sir."

"I understand you sometimes stop at the river to swim. I mean to wash the Jeep, of course."

"Yes, sir."

"And you always stop at a restaurant to eat and flirt with the girls."

"Yes, sir. I can see why you were made the intelligence officer."

"Do these people talk to you, ever reveal anything of value?"

"That's a good question. Captain. No one has given up a V.C. cadre member or warned of an immediate attack or anything like that."

"But?"

"There's a man I think you should meet. He can round out your true knowledge of Vietnam, of the politics and personnel, both military and civilian, here in I Corp."

"You speak Vietnamese?"

"Yes, sir, some. Enough to get by."

"So, the time you spend at that restaurant is really a cover for running a low-level intelligence operation?"

"Oh, yes, sir. Absolutely!" Steve said with a serious face, understanding that the captain was essentially providing an officially sanctioned reason for Steve to continue his activities at those otherwise out of bounds locations.

"You will continue to attend those briefings as our chief scout."

"Yes, sir." Steve realized he was saying that a lot.

"It won't cramp your style if I ride along from time to time; will it be, corporal?"

"No sir. I may need some supervision washing that vehicle."

"The battalion is not back up to full strength yet, Kowalski. A lot of people are holding down more than one job."

"Yes, sir," Steve responded, wondering if the captain was going to palm him off on someone else or make him work in administration as well. God, I'd hate that, Steve thought.

"The battalion needs a civil affairs officer and a civil affairs program and project."

"Yes, sir." It was obvious the captain had already been briefed on a higher level.

"The civil affairs officer must speak Vietnamese."

"Yes, sir." Steve was aware that he was sounding like a robot.

"The two shop maintains records on the battalion personnel who speak foreign languages, right?"

"Yes, sir."

"How many speak Vietnamese?"

"One, sir."

"You?"

"Yes, sir."

"Well, then. That makes you the battalion civil affairs officer."

"Acting."

"Acting, of course."

Steve's first thought was about how this was going to look in his service record book. A corporal and first appointed as the battalion's acting intelligence officer. Then an immediate appointment upon relief as the unit's acting civil affairs officer. What doors might that open? He thought he might have a chance if he applied to become a warrant officer, but he shelved that possibility as he gave thought to the civil affairs position. Each command was encouraged to develop such a program, which was quite a low priority for a rifle battalion with a majority of its personnel constantly on the move in the field.

Relocation and pacification programs were not working. They were truly making more enemies than friends. In an effort to win the hearts and minds of the Vietnamese people, programs had been established to introduce higher-yielding types of rice, better stocks of beef and pigs, and other agricultural support.

"With you in charge, Thach Hanh can easily become the battalion's civil affairs project. That will have to be approved by the regimental and division civil affairs officers. I will make the appropriate appointments and recommendations. There should be no resistance as you will have a head start in undertaking such a program in Thach Hanh."

Steve's mind was churning. Thach Hanh was a village in the middle of a prolonged war. It was located in a hot combat zone. Loyalties were divided. While his primary mission would remain military, Steve would have to embrace the civil affairs aspect of the assignment. Pacification programs had worked with only limited results in the jungle and rural environs where Steve had spent the majority of his time in Vietnam. He hoped for more positive results in the urban setting but realized that he would need to spend a significant amount of time in the village, perhaps days at a time.

"We'll have to run a security program first, mostly likely a country fair and set up a self-defense force. That will fulfill the military requirements of this type of operation."

Steve addressed a concern to Captain Maxwell. "There's a SEAL team and a Recon team based on the river near the village. I'll need their assistance from time to time. However, they are not allowed to enter the village."

"That shouldn't be a problem. Once they are officially participating in a civil affairs program approved at the division level and higher, they will be relieved of that restriction."

"Captain, why not move their base camp?" Steve asked. "We could all live in one large general-purpose tent. As they are available, that's where instructors and other visitors will stay.

"In the meantime, with the battalion still short of S-2 scouts, as soon as that cast is removed you will report to the companies and staff in the field and carry out instructions set forth as I dig into this job. You may have to fill both roles simultaneously."

CHAPTER SIX
QUANG TRI COMBAT BASE

Uneventful weeks passed as the intelligence section went through a period of transition. Fully healed from his wounds, Steve remained the Chief scout. Tsoi, Hoskins, and Dykus had returned from hospitals. After short periods of recovery, performing light duties such as sitting radio watches and reading through volumes of intelligence documents daily, they were returned to full duty status in the field. Steve wondered but did not ask how the civil affairs program Captain Maxwell had proposed was coming along.

The battalion returned to near full combat strength as more of the wounded returned, although most were ready for duty on a limited basis only. There were also new arrivals. Orientation and an extensive training program were instituted while the battalion was held in reserve and given responsibility for the perimeter defense of the sprawling combat base.

The battalion remained in tent quarters at Quang Tri, manning the perimeter lines constantly while conducting the required range of patrols in spite of the load it put on the intelligence section, which was still at only half its authorized personnel level. A scout was required to accompany every patrol and field operation. Small unit operations commenced in Quang Tri Province, primarily for training purposes but also to protect the base. Steve continued to lead patrols himself. He also attended the daily briefings at the Citadel in Quang Tri City and conducted his own at the battalion level afterward. Making an ice run became a part of the routine. Other opportunities presented themselves.

The port facility was busy twenty-four seven unloading supplies of every kind for the war effort as well as civil needs. Anything that was spilled or dropped during the unloading process was fair game for the taking. Units from every branch of military service throughout I Corp sent their scroungers to the docks on unofficial supply missions.

Steve arranged for use of what looked like the military version of a pickup truck bed which could be towed behind a Jeep or other similar vehicle. The loan was more or less permanent given a standing request for 100-pound blocks of ice from both the mess sergeant and the club NCO.

Although they competed seriously for any available goods, the scroungers knew one another and were friendly enough. They policed themselves as they didn't want their activities to be officially shut down. Steve and Gary soon became accepted as part of this irregular supply source. The Marines quickly became friendly with the civilian work force. Steve was putting together an idea that would require the cooperation of one of the civilians. Gary had talked to other drivers who trusted him enough to give him a name. He passed it on, pointing the man out to Steve. The stevedore was a burly, hirsute rather imposing figure. Steve wondered what he pulled down monthly for working in a war zone. Where and how does he live? Like a king, probably. Not in a tent, that's for damn sure. Does he have a beautiful young live-in companion? Most likely.

Steve introduced himself and engaged the man in conversation at the first opportunity to do so. Their exchange was obviously guarded by both parties. Steve led the man to his Jeep where he revealed a captured SKS rifle that had been wrapped in a blanket. Steve could see that the man wanted the weapon. Still, he hesitated. The Marine raised his shirt. Tucked into his belt was a pistol, a rare NVA officer's personal weapon. Steve laid it beside the rifle, knowing that would seal the deal he wanted to make.

Steve explained his idea. The stevedore wrapped the weapons in the blanket and left. A short time later, a cargo net was overloaded with beer, sodas, frozen lobster and steaks, cases of canned shrimp and chicken, candy, and an assortment of canned fruit. The net was piled high, too high. Steve watched as forklifts sealed off access to what would become the spill location. The other drivers didn't complain. They'd seen this happen before.

An overhead crane was moved into place. Three corners of the net were hooked up. One of the stevedores gave his signal to the crane operator. The crane lifted. Boxes of goods spilled out through the opening where the fourth corner of the net should have been hooked up. In spite of the shouting, the crane continued to lift until the net was completely empty.

"We'll have to survey this shit," the stevedore shouted as the net was lowered and unhooked. Then he walked off. Gary and Steve began loading their "salvaged goods." The watching scavengers did not interfere. They knew what was happening, that an arrangement had been made. Many of them had done it themselves. The pickup body was soon filled. The back seat of the Jeep was full. Everyone in the battalion who was not in the field would benefit in some way from this activity. A significant amount of goods was left behind for the other scroungers to pick through.

Hurrying and sweating, the Marines drove to the combat base without stopping at Thach Hanh or the ice house. At the guard gate they were waved into the base without being stopped. With eyeballs on them, they unloaded. The S-2 tent was soon filled with boxes. Steve stepped back and viewed what they had done. He had to think. There were decisions to be made. Although he didn't anticipate problems, he had to cover himself. There were questions to be answered. Who can I trust, he wondered. Who will make me the best deal? Steve had already decided to make four of them. He began chasing down the people he needed to talk to. The mess chief took a box of steaks. In exchange, he cooked a full steak and lobster meal for the scouts. It was delivered hot in canisters. There was a risk involved, but for an added case of beer the mess chief agreed to hold the frozen goods for Steve. They both knew he would be paid again to cook for the scouts when they came in from the field. Steve donated a gallon of shrimp and a case of chicken breasts to the officer's mess.

A similar deal with the non-commissioned officer in charge of the enlisted men's club cost Steve a case of Budweiser and two soda pops. At the last moment, Steve decided to split the liquor he'd salvaged several ways. For six bottles of Jack Daniels donated to the officer's mess, the lieutenant in charge agreed to store half of Steve's beverages. There was a bottle for the lieutenant and another for the battalion commander. Steve set five more aside.

One bottle was for the helicopter pilot who would deliver Steve and his goods to the field. Another went to the supply sergeant, who had agreed to issue completely new equipment and uniforms to all the scouts. He would provide boots, underclothing, towels, jungle utilities, socks, ponchos, packs, full web gear, and shelter halves. For an exchange of new weapons, Steve added a case of Black Label beer.

He gave his former S-2 officer, now the battalion's executive officer, his own bottle. Steve presented the battalion's sergeant major a bottle of Scotch with another to the Headquarters and Service Company commander. That done, the intelligence chief returned to his tent to begin selecting and sorting the goods to be taken to the field.

Steve now had eight scouts in the field with rifle companies. Two scouts were assigned to each company. Not a part of the company to which they were attached by headquarters, the scouts operated with a minimal amount of supervision and a great deal of independence. They were paid and supplied separately, allowing Steve to legitimize his deliveries. On the flight out, Steve would deliver the new issue of clothing and weapons while having a word in private with each of his scouts. He put a case of beer, two cases of soda, and a variety of canned goods under each man's bunk.

The radioman and driver assigned to the intelligence section would remain in the rear headquarters at Quang Tri Combat Base. They would be in charge of the goods during Steve's absence.

"Whenever they come in, the scouts can take care of their own goods," Steve instructed as he issued their portion. Perhaps half the salvaged goods were thus allocated. What remained was stacked in Steve's quarters and under his cot, not all for his personal use, of course. He wouldn't sell any of it. The Marine was not in the black market business and had not gone to all this length for personal gain.

There were still decisions that had to be made. The most choice and perishable foods had to go first. The chief scout asked Major Small and his company commander to dinner over a briefing at the S-2 tent. They had steak and lobster again, mashed potatoes with mushroom gravy, green beans flavored with bacon, buttered corn, and a fruit medley with whipped cream. It was almost like eating at home. After the meal, Steve brought the officers up to date on intelligence matters in the battalion's area of responsibility. Both officers and the mess sergeant departed with a case of Budweiser. I'm covered, Steve thought. What made the event memorable is that it was a singular event, a blink of time in the long Vietnam War.

Steve arrived early at the helicopter landing strip. A cargo net had already been spread out. The supply sergeant had kept his end of the bargain, as did the mess sergeant. The regular issues of supplies, ammunition, and rations were carried inside the two vessel flight of Chinooks. Included were insulated food containers. The choppers lifted off, each hovering to pick up supplies. One of them lifted two water bottles. The other was a net full of supplies Steve was providing. For the rifle companies, it appeared to be a routine resupply mission. For the scouts, it was more like Christmas. The following day they would all face death again.

Major James Hamlin, a VMI graduate and two-tour combat veteran, was currently serving as the Third Marine Division's Civil Affairs Officer. In addition to a great deal of tact and political acumen, the position required close coordination and cooperation with psy-ops, intelligence, logistics, and operations, as well as supply and medical units of combined American and South Vietnamese commands.

Steve had prepared a report for Major Maxwell based upon his observations of Thach Hanh and his interaction with the residents. In his summary, he noted that Thach Hanh was bisected by a strategic bridge. He reported that he had heard the village to be frequented by enemy tax collectors and political cadre. He found this to be somewhat alarming in that the village was in the shadows of Quang Tri City. The report was given a high probability of truth from a reliable source, qualifying it for immediate action. The captain passed the report on to Major Hamlin with his request for the civil affairs program to be located there.

"There's eyes in that village, monitoring every movement we make across that bridge, major," Steve emphasized at his interview with the division's civil affairs officer. "A small V.C. unit from within that village could take the bridge within ten minutes; rig it for destruction within an hour. It could be done in the middle of the night with a high probability of success, at least ninety percent. And it could all be accomplished by four sappers."

The former VMI linebacker, who was much more stiff and formal than Captain Maxwell, looked at his wall map of I Corp as if looking for something that he hadn't seen before. He took a deep breath. "That wouldn't be good at all."

"No, sir, it wouldn't."

"Sit down, son." The major offered. "We've got a lot of work to do."

Although he didn't understand why and didn't question it, under the major's tutelage, Corporal Kowalski received from the ground up lessons in the planning of psy-op/civil affairs operations, including a CIA investigation. In addition, after ascertaining that the scout was proficient in map-reading, scouting, patrolling, and calling in air and artillery strikes, the major provided lessons in small unit leadership in the form of instructions and conversations. Then he sent Kowalski for two weeks of on-the-job training with the Combined Action Platoon at Cam Lo. Steve returned from that assignment in time to attend the operation's first planning session.

The day before the operation was scheduled to commence, the major reported to his commander, Colonel Edward Jenkins.

"Everything in place, Jim?" the colonel asked, knowing it would be. Otherwise, he would already have heard about it. Plus, the major had a reputation for his meticulous attention to detail.

"All set, colonel. Security on this is as ironclad as anything you'll see in Vietnam. The Vietnamese expect to be loaded aboard helicopters for a joint operation northwest of The Rock Pile. We'll be in control of all communications. They won't be told anything until we're in the air and away."

"What about the Vietnamese police?"

"They think they'll be escorting a convoy through Quang Tri City to board troop ships as part of the drawdown."

"And the troops and commanders?"

"All confined to a secure bunker, debriefed and ready to move out."

"This type of operation has never been conducted adjacent to a large city. It could be a model for success...or failure."

There was really no answer for that statement. The major chose to remain mute.

"And we are leaving execution of this operation in the hands of a corporal?" The Colonel shook his head in disbelief. He gave away his feelings by clamping down on the tip of his tongue with his right canine, a personal habit he was well known for.

"This corporal is as good as any second lieutenant I've ever served with, colonel. And better than most. He'll do just fine."

"He'd better," the colonel replied sternly.

The major left the colonel to hold his final debriefing on the County Fair Operation code-named Thach Hanh Dawn. All the American participants were present. The major's briefing was extensive.

"County Fair Operations are designed to swiftly isolate hamlets, usually by heliborne forces. Once we've established a perimeter and cut the village off from movement in and out, the Quan Chanh will move in and conduct a census. Any male of military age, and in Vietnam that means eight to eighty, will be taken away for questioning. That's purely a Vietnamese phase of the operation, and no matter what you see, don't involve yourself in it. Don't try to stop it or protest it. Report anything you believe to be wrong to your squad leader. He will report it to me.

"There is going to be a lot of crying children and weeping women. Don't let it unnerve you. Security of the perimeter is your primary focus. The village is to be sealed off tightly. No one comes in; no one goes out until I give the word.

"The attached medical unit will enter the village and hold a clinic with emphasis on taking care of the children and any pregnant women. The cooks will establish a kitchen and provide a hot meal.

You men should be able to take advantage of that. I believe they'll be serving hamburgers and hot dogs with chili, potato salad, and baked beans."

That would be a treat even for the Marines.

"The search team will go through the village looking for weapons, people hiding out, documents, that sort of thing. After the operation ends, a squad of Marines usually remains behind, forming a Combined Action Platoon such as we have at Cam Lo. The CAP units primarily train a village self-defense force. We don't have a squad to spare. What we have is Corporal Kowalski. He will remain behind and perform the function of that squad. He will be in the village during the operation and will appear to be in charge of the cooks and the medical staff but not of the security forces."

Final orders were issued. The County Fair Operation for Thach Hanh began with the driver leaving the corporal behind at Le Kinh's house while the major made a courtesy call on the village chief. Greeted by the usual crowd of women and children, Ha Shi Cau hung his M-16 over his shoulder and, with some degree of difficulty due to pains he still experienced in his legs, walked the length of the southern half of the village. Both hands were being held by children. Happy to see Steve, Lan rode her bicycle in circles around the advancing group. Steve could feel the barber's hot eyes boring into him as he passed his stall. The man had a military bearing even down to his short-clipped hair and posture. Steve knew he was V.C. He hoped the security force could prove it and remove him and his influence from the village.

A green Marine Corps six-by transport truck with a high canvas cover pulled off the asphalt bridge road and slowly ground its way down the red dirt road toward Steve. This surprised the villagers. Steve dropped the hands of the children and rushed forward past a huge sow sleeping in a large muddy rut in the path of the vehicle. Fortunately, he didn't have to move the sow. He halted the truck with a held-up hand. Steve directed the driver toward an open space near the restaurant and in close proximity to the river and the bridge. It was the most logical place for the Marine to set up his base of operations.

The villagers watched in quiet curiosity with a great deal of whispered speculation as four Marines unloaded and quickly erected a large green all-purpose canvas tent complete with flooring made of wood pallets. The tent was twice as large as most of the thatch-roofed huts in the village. Equipment and supplies were unloaded and stacked nearby. They included a stove; cots; radio; ammunition, including small arms rounds; and grenades, Claymore mines and explosives; C-rations and other items a Marine living isolated from his post might require. Steve was not the only person who realized that this lightly defended supply source might make him a target for local V.C. or for enterprising criminals.

The Marines and their truck departed, leaving Steve as the sole American in the hamlet. Steve spent a nervous first night in the tent, which was large enough for a platoon of Marines. He slept with his rifle in the cot beside him and a pistol under his pillow. There was reason for his nervousness. He was alone in what could turn into a hostile situation at any moment. The enemy might wish to display their strength. A local agent might report his presence to a cadre member who would arrange to have him killed or captured. An individual might take action seeking vengeance for a relative who had been killed or taken into custody. He might already be a target simply because of the stack of supplies in his tent. The criminal element could be just as dangerous as the military threat. The Marine was not used to having no one to share duties with or to watch while he slept.

Steve fell asleep with the natural sounds and smells of the river and the village quieting his fears and doubts. Up at four thirty without being awakened by an alarm clock, the Marine shaved with his helmet serving as a water basin. He had been provided a lister bag of water which would be replaced weekly. A flickering candle served as his light.

Although he did not actually expect to need it, Steve shouldered his rifle. He couldn't leave it behind in the unguarded tent. It would surely disappear. He strapped his web belt on. Hung from it were the tools of his trade, four ammunition pouches, his bayonet and his sidearm, which he could not leave behind and might actually need, and a canteen of water. He filled his pockets with hard candies in butterscotch, cherry, and lemon flavors. The candy was a personal purchase, not something provided by the Marine Corps. Finally, Steve pulled the heavy radio harness on like a pack and checked in on the regimental frequency.

"Red Clematis, Red Clematis, this is White Clematis One, over."

The answer came immediately, as if Steve had been late rather than on time in reporting in.

"Red Clematis. We have you five by five. Operation on time, over."

Steve didn't respond. He didn't need to. He was ready. He leaned over and blew out the candle. The small flame had destroyed his night vision. The village was still dark and quiet with sleep. Steve would have to wait at least ten minutes until his night vision was somewhat restored. He sat in the dark and unwrapped a lemondrop as he considered how to implement the plans for organizing the village's self-defense force. A stack of flyers he could not read were in his pocket. Prepared by the psy-ops office, they explained in Vietnamese the intent of the county fair operation. The execution of matters following the operation had been left up to Steve.

As he sucked on the sugar-coated tart candy, Steve had a moment of reflection. Dallas in 1962 had a small town attitude with corresponding conservative values. It was truly not just a town and time of innocence but of naivety, of belief in government institutions, and such concepts as upward mobility, sock hops, Friday night football, ponytails, and jeans with the cuffs turned up had been the norm for Steve in Dallas. There was nothing like that in Thach Hanh.

Jerry Lee Lewis, Fats Domino and Elvis, the Twist and the Hully Gully, Dick Clark, and Bandstand. Drag racing, Chinese fire drills, and making out were all part of the past now. The veneer of Steve's innocence had been worn away like that of the hot high school cheerleader who'd had too many sizzling dates with older, more experienced boys. Steve's own experiences seemed to have run the gauntlet from polite and restrained upscale Westbury to the savage jungles of Vietnam, from giggling high school girls to aggressive Saigon whores, from the Pledge of Allegiance to Fuck the War, the Army, and any other institution that pissed him off. It was a war-hardened attitude.

Steve Kowalski was not an angry young man. He was simply becoming something of a realist who'd begun to think for himself and question what he'd been taught and once accepted as true. Throughout high school, he had been known as "Little Steve." His father was not Big Steve, but Big Don.

The name wasn't used the way "Tiny" is often attached to a big man. Steve stood six feet three and, at 240 pounds, considered himself to be a "lean, mean, Marine fighting machine."

"Little Steve" Kowalski's high school buddy and teammate was even larger in every way. At six feet, seven and 320 pounds, "Big Steve" appeared to be a small elephant to the defenders he blocked for "Little Steve," a bruising fullback who only played football in one direction, toward the goal line.

"Can't run over him and takes three days to run around him," their coach had said of Big Steve with a wide grin on his Irish face.

Steve thought for a moment of the plans he had made with his oversized teammate. They would be going to the University of Texas together to win a national championship for the Longhorns. It was a goal they had talked about and worked toward on the field, at the track, and in the gym for five years. First, however, Big Steve had to finish junior college to raise his grade point average. In reality, Steve had just been along for the ride, infected by his friend's enthusiasm, so he attended the junior college with him.

A drunk driving charge, accident, and near-fatal brain damage had ended Big Steve's dreams of a college and NFL career. Kowalski felt guilty for having survived the accident without suffering serious injuries. He did develop an aversion to alcohol. Steve had no real drive to attend college or to play professional football. He certainly couldn't go to UT without Big Steve. Perhaps there was an element of self-punishment involved with the heavy burden of guilt he felt, but Little Steve took his black eyes and sore shoulder straight to the recruiting office and joined the Marine Corps.

Steve had passed on the offered delay entry program. He wanted to leave as quickly as possible. The smiling recruiting sergeant made that easy for him. From that office, Steve called home, told his mother what he had done, and a short time later was on an airplane bound for South Carolina. During four months of rigorous training during boot camp, Steve thought frequently of returning home and "beating that lying ass recruiter to a bloody pulp." That notion was forgotten the first time someone called him a Marine instead of puke or maggot, his drill instructor's favorite term for boots who were not yet Marines, who would "never make a pimple on a real Marine's ass." Steve would never forget the feeling of pride and accomplishment, of becoming part of something bigger than himself, that he experienced at graduation after having earned the right to be called a Marine.

Bootcamp and his training experiences were something of a blur, easier to forget and put behind him than Steve had thought they would be. With advanced infantry training and his assignment to an infantry battalion, nothing of import happened to the young Marine until he was assigned to Vietnam for a thirteen-month-long tour of combat duty. It was something he had worked and trained for, an assignment he relished, thinking more of the adventure than the dangers of being in a combat zone. That he might be killed was only a remote thought in the depths of his mind. Through the attrition of combat and routine transfers, Steve quickly became a corporal and the chief intelligence scout for his battalion. He was effectively in charge of a platoon of seventy-two men. Heady stuff for a twenty-year-old kid.

Although he had always been popular, Steve had never made friends quickly or easily. He had few buddies outside of the Marine Corps. He considered himself a loner who didn't need anyone else and, naturally, a love 'em and leave 'em type of guy. Steve had never felt lonely. He always had plenty of company. Mary Ann, the delightful red-headed ditzy artist and model; Twyla, the buxom blond high kicker from San Marcos – "If tits had been brains, she'd be a fucking Einstein," he told one of his companions. Trisha Dawn is a freaky Dallas beauty with a touch of Cherokee wildness and beauty in her. Kathy Crittenden, "a girl with a pussy that knows more tricks than a circus monkey." Cayla Hogue, the untouchable dream, the most gorgeous of them all. Cayla wasn't untouchable because she was out of Steve's league. He played in the majors as far as women were concerned. But Cayla was out of his age range, way too young.

There were some parallels where Cayla and Lan were concerned. Both were considerably younger than Steve but exhibited enough interest to make him wonder about them, to think of them, and to tempt him to push the boundaries beyond mild flirtation. Both were dark-haired beauties with brown eyes. Their fathers were both doctors and influential members of their community. Both fathers were quite protective of their daughters.

Steve thought of Cayla as much as he thought of Mary Ann now that he was ten thousand miles away from both of them. He had been home on leave when he spotted a moving van at one of the newly built houses across the street. He'd watched with natural curiosity as anyone would, wondering about the new neighbors. He saw a nice car and furniture. And then he spotted the daughter. That Playboy Bunny body was a male magnet, and Steve was in a position to be the first to meet and greet the woman.

Steve quickly made a large pitcher of cold lemonade, grabbed some plastic cups, and headed across the street. The closer he got to the girl, the more clearly defined her beauty became, from the perfect nose, pouty lips, and big brown eyes with heavy long lashes to her voluptuous curves. The family was watching Steve as he approached as well.

"Thought you folks might like a cold drink, doing all this hard, hot work."

The girl thanked him, taking the pitcher and looking up at him from her height of five feet, two inches. "You seem to go up forever," the girl said, just short of a giggle.

Steve had to force himself to shut his gaping mouth before he could talk. He wondered if he was drooling. Wouldn't that make a good first impression? She'd take him to the village, idiot.

"Steve Kowalski," he managed without stuttering. "I live across the street. Well, that is, my folks live across the street. I live in South Carolina."

"You a college boy, Steve?"

"No, a Marine."

The girl seemed a little disappointed. She recovered quickly. "My name is Cayla, Cayla Hogue." Steve offered more than his hand. He lent his strong back and helped the family move in, exchanging information with them in their presence. Doctor Hogue was a surgeon who would be practicing his trade at University Hospital. Her mother, Donna was a former nurse who no longer worked. Cayla was their only child. The doctor was an LSU graduate and had the same Cajun accent and manner of speaking that sounded so much better coming from Cayla's lips.

Steve knew not to overstay his welcome. He returned home in spite of his desire to stay. He and Cayla met again a few days later, in her yard, where Steve had kicked a football, not quite by accident.

"So, where do you go to school?" Steve asked her, expecting perhaps to hear Rice, Texas, or even LSU.

"I'll be going to Madison."

That was a shock. Steve had attended Madison. "Madison Middle School?"

"Yeah. You thought I was a college girl, right?"

"Yes."

"I get that a lot. I'm only thirteen. I'm in the eighth grade. Daddy threatens to hang a sign around my neck that reads 'Jail bait' every time we go out anywhere."

"I can understand that," Steve said, thinking, Wow, how precocious. That body can't be baby fat. What is she going to look like in four or five years? She'll be so beautiful no normal man can look at her without going blind.

"He warned me about you, about older boys, that is. I can only talk to you for five minutes at a time and only in the front yard."

Steve went home, a bit stunned, thinking, thirteen years old, and a very ripe thirteen at that. A lot of older girls, and women, in this neighborhood and her school will be quite envious of her, and could even hate her and be mean to her. At other times in history, they might have run her out of town on a rail or burned her at the stake as a witch just to get rid of the very unfair competition.

Steve sought Cayla out for five-minute meetings in spite of her age during other leaves. That was the extent of their relationship. He watched fascinated as she grew. Cayla was too young for him to even write. Her father was never far away from them when they met in the yard. They only spoke briefly or waved and nodded. He didn't talk about the Marine Corps.

At that day and time, a few years of "seasoning and maturing" in the military was the norm rather than the exception for young men who were not going to college. Steve had never heard of Vietnam or even Indo-China. He couldn't imagine killing anyone, no matter what kind of training he'd had for doing just that.

Killing, however, came easy. It wasn't like times past when you faced a man's blade or pike, when you would feel the cold steel bite muscle and bones or slide completely through your body. You didn't often hear the enemy's pain-filled cries at the moment of his death. You rarely saw the anguish on his face as his hopes and dreams died. Your arm was not battle-weary afterwards, and you rarely had enemy blood on your body or clothing. You were more likely to come away from a modern battle with a ringing in your ears.

In Vietnam, you killed with bullets at three hundred yards, or with mortars, artillery, mines, and bombs at a much greater distance. Afterwards the enemy lay where they had fallen like dead dogs in rictus, with all their suffering and pain frozen on their faces. Outwardly, the survivors did not seem to be affected. Him or me was the prevailing attitude. All too often, the threat was only imagined while the killing was very real.

"I shot him because he ran. He must be V.C." was an acceptable explanation, as was "He was in a free fire zone."

During his last leave home, Steve worried about how much of that warrior ethos he'd brought back home with him. How much bullshit would he put up with before he used that killer instinct and training and hurt someone who was innocent? He was edgy. Noises in the night woke him and set him off. Worse, an unexpected touch caused Steve to whirl and strike out before he could restrain himself. His friend with the broken nose avoided him forever after that incident.

T.J., a lovely redhead, thought she could tame Steve. The girl was a long-legged, full-breasted wasp-waisted wonder. She seemed to drip sex without even being aware of it. Steve told a friend, T.J.'s got a pussy like a Maytag washer on spin dry and a mouth like a velvet-lined oven." The Marine knew that all this girl saw were his dress blues and the Corvette convertible he'd purchased with money saved from his combat pay. She didn't really know him at all, and he didn't care to know her on more than a physical level.

Cayla, however, was different. She seemed completely unimpressed with the car or the uniform. Yet, there was something. The two of them were like a teaser and a stud on a breeding farm. The nubile fifteen-year-old began her baton and kick routines every morning about the same time Steve did his exercises, both in front yards facing one another. It seemed to Steve that as the days passed, Cayla's shorts got tighter and shorter. The bottom of her pullover got higher. Steve's eyes grew larger and his mouth drier.

No matter how grown up she looked and how tempting she might be, Cayla was out of bounds and strictly off limits. There were no hellos, no conversations, just a wiggling ass and bouncing boobs that took Steve's breath away again and again. Heat and sexual tension. The morning Steve drove off to return to duty at Camp Pendleton. Cayla was standing in the middle of the street around the corner, flagging him down.

"Hurry up!" she said, opening the passenger side door and sliding into the front seat beside him. She leaned down, saying, "Hurry up; get away from here. I can't let anyone see me with you."

Steve complied. "Take me to school. Drop me off a couple of blocks away." Her high school was only a short distance away, perhaps half a mile. Cayla kept down out of sight.

"I hear you're going back to Vietnam."

"That's right."

"You volunteered." It was not a question but almost an accusation.

"Right again."

Then Cayla sat up and scooted across the seat with her mouth close to Steve's ear. "Listen to me, you big dummy. Take care of yourself. Don't get hurt again."

Then she pulled away, saying, "Pull over' in a completely different tone of voice.

Steve stopped the car. Cayla dug in her purse for a white envelope, which she handed to the Marine. "Remember, when you come back home, I'll be almost seventeen," punctuating her message with a quick but burning kiss. Then she slid across the seat and was gone, just another girl walking to school. Steve held his breath as he watched her hips sway. She turned a corner. After she was out of sight, Steve remembered to breathe while he ripped the envelope open, expecting some sort of note. Instead, it contained photos, each marked by red lips and a scrawl that read, Luv, Cayla.

Almost seventeen and she'll still be off limits, still jail bait, Steve thought as he drove away, his thoughts now on Vietnam. Steve had been the leader of a twelve-man rifle squad in combat. With attached men from the weapons section, a corpsman, a radioman, and scouts, he often had twice that number on his patrols. That had made him responsible for two dozen other Marines. He had the stripes and medals that reflected his level of performance in accepting that responsibility and carrying out the often tough duties assigned to him and his squad, nothing gaudy, mind you. His purple heart drew some respect. It revealed that he had been wounded in combat. Three rows of decorations weren't bad for a twenty-one-year-old kid with four years in the Corps.

Now though, Steve was beginning to question where the Corps was taking him. Who was risking who and to what advantage, he wondered. Should he stay in or get out? Was architecture what he really wanted to do? Should he drive a truck, run a machine in a factory, or suck on the federal tit as a postal worker? Or maybe even take advantage of the G.I. Bill and go to college? If so, what would he study? What would he become? He'd never make a doctor or a lawyer, nothing like that. He couldn't see himself as a bean-counting accountant, a teacher, or a scientist. Perhaps a manager of some kind? Would he ever be able to do anything normal again? Was Mary the right woman for him, or should he wait on Cayla?

A lot of former Marines became cops. Steve wondered if that was because they couldn't give up being in uniform or because of the weapon. Perhaps both. Steve didn't think he had the individual courage it took to be a cop. "What am I going to be besides walking hard on?" he muttered.

Steve wondered what good he was doing in Vietnam while life was passing him by ten thousand miles away. His goals and dreams had begun to fade, to seem unattainable. Shortly after his return to duty, a friend from the neighborhood had written to tell him that the day he left Cayla Hoque's front yard routines ended as well. The guys had all hated to see him go, except for Jimmy, who seemed to be getting a little too close to Mary.

An opportunity missed, Steve thought. I wonder how many more I'm missing. Vietnam is going to fall to the Communists within months after the last American leaves anyway. What the hell am I risking my life for? Glory? Honors? National pride? Duty? The fucking experience or the awesome rush of combat? What good is my killing another truckload of gooks going to do to the world? Let's see. If I kill fifty of the gook bastards and they multiply at the rate of whatever, expanded, squared, and squared again at the end of one hundred years I'll be responsible for a shitload of fewer gooks in the world. In that case, they should send my ass to Africa and declare open season on fucking jungle bunnies.

Steve Kowalski was not a radical racist. He would, however, live his whole life keenly aware of racism, saying such things among his white peers while having black friends. The political element of life is the liberal minority forced upon society by evolution and enforcing laws. It was not something that came from his heart or his conscience. Steve Kowalski was a very human, very flawed individual.

Steve wondered if anyone would have hired him to go back to Vietnam and write about the war. Not more of the rewritten lies handed out at the five o'clock follies by MACV. Not more political postulating but more Ernie Pyle type of blood and guts reporting about the soldiers' stories from the front lines. Some pieces on the doctor and nurses and even the Red Cross, and the Vietnamese themselves, maybe. A good idea came too late, probably, he decided.

So here I am, right back In the middle again, Steve thought. Gooks are going to leave my village alone. They're going to learn this ol' dog's got teeth. Night vision's back. Time to go to work.

CHAPTER EIGHT
THACH HANH, SOUTH VIETNAM

Steve walked up the middle of the hard-packed red dirt road past darkened straw and flimsy thatch hootches. The peasants had scrounged whatever they could to make the poor structures more livable. Although this was not his first tour of duty in Vietnam, the American Marine continued to be amazed at the simplicity of life in Vietnam and the general acceptance of their meager lot in life. Steve noticed that more of the walls were covered in a scale-like pattern with tin from beer and soda pop cans, adopting the idea that Le Kinh had brought to the village. A crippled old man who could do little else cut the tops and bottoms off the cans. He cut them up the side and flattened them with a hammer against a flat rock.

Steve passed the closed restaurant and came to the pavement. "Comin' in!" he called to let the MP at the bridge know he was an American. The MP waved him on. At the bridge road he turned left and crossed the three hundred-meter-long bridge. He was met at that end by another Army MP who was expecting him.

"You Kowalski?"

"That's me."

"Your convoy's just out of sight. They arrived with lights blacked out just like you ordered, sir."

The Marine didn't correct the sergeant who outranked him. Instead, he began walking down the road toward the convoy of trucks that had stopped and lined up on both shoulders of the road. He pulled himself up to the cab of the lead vehicle. He introduced himself.

"Captain, I'm Kowalski," he said, jumping down to give the captain room to exit the vehicle.

The captain joined the corporal on the road, handing him a package. "Your flyers from Psy-ops. I've got a squad spread out quietly on the west bank of the river, opposite the village to the north and another to the south."

"They're already in place?"

"For about five minutes now."

False dawn was creeping over the horizon. The village would be waking soon.

"Let's get the next four squads on the move as planned," Steve suggested. The captain turned and made a signal over his head. Four thirteen-man squads of Marine riflemen quietly but not silently departed the vehicles and marched across the bridge. They were not wearing their packs. They didn't need their entrenching tools. They weren't going to be digging in to stay. They weren't wearing their flak jackets. They weren't expecting resistance or to be hit by mortars and artillery.

As planned, the Marines crossed the bridge and entered Quang Tri City and peeled off, two squads to the north and two to the south along the first street parallel to the village. On the east bank of the river, they established the eastern corridor, which was most likely to be problematic. They would have to deal with civilians and perhaps hostiles to both their front and rear.

These troops also provided the flanking cutoff teams of the well-planned and executed operation. They were in place without anyone raising an alarm. Within fifteen minutes, as gray streaks of dawn peeked over the horizon, a convoy of six Jeeps full of South Vietnamese policemen was stopped by the MP at the eastern end of the bridge. A liaison officer who was there for that purpose explained the changes in orders to the Vietnamese. The upset commander of the unit, who had expected to pass the checkpoint unmolested en route to Quang Tri Combat Base, threatened to blow the whole operation with his high, shrill-voiced complaints and refusal to cooperate.

Part of the Vietnamese captain's ire was due to the fact that he understood immediately that the Quang Tri-based military police unit had not been trusted by the Marine planners of the operation.

At about the same time this argument was taking place, the Vietnamese military commander in Quang Tri City was also being informed of the change in plans and the scope of the operation. While his feelings were much the same as those of his subordinate, the commander handled the event with more tact and diplomacy. He radioed his MP commander at the bridge to confirm his consent to the change in orders.

Two Vietnamese policemen were assigned to each of the U.S. Army MPs at the ends of the bridge. They would seal off that possible route into or out of Thach Hanh while continuing to allow traffic to pass on over the river. A team of SEALS was already in the water looking over the piers of the bridge. By the end of the day they would have the piles wrapped in a bell-shaped pattern of concertina and razor wire to at least make it more difficult for enemy sappers to bring the bridge down by blowing up the support columns.

The villagers woke to find themselves surrounded and sealed off. Vehemently protesting fishermen were not allowed in their boats. A team of SEALS was already searching the vessels. One of the fishing boats was found to have a cache of weapons and ammunition aboard. Steve was asked to identify its owner. He was surprised as it was not a man he would have suspected of being a V.C., but there was no doubt about that now. A fire team of four Marines with rifles in hand were directed to his house. They rushed inside from front and back, their fingers on the triggers of their weapons. A shot was fired, followed immediately by a burst of gunfire. Bullets punched with little resistance through the thin walls of the hootch. It was fortunate no one outside was injured. The Marines dragged a torn, bleeding body into the street by its legs. A dazed Marine examined the fresh gash in his helmet where it had deflected a round fired at him by the pistol-wielding enemy. The operation had suddenly taken a very serious turn.

The villagers had become nervous when the laborers going to the rice fields were turned back by soldiers. With the exchange of gunfire, the women of the village began wailing. Children were crying. Several V.C. raced to their hideouts. The helicopters carrying the reserve body of the search troops arrived, landing in the road behind the truck convoy. They had been on call only if there was opposition to the operation. The combat-loaded Marines crouched low as they ran under the whirling rotors of the chopper. Doorgunners were prepared to provide covering machine gun fire if the troops were fired upon. Other helicopters unload medical supplies and personnel and cooks with their supplies and equipment. The choppers were in and out quickly.

The operation was running smoothly, with one V.C. already being ferreted out and killed. Although that would complicate the operation and rob it of the festive atmosphere hoped for, Steve thought the County Fair Operation was going well, better from a military point of view than for the civil affairs effort, which would now be more difficult.

The Marines gathered the residents, separating the men and making them march to the south end of the village. An interrogator/translator team began questioning them individually. The women feared what would happen to their sons and husbands. Men who were marched away in South Vietnam seldom returned. Children clung to their mothers. The women wailed and cried. They pleaded and begged. They knew death was only a trigger pull away from them all.

The Vietnamese MPs set up a table where they began conducting the official census of the village. Steve was a bit surprised at the population of the village with residents from both ends all collected together. The search teams continued to move carefully through each yard and structure, including the restaurant. They exempted only the Catholic Church, guarded by the withering glares of the Mother Superior. "Sister Gargoyle," one of the Marines called her.

Two Marines escorting an elderly woman carrying a naked infant on her hip passed on their way to the gathering point. She was so thin; barely able, it would seem, to support life. An old man with long grey chin whiskers was being prodded into the street at rifle point by one of the Marines. Across the left shoulder of the American was draped a cloth Steve recognized by its colors. It was the blue and red of the North Vietnamese flag. Is this the face of our enemy? he wondered. The prisoner was shoved roughly to the ground. The Marine's knee was in his back the way this was taught in combat town training. Another Marine rushed over to bind the old man's hands behind his back.

Another wrapped a t-shirt around his head, completely enclosing his face from beneath his chin to above his hairline. He was led away to be turned over to the South Vietnamese military police.

The villagers had watched the capture and treatment of the prisoner. It subdued and frightened them. Steve knew they were all wondering if the Marines will now consider them all V.C., will they all be taken away as prisoners? Would the village be destroyed? The Marines grew more cautious. The search intensified.

The Marines now worked in pairs, one covering from outside while the other entered the huts. Clad only in a loincloth, looking very primitive, a man was dragged from his hut. It was another old man. A Marine posed for a photo, his arm around the waist of a young girl, pressing her to his side. She was obviously discomforted by the action. Steve saw it happening again with a different girl. With a stern command, the captain put an end to taking photos. Good for him, Steve thought.

Steve was surprised by a number of things the searchers found in Thach Hanh. One was the number of people in the village given the number of structures. Also, the number of undocumented young men of military age the Quan Chanh were taking captive as V.C. suspects was shocking. Steve thought he had known the village well; however, it was evident that he did not. Most of those men were assuredly at least V.C. sympathizers. A Marine escorted two men of such age to the South Vietnamese officer in charge. He had secured their hands behind their backs. POW tags had been tied to button holes in their black shirts. Their eyes and mouths had been covered with wide strips of duct tape. Those men looked like soldiers. Steve wondered if they might be South Vietnamese deserters.

They were being followed by what appeared to be family members. An older man had his arm around what must be his wife and daughter. There was abject fear on their faces. They knew what the South Vietnamese did to prisoners. The small, older woman carried a child half her size on her hip. A big-headed, naked baby clung precariously to the younger woman as the family tried to follow the prisoners. They were, however, pushed away by a Marine who shoved them as a group with his rifle.

Half a dozen Marines responded to a cry. They converged on one of the more substantial of the structures at the north end of the village. Stacks of wood and coconuts appeared to have formed a type of fortification around the house similar to the way Marines sandbagged their emplacements. A smiling blond-haired Marine sergeant came out of the home carrying an AK-47, the enemy's primary infantry weapon. The triangular blood-groove bayonet was extended. Steve noticed a curved, thirty-round banana clip. The weapon was not new, but it had been well cared for, surely recently used. With what the Marines were finding, had this been a village in the jungle it would undoubtedly have been torched, burning it to the ground and destroying all assets.

A struggling, loudly protesting man who had been blindfolded and whose hands had been secured was dragged roughly from the house. There was no doubt about who he was. A stern-faced young woman with hands secured in front of her was led from the same structure. She was detainee. He was a POW.

A protesting older woman, her yellowed dry skin stretched over gaunt features, was escorted from her house. Her deep-set hollow eyes had a vacancy to them, a shocked look perhaps. The morning's events seem to have taken her within herself. Steve spotted a youngish woman squatting on her heels in the Vietnamese way. She sat in the doorway of her home, waiting, resigned to being searched or perhaps worse. There was nothing distinctive about the woman. She held a standing child of what, three maybe, between her legs. The baby wore jade bracelets on each wrist. Both of them wore medallions hung from thin gold chains around their necks. The woman also wore two broad gold rings on the first and third fingers of each hand. Steve had seen that before but did not know what it meant.

There were tears coursing down the woman's cheeks. The child took a hesitant step toward the Marine. Steve offered a bit of hard candy. The child grasped the treat in his grubby little hand. Steve noticed that he also wore jade anklets on each leg. The Marine took the child in his arms and swung him up to his hip. He held a hand out to the woman.

"Lai Dai, come," he said in Vietnamese. He was quite surprised when the woman took his hand. He pulled her up. She held tightly to his hand as he escorted her to the gathering point. It was a good thing given his future presence and mission within the village.

Another Marine was kneeling, talking to a squatting young woman. There was a lost expression on her face. Two crying children sat nearby. She held another child in her arms. Oddly, Steve noticed the child was wearing new cloth shoes. He stopped. "You must come with me, he told the woman. He gave each of the children a piece of candy. He took her smallest child on his other hip. That group joined his little convoy. Another woman, pregnant and with a wide-eyed toddler strapped to her back, got to her feet and joined Steve.

They passed an elderly woman. With one hand she clung to a small girl who was wearing real gold earrings through her pierced earlobes. In the other hand, there was an orange teapot and a fat-lighted cigar. A cigar-smoking peasant woman was not all that unusual a sight in Vietnam. A very old couple, grey hair, prominent cheekbones, brown age spots, deep wrinkles, fell in with Steve's procession. It appeared that he had built up some trust among the villagers. The old woman wore her straw hat. He carried a small umbrella to shield himself from the sun. Steve thought they looked eighty but were at least twenty years younger and near the end of the life expectancy of Vietnamese peasants.

A group of combined forces, Marines, South Vietnamese military police, and civil authorities, had surrounded a young man. Nearby was a North Vietnamese weapon. An RPD-50 machine gun is a major piece of business. His hands were tied, of course. He had been striped to a pair of shorts. He was undergoing a serious interrogation. Steve wondered what they had stumbled upon in this tiny village.

A policeman harshly asked a question. The prisoner didn't answer. The MP slapped him hard across the face, bowling the kneeling man over. Steve knew that was just the beginning of the brutal interrogation the prisoner would undergo. Not my business, he thought as he continued past.

The doctors and dentists set up their clinics in Steve's large general-purpose tent. In order to solidify his position after the operation ended, the corporal appeared to be in overall command of the operation. Steve separated pregnant women and women with children to go through the clinic first. A triage system had been set up. Each person was examined by a corpsman who filled out their needs on a card for the appropriate medical doctor. Each person went to the shot line next for basic inoculations. From there, each was sent to a specialist according to his primary needs, as indicated by the colored cards they had been given. Almost everyone had to go to the dentists, while many were sent to one of several specialists. They all attended lectures on hygiene and the use of soap or saphong, an item many had never used in their lives.

Villagers who had hidden in makeshift bomb shelters were rousted from their hiding places and escorted firmly to one end of the village or the other. Any young man who was of the country's broad military age range found to be hiding was handcuffed, blindfolded, and taken away by the White Mice, the Vietnamese Military Police, for a rather harsh interrogation and imprisonment or induction into the Army.

"Fire in the hole!" someone yelled. The Marines all dropped to the ground, expecting an explosion. The more experienced men had their hands on their balls or on the backs of their necks and between their legs. Some risked shrapnel in the head or eye by looking around. Others pointed their rifles this way or that, looking for someone to shoot. The Vietnamese didn't seem to know what to think about this odd behavior. There was no explosion. The Marines sheepishly crawled to their feet.

"Engineer up!" the man who had shouted "Fire in the hole!" called.

A man with special training in the disarming of mines, booby traps, and other surprise firing devices came forward. He did not wear the heavy protective suits a civilian or police agency would provide for their demolition expert. He was wearing a flak jacket and, most unusually, the crotch vest. Carefully, he entered the barber's hootch, probing every likely place for a trip wire, a pressure pad, or a release device. He opened the lid of a wooden ammunition crate. Inside he found an old French rifle and the trappings of a soldier a pack, a web belt, ammunition, and canteens.

At the south end of the village where the men had been gathered for interrogation, the graying barber broke from the group, shoved one of the guards aside, turned over the table, and raced toward the rice fields. A Marine member of the cutoff team calmly raised his rifle into an offhand firing position. As if his drill instructor were watching him at the rifle range, the PFC tucked his arm in tight, he aimed and fired a three-round burst from his M-16. The barrel jumped up and to the right slightly as each round was fired.

The bullets impacted almost as one, tearing through the Viet Cong cadre member's left kidney, his heart, and his right lung. Tossed to the ground by the impacting bullets, the discovered enemy soldier twisted convulsively. He quivered as vital fluids flowed from his body and became part of the rice field, part of Vietnam. Two Quan Chanh drug him back to the village by his feet. They dropped his body on the road in the middle of the village.

The keening of the frightened women rose like the howl of wolves missing a member of the pack. Marines with hammering hearts held their breath, anticipating what might happen next. Would V.C. spring from hiding places, rifles firing? Would an enemy squad charge out of the nearby brush? They listened for the hollow thunk! Thunk! Thunk of mortars being fired, combat sounds the Marines knew well.

None of that happened. Almost sheepishly, the Marines regained their feet, and their poise. With a renewed sense of mission, the searching continued. A printing press and V.C. propaganda documents were discovered at the north end of the village. The location of a rifle was provided to the interrogators. Another hard-eyed man was handcuffed and escorted away.

"Your quiet little village seems to be a hotbed of V.C. activity," the captain noted.

"I think it's probably like this all over the country," Steve observed, noting that even the bold girl who sold Coca-Colas at the bridge was a confirmed NVA soldier who had made the trek from a village in Hanoi down the Ho Chi Minh Trail to South Vietnam. Her once teasing eyes were now hard as she spat and kicked at the military policemen who had wrestled her roughly to the ground and handcuffed her. There was no doubt that she had been reporting on military traffic passing over the bridge. One of the Quan Chanh slapped her viciously across her pretty face. True to their orders, the Marines did not react. It was two more hours before the interrogators completed their tasks and departed. The Vietnamese military police loaded up their prisoners and evidence and returned to Quang Tri City. The remainder of their business was not for public eyes.

A line had formed at the tent where the medics were working, it seemed, on every ailment known to man. Steve joined the medics, doing small, simple things under their careful instructions. He washed sores with antibiotics, held trays, and emptied others. His presence was more important than anything he actually did. The crying children who received shots were given a ten-cent bag of candy straight from Steve's pockets. Steve slipped a handful of gumdrops into his left breast pocket for Lan.

Dr. Quoc had come forward with an offer to help the American doctors. The offer was genuinely and gratefully accepted. With a trained professional acting also as an interpreter, the MEDCAP, as it was called, ran smoothly. Steve noticed that Lan was not with her father or with her mother, who was also assisting the corpsmen. Is she in her hiding spot? Steve wondered. He decided her parents must know where she was, as they didn't seem concerned by her absence. They didn't appear to be searching for her. Could she be a V.C.? Many her age, like the Coca-Cola seller, were.

Every adult who was seen by the doctors or dentists received a package of Kool cigarettes, which proved to be an inducement for the entire population of the village to visit the medical team. Similarly, none of them missed the meal that was prepared. The villagers had all eaten C-rations, which were sold and traded on the black market. They were expecting that type of meal. Instead, they had a real cooked meal: hot dogs with mustard, relish, onions, cheese, and chili. There was an equal amount of cheeseburgers with lettuce, pickles, onions, and tomatoes. Side dishes were baked beans and a loaded potato salad, none of which the Vietnamese had ever eaten. Everyone ate until they were full. Nothing was wasted. Even the sow feasted for two days on the scraps.

The doctors began packing up. Steve pulled the senior naval officer aside. "Commander, you see how little these people have. We're trying to build a relationship here to win the trust and confidence of these people."

"The hearts and minds program."

"Yes, sir. You've met Doctor Quoc."

"Yes. He seems knowledgeable and skilled."

"We have a doctor but little in the way of medications or even bandages. I'm asking you to leave him what you can."

"Can you assure me the items we leave behind won't find their way to the black market, or be abused?"

"Yes, sir. I'll keep it all locked up in my tent. The doctor can pull what he needs as required."

"And no one is to be charged for any of the medications?"

"That will not happen. Commander, in this village, Doctor Quoc does not charge for his services."

The medical unit was more than generous. They left all their instruments with Steve, as well as pills, vials of medications, bandages and tape, and even syringes. Dr. Quoc was teary-eyed as he accepted the gifts. The cooks had heard Steve's request and saw the reaction. Without being asked, they responded in a like manner. They left behind cooking oils, buns, vegetables, and meat in a large ice chest. A section of the tent was stacked four feet high with canned goods, cases of soda, and bags of staples such as wheat flour, cornmeal, and sugar. There was even a box of chocolate bars.

The search was over. The Marines were more relaxed than Steve thought they would have been given all they'd found. A squad rested, unconcerned, their primary mission over. Two men were napping. Only one of them still wore his helmet. Rifles lay on the ground beside them. Some were even holding children who were seeking candy or other items from them.

A sergeant called out. "Mount up!" The men stood, retrieved their helmets and weapons, and in a loose column of twos, began marching up the dirt road toward the bridge. At the head of the column was a bound Vietnamese man. The Marine behind him had the barrel of his M-16 pressed to the prisoner's neck. Third in line was another Vietnamese man. He had a large pack on his back. Steve wondered what was in it. Intelligence documents most likely, he assumed.

Behind him, also bound, was one of the village beauties, a schoolgirl. She wore nothing but a pink bra that clung to her firm, salient breasts and a pair of pants. The only other thing she wore was a defiant expression. Behind her was another bound man, followed by the columns of Marines. The South Vietnamese quickly departed as well, taking their cue from the Marines. It would appear they were anxious to begin their interrogations. The only thing Steve found surprising about the departures were the prisoners the Marines had taken instead of the Vietnamese.

He watched as all the security forces boarded their vehicles and drove off. Now his job would begin in earnest. Scared, the villagers remained huddled in their family groups at the gathering point. "Go," Steve told them. "See to your homes."

The shocked and still frightened villagers dispersed. They were righting their homes, throwing out clay pots that had been shattered, clothing and bedding that had been ripped and food that had been contaminated or dumped onto the ground. That was swept into the street for the roaming pigs. The village would recover quickly. Steve was determined to help them in that process. But for now he knew he needed to give them some time and space.

A South Vietnamese government propaganda team that included several women in military uniforms arrived on the heels of the departing Marines. Steve watched as they set up a stage. He found their commander and turned over the psy-op fliers he had been provided, knowing the Vietnamese would pass them out and explain the role he would have in the future of Thach Hanh. Well fed and reassured that the Military Police and the Viet Cong would not return, the villagers did not protest as they were gathered again in front of the stage.

As the men and women passed him, Steve met their pleading eyes boldly. With the departure of the security forces, the level of tension within the village decreased. Reassured that the V.C. would not return, the propaganda team launched into a series of lectures on a woman's duty to the government.

A movie with that theme was shown as daylight faded.

As Steve watched the movie, making up his own ridiculous dialogue, a small, cool hand slipped into his own. Lan! He didn't need to look. Although it was the first time anything like that had happened, it couldn't be anyone else but her. Everyone was watching the movie. Steve had moved to the rear of the group. There were no eyes on him. He gave Lan's hand a reassuring squeeze. She leaned in and clung to him as if scared. How much had she seen? Or missed? In America, they would have stolen away to find a private place to talk. But not here, not in this culture.

The movie ended. A woman spoke harshly into the speakers like a Baptist tent revivalist chasing the devil. Steve did not think the haranguing nature of the propaganda team would prove to be particularly effective. After a while, the propaganda team passed out the fliers and explained Steve's continued presence.

"Ha Shi Cau will live among you. He will organize and train a military self-defense force. While your brave fathers and brothers resist the invasion in our regular armed forces, you at home must provide for the security of your own village. You must not only be prepared to fight when the NVA tax collectors come to take your rice and to recruit your sons and daughters, but to prevent infiltration by V.C. agents such as those who were arrested today.

"Those of you accepted for the defense team will be paid by and report to Ha Shi Cau. You will obey his orders. Certain duties and times to perform them will be issued," the woman who seemed to be in command charged. She stepped down and opened the large crate that had served as her stage. She took out a base plate, bipod, and tube for a 60mm mortar. She assembled it quickly and with a confident, even expert, manner. Steve was impressed.

The woman pointed the mortar toward the north. The other female members of the propaganda unit performed a similarly impressive operation with an M-60 machine gun . Although he couldn't understand a lot of what the women were saying, Steve knew the message being relayed.

"The V.C. has been taught a lesson here today. They will not return to Thach Hanh to take your sons and daughters. The V.C. tax collectors will not come in the night to take your rice. Why? Because you will not let them! They know what we have done here. The government will provide you with the means and the training, but you must cooperate with the government's program and defend yourselves while our valiant soldiers defend the country."

The speaker continued at length with patriotic speeches, even music, and an appeal to volunteer for service in the Army or the self-defense team. "Ha Shi Cau will live among you. He will become your neighbor. He already knows many of you. He will choose the fifty-four who will become the paid self-defense force, men too old for the regular Army or disabled, and women, a platoon of citizen soldiers who will be paid according to their accomplishments and rank. Le Kinh, whom you all know, has been appointed your platoon sergeant.

"The government will supply each of you with rifles and two mortars and two machine guns for the company."

The woman waved a form in the air. "Come! Anyone who wishes to be a part of the defense force for your village, step forward! Women, you can be brave too! Remember the Truong Sisters!"

Lan turned loose of Steve's hand, taking a step to the side, separating herself from him. "Me. Lan Thi Quoc. I will join to fight!" Lan called, stepping forward. There were many more volunteers than Steve was authorized to accept. The Marine, intelligent and resourceful, had the germ of an idea on how to use all of them.

Steve watched Lan sign the roster. Other girls began to come forward. All of the girls remaining in the village, several young boys, a couple of disabled and elderly men, and women, mothers of every age, came forward. Steve would have to make his choices tactfully and with diplomacy while selecting the most capable of the lot. The villagers were still somewhat in shock over the military operation that had just been conducted. Some were still angry. Others were resentful. A small percentage was pleased. Steve would have to win them all over. He knew that was not going to be easy. The Marine wanted to get his program started right away to offset some of those feelings.

It had been a long day, but while the villagers retired to their homes to discuss the events, the corporal asked Dr. Quoc to set up a meeting with the village leaders. It seemed that there were three of them: the doctor, one of the rice farmers, and one of the fishermen. That seemed to be a fairly representative group. They met at the doctor's home.

In Vietnam, most serious meetings, and this one certainly qualified as serious, were conducted over dinner and drinks. In spite of the meal they had all eaten earlier, Lan served her father and his guests tasty shrimp spring rolls with a variety of sauces. This appetizer was followed by fresh fish soup, tangy curried chicken, and a huge bowl of fried rice featuring chopped shrimp, chicken breasts, and fatty pork bits.

The main course was lobster with shrimp paste and black bean sauce served over white rice. A beer the Marines called 'Tiger Piss" was served throughout the meal. During dinner, Steve answered questions about his home, his family, and his lifestyle by the curious Vietnamese. It was only after the table was cleared and everyone had belched and picked their teeth that business was brought into the discussion. In the Vietnamese tradition, the women ate in the kitchen after the men had completed their meal. Steve stood to address the leaders. He knew Lan would be listening.

"The United States wishes to help the Vietnamese people not only in military matters but in areas of public service as well. I wish to know the greatest public need of your village so I can obtain funds and personnel to meet those needs."

The doctor translated. The men immediately began arguing heatedly among themselves, each pressing for his own project. Steve did not take part. He sat back and listened, making out as much of the conversations as he could understand. He finally spoke up when he felt it necessary.

"A privy, I doubt that project would get approved. A hospital? Not for only a few thousand people, and not with Quang Tri City's hospital so close by. A church? I see little chance of that. Electric plant? Too much cost for such a small village."

In the midst of the shrill verbal chaos, while serving hot green tea, Lan brought the meeting to a close by asking, "What about a school?"

"I think I can get a school project approved," Steve said. Heads were nodding in approval.

"I'll present this request tomorrow," the Marine announced happily. He shook hands with the smiling Vietnamese who had all quickly agreed that a school would be a good thing and be looked upon as an accomplishment of their leadership.

In spite of the successful meeting and the County Fair Operation, as he walked through the village toward his tent Steve wondered how many of the villagers might still be Viet Cong or V.C. sympathizers, or even North Vietnamese soldiers or agents. Did one have him in the sites of his rifle right now? It was possible, but he would show no fear.

When informed the following morning of the quick progress, Captain Maxwell's reaction was gratifying to the corporal, who felt a bit out of his element.

"A school? Excellent," beamed the S-2 officer. He immediately forwarded the proposal up the chain of command to Major Hamlin with his endorsement. The request was quickly approved. Steve was ordered to oversee construction as a part of his civil affairs program.

CHAPTER NINE
THACH HANH, SOUTH VIETNAM

The civil defense force Steve was now in charge of was a co-ed mixture of part-time civilians of limited abilities. The organized Marine had begun his own form of population control under the tutelage of Major Hamlin. In a three-ring notebook, Steve created a file on every person in the village, men, women, and children, including the nuns and any visitors he happened to see.

Civil affairs was a new added mission of military units. It involved psy-ops, medical aid, military training, intelligence, and numerous civilian aid programs and possibly the CIA, as well as South Vietnamese military, civil and political elements. It took a great deal of organization and tact to deal with the various factions, including their jealousies and posturing.

Steve saw his first task as establishing a table of organization for the self-defense force. He interviewed the volunteers individually, asking not only questions about themselves but the other applicants and villagers. After each interview, he updated his census files while the information was still fresh in his mind. Although there were still questions and blanks to be filled in as well as conflicting information, the Marine soon had an astonishing insight into the makeup of the village. His interviews completed, Steve made an announcement to the village.

"I will begin training the defense force tomorrow. I have made an organizational chart. Truong Ngock will be your commander."

Truong was the most respected man in the village. He was not a military man. He was not political. The village had no mayor or formally elected chief. Still, this was a necessary political decision rather than a purely military choice.

"I am not your commander. I am simply an advisor," was the official status of the Marine, although there was no doubt that in any military situation Steve would be the actual commander.

"Bui Vao Tham" will be our first sergeant. He will assist me in training you."

Bui was a former Vietnamese Marine who had lost his left leg just above the knee in combat.

His politics were sound. His training, experience, and maturity would be invaluable to Steve and to the defense force.

"Le Kinh will serve as my aide and liaison officer between the United States military and the South Vietnamese government, which includes the Army and the Military Police.

"The structure of our defense force will be based upon that of a U.S. Marine Corps platoon. A platoon is commanded by a lieutenant with the assistance of his experienced platoon sergeant. Under them are three rifle squads. Each squad is made up of three four-man fire teams. In each team is a corporal fire team leader, a lance corporal automatic rifleman, a PFC, and a private, both basic riflemen.

"A squad is usually accompanied by other people scouts, radiomen, corpsmen, and grenadiers. Also weapons personnel from the company's weapons platoon. Our last squad will be the weapons squad, consisting of two machine gun teams and two mortar teams.

"Selections for the team will be made primarily upon ability, but attitude and character will also be considered. These factors will also determine your rank and position within a squad, and therefore, your pay."

There were murmurs and speculation about that. Steve left the villagers to their speculations. He began training the following morning. He had located a high bank on the river near the village that would serve as an impact zone for marksmanship training. At present, they only had thirteen World War II-era M-1 rifles for training. Therefore, he trained thirteen applicants at a time twice daily for a full week.

Being a Marine, he naturally began with the weapon itself. He taught the applicants how to care for the rifle, to disassemble, clean, and reassemble it. Then he taught them how to use the site and windage knobs. He taught them to aim the weapon properly. There was no time for snapping in or dry firing. Steve taught at only three hundred yards and firing from prone positions. Then he dug holes and taught his charges to shoot from a fighting hole, something the Marine Corps had not taught him but that he had learned well. Finally, he requested the services of a trained marksmanship tutor for one week. During that time the applicants rotated the hourly training periods so that by the end of the week Steve had 67 trainees who could hit a stationary eighteen-inch circle at 300 yards, standard combat range.

Although he would only be given enough weapons to arm the authorized 54-man defense team, there was a positive aspect to training more than enough volunteers. Weapons were readily available in Vietnam. Those who did not make the cut would still have some training. If the village came under attack, they could reinforce the defense team, even pick up and use the weapon of a casualty.

Over a period of a month of training in two-hour rotations every day, correcting mistakes and watching improvements or the lack of the same and the interactions of the trainees, Steve had developed a system that allowed him to fairly evaluate and grade all the participants. From the fighting holes he had dug for marksmanship training, Steve taught the villagers to throw grenades. A side benefit of throwing the grenades into the river was that the explosions stunned fish that floated to the surface where they were collected for cooking. Although he only had one M-79, Steve taught everyone to use the grenade launcher.

Patrolling was a part of self-defense. The Marines taught squad tactics and maneuvers. He led the volunteers on low-risk training patrols. On every patrol, Steve had the squad members carry long poles with painted triangles attached to the top. At approximately 1,000 meters, they pounded a stake with a blue triangle into the ground. At 2,000 meters, they placed stakes with yellow triangles; at 3,000 meters, white triangles; and at 3,500 meters, red triangles.

Steve used those markers for ranging purposes as he trained the villagers to use the 60mm mortars, firing non-explosive blue-coned rounds. The villagers had to quickly learn to recognize the difference between HEAT (high explosive anti-tank) rounds, white phosphorous, and illumination. They had to know how to register the weapons and how to aim them. They had to learn how to set the nose fuse and clear malfunctions.

Steve used the ranging stakes in teaching them all to fire the M-60 machine gun. It was not just pulling the trigger and firing the weapon but, like the rifles, caring for them, learning how the various parts functioned, how to take it apart, clean it, and put it back together again. That led to learning how to clear and prevent a misfire. It was a repeat of the process they had gone through with the mortars.

The marksmanship training had gone so well Steve asked for the services of a senior NCO, a gunnery sergeant named Reynolds who had twelve years' experience serving in a light weapons platoon. Since he was in country on his second tour of duty and had not been assigned to a combat unit, he could teach both machine guns and mortars. Gunny Reynolds arrived in a Jeep with a nervous driver who did not linger long. The gunny stood in front of Steve's tent, observing the village, its layout, vantage points, and the activity of the people. He was soon surrounded by shouting children.

"Hey, G.I.! You souvenir me one cigarette." The gunny ignored the request. "G.I., you numbah fuckin' ten!" "Hey, Marine! You give me chop-chop."

"You want bang-bang?"

"Welcome to Camp Kowalski, Gunny."

Gunny Reynolds turned at the sound of that voice to the face of the young Marine who was standing at the tent's entrance. He was holding the hand of a very young girl, maybe four years old. Exceptionally beautiful, the child clung to the Marine and peeked at the older man shyly.

"Who's your friend, Kowalski?"

"This is Hanh. Her mother cooks and washes for me. Drop your sea bag on any cot and I'll show you around."

The gunnery sergeant picked his spot and looked around the tent, giving it a visual inspection with the seeking eyes of a senior non-commissioned officer. What he saw was an orderly, clean tent firmly in place with its stakes and poles properly set. There was an abundant supply of rations, ammunition, and weapons. The Marine was freshly shaved and properly uniformed, although his hair was a bit long by Marine Corps standards.

Steve knew what the Gunny was doing, trying to find something wrong so he could assert his rank authority over the younger Marine. Without commenting, the Gunny joined Steve in the street. They began their tour of the village. During the walk, the Marines were followed by crowds of children. Kowalski would pick up one or two of them, carry them a block or so, and hand them off to a woman or girl who smiled at him or spoke to him in their language.

"You speak Vietnamese?"

"Poorly, but enough to get by. I learn more every day."

The sergeant toured the firing range and, from the bridge, noticed the distance markers both to the east and west. Although he was impressed, the sergeant had to comment. "You could use some trenches and fighting holes, some sandbagged positions."

"That's on the list, but these people have to make a living in their fields or on the river most of the day. They have to learn to defend themselves next, while their enthusiasm for it is high. Then we'll dig some fighting holes and trenches; fill some sandbags." Kowalski understood military protocol quite well. He tossed the senior sergeant a bone.

"Maybe after you've looked the place over, you can help me select the locations of those for when we get to that point."

The sergeant agreed. Steve led the senior non-com to the pink restaurant.

"This is the most stable structure in the village. In case of a battle to defend the bridge, this will most likely become my headquarters."

A chorus of greetings in French, Vietnamese, and English met the men at the door. Kowalski had given the girls American style names to help him remember them. It also pleased the girls. They were good Vietnamese school girls, a world apart from the painted twelve-year-old whores who plied their trade on the streets of Saigon and other locations where U.S. servicemen were allowed to spend time off.

Two diminutive girls took the men by the arms and led them to a table with a cloth displaying red flowers on a white background. Connie, who was on the sergeant's arm, was a slender girl with brunette hair and dark eyes. She wore a fashionable watch on her left arm. Her orange summer dress was printed with yellow flowers and green leaves. Neither she nor Lan, who had taken Steve's arm, were typical Vietnamese peasant girls. They were more like orchids among weeds.

The war and America had brought the world to the village. Lan wore a strapless black top that clung to her bosom, hugged her small waist, and flared at the hips. A tight black skirt ended just below her knees. She wore a jade Buddha set in gold around her neck and a gold watch on her left arm. Her long hair, lighter than Connie's, was parted down the middle. It reached just past her shoulder blades. She did not wear bangs. The color of her eyebrows matched the color of her hair, perhaps inherited from her French grandfather. Her features appeared more European than Asian. Her nose was not as flat as most Orientals. Her brown eyes were shining with pleasure at seeing the Marine. Her dark lashes might have been too long to be real. Her lightly colored lips were neither overly full nor too narrow. She seemed to be a young woman without a flaw. She would look quite natural in a lineup of UCLA cheerleaders.

"I get you, pho," she said to Steve. Pho was the Vietnamese national dish made with many variations, a hot soup full of spices and flavorings poured over bean sprouts and thinly sliced meat that was raw when the boiling soup was poured over it, cooking the meat in the bowl. It was served with a sprig of tasty leaves, slices of lime, and peppers on the side so the customer could make the basic soup further to his own tastes.

The girls served without the mincing steps, the formalities or traditions of Geishas, which both Marines had experienced numerous times in Japan. Their movements, still delicate, were more natural and flowing. The sergeant followed Kowalski's lead as he used the leaves and peppers sparingly but squeezed the lime dry, stirring the steaming mixture with the plastic chopsticks provided. The girls served themselves as well. Gunny Reynolds copied the younger man as he began eating the soup with the chopsticks. Crisp bean sprouts first, leaving the meat to finish cooking. The medium-cooked meat was quite tasty; however, it paled in comparison to the flavorful broth.

The girls ate in the common Vietnamese fashion. They slurped the broth and tore at the meat with their fingers. They chewed with their mouths open. They belched and later, with one hand in front of their mouths, picked their teeth at the table, all polite manners in Vietnam.

The second course was a platter with a huge mound of spicy fried rice. It was set before them with a whole crab facing each diner. A delicious black bean sauce had been poured over the crabs. The sergeant ate with obvious enjoyment. He drank two bottles of Ba Mui Ba, Beer 33, a Vietnamese brand. Steve and the girls drank Vietnamese lemonade, which began with a glass one-third full of sugar.

"This is excellent," the sergeant said. "Do they treat you like this all the time?"

"Pretty much," Steve admitted.

"Good duty in a war zone...or not. You seem to have connected with these people. You have a good rapport with them. As close as they are to the city you are still in a great deal of danger out here. The V.C. have eyes everywhere. They know what you are doing. They won't let it go for long before they have to take action. They might even try to take you alive."

The Marines talked late into the night, even after escorting the girls home and returning to their tent. Steve knew there were enemy soldiers on the other end of the village as they talked. Early in the morning, the village stirred. Women lit their cooking fires with pieces of wood gathered from the nearby forests and jungles.

The Marines woke with the village. They shook out their boots before pulling them on. "Shake out your clothing, Gunny," Steve advised. " Every excursion, for whatever reason, into grasses, the water, the forest, or the jungle risks an encounter with any of fifty varieties of poisonous snakes, such as the banded krait, which are indigenous to Vietnam. The deadly cobras would rather attack and strike than flee like most snakes. Well-camouflaged green vipers can strike from tree branches above. Many of the spiders and scorpions that will crawl into your boots or clothing are poisonous.

"Upon awakening, the locals search their homes thoroughly for those dangers. Some even keep a pig in the house overnight, as they will seek out and eat all of these pests and are immune to most of the poisonous bites. And the Vietnamese have another weapon. You are going to experience it shortly."

As the cocks began crowing, a team of five monks in their gray robes walked the main street of the village from north to south. The monks all had a similar look: shaven bald heads and wire-rimmed glasses. The lead monk prayed. Another beat a drum loudly. Another rang bells. Two held burning incense, which they wafted toward the homes of the villagers as they passed.

"This rite is one of protection," Steve explained. "They are seeking the Buddha's blessing on the village and its people. At the very least, they scare off numerous snakes."

The Marines watched and waited respectfully until the monks had gathered rice bowl offerings and departed the village. A squad of volunteers gathered outside the tent. The gunny looked puzzled.

"I've established a boot camp of sorts. This force is not trained to march or run obstacle courses. Neither are they expected to learn such things as rifle drills. Their training is focused upon the mastery of infantry weapons."

Steve gathered the available volunteers. The gunnery sergeant stood tall among Americans. Among the Vietnamese, he was a giant and therefore an object of great curiosity. Steve stood there among the loose formation of rag-tag self-defense soldiers, mostly young women, preparing to inspect their weapons as if they were U.S. Marines. He did not look the part of a parade ground spit and polish Marine. His combat boots were worn. His camouflage uniform hung limply from his shoulders and hips. He had lost weight due to the rigors of combat and the C-ration diet.

The Vietnamese barely came to his shoulders. None of them wore boots or even shoes. They all wore shorts and shirts buttoned no more than once. Most of them wore some sort of cloth cap. There was no sameness to anything. Even their weapons were a mixture of cast-offs and captured rifles from various sources. In addition to the M-1s, they carried French, U.S., Japanese, Czech, and Chinese weapons, as well as Chinese copies of the Russian AK-47.

Supplying ammunition for the various caliber weapons had been an early problem for Steve. It wasn't just rifles but machine guns and mortars as well. Steve had solved the problem with a visit to the division's G-2 officer. The colonel gave him first choice on any captured ammunition, explosives, and weapons. Steve sought North Vietnamese AK-47s and SKS rifles and ammunition. He also took all of the RPG-7s he could get his hands on. For his unit, they would be the most effective weapons on the battlefield.

Lan came running up, reporting late, an AK-47 slung over her left shoulder. She held a loaded RPG over her right shoulder. She wore a North Vietnamese tan pith helmet. The ceramic emblem had been removed. Her long, black hair was tucked up under the helmet. This is so wrong, Steve thought.

This young beauty should not have to be fighting for her country, for her village, her family, and her home. Yet here she is with her smooth face, her pouty lips, and those beautiful brown eyes full of trust in a face set not for a party or a ball but in determination, in rock solid resolve. Steve couldn't begin to imagine how Mary would react in a similar situation. She'd probably be afraid of breaking a nail.

The Gunny began his first class in the use of the machine gun . Most of the little girls could not handle the heavy automatic weapon. Although they would not become the machine gunner or the assistant machine gunner, the team's ammunition carriers would have to know how to fire the weapon, how to load the belted ammunition, change the hot barrels during a firefight, and clear jams. Several of the girls surprised the gunny by grading high enough at the end of a week to be considered for the positions of gunners and assistants.

Indoctrination on the 60mm mortar began on the eighth day of training. In this case, due to the heavy loads, the ammunition carriers were all young men. Using the range indicators, all of the prospects fired the mortars. The practice rounds weighted the same and had similar flight characteristics to the live rounds. Surprisingly, the person who came closest to the target with the greatest consistency was Lan. Steve had planned for her to be their corpsman; however, due to her proficiency with the weapon and her standing in the village, the young beauty was promoted to corporal and placed in charge of a four-man mortar team. By the fifteenth day, the mortar and machine gun teams had been selected and began training as units.

Gunny Reynolds had been given a month to teach the civilians of Thach Hanh all he could about the crew-served infantry weapons. "With the head start you've provided, I feel confident that at the end of a month, several of these villagers will become as good as serving Marines on these light weapons. Good job, Kowalski," the Gunny said upon his departure. A week later, he returned with weapons.

M-14 rifles were delivered, 54 of them. The mortar and machine gun crews were given their rifles first. The remaining roster was announced. As each person's name, rank, and position were announced he or she stepped forward to take possession of their rifle. The Marine Corps had not asked for the return of the World War II-era M-1s. Steve was not going to voluntarily give them up. With the weapons they had used for training, Steve established a reserve squad. There was no budget to pay them from. They were an unauthorized off-the-books force. Several members of the self-defense force owned their own weapons, as did others who had not been chosen as part of the defense team, enough for two fire teams to join the reserve force, bringing their numbers up to 21, almost half the strength of the authorized force.

Gunny Reynolds taught the selected teams and interested parties to build concealed bunkers that were dug into the ground, overlooking a likely avenue of enemy approach. The cover was a layer of limbs and branches laid across the hole. Another layer of limbs was laid ninety degrees to the first. The sides were anchored by the earth that had been removed. The whole thing was covered with a foot or more of earth topped with leaves and debris, even planted foliage.

Numerous bunkers were built to practice constructing them. The platoon then practiced assaulting them and destroying them, principally with shoulder-fired LAAWs, the best use of the generally ineffective anti-tank weapon. From people who had not been selected for the defense force and still wanted to participate, Steve sought applicants to carry the M-79 grenade launcher. A stooped, prematurely gray middle-aged woman who worked all day in the rice fields won that shootout.

The engineers who had inspected the bridge were called upon to give classes in the use of explosives, mines, and booby traps. Steve and the Gunny learned right along with the Vietnamese.

The best English speakers were taught individually to use the PRC-10 radio. They also had to learn map reading so they could call in artillery and air strikes.

From time to time, a riverine patrol boat passed the village. An idea began to form in Steve's mind. The Marine began to take his teams out on patrols more to enable him to familiarize himself with the terrain than anything else. But the patrols were also a training tool that built skills of all types while boosting morale and military discipline. Soon the teams were running night patrols and establishing listening posts.

After hearing of Gunnery Sergeant Reynold's experiences in Thach Hanh, the battalion's Marines were soon competing for an opportunity to help train the self-defense force. They had little opportunity otherwise to mingle with the local populace, the city being off limits to most Marines. Kowalski took advantage of the offers to provide top-notch training of all kinds for his self defense force. The young Marines naturally attempted to get personal with some of the attractive village girls. Lan was often heard saying or shrieking sometimes, "I no say for you!" I no say for you became a catchphrase among Marines of the First Battalion.

Although new mortars and rifles earmarked for the program had been provided by the supply sergeant with the approval of his commanding officer, he substituted them with weapons that had seen heavy duty by the Marines. Every armorer has a collection of "combat lost" weapons he often used for parts. Some of these rifles were supplied to the Vietnamese.

In small groups, all the cadre had eventually trained to at least a minimum level of acceptable proficiency on the 60mm mortars. Surprisingly, Lan had continued not only to have the best eye for mortars, understanding the function of the range and elevation knobs and of factors such as wind, but for the range cards and aiming stakes.

Calling upon various squads of the Indigenous company for duty outside the village at night, the Marine walked the lines and retired to spend the night with a different family each evening. Part of that was due to the wonderful hospitality of the Vietnamese. It was also a security issue. No one ever knew where Steve was going to be. After leaving a home to tour the lines in the middle of the night, Steve did not return to that home. The V.C. would never know where he was going to spend the remainder of the night. He showed up unannounced and sometimes slept on the floor.

Early one morning before dawn, he was rudely shaken awake by Lan. She was wide-eyed and breathless.

"Lan. What is it?"

"V.C.I. You come quick!"

Steve slept fully clothed. Due to his combat experiences, he slept lightly wherever and whenever he could in places and situations that would appear impossible. He was awake and alert instantly. His mind was racing. Where are the V.C.? How many of them are there? How are they armed? Where had they come from? Where are they going? There were other questions he would need to answer later.

Steve knew he had only twenty members of his self-defense force on duty.

Confident they knew after many hours of instructions and practice how to operate the weapons and at least come close to a target under perfect classroom conditions, Steve worried how the old men, the young boys, and the girls and women would react once bullets started flying their way.

He grabbed his rifle and followed Lan to the south end of the village. They approached quietly and slid into a machine gun position manned by two teenage boys and a girl. She would have been a high school sophomore back in the States. The girl, Huan, who was the gunner, had the long-range ring site raised. She was hunched over, sighting down the long barrel of the gun. As instructed, her finger was off the trigger and would remain so until the moment she was prepared to open fire.

Steve placed a finger across his lips to indicate silence. He raised his hand and gave Huan the signal for Look! He cupped his hand to his ear, the signal for Listen! Steve knew after months of training and practice the self-defense cadre was anxious to prove their mettle and defend their village. Steve was most pleased with their courage and eagerness to stand and fight but more so with the discipline they were exhibiting.

Steve used a Starlite Scope to watch the eerily green figures Huan had pointed out as they moved from hut to hut a short distance from the river. V.C. tax collectors gathering rice, he correctly surmised. Steve watched, gathering information. He gave the enemy a "pass" as they came under the guns of his waiting defense force.

Discipline held. No one fired off a nervous round. They watched as the last of the enemy disappeared into the nearby woods. The Marine and the villagers waited. When it appeared safe to do so, Steve stood. Lan, who had attached herself to the Marine from his first visit to the village and always seemed to be in his presence, stood and angrily faced the Marine. She slapped him hard across the face, spitting out hateful words. "You big coward!" The accusation stung more than the slap. Steve watched the girl stomp off without responding to her accusation.

Steve retired to his tent. At first light, he sought out Le Kinh. Pink climbed into his lap. "Cau?" she asked, digging in Steve's pockets for a piece of hard candy she knew would be there. Her mother would allow her only one piece. From another pocket, Steve slipped the girl a second piece of candy as he put her down. Le Kinh invited Steve to share breakfast with his family, boiled white rice sweetened with condensed milk and sugar. Over the meal, Steve shared with the staff sergeant his reasons for not firing upon the enemy tax collectors.

"They know about us, Le Kinh. They know our weapons and positions, our displacement and strength. We saw the tax collector because they wanted us to see them. I did not see the soldiers that always accompany them. I'm reasonably certain they were prepared to fight us with the odds being in their favor. Many villagers, perhaps women and children, would have been killed. We are a self-defense force. For now we fight only in self-defense of this village."

Steve knew Le Kinh would inform the village leaders of his evaluations. The entire village and the local V.C. cadre would hear of it by noon. The Marine was counting on it. He left the Kit Carson's home and made his way from house to house, alerting the twenty self-defense force members who would be on duty the following evening and instructing the remainder that they would be required as well.

Steve checked on the construction of the school being built for the village. MCB-3, a Seabee unit, was responsible for the project. Their heavy construction equipment could become a target. Steve explained the situation to the master chief in charge, who reluctantly agreed to stage his equipment and men within the walls of the nearby Quang Tri Citadel when not engaged in construction. The travel time from there to the city before and at the end of the day would delay the timetable of the construction; however, Steve was more concerned with security than with keeping a construction schedule.

Steve called for his driver who was enjoying sweet South Vietnamese coffee and sweeter Vietnamese girls at the roadside restaurant.

"How many times have you fallen in love here, Gary?" he asked.

"Twice...this morning...so far," the driver answered, grinning. Being assigned to the S-2 and S-6 sections was a true blessing for the Oklahoman. "You lost your shadow," he noted.

Steve didn't comment. He was thinking, putting together a plan for action. He didn't say a word all the way to the Quang Tri Combat Base where he reported immediately to Captain Maxwell, explaining to the S-2 officer what had taken place the preceding evening.

"I assume you have a plan of action."

"Yes, sir."

"It will need my approval, and that of the regimental S-6."

"And the colonel's, I expect."

With his hands laced behind his head, the captain leaned back, put his size twelve boots up on the desk, and said, "Lay it on me, chief."

"The tax unit was made up of nine local V.C. out of Quang Tri City and two uniformed NVA officers. They were lightly armed."

"Operating in uniform right under our noses," snorted the captain.

"With the assistance or at least the blind eyes of the local military and police. I'm sure there was an infantry force nearby. I think they were planning on surprising us."

"But you didn't see them?"

"No, sir, but I know how these people operate."

"And you didn't send patrols out to look for evidence?"

"I didn't think it prudent, sir. A part of my plan is to let them think we're taking no action."

"And the rest of this plan is?"

"I can't involve the Vietnamese or go through any Vietnamese channels."

"Touchy, but completely understandable."

"I can't lay on artillery or air strikes that close to the city."

"You'd never get approval for that. So, it'll be small arms, close quarter fight. Can your people handle that?"

"No, sir. Not these boys and girls and cripples."

"What do you need?"

"My driver and all the scouts in house."

"Three new guys, no combat experience."

"They're Marines, Captain. They'll do."

"And the plan?"

"Have the scouts join a convoy headed for Quang Tri City. At the bridge, they get out and visit the whorehouse at the north end of the village, and stay there."

"Typical Marines."

"The recon team will make contact with them after dark. In two rubber boats, a team of seven Marines and five hand-picked members of my self-defense force will travel to the north of the last hut the tax collectors visited last night."

"What about the infantry force you expect to be guarding them?"

"I have to be with my people on the ambush we'll be setting up. Me, two scouts, and five villagers. I want the other scouts and the recon team in position to observe the V.C. as they come out of the city and join up with the NVA. They'll follow the infantry and use their own discretion to ambush them immediately upon hearing us initiate our own ambush."

"What if you are outnumbered?"

"We expect to be outnumbered but not outfought. We'll have the advantage of surprise, which will include using some Claymores on that trail. But if we need them, we have two routes of egress, one by river and the other through our lines to the village."

"What about support?"

"I'll have some pre-registered mortar fire laid out, all firing away from Quang Tri City, so that won't be a problem. We need a gunship, a medevac helicopter, and a reaction force; a reinforced squad should do it, standing by at the helipad."

"That's a well-thought-out plan, Kowalski. I can get all that approved for you. If the dinks bug out to the south away from the city, I think I can lay on some artillery without letting the cat out of the bag."

"I think that covers it then, sir."

"It appears so. You didn't by any chance flunk out of OCS, did you, corporal?"

"No, sir. I just like this shit."

The operational plans were presented to headquarters. They were quickly approved. Anticipation built as the afternoon crept past. Steve attended the briefing at the Citadel, carefully listening to each unit's report for impacts upon or conflict with his own plans, which were not revealed. The entire general staff and intelligence officers of both the South Vietnamese and American commands seemed completely oblivious to the combined V.C./NVA operation taking place right under their noses.

Steve returned to Thach Hanh where he and the driver "washed" the Jeep under the bridge. Surreptitiously, Steve observed as the scouts departed the convoy with the appearance of paying the prostitutes a visit. No one seemed to be paying special attention to them. One of the men purchased a bottle of whiskey from a roadside vendor. Nice touch, Steve thought.

The operation was proceeding as planned. The reconners had put on their SCUBA equipment and were routinely checking the bridge pilings, diving from rubber boats that would be employed to transport the ambush team in just as few hours. Steve left the driver and walked through the village to check on the construction site, a normal part of his daily routine. The Seabees were packing up to pull out for the day. Everything appeared normal.

Fat pigs grunted deeply as they waddled down the village streets, wrinkling their snouts, sniffing with curiosity as well as hunger. A dog, hit by a stone thrown by a mischievous child, yelped and ran into the bushes. The new barber was closing his lean-to shop. The laborers, mostly women, were coming in from the rice paddies.

The women chewed a mixture of betel nuts, lime, and pepper, which formed a mild stimulant. It stained their lips, gums, and teeth an ugly black color. Steve tried to imagine Lan appearing the same way. He wondered if one of those haggard, emaciated women had once been considered beautiful. Had she dreamed of a life beyond Thach Hanh or Quang Tri?

At dusk, the self-defense force gathered at Steve's tent for inspection and instructions. Steve went through the procedure with a careful eye, making sure all the weapons were ready for service. He did not wait until it was dark to place his personnel in their defensive positions. Any watcher could easily note the location of the defenders and especially that of the crew-served weapons.

Deep darkness never quite fell on Thach Hanh the way it did on most villages without power. The low-wattage power grid of nearby Quang Tri City bathed the village in a dull yellow glow. Steve went to Le Kinh and explained his plan. The sergeant wrote out a firing schedule for the mortars in Vietnamese so there would be no uncertainty about the orders and the numbers. Together, they went to the defensive positions as quietly and as covertly as possible, changing the location of both machine guns and mortars. Steve "set" both mortars for the first firing schedule to be commenced by a green pop flare. He gave instructions for the second schedule to be fired upon seeing a red pop flare and for the third by a white pop flare. Lan, who was the gunner on one of the mortars, would not look Steve in the face.

Le Kinh agreed with Steve's choice of personnel and pulled four men off the line of perimeter defense. They were given no explanation, only instructions to follow. The team was soon assembled in a hut near the river. Steve explained the mission and stripped everyone of everything not essential to the patrol. The Marines taped their dog tags to their chests to prevent their tinkling like wind chimes against one another at an inopportune moment. They wore soft "bush hats" rather than their helmets. Rifle slings and swivels were tied and taped down. All exposed parts of their bodies were covered in black, brown, white, light, and dark green grease paint to serve as camouflage.

One new Marine who smelled of after shave was sent to the river for a quick bath. Upon his return, he was instructed to roll in the mud to complete camouflage of his scent. Steve issued his final instructions.

"Once you are in position, make no movement, no sound. Do not cough, belch, burp, or fart. Don't whisper or pray out loud. Don't slap at bugs or scratch whatever itches. Keep your eyes moving but otherwise freeze as if you are a marble statue."

Steve led the teams down to the water. They crouched down in the rubber boats. Motors were not used. The reconners in the water provided guidance and propulsion. No oars were taken. The short trip was necessary to prevent anyone in the village from seeing the team moving beyond their defensive lines. After a few moments, the boats swung inward and scrapped the sandy bottom of the river.

The swimmers rose out of the water and tugged the boats ashore. They moved as silently as a fish swimming in deep water. There was no splashing noise to give them away. The men stepped out of the boats onto the dry bank, advanced to the tree line, and took up defensive positions in case they had been spotted. Plugs were pulled. The boats and expensive SCUBA gear were pushed into the water where they sank. The swimmers planned to retrieve them the following day. Steve waited a short time and then moved to the trail he had marked on his map, searching for an alternate route inland. Communicating by hand and arm signals every Marine learns early in his career, the patrol leader dropped one of the Marines off to serve as the cutoff man on that trail. He sent another man up the trail past the juncture where the ambush would be set up to serve as the other cutoff man on that end of the trail.

Once in place, the man flashed a red pen light toward the others to indicate their positions. The ambushers established their killing zone. Fire limit stakes were pushed into the ground to prevent them from shooting one another, and especially the cutoff men who they could not see. Steve knew how alone and vulnerable those men were feeling. He'd been in their shoes many times as a scout.

The reconners were placed at the opposite ends of the adjacent trail. There are a number of different types of ambushes. Each calls for a different level of sophistication and training. A reinforced recon patrol would have established an X-shaped patrol at the trail junction. An infantry squad might have employed an L-shaped ambush. Steve selected a straight-line ambush with his riflemen on the south side of the trail. As his reference point, Steve had chosen a large tree growing close to the footpath.

Quickly, but with practiced efficiency, the scout positioned a Claymore mine in the tree's branches so it would discharge downward. Three others were placed at ground level with a slight upward angle. The "killing zone" he created was twenty meters long. The effect of a single Claymore mine exploding 750 marble-sized chunks of steel at better than shotgun velocity is utterly awesome. Steve wired the four of them to fire simultaneously. He rigged two more as booby traps along the north-south pathway.

Steve covered his tracks and mines with leaves and grass. He then joined the line of riflemen: four Vietnamese villagers, a young Marine who had no combat experience, and himself, a two-tour veteran. Steve lay still, hardly breathing, aware of every movement, every sound. None of it was coming from his people.

A frog croaked. It seemed quite loud. Then its mating call was answered. A cricket chirped. A lizard in a tree boomed, announcing his availability to mate or defend his territory. They were the natural sounds of the environment. Steve's mind wandered. He thought of how nice it would be to sleep in his own bed again, on a mattress with clean sheets. It would be a real luxury to bathe every day and brush your teeth after every meal. Steve wondered how his experiences in Vietnam could compare to his father's infantry service with Patton's Army during World War Two. How would their relationship change when he got home as a result of his Marine Corps experiences?

Steve's thoughts drifted to Mary. He recalled walking on a beach in Galveston with her, hand in hand, her tiny bikini turning heads every step of the way. He thought of the sound of her laughter and of all the things he wished he had said to her but did not. He wondered what they really had. Was it love or youth? What did his attraction to other women mean? Would their relationship be changed when he returned home?

An hour passed. The Marine began to wonder if he had been wrong. Could the NVA tax collectors be behind them? Could they have learned of Steve's plans and set up their own ambush? More time passed, and then, a whisper. The scout held his breath, his eyes searching the trail in peripheral vision as he dared not turn his head. A movement, perhaps just a shadow, and the breeze in a tree caught his attention. And then a flash of movement and a sound that puzzled him. Without moving his head, he cast his eyes about. There! Entering the killing zone was an NVA soldier in uniform, grass stuck in his pith helmet to break up his silhouette. His AK-47 rifle was extended to the front at waist level. The extended bayonet appeared to be probing the air. The assault rifle swung left to right as the soldier advanced. Ten meters behind him were seventeen V.C. and NVA soldiers. Four more pushing bicycles, heavily laden with the rice they had collected as taxes brought up the rear. The tires on the path had created the sound Steve had not been able to identify.

Steve's heart was hammering. His finger was poised near the trigger of his rifle. The Claymore detonator was clasped in his left hand. The NVA scout was directly in front of him now. The Marines could smell the enemy, their sweat, their breath. Steve held his breath and waited. Another enemy soldier came into his line of vision, and then two were walking abreast. They were followed by a man guiding a bicycle. Steve could not see the tail end of the enemy patrol without turning his head.

He would have to trust the cutoff man to take care of any enemy soldiers who escaped the killing zone of his ambush. Steve took two deep calming breaths. The enemy scout was near the front limit of the killing zone. It was time. Steve depressed the switch in his left hand. Four thundering Claymores ripped the enemy column to shreds with flashing explosions and three thousand steel projectiles. Twisting with shock and pain, the NVA soldiers fell to the ground. Shielded by the baskets of rice on the bicycles and other men, two enemy soldiers survived the initial blast from the mines.

With the explosions, the ambushers opened up with their rifles, releasing their pent-up anxiety and nervousness in a fierce fusillade of bullets. The enemy soldiers jerked with multiple bullet impacts and fell to the ground. The NVA had not fired off a shot in return. Shouting "Cease fire! Cease fire!" Steve quieted both the guns and the ebullient voices from his riflemen. He had them go through their after-action security drill while he approached the bloody bodies on the trail.

Steve gathered the enemy soldiers' weapons and presented them to the Vietnamese members of his patrol, each of whom bowed low and smiled broadly when accepting the rifles. Steve searched the bloody bodies. He stuffed the documents he found in packs and pockets into his own large thigh pockets. One document, however, piqued his interest more than the others. He folded that one and put it in his breast pocket.

Rifle shots suddenly rang out to the north. Steve took a thin pop-up flare from his pocket. It looked like a high-priced cigar in a silver container. Holding it firmly In his left hand, he slapped the bottom of the flare into the palm of his right hand. Four streaks of green shot skyward. Mortars began firing from the village. Again, a dozen explosions ripped the calm of night to shreds.

Steve retrieved his booby traps from the trails. He collected the nervous cutoff men and quickly extracted the patrol. Returning to Thach Hanh, just outside the perimeter, Steve heard the metallic charging of a machine gun .

"Toi Mai!" he yelled. "Toi Ha Shi Cau!" It was the first thing that came to mind. "It's Mai. It's Corporal Candy. The Vietnamese chatted excitedly as the captured weapons were displayed. Every man told his personal version of the event. Steve left them to celebrate their victory. The radio in his tent was buzzing when he arrived.

"Who's firing up Quang Tri? Over?"

"Are we under attack? Over."

The various commands were stepping all over each other in their quest for answers. Steve heard transmissions from Army and Marine Corps units at all levels. Finally, he keyed the mic.

"All units this channel, all units this channel. Stand by for an after-action report, over."

The radio was suddenly silent, the various operators waiting and listening. They knew an after-action report would answer all their questions, but it was highly unusual for a unit to provide an after-action report over the radio.

"Candy Tuft Sierra Two Six. Candy Tuft Sierra Two Six; this is CAP six. Viking six, over."

That coded transmission alerted all units that the S-6 officer of the First Battalion, 3'" Marine Regiment, was reporting to the battalion's S-2 officer, civil affairs to intelligence.

"Sierra six six, send your traffic. Over." Steve recognized Captain Maxwell's voice. He would have bet a dollar on a donut the battalion commander was standing next to him.

"Be advised, civilian Indigenous self-defense force has completed planned operation in the vicinity south of Quang Tri City, east of Thach Hanh village adjacent to the Thach Hanh River. All requested support units stand down, over."

"I copy your stand-down order, six. Will join at your location at 1300 hours for a verbal briefing, over."

"Negative. Request an 0800 meeting. Over." Steve did not want to wait until early afternoon for the captain to become involved in the follow-up. The captain agreed. Before he could rest, there were captured documents Steve would have to translate. It took several hours to complete that task. Physically and mentally exhausted, the scout fell onto his hard cot and slept as soundly as if it were a mattress he had longed for. Steve was awakened by a heavy foot kicking the braced legs of his cot. He sat up, rubbing the sleep from his gritty eyes.

"You stirred up quite a hornet's nest with that ambush, Tiger," Captain Maxwell informed him. Over a cup of ration coffee, the scout debriefed the S-2 officer. They went through the documents taken from the NVA soldiers. Captain Maxwell became a bit bug-eyed when Steve explained what they were. The Marines implemented follow-up actions until it was time for them to attend the daily intelligence briefing, knowing they would be the stars of this day's meeting.

At the daily briefing, Captain Maxwell arranged for a projector to be placed so he could make his presentation. That alone caused murmurs and speculation to spread throughout the room. Long-established protocols remained in place as unit by unit the intelligence representatives gave their briefing. When the battalion's number was called, Steve stood.

"Corporal Kowalski, acting civil affairs officer and chief intelligence scout. Based upon intelligence developed in a joint operation with the Indigenous self-defense cadre at Thac Hanh, One Three conducted an ambush at 0200 hours this day of an NVA/VC force operating out of Quang Tri City. The ambushed force consisted of eighteen individuals who have been collecting taxes throughout Quang Tri and Thua Thien Provinces since the rice harvest began.

"In a collateral action in support of the ambushing force, our security force at Thach Hanh conducted a support by mortar fire mission against what was estimated to be a squad in strength. Patrols sent out this morning noted five blood trails and drag marks in the vicinity of the mortar strike conducted by the defense force in support of the ambush unit; however, no casualties can be confirmed. Our S-2 officer has additional information of interest to all units operating in I Corp." Steve sat.

Captain Maxwell stood, the captured documents in his hand. He began by reading the date, time group, location, and results of the event in bare bones, dry military language. "Corporal Kowalski," he said, pointing to Steve, "who has been our acting intelligence officer and chief intelligence scout, initiated this operation based upon intelligence provided through a network he has established. He captured the documents I am about to show you from an NVA lieutenant who was accompanying the local tax collectors. We believe he was in a liaison position to coordinate North Vietnamese Army attacks against certain bases with the local Viet Cong units.

"These overlays will be sufficient evidence of that and the cause for my concern." The captain placed one of the documents on the projector. A contour map image was projected in faint colors on the wall. "What you see here is the location of the 1st ARVN Division's Combat Base at Ai Tu. I believe we all know where that is." He replaced the document with another.

"This is a blowup of that base. As you can see, the locations of the unit's artillery pieces and major assets, such as communications and command centers, are noted, complete with distances. That leads me to believe an attack against Ai Tu is imminent." The captain again replaced the document with another. "This is similar to the first overall map you saw. Only this reveals the location of the U.S. Army's American Division at Than Hua."

The captain displayed the last of the captured documents. "This is a close-up layout of the American Division's assets similar to those at Ai Tu."

There was a general drawing of breaths at the revelation. The Marines had embarrassed the Army while at the same time possibly saving them. It might have been more politic to have made the announcements in private to the involved base commanders; however, the captain had a general statement to make.

"In view of this intelligence, all Allied bases in the I Corp should consider relocation of their primary assets. At Quang Tri, we are reviewing our policy of using indigenous personnel for such tasks as laundry and the filling of sandbags. We welcome any additional suggestions."

On their way out the door, an Army colonel with the name tag Neuman over his chest pocket stopped the Marines and introduced himself. He spoke to Steve. "Son, If you were in my command, this would be automatic, but since it is interservice, I need another endorsement. I'm putting you in for an Army Commendation Medal. You will hear from our headquarters."

Steve was surprised. In the Jeep as they returned to Quang Tri, he told the captain, "If they award it, I won't wear it."

"That is certainly one attitude, but you earned it, and an Army medal would be a little unique for a serving Marine. I think you should reconsider."

"Yes, sir," Steve answered. There was often nothing else to say to an officer when he made a suggestion or observation.

The residents of Thac Hanh had a new sense of pride in their self-defense force. Kowalski enjoyed a high degree of renewed respect. Lan, however, was somewhat certain she had shamed the Marine into taking action against the tax collectors. She continued to keep her distance from Steve.

CHAPTER ELEVEN
THACH HAHN

Halfway through his second combat tour, Steve was growing restless in the village. It would generally have been considered a choice assignment. No inspection. Little supervision. Drawing combat pay without having to fight for it. Enjoying the freedom to come and go as you want with plenty of time to get to know the villagers, the mischievous children, and the slender exotic schoolgirls. During one of Major Hamlin's infrequent visits, Steve brought forward an idea that he had tossed around mentally for a week.

"How's everything going?" The major asked as if he had not read the routine report Steve supplied.

"All quiet, sir. Initial training has been completed. I've begun cross-training the entire unit. I'm including civilians who own their own weapons and don't expect to be paid."

"Is there anything you need out here?"

"Well, sir, I do have an idea."

The major almost groaned as he said, "Let's hear it."

"My people are becoming proficient soldiers. They are well trained. But let's face the facts, Major. With two individual combat bases so close and other major units in Quang Tri City, the only way we will be attacked is if the NVA rolls over us on their way into Quang Tri, and that would be an entire shift in the war."

"Fundamentally, I agree."

"Basically, I'm here because we needed this program on paper," Steve said, having read some impatience and resistance in the major's short response.

"Most villages aren't large enough to support a CAP Unit or a self defense force."

"You are right there. We can't put Marines in every little hamlet and village."

"My people won't maintain sharp skills, continue absorbing the training, or build pride without some sort of edge."

"You mean another combat operation?"

"No, sir, not exactly."

"What about the patrols you are running?"

"There was an edge to them at first, but they've become so routine the edge has worn off."

"Exactly what have you got in mind, Kowalski?"

"I want to expand our operations in several phases. Phase one will be intelligence gathering."

"You seem to have thought this out. How are you going to accomplish this intelligence operation?"

"This is all based on that map study we did of the villages with the red and blue pins. I've used an older woman, a wood gatherer who wanders from place to place almost without being noticed, with success in the past."

"That's a good ploy."

"And I have a peg-legged veteran who is also a barber. These hamlets and small villages can't support commercial enterprises the way a larger village can. They rely upon traveling barbers and other goods merchants, knife sharpeners, and pot sellers."

"You intend to use these people as your eyes and ears?"

"Not quite, not those people. I don't know many of them well. I can't trust them. I'll use our people in those roles."

"What type of support do you require?"

"Minimum really. I need the proper approval. We'll need to arrange some funding for the program. Seed money to set up the pot seller with goods and a pony to carry them. Barber tools. And some cash for these people who will have to give up their livelihood for this program."

"You will have to operate within some limits."

"Such as?"

"Confine your activities to Quang Tri Province. Share your intelligence with the battalion, regiment, and division G-2 officers. Conduct no offensive actions without obtaining prior permission. Notify my office any time you leave the village."

"Yes, sir."

Approval of the division for the intelligence operation was quick in coming. Funding was to be provided by a CIA front. The amount made available was surprising. American tax dollars from some secret slush fund, Steve assumed. Rather than pay his agents extravagantly, the Marine expanded his program. Saah readily agreed to participate as a wood gatherer, which was how she made her living after she got too old to work in the rice fields. As a CIA operative, although completely unaware that this was her new status, she was paid twelve dollars per month, twice what she made as a wood cutter. She would keep those earnings as well.

Steve met secretly with the elderly woman to explain her role but nothing more of his overall plan. He paid her monthly wages in advance. "Report only to me or Le Kinh," he instructed. The barber received similar instructions and slightly more pay. The pot seller was another rung up the ladder in the pay scale. The additional funding allowed Steve to expand his operation. After giving it considerable thought, he hired a fisherman and his wife to ply the channels and waterways selling fruits and vegetables the Marine bought in Quang Tri City. Another man was hired to sell chicks, ducklings, and piglets.

There were no group meetings. No team was told what the others were doing. Steve sent them out in separate directions daily. There were two more women he needed to hire. An elderly woman was sent to fill sandbags at the Quang Tri Combat Base. Her mission was to listen to the gossip of the women, to observe and report on anyone who appeared suspicious.

His final hire took place at Dr. Quoc's house over dinner.

"Hello, sweetheart," he greeted Lan, who smelled fresh and wonderful. Anticipating the visit, the girl had crushed fragrant flowers and rubbed the petals through her raven's wing dark hair before brushing it over one hundred strokes. After vigorously scrubbing herself clean, Lan used a coconut oil-based lotion on her body.

"I no say for you," she responded rather flatly, as if she were not expressing her inner feelings. Her mother, though, knew her daughter well. She smiled, pleased at the developing relationship between her daughter and the Marine. She was more pleased when after dinner Steve asked to sit alone with Lan on the porch.

Steve's intentions, however, were not romantic. "I want to pay you," he explained.

"For what?" Lan spat, fearing the Marine was offering her money for sex, which was typically what the American soldiers she had met did.

"I need for you to ride buses every chance you get from Quang Tri to Dong Ha to Gio Linh, Cam Lo, and Da Nang."

"Why?"

"I need you to just ride from place to place. Be shy and quiet, but listen. Report back anything you hear that might be of interest to me militarily."

"You want me to be a spy?" Lan seemed shocked at the idea.

"Not a spy. I just want to know what people are saying when they don't think anyone is listening."

"About Thach Hanh?"

"No, about everything going on in Quang Tri Province."

"It will seem strange if I spend so much time on buses."

"Not if you are selling soaps and perfume from village to village."

"I can do that."

Steve explained how the program would work, about reporting only to him and paying her fifty dollars per month, more than her father made. Perhaps she read more into it than was intended, but Lan readily agreed to participate in the program.

By foot, along the waterways, by bus and pony, Steve spread his thin intelligence network throughout the province. Sometimes intelligence information comes in an almost complete package. Most of the time, however, It comes in bits that have to be put together like pieces of a puzzle. Patience, diligence, and meticulous attention to detail are required.

At the end of eight weeks, Steve had sent his agents one by one into a dozen different villages. He kept a notebook in each of the villages with the comments of the various agents on every village. The major supplied aerial photographs and blow-ups of topographical maps. The results so far were inconclusive.

When the first important piece of intelligence data came to Steve's attention, it did not concern Thatch Hanh or any of the target villages. Le Kinh came to his tent early one evening, escorting the gnarled older woman he had assigned to fill sandbags at the combat base.

The excited scout was in a hurry. "We must go to the combat base. Right now!" he emphasized. Steve trusted the scout. He called for his driver. Le Kinh explained his urgency on the way. When the driver heard what the Vietnamese scout had to say he sped up. He understood why the radio couldn't be used. They rushed to the civil affairs office.

When he heard the basics of the information, the major rushed with Steve and his companions to the division G-2 officer, calling for the regimental intelligence officer to join them. At headquarters, Steve briefed them all.

"With our intelligence operation approved, I sent a paid agent, Yahn, here, a lady of seventy some years, to seek employment at the base filling sandbags."

"Rather strenuous work for a woman of her age," the regimental S-2 officer said as if he disapproved. Perhaps he was a bit defensive as he realized his presence was only a superfluous afterthought.

"Several of the women from Thach Hanh and a bus load from Quang Tri City come in every day to perform various duties here on the base."

"They fill sandbags, cook, and do laundry," the major added, although they all knew what the "mamma-sans" did.

"I told her to be observant and to keep her ears open for anything we might need to know."

At that point, Le Kinh stepped in as interpreter. He spoke rapidly to the old woman. She told her story through him.

"I watch every day. I see who works hard and who is lazy. Who goes to tents with soldiers. I see one young woman. When we eat at noon, she walks. I see her counting steps, this way, that way, stop to flirt with soldiers."

"What soldiers?"

"Soldiers at big guns, at tanks, at some bunkers."

"She was measuring distances," the major interjected.

The G-2 officer, a full colonel, nodded in affirmation. "Do we have an I.D. on her?"

"We know who she is and where she lives along the river. A perfect snatch job for the SEALS," Steve suggested.

"Put that in motion," the colonel ordered. "Have her brought here. Good work, Kowalski," he said, rising as if to leave.

"That's not all, Colonel," the corporal told him in a serious tone. The colonel sank back into his chair.

"Let's get on with it then."

Le Kinh continued the interrogation. "She also listens to gossip. Women's talk mostly about soldiers and children. Sometimes a girl stays overnight on the base with a boyfriend or with a provider."

"A pimp."

"I do not know this word. I think it is the same." Le Kinh said, continuing the exchange with the intelligence source. "She said this same woman warned girls not to stay at base tonight. There will be an attack."

"By who?"

"North Vietnamese soldier battalion and sappers with local V.C. cadre."

"How many?"

"Six hundred in a battalion, maybe another one hundred V.C. with them."

"So this is no probe or simple sapper attack?"

"No, sir. It is going to be a full-scale attack."

"That's kind of a light force to take on this headquarters."

"They are undoubtedly counting on the element of surprise."

"He say base soldiers not real soldiers, no go to field, no fight, too soft, no, too weak, to defend against real soldiers from north."

"It's probably a hit-and-run mission. Breech our defenses, cause as much damage as possible, and disappear."

"Does she know anything else?"

Le Kinh asked more questions. The Americans waited. Finally, the woman seemed to have run out of things to say. "She says attacks come at deep, dark hours. From the west, through jungle, across river."

"Coincidentally, through the perimeter closest to the artillery assets. These are their targets."

The colonel went into action. He began issuing orders.

"Have the base quietly go on fifty percent alert. Get the unit commanders in here. After dark, have all the perimeter security move to their secondary positions as stealthily and quietly as possible. Have the Army reinforce the Marines on perimeter, man for man. Don't move any major units or assets.

"Alert the artillery to have beehive rounds available. Load some clerks and cooks on the helicopters. Make it look like a combat operation. Get those choppers out of here. Good work, Major. We'll take it from here."

Steve felt slighted. Basically, he felt the colonel had diminished his role in the intelligence coup due to his rank. The major didn't miss it himself. As the Thach Hanh contingent prepared to return to the village, the major attempted to make things right. "That was good work, Kowalski. Your part won't go unnoticed in my report. When this is over, I'll be writing up my recommendation for your Naval Commendation Medal."

Steve returned to Thach Hanh, his mind racing. This bit of intelligence was a huge coup for him, for the entire program. He wanted the villagers to know, but to do so would endanger his asset. He knew how she would feel if she were not recognized. If the attack developed as she had reported and it was repulsed successfully due to her intelligence, Steve would ask the CIA for a cash reward. But how could he give that to her without bringing suspicion upon her?

Le Kinh provided the answer. "She has a son in the army. He can visit; present her with water buffalo and other small gifts. Maybe he visits every two, three months with gifts."

Life in the village would continue. Tongues might wag, but suspicion would not be raised against the old woman. The sandbag job would continue, as would the intelligence operations. Knowing an attack of major proportions was imminent, Steve could not sleep. He walked the lines of Thach Hanh's security perimeter, talking to the guards on duty. Two o'clock came too slowly. Steve took up a position on the bridge facing west toward the combat base. He waited, wondering if the gossip he'd reported was only talk and speculation. At nearly three a.m., the SEAL team arrived, reporting a smooth operation in the extraction of the V.C. agent. One of the SEALS had deep scratches across his face. He answered Steve's question before it could be asked.

"Little hundred-pound bitch fought like a three hundred-pound wildcat."

"You could get a purple heart for that wound."

"I'd never live that down," he said.

A roll of popcorn-like bursts caught the group's attention. The men all looked to the west. Mortar flares lit up the sky over Quang Tri Combat Base. Streaks of green and lines of glowing orange marked the locations of automatic weapons. The assault was under way. Mortars were added to the mix by both sides. The base was too far away for the men there to hear the shouted orders, cries for a corpsman, or for ammunition. All the veterans could easily imagine artillery commanders calling out ranges and corpsmen answering the cries and moans of the wounded.

In spite of knowing that men were being killed and wounded in the battle, some of whom would suffer various types of pain for the rest of their lives, Steve was relieved that the attack had taken place. From the sounds of the prolonged battle, Steve knew it was a major event. What does that mean for I Corp? he wondered. And what did it mean for Thach Hanh?

The following day Steve was called to a meeting at the division intelligence office. The base was cleaning up after the pitched battle. Craters where mortars had struck were being filled in. Tents that had caught fire were being pulled down to be replaced. Burned and shot-up vehicles were being hauled away.

Sandbags were being replaced. The pall of battle hung over the combat base. The major, three battalion commanders, and the commander of the Third Marine Regiment were present with a similar number of Army officers from the 5th Mechanized Division.

The smells of the previous night's combat lingered even in the headquarters building. Steve had noticed an artillery piece that had been destroyed, most likely by a sapper. The NVA had walked on their own bodies to get through the minefield and then the perimeter wire. The battle had carried into the compound itself.

"Seventeen killed, thirty-two wounded." The colonel read from a typed report. Three hundred NVA KIAs who weren't dragged off. The attack was led by the 88th Sapper Company. The Third Battalion of the 106 Star Regiment was the main infantry force. Other elements as yet to be identified acted in support.

"This was a major effort, gentlemen. Had it not been for the early warning provided by the corporal here, we might have lost this base."

"Our losses would certainly have been much heavier," the Major added.

The colonel briefed the gathering on the CAP unit's activities with emphasis on their intelligence gathering program. As a result, Steve was awarded not only the Naval Commendation Medal but another Army Commendation Medal as well.

He returned to duty in Thach Hahn with the enthusiastic, unanimous support of the command structure at Quang Tri Combat Base. His model was adopted for use by CAP units near Dong Ha and Da Nang. That support was manifested by increased levels of assistance from the Army and the Marine Corps through material and training efforts.

The Army rented a building at the north end of Thach Hanh. Six men moved in. Their first overt act was to secure the building with barbed wire. Gun positions were established. Sandbags were placed around the gun pits and in places to reinforce the building. The Army unit was to assume responsibility for expanding the CAP program's reach to that end of the village and provide security for the residents. The soldiers were attached to and subservient to Steve's CAP unit. The Army brought resources the Marines did not have. The Navy SEALS, Army Rangers, and Marines were now working in a joint operation from Thach Hanh. The V.C. would no longer own the night in the north end of Thach Hanh.

Steve knew he had to make some changes in the things he saw the soldiers doing before that could happen. "You should be in a fifty percent alert situation at all times," he instructed the soldiers. "That means three of you will be in your headquarters at all times." Steve could tell the soldiers didn't like taking orders from a Marine. "One of you will always be on duty with the CAP unit. One of us will lead a training patrol daily.

"So, you all know who I am and what I do. So tell me, who are you? What are your specialties?"

A tall, pimple-faced soldier stood. "I'm Sammy Middlebrook. I'm a medic."

"Good. You're going to run what we Marines call a MEDCAP. Set up a clinic, not in your enclosure. Establish regular hours to see patients. Requisition whatever you need. Take care of all comers, but keep your eyes and ears open. Practice weapons and personal security at all times."

Sammy sat. Another man stood. His nickname was Pinocchio for the obvious reason. "I'm Ed Miller, communications specialist."

"Ed, get us another radio. We'll have our own frequency. Make sure all the commands and supporting forces know what it is. Stock up on batteries. Teach someone to back you up on the radio. You'll be responsible for training two of my people and familiarizing as many of the rest as you can on radio procedures."

Another man stood, sturdy, blond, medium. "Gary Presley, demolitions," was all he had to say by way of introduction.

"Gary, can you rig mines and booby traps?"

"Absolutely,"

"Requisition everything you need. Surreptitiously set up a mine and bomb trap defense for this entire village. It will have to be command detonated. You'll also be teaching my people as much as you can about your specialty."

Next was a broad, short man who needed some exercise. He had a high forehead that met a thin hairline near the crown of his head. He was pale, reminding Steve of a grub worm. "I'm Jay Thomas." His voice was a girlish squeak. "I'm the armorer."

"Make sure you have plenty of spare parts for our variety of weapons. Requisition whatever replacements you deem necessary. Keep our weapons in tip-top shape."

"Of course," he said as he sat.

A man who was ordinary in every way except for his carrot orange hair stood. Steve immediately thought of Mary. "Roger Edwards, weapons expert," the red-head announced.

"What is an Army weapons expert, exactly?"

"I am proficient with every weapon carried by a light infantry battalion."

"Rifle?"

"Expert."

"Sniper qualified?"

"Yes."

"Pistol?"

"Yes."

"Machine gun?"

"Yes."

"Light mortar?"

"That too."

"By now you know what I want from you."

"Yes, to train your people."

The last man stood. He reminded Steve of the SEALS. Same broad chest. Bulging biceps. Thick neck. Steel-eyed look. Now this one was more like the warriors Steve had expected to be sent.

"Michael Wise. Martial arts and combat knife fighting

A well-rounded lot, but not an intelligence specialist among them. Steve addressed the group. "When I ask you to train everyone in your specialty, I intend for that to include each other, with myself being no exception." That seemed to mildly surprise the soldiers.

"I'll make up some training schedules. You have three days to get your house in order before the training schedule begins." Steve turned and left the Army to their own devices.

The children who had free run of the entire village had found new and perhaps more gullible targets from which to beg candy and cigarettes. They were new customers for the cold soda pop girls, the baguette baker, and the restaurant. Steve left the Army largely alone. He busied himself with making the schedules to the best benefit of all. He ran his intelligence operation. He patrolled the village at random times. Slowly, the village adapted to the presence of the small contingent of soldiers. But these men were more what the residents were used to. They spent their money more freely. They drank Ba Mui Ba, a potent local beer, in large quantities. They often stumbled to their quarters before the ten p.m. curfew Steve had insisted upon but had no authority to enforce.

Life in Thach Hanh went on for the most part as it always had. The farmers planted and harvested rice the same labor-intensive way they had done for generations, behind the Asian tractor, a plodding water buffalo. Fishermen cast their nets early in the morning so as to deliver fresh fish to the market by noon. The wood gatherers spread out into the nearby forests to gather what each could strap to his or her back. The commerce that sprang up to serve each occupying army, Chinese, Japanese, French, and American, serviced the soldiers.

The whore at the north end of the village was busier than ever. The restaurant sold considerably more beer. The ice house gained a new steady customer. The nuns were more reclusive; however, they were pleased to take in the increased donations in cash or goods for teaching the villagers to speak English.

Daily, a dozen Vietnamese were split into teams of four, each group being instructed in different subjects by the various American specialists. The training was as intense as boot camp without the emphasis on discipline, uniforms, and such things as close-order drill. Patrolling continued as well.

In twelve weeks, almost 100 villagers were as well trained as any U.S. soldier, better than most, in the basics of light infantry weapons and tactics. They were better cross-trained than any of those soldiers who were trained as basic riflemen and only "fam-fired" support weapons.

The intelligence operation that consumed most of Steve's time was creating a comprehensive mosaic of the enemy's presence and activities throughout Quang Tri Province. It was all developed by low-level "eyes and ears" intelligence. The first bit of intelligence requiring action came from Lan as a result of her travels.

Steve was sleeping, not exactly with one eye open but with that "aware" sleep of those who live in danger-filled environments. He woke, aware of a presence in his tent. He began sneaking his right hand up under his pillow toward his pistol.

"No, Ha Shi," came the whisper of a voice he knew well.

"Lan?" he questioned.

"Yes. Please speak quietly. No one must know I am here."

"Why? What's going on?"

"We have V.C. in village."

"Where?"

"I do not know. I hear. They watch. Make reports. Make plans."

"You heard this on the bus?"

"Yes, from Quang Tri to Da Nang. They do not know I am from Thach Hanh."

Steve thought a moment. "After consideration, I assume that to be true."

"There is more."

"Good. What have you got?" Steve asked, sitting up.

"An NVA paymaster is on his way from the north with money for all the agents in Quang Tri."

"Who is he?"

"I do not know. No name was given."

"Where is he coming from?"

"I did not hear."

"When is he due to arrive?"

"Soon."

"Thank you, Lan." Impulsively, Steve reached out, pulling the girl to him, kissing her quickly but fully on the lips. She was surprised. Steve was also surprised by his action. He ended the buss quickly. Lan reached out, her hands finding his head. She tugged at him and returned the kiss, fully, passionately. When she finally had to take a breath, the girl broke away completely and quietly disappeared into the darkness.

"Oh my God," the Marine muttered. The only reason he didn't consider the implications of that kiss deeper was because of the questions raised by the intelligence Lan had delivered. Finding that paymaster would be like finding a needle in a haystack at harvest season in Nebraska. If he delivered this intelligence to anyone, there was a very good possibility it would find its way back to the North Vietnamese. They would change their plans. Doing so might also endanger Lan. Steve slept fitfully as he considered the possibilities. Lan also slept fitfully, her lips burning as she thought about that kiss and the possibilities. Steve wondered how often those paymasters made their routes, as he had already captured one of them in the recent past.

The next morning Steve called a meeting of his joint team at the Army's secure compound. Six soldiers, four SEALS, and one Marine. Using the resources they had trained, they could count on six twelve-man squads for patrols, with about two dozen of the most minimally qualified left behind to guard the village. Steve explained the situation. He asked for suggestions and thoughts.

Scott, the bulky SEAL, spoke first. "This paymaster, I would think he would be traveling with an armed guard."

"Probably a squad," Steve responded. "Anything larger than a squad would be too likely to attract attention."

"And they'll be moving at night," Gary added.

"We'll have to watch all the roads into Quang Tri," Sammy said.

"There's too many roads and not enough of us to cover them all," Tom, another SEAL, noted.

"So far, it seems we're looking for a squad moving at night toward Quang Tri," Ed summed up.

"Right," Steve affirmed. "It seems unlikely they'll be coming from anywhere but north.'

"They might come in from the sea." It was only natural for a SEAL to think that way.

"If they come from the north, the most logical place to find them is Glo Linh."

"The place is a maze of bunkers and tunnels. If we mount an operation against the village, the people we're looking for will simply disappear underground."

"Gio Linh is notoriously dangerous. I've warned my agents to avoid it," Steve said.

"What I'm thinking," Scott proposed, "is six nightly squad-sized ambushes established at likely routes between Gio LInh and Quang Tri."

"There are dozens of routes when you consider the indirect approaches."

"That's the most likely scenario," Steve agreed. "We increase our chances of intercepting these guys by establishing our ambushes where trails and footpaths cross."

There was general agreement on the plan. "When do we start?"

"Immediately. Tonight," Steve decided.

"How long do we give ourselves for this guy to show up?"

"Yeah, sitting in ambush all night and working all day is going to get old very fast for these people."

"Two weeks, then we'll turn it over to someone else."

"How do we explain not reporting it for that length of time?"

"We don't. I'll bring the major in, but only him."

It was agreed. The six patrol leaders spread out through the village to inform their squads they would be going out on a night combat patrol. Le Kinh was brought into the plan. He would be in charge of those left behind to provide support and guard the village.

Steve rushed to Quang Tri Combat Base to inform the major of the events. Major Hamlin heard him out and immediately arranged for a private meeting with the division's 6-2 officer.

"My first concern is security. Frankly, Colonel, there is none where the South Vietnamese are concerned." For a moment, Steve thought he had said too much.

"Well," the colonel replied, "we don't inform them of every squad-sized patrol action we initiate," in effect providing his permissions to conduct the operation as outlined.

The Marines then set to the task of planning, support, and execution. The colonel had maps and aerial photographs of the area between Gio Linh and Quang Tri. Using an acetate overlay, they plotted every road, path, and trail between Gio Linh and Quang Tri. There were dozens of interesting points, which was a bit disheartening to Steve. The colonel, however, had an idea. "Gentlemen, we are going to brainstorm this issue. Each of us will individually assign a numerical value, starting with one, your most likely location to intercept this squad. We add up the numbers and average the values for each location. Prioritize your ambushes accordingly."

"That's a great idea, colonel," Steve said. He'd never heard of the brainstorming concept of problem solving before. Of course, he had not attended a variety of war colleges where such concepts were taught.

Steve returned to Thach Hahn with an acetate overlay and explanation of the plans. Map grid coordinates in six-digit numbers were supplied for each potential ambush point. Code names and radio frequencies were established. Potential supporting arms, communications, intelligence and artillery were prepared on a need-to-know basis only.

The maps were studied. Each squad leader was assigned an ambush location, one of the top six selected by the brainstormers. As a group, the Americans evaluated each location, deciding upon which type of ambush would be best suited for it. They then decided upon which squad was the best at executing that type of ambush.

Steve would not lead a squad. It was time for him to trust the men who had trained the squads and to reward them for their labors. Each of the four SEALS and two Army staff would lead the first night's ambush teams. They would alternate with the remaining five Americans and Le Kinh as patrol leaders. The ambushers waited until dark to move out.

It was a long, tense night. Each patrol leader had a radio, thanks to the Army and Ed Miller. Radio discipline was strict. Each patrol leader depressed the send button when they arrived on location. At staggered five-minute intervals, the teams reported in hourly with a single depression of the send button.

Steve didn't sleep. He couldn't. At the beginning of each hour, he counted the radio clicks. The squads had to exfiltrate unseen from the ambush locations before dawn. Four thirty was the time selected for departure. Steve met each of the teams as they returned. Many of the Vietnamese had to go straight to the fields to begin their day's labor. The Americans rested for four hours before reestablishing their daily routine for the benefit of any watchers.

The patrols ran for six nights without any results. It was frustrating. "Maybe they've already delivered the money. Beat us to the punch" proposed Rocco.

"Or took another trail."

That led Steve to revise his plans. "We have eleven Americans and Le Kinh. If we split the squads, we can cover twice the number of crossings. With the element of surprise, a seven-man team should be able to handle a ten- to twelve-man squad. Any force larger than that should be allowed to pass. Note their direction of travel, call in artillery, and bug out. The Marines at Quang Tri will have a search team with dogs on site within minutes."

For three more days, the split squads sat in ambush positions, fighting bugs, sleep, nerves, and attitudes to remain quiet and alert throughout the night. Steve was not ready to give up despite the "nothing to report" messages he sent to the major every morning.

On the seventeenth night, Le Kinh's patrol was set up in a line ambush just south of a Y intersection east of Xa Cam Tuyen when they spotted movement. The ambushers watched nervously as four men with AK-47 rifles approached. They were walking bicycles loaded with baskets of rice. They were V.C. "tax collectors," but the paymaster could have been among them.

The scout hoped none of the inexperienced self-defense force soldiers would allow his nerves to give away the ambush early. All the symptoms of nerves and fright surfaced in every one of the ambushers; however, their discipline held. They trusted Le Kinh and the men who had trained them. And they believed in themselves. They waited, listening to the sibilant sounds of the bicycle tires on the dirt path. The enemy patrol was back lighted by the near full moon. A scout in front of the patrol, his rifle held forward at the ready. He alone was in the squad's kill zone when he signaled for the patrol to halt. Had he heard or seen something? He moved forward cautiously, deeper into the ambush killing zone. Eyeballs and rifle barrels tracked him. In spite of his caution, he led the tax collectors into the ambush. His M-16 on full automatic, Le Kinh fired, sweeping his weapon from left to right. All four of the enemies took at least one round from his rifle, although they weren't all kill shots.

The six squad members had not hesitated to follow suite when Le Kinh sprang the ambush. They fired their weapons much longer than necessary, until triggers clicked on empty. The NVA soldiers never had a chance. They didn't fire a shot in return. They were searched thoroughly. No documents of any kind were found.

Rather than a failure, the ambush proved to be a success in that it served as a morale booster for the entire self-defense force, including the Americans. The ambush site was abandoned. The squad would move to the next crossing in order of priority. The village, of course, was abuzz with the news of the ambush. Four men, discounting Le Klnh, and two girls were touted as heroes.

On the 23rd night, with hopes of discovering the paymaster waning, Steve led a patrol to a crossing that had been designated as number five on the probability list. Xa Gio Binh was southwest of Gio Linh. The crossing was paths leading from both villages that came together north of Quang Tri City. Looking over the site, Steve set his team in along the stem of the Y. Carrying a load of Claymores, he quickly established a mine killing zone on each branch. There were two Claymores on one side, with a third in the middle on the other side of the path. The mines were to be command detonated. They were extremely deadly to man, beast, or vehicle.

Steve rejoined the team, reminding them to fire their weapons only after he fired his, saying, "Remember, total silence. No coughing, sneezing, belching, or burping. And no farting either. No movement at all. Don't slap at bugs or swat mosquitoes. Any of these could cost all of us our lives."

The patrol settled in to wait. There was nothing left to do. Clouds obscured the moon. Mosquitoes buzzed loudly in ears. A frog croaked. More waiting. The Marine daydreamed. He was on the beach with a girl, a spectacular girl, of course. Not Mary, and not Lan, but a girl he had never met, never seen in a photograph. It was his perfect dream girl. The girl who was just right for him in every way. She was madly in love with him. Why wasn't it Mary? he would later wonder.

There was a sound that caught his attention. Had someone moved? He listened. For a moment he wished for ears like a jackrabbit. Where had the sound come from? Had the others heard it? Which branch of the trail did it come from? He looked to the northeast. Nothing. To the northwest. Nothing again. And then the sound was repeated. It was a small metallic sound. Not repetitive. The swivel of a rifle maybe? A canteen bouncing? The sounds became multiple and varied. Steve heard them as distinctly as if he actually had the long ears of a donkey. Then he smelled them, their fishy breath, and their combined sweat. He could almost feel the heat coming off their bodies.

And then he saw them. Christ! There are a lot of them! It was a platoon at least, seventy or more soldiers. Shit, they're armed to the teeth and searching. But from the wrong direction, from the south. Steve could make them out clearly. They were not V.C. but uniformed North Vietnamese Army soldiers. Pith helmets, web gear, but no packs. This was a combat patrol, not tax collectors or infiltrating soldiers. Were they on the prowl as a result of Le Kinh's ambush?

The ambushers were in terrible danger. The enemy platoon seemed to move in slow motion. Sweat trickled down the Marine's face. Death whispered in his ear. Come. Come to me. Softly, but not urgently. Scared into immobility, the ambushers froze. Eyes closed. Prayers were sent to Buddha and to God. The enemy patrol paused. A young lieutenant who wore the red shoulder tabs of his rank pointed up one trail and then the other. Half the men went up each branch. Had they entered the killing zone simultaneously? Steve would have initiated his Claymore ambush only if he could be certain all the men were within the kill zones. But one was through their killing zone before the other even entered theirs. Steve exhaled with relief as the soldiers disappeared from sight. He glanced at his watch. It was nearly four o'clock. Almost time to bug out. But what were those people up to? He wondered. And then it came to him. Jesus Christ! They were clearing the path for that paymaster. They are moving back from Quang Tri to Gio Linh. The bastard has been hiding out in the tunnels. He'll be ditty-bobbing down the trail shortly.

Four thirty came. The ambushers remained in place. Nothing happened. Five o'clock. Five thirty. Steve was sure he was right about the paymaster coming along just any time. The sky had grown visibly lighter. It was time for the laborers to wake, to heat their pots of rice, and to make their way to the fields. That's it, Steve thought. He'll come down the trail disguised as a farmer. He'll join a group walking to the fields. He'll blend in and walk right past us. How will I know him? I don't know, but I'll know him when I see him. He'll be coming down that trail from Gio Linh as bold as brass, but he's going to do something to give himself away.

Soon, there were villagers on the path, negating the Claymore ambush. Boys rode fat big horned water buffalo past the ambushers. Women carried goods to the market on chogi sticks balanced across their shoulders. Was it a man? It could be a woman. That would complicate things. Could it be a woman carrying the pay in one of those baskets suspended from the chogi sticks?

But then Steve spotted a man and somehow knew instantly that this was the paymaster they had been waiting for. He was dressed in black trousers and a wrinkled plaid shirt like the workers he was trying to blend in with. His sandals were the same. But he was more erect, of a different attitude, less downtrodden by life. His hair was short and clipped neatly in a military fashion. And he carried a backpack casually, as if it were perhaps his lunch. His eyes, though, were the final giveaway. They were furtive and searching.

After the man had passed his position, Steve sprang out of hiding, his rifle in his shoulder, and ready to fire. The ambushers, although surprised, came out of hiding as well. The shocked villagers stopped in their tracks, knowing Americans often shot at anyone who ran.

"Lan, tell them to put their hands on their heads."

That done, Steve issued another instruction. "Everyone on their knees." He had locked eyes with the suspect, daring him to defy one of the orders. The man calmly dropped to his knees. "Now, on their stomachs." That done, he ordered them to assume a spread eagle position. Steve's rifle barrel had not wavered an eighth of an inch from his suspect.

Steve instructed Lan and two others to flank the people on the ground. And then one by one, using descriptions such as "the woman in the purple blouse," he had Lan tell them to go. He was thinning out the number of people he would have to deal with if this thing went bad. Steve would not give this man a chance to get away. He walked up behind him and struck him a vicious blow between the shoulder blades with the butt of his rifle, following up with a club to the head. The enemy soldier was unconscious. Steve moved in quickly to bind his hands tightly behind his back. He then used medical wrapping to blindfold the man. The enemy soldier was slow to come around, but by the time he did, Steve had opened the pack he'd been carrying. It was full of bundles of South Vietnamese bills. A helicopter was already inbound to pick up the prisoner and the patrol.

None of the Vietnamese had been on a helicopter before. Steve assured that each rifle was cleared and safe before they boarded. Lan leaned into him, shuddering with fright during the short trip to the combat base. There was more than just body heat being exchanged between them. The helicopter was met by Major Hamlin and the G-2 colonel. Both were smiling. A pair of Marine MPs took custody of the prisoner. A Vietnamese officer escorted the ambushers to the chow hall where they were served a special meal. Steve was escorted to the intelligence office.

The major unhooked the captured pack, saying, "Let's see what we've got."

He dumped the contents onto the desktop. The men began counting, bundling the money in stacks of $1,000 each.

"Two hundred, thirty thousand dollars," the colonel said. "That's quite a payday."

The major began inspecting the pack. He found a poorly concealed compartment. Inside, folded, were three pages of typed documents. He read for a moment, growing big eyes. "Son of a bitch!"

"What is it?" the colonel asked.

"The payroll list. This is the name and address of every enemy cadre member in Quang Tri Province. South Vietnamese Army officers, government officials, policemen, women, the whole gauntlet."

Two hundred-seventy-one parties were named along with the amount they were to receive. Some would obviously be paying others down their chain of command. The highest-ranking judges, police officers, and Army commanders not on the list were quickly located and delivered to Quang Tri Combat Base for their protection. Two trusted but guarded judges signed arrest warrants for all the parties listed.

A plan to arrest as many of the named parties as possible without alerting the others was quickly set into place.

"Some of them will undoubtedly get away," the major told Steve. "But we'll get the majority of them, and the others will have been exposed. Well done, Corporal."

Many of the arrests were to take place at the daily briefing at the citadel in Quang Tri City. The briefing known as the five o'clock follies in Saigon was much less a circus in the serious venue at I Corp. Fewer news reporters and senior commanders usually attended the intelligence briefing at Quang Tri's Citadel. The night's action, however, had sparked interest and curiosity. Intelligence officers and commanders themselves were in attendance. They usually sent very junior subordinates to handle the boring details of what other units in I Corp were doing on a daily basis.

Unit by unit, the representatives stood and reported, usually with "nothing to report," as they were anxious to hear from the First Battalion, 3rd Marine Regiment, which had been purposely left for last. Looking around while waiting to report, Steve observed that the G-2, the Third Marine Division's top intelligence officer and a full colonel, was in attendance. He was the ultimate commander of all Marine Corps S-2 units in the division.

"The First of the Third," the ARVN general who conducted the briefing miscalled the Marine battalion.

Captain Maxwell stood. "First Battalion, Third Marine Regiment, S-2. I will defer to the battalion's S-6."

He sat. Steve stood. Colonels, majors, and captains shifted in their seats.

They could all see the insignia of Steve's rank on his collar. After months of representing the battalion at these meetings and then debriefing his own battalion's officers, the young Marine had become a confident speaker whom the attendees had come to trust.

"Corporal Kowalski, acting civil affairs officer and chief intelligence scout. You are aware from previous reports of the activities of the CAP unit at Thach Hanh and the intelligence operation we run from that location. Acting upon that intelligence, we conducted an ambush at 973481 early this morning."

Steve reached down to retrieve a small packet from his chair. He walked over and handed it to the Marine G-2 officer, who looked at him questioningly. The corporal continued speaking.

"Results of an ambush conducted by seven U.S. Marines supported by Seal Team Four and five South Vietnamese self-defense force cadre was the capture of Lieutenant Duong, supply officer for the B-5 Front. Almost two hundred, fifty thousand dollars in currency was recovered from his pack," Steve said, pointing to the pack he'd left in his chair.

"This building has been quietly surrounded by U.S. Army Military Police."

The announcement seemed to startle everyone except Captain Maxwell. It was a bold move with potentially serious political consequences. While attention was focused on the corporal, the captain had quietly moved to place his back against a wall. He unhooked the holster flap of his sidearm as Steve continued with his surprise announcement.

"Along with the cash and other documents seized, a list of V.C. cadre and agents in the immediate vicinity of Quang Tri City was recovered."

Amid the gasps of surprise at the magnitude of the intelligence coup, Steve extracted the list from his pocket. "With the cooperation of the Division's Provost Marshall and the Quan Chanh, these individuals are currently being arrested...including several presently in attendance at this briefing."

The room was suddenly in a state of turmoil as faces were examined, accusations were leveled, and fights broke out as several South Vietnamese officers attempted to escape. Others tried to get their weapons out of holsters. The one who did manage to do so took his own life.

The arrests, trials, tortures, and executions resulting from the intelligence coup were strictly a South Vietnamese issue. Corporal Kowalski was awarded his second Naval Commendation Medal. His presence and work in Thach Hanh continued. However, the villagers had a new sense of pride in their self-defense force. Kowalski enjoyed a high degree of renewed respect.

A week later, the major, Captain Maxwell, and a Marine Corps general with his entourage arrived in Thach Hanh. Steve was instructed to form ranks as if for a parade. With everyone watching, all the Americans and Steve's ambush unit were awarded commendation medals. The Army rewarded their success with a largess of military and comfort goods. With the captured funds, several programs were initiated to benefit the villagers. Under the guise of U.S. Aid, agricultural machinery was delivered. Some villagers received gifts of cattle, others pigs, and many were given sacks of rice seed, all of an "improved" variety according to American standards. It provided Steve an opportunity to pay off his agents in larger sums. A significant number of thatch huts were torn down and replaced with simple concrete block structures. The Army annexed the building next door to their location and turned it into an armory. The clinic, living quarters, and armory were turned into a complex. A floating dock and quarters were established on the west bank of the river near the bridge for the SEAL unit. Two members were added to the Navy team and four to the Army roster. At least half those men outranked Steve, yet he remained in charge of the Marine Corps program.

Through CIA funding, a sub-unit of twenty-six paid citizen soldiers was added to the CAP unit ranks. Along with that, new weapons were issued. Training continued with the new recruits being brought up to date. That training was excellent, being conducted by the best the Navy, the Army, and the Marines had to offer. Intelligence efforts continued. Additional agents were recruited. One of them was the old lady who baked the French bread sold near the bridge every day. She routinely traveled to the city to purchase flour and other products.

A fisherman who traveled up and down the river daily was also recruited. A bus driver completed the additions. As well placed as they might be, Steve worried about the Vietnamese possibly being double agents. The moves, however, did have almost immediate benefits. The fisherman reported a village downstream, Xa Hai Truong, had suddenly begun buying much more fish than the villagers could possibly eat. Steve paid the fisherman a small bonus for this bit of information.

The Marine mulled over the information, considering the possibilities. Over dinner, which he had begun to have with the Quocs more frequently, he mentioned the fisherman's information to Lan. The girl took him by the hand and led him to the kitchen. She opened a cabinet, revealing half-gallon-sized glass jars. In each was some type of fuzzy flakes. The jars were labeled in Vietnamese, which Steve could not read. Lan took the jars off the shelf one by one. "Tuna...tilapia.." and so on.

"How?"

"We cut fresh fish into steaks. These are grilled slowly. As they cook and dry out, they are gently separated into flakes. The flakes are totally dehydrated. The fish lasts a long time that way." She pulled down a jar of thick liquid. "The oil is gathered and used as a flavoring for rice and noodles. You see, we buy goods when they are available. When there is a good catch, we buy and preserve it for those times when food is less available."

It was a reasonable explanation, one that explained the stores of goods such as bags of rice in most homes. Steve wanted to trust Lan, but at this point he was not absolutely sure of who he could fully trust. Without telling Lan or anyone else, he quietly sent Saah on an intelligence gathering mission to verify a vague report he had received of V.C. activity in a nearby village. After two trips, the elderly woman's reports were inconclusive. Steve sent the fruit sellers with a boatload of fresh goods to call on the village.

"They reported a lot of young men who tried to remain unseen, "Steve reported to the major.

"Is this village within five hundred meters of a waterway?"

"I believe it is, sir."

"Then it will come under the Navy's authority. Of course, if requested through proper channels, you will render all assistance possible."

"I understand, sir." What Steve understood more than anything else was the convoluted chain of authority that often shackled all types of operations except when under direct attack, even to the point of not firing upon the enemy until he fired at you first. The reasons for this were what Steve could not understand.

"Well, keep up the good work then, Corporal."

Steve took his leave and his cue. Without actually saying so, the major had told him to work through the SEALS. Upon returning to Thach Hanh, Steve presented himself at the SEAL compound.

"Pass me a cold one and gather around, heroes," Steve requested.

A beer flew through the air. Steve caught it with one hand.

"Show off," Scott said.

With the SEALS gathered around, Steve related his suspicions about the village and his predicament, the need for them to undertake the operation, and to request his assistance.

"What are you thinking?" Scott asked.

"A recon by you guys first. Find out the truth about what's going on in that village. We'll go from there."

The SEALS studied the map. "Has to be a nighttime operation."

"Of course."

"We can't give them any warning of what's to come, so we have to avoid contact. We don't even want to run a routine patrol in the vicinity. In and out without being seen or heard."

"They'll never know we were there."

"This is a Navy operation. You'll have to formally request our assistance if there are enough enemy soldiers in that village to warrant it."

"Not before the attack. It would never be approved."

"I can have a nighttime ambush set up in the next village over. We'll be the closest unit able to respond to your cry for help."

"Make that request for assistance," Rocco insisted firmly.

The SEALS picked an overcast, stormy night for their reconnaissance. Four dark-clad divers dropped into the water south of the village. Their faces were camouflaged with grease paint. They were swimmers, not divers, on this operation. Lightly armed with pistols and fighting knives, they carried no explosives or other equipment. It was just about as "naked" or "slick" as the SEALS ever get.

They drifted in rafts with the current toward the village. The SEALS dropped into the water half a mile from the objective. The SEALS were not the only predators in the water. Another even more silent danger with better senses became aware of the intrusion of his hunting grounds. With barely a ripple, he slid into the water. He was quieter in the water, more streamlined, and faster than his prey. The prey was swimming in a herd, giving off heat, which helped to locate them as a group and individually as he moved closer. They dove and swam clumsily, then rose for air. Perhaps the prey had been injured. The twenty-two-foot-long, three hundred-pound poisonous blood python had lived many years in this marsh and jungle. He had taken every kind of prey in his environment, including humans.

The python sensed the swimmers positioned in a row. He perceived the last in line to be the slowest, the weakest, and the easiest to take. The python's timing was perfect. He caught up with the swimmer and angled toward him. As the man dove the python's wide jaws clamped down on his left leg. The incredibly strong reptile used the prey's momentum to continue carrying him to the bottom of the river as he coiled his long body around the smaller creature. The incredible force of the snake's constrictions broke ribs and forced lungs to empty. There was little chance for the man to struggle. There was even less chance for him to survive.

Three SEALS, unaware of their teammate's plight, swam on, focused on their mission. They came out of the water at twenty-second intervals, separated, still unaware that one of their members was missing. The SEALs had assumed there would be guards. Stealth was one of the many attributes of SEALs. The ability to operate alone if required was another. The Americans came ashore silently, unseen. They began searching for those guards. They looked. They listened. They sniffed the air. They moved quietly. They were not rushed. They worked independently, planning to compare notes on their findings at the rendezvous point half a mile down the river.

Scott heard a guard making his rounds. He made no attempt at stealth as he walked his post. He broke twigs and crushed them under his feet. Rocco avoided a guard who gave away his location by sneezing. They were the only guards on duty. The SEALs crept as silently as shadows into the village. They fixed locations and distances in their minds.

Trained to be observant, the SEALs missed little. Like savants, they counted everything. The number of cooking pots, the pairs of shoes left outside the hootches. They looked for signs of women and children. They looked for baskets of supplies and bundles of rice, for weapons, at all the signs of activity. They noted newly dug trenches and fighting holes. Two recently constructed bunkers were discovered. The SEALs didn't take anything. They didn't move anything. Once each man was satisfied that he had covered the village completely, he melted back into the river, stroking strongly under water to get as far away from the village as he could as fast as he could without being observed.

Within an hour of one another, three SEALs had gathered at the rendezvous point. They waited in silence for their missing team member, their concern growing by the minute. An hour passed. They would have to move soon. There had been no shots fired. No shouts of discovery had been heard. Scott wondered if the mission had been compromised. Had the enemy been alerted? The team wondered and waited as long as they could.

"He's a big guy. He'll find his way back," Rocco assured the men. It was past dawn when the SEALs reported to Steve.

Informing him of the missing party, Scott told Steve, "We can't search for him. We can't even run a boat upstream, not tonight, not tomorrow. Not until after the operation is concluded."

"It's still on? You know it could be compromised. You could be walking into a well-planned trap."

"I say bomb it and forget it," Sammy said.

Steve stood. "I'm going to send one of my agents in for a look tomorrow."

"Very dangerous. They might be looking for someone to come nosing around."

"Saah is a stooped eighty-year-old woman with cataracts. No one will suspect her if they see her gathering wood."

"Send her in, but not directly. Have her gather wood nearby, but keep an eye on the village." "And be on the lookout for our missing man. He may be injured."

"If she spots him, tell her to run away, not to approach him, but to act as if she is scared of him."

"I'll have her come straight back and report his condition and location to me."

"So, we'll know by tomorrow night if this thing is a go?"

"If everything goes right with Saah."

Saah, staunchly anti-communist, seemed to relish her role as Steve's eyes and ears. In spite of her physical limitations, she readily agreed to undertake the dangerous reconnaissance mission. She refused to be ferried part way by the SEAL team. Dressed in the peasant fashion of clothing she never seemed to change, the woman tightened her coarse gray hair into a bun, donned her straw hat, and strapped on a wood gathering pack. She shuffled out of the village at first light. Steve admired the wizened old woman. He thought her quite heroic.

But Steve worried about his agent throughout the day. He continued his daily routine of interacting with the SEALs and paid a brief visit to the Army compound. He walked the village streets.

He learned that the long, unmarked dirt road paralleling the river was Phan Chu Tinh Street. He greeted people, all the while watching and learning. He stopped to talk and gave a cigarette to a man who was too old to work in the fields. He swept doorways with a home-made broom.

Steve delivered a case of C-rations to the nuns. He had lunch at the restaurant, supplying the basics from his own rations. Spaghetti and meatballs, a dish that was new to the Vietnamese. The cook added garlic, French bread, and a salad with a bit of an unusual taste. The greens were different than anything Steve had tasted before. Some of them had a touch of pepper like heat, others a hint of mint. The salad included mung beans, bamboo shoots, bean sprouts and crushed peanuts. The dressing was a mixture of olive oil, vinegar, and soy sauce. The blended tastes appealed to the Marine.

Late in the afternoon, a heavily burdened, obviously exhausted Saah slowly worked her way toward Thach Hanh, stopping to drop off the day's gathering at her regular customers who would burn the wood she had delivered in cooking their evening meals. Steve wanted to hustle her into his tent for a debriefing, but appearances had to be maintained. Saah was in no hurry. She would not report directly to Steve. The wood she had gathered was from one to two inches in diameter. It had been chopped into three and four foot lengths. The old woman was obviously tired. There were large sweat rings at her armpits and around her neck. Steve watched but didn't move to help her as the old woman delivered a bundle to the baker, saving the last, as always, for the restaurant.

Saah typically sat and drank a Vietnamese coffee, a mixture of half cream, one quarter sugar, and thick local coffee over ice. At some of her stops, Saah had been paid in rice. At others she was paid a fish or a cut of pork. She was seldom paid in cash, but from time to time she was able to sell her goods for a bit of cash at the restaurant. Her presence there was normal, completely routine, as was Steve's. She did not approach or communicate with the Marine who flirted with the young waitresses throughout his meal.

The daily parade of schoolgirls returning to their homes passed by. A bus from the combat base discharged its load of women who worked for the Americans there. Fishermen delivered their fresh catch. Fires were lit, burning Saah's wood as meals were cooked. Laborers returned from the rice paddies.

The sun set. Dogs yawned widely, stretched, and curled up for sleep. Steve returned to his tent where Le Kinh and Saah were waiting for him. The Marine fired up the cooker in the center of his tent. The Vietnamese watched silently as Steve prepared sweet cocoa drinks from his C-rations. He offered them cigarettes. They sat down to discuss Saah's observations with Le Kinh translating.

"She says she gathers wood slowly, like an old woman. She watches and works her way slowly toward the village. She stops often to chop wood, rest, and watch."

"She's crafty and fearless," Steve commented.

Saah smiled and cackled at the translation.

"She moves into trees, gathering wood. Two young men dressed in black come to talk. They are soldiers but carry no weapons. She knows they V.C. They give her fish for wood but ask her questions."

"What kind of questions?"

"Who is she? Where is she from? What does she do? And political questions."

"I assume she satisfied them."

"She is a right-thinking woman. She says she will report on Americans."

Steve was almost shocked. Perfect! He thought. Now he would have an agent inside the enemy camp.

"The soldiers will help her. Gather wood for her. She must report."

"That's good. Is she up to this?"

The Vietnamese chatted a moment before Le Kinh translated. "She will tell them lies."

"No!" Steve said emphatically. He could see the surprise and questions on their faces.

"We must not put her in such danger. We know V.C. agents must be reporting our presence here. She will report to them what they already know. What anyone can see. How many of us there are, what combat weapons we carry, what we do daily, the things every villager can see for themselves. In this way she will earn their trust."

Saah smiled widely through betel-stained teeth and lips at that and even wider when she was given ten dollars in military payment currency and two C-ration meals. The intelligence was worth much more. Steve did not tell Saah what to say or what to tell the soldiers who questioned her. He wanted her answers to come instantly and naturally. It took only a brief time for this approach to return positive results.

On the following day, Saah approached the village directly, observing it from another point of view. Again, one of the soldiers came out to confront her. Saah revealed the number of Americans in Thach Hanh, their weapons and location, and what she had seen of the weapons they carried. She revealed the location of bunkers, trenches, and fighting holes, each of which would be moved soon.

Saah had little to report to Steve for several days. Finally, as he had hoped for, the pair of soldiers had allowed the old woman into their buildings. She was given a small package to deliver to a person they named who lived in the north half of Thach Hanh.

"Bingo!" Steve said. He now knew the identity of at least one of the enemy agents in Thach Hanh. He knew it was the lean, rough-faced man of early middle age who worked at the nearby ice house.

"We will remove him," Le Kinh said in a quite deadly manner.

"No," Steve warned. "That will point to Saah. We know who he is. We will use that knowledge. Tell Saah to deliver the packet. We'll keep an eye on this guy; see where he goes, what he does, who he visits, and who visits him. We'll gather him up when the time is right."

There was an element of risk and danger in this course of action. Steve felt they were outweighed by the potential benefits. Several days passed, enough time for a report of Saah's delivery of the packet to return to the senders. On her next visit to the village, Saah was surprised by the activity she observed. In the forest where wood had been stacked for her to gather, the elderly woman spotted a newly constructed machine gun bunker. She reported to Steve on this and on counting twenty-one soldiers, recalling a surprising amount of details about them.

The questions remained: who are they and what are they doing there? Steve reported to Major Hamlin.

"That's incredibly good work by all of you," the major complimented him.

"We plan to hit them within a week, major. I'll need some clearances for what we are going to do and some support during training but none in the operational phase."

"Keeping in mind that this is a naval operation, what is your plan?"

The SEALS are going in under cover of darkness. Their first objective is to take that bunker, silently if possible. I'll have a CAP unit on ambush about 4,000 meters away."

"Along a fast relief route, I assume."

"Yes, sir. We'll arrive pretty much on the run. The SEALs won't call us up until they have to or until first light when my ambush team would be pulling out. First they'll put in a call that they are under fire and need assistance."

"To which you will respond with your proximity."

"Affirmative, sir."

"Show me." The major stepped over to the current situation map. Steve picked up a pointer.

"Here's the village. The SEAL team will swim in. Here's our ambush point. It will take an early night march for us to get there."

"What's your strength?"

"A couple of dozen at least."

"And the SEALs?"

"Four going in. Two behind at Thach Hanh.

"Your force?"

"Myself, two Army, my experienced scout, and a thirteen-man CAP squad reinforced by a machine gun team and a mortar crew."

"I don't like those numbers, Kowalski."

"It is a little light, major, but it has to be in order to be plausible."

"Well, you do have the element of surprise."

"And I expect those SEALs to even the numbers out a bit before the major action begins. And I think we'll have a second element of surprise with the swift arrival from another direction of my forces as well as the supporting mortar."

"So, the SEALs in that bunker would be firing from the south to the northwest. You'll be north of them and approaching and firing from the northeast."

"We'll have them in a crossfire."

"Can you get some more help from that Army detachment?"

"They are providing significant support using all their personnel. Two of them will be with us. Two will remain in Thach Hanh to secure their compound. The other six will split into two teams. They will arrest the two V.C.s we've identified in the village."

"I can't fault that plan. Your night ambush at the indicated position is approved."

Steve returned to Thach Hanh to set the plan into motion. All the way back to the village, Steve worried about this operation. What would happen if the SEALs were discovered? What if they couldn't take the bunker without alerting the enemy unit in the village? What if he lost a member of the CAP unit? How would his irregular defense force react to adversity under fire?

Who was to be taken on this mission? He needed the best of the lot. What message would that send to the persons who were not chosen? For the sake of morale, he would have to include at least two women in the assault force. What if one of them was wounded or killed? How would the village react?

Security was an issue. Not only would he have to carefully brief the reinforced squad he was taking with him, he would have to conduct practice assaults. That couldn't be done in or near the village. Steve decided on a rather elaborate ruse to solve that problem. He had some help from the major with the logistics and clearances required. Steve then met with the CAP unit to explain the operation and make choices.

"We are going to provide a reinforced squad for an operation. There is a strong element of danger involved. We will be gone from the village for four to six days. I will only select the team from those who volunteer. All who wish to volunteer, please step across the street."

The Marine was not surprised when every CAP member and the trained volunteers with weapons of their own gathered in formation on the opposite side of the street. "Now comes the hard part," he told Gary.

"Lan," he announced. Everyone knew she was the best mortar gunner among them all. Steve motioned for her to join him.

"Hanh." She was the best rifleman among the women. Steve chose twelve others judged to be the most stout-hearted and best-trained riflemen to fill out his basic rifle squad. He appointed Le Kinh as their squad leader. He chose another female, an unusually stout woman, a mother with a six-month-old child, to be his radioman. His last selection was the best machine gunner among the unit. The gun and mortar crews were selected by those he had chosen to be in charge of the crew-served weapons.

The selected personnel gathered in Steve's tent where he conducted his first briefing. He gathered the complete team: four SEALs, two soldiers, Le Kinh, Lan and her three-person mortar crew, thirteen riflemen, and the machine gunner and his three-man crew, twenty-eight total.

Through Le Kinh, Steve issued his instructions. "This is our combat loadout. Nothing more, nothing less."

He picked up a set of camouflaged utilities. "You must not look like villagers. You will wear this uniform." He set out a pair of American jungle boots. He held up an M-16 rifle. "Your footwear. Your primary weapon. Eight clips of ammunition. A bandolier of one hundred extra bullets. Two canteens of water."

Steve paused a moment. "We won't need packs. This action is going to be short and swift. You will not need rations." He picked up a white canvas vest. The vest was full of sewn pockets. He slipped it over his head like a poncho. Le Kinh helped fill three pockets on the Marine's back. Steve filled the two on the front. "Each of you will carry five sixty-millimeter mortar rounds. We will leave them with Lan prior to moving into our final assault positions."

Steve looked at his watch. "We will board a U.S. Navy ship in the Port of Quang Tri. Be back here ready to go in one hour."

By loading aboard a ship and by not revealing the target or other forces involved, Steve knew he would create more questions, confusion, and gossip. That was intended to get back to the North Vietnamese via their V.C. agents in the village. Going out by ship would lead them to think the operation was to be conducted some distance from the village, perhaps on the coast.

Two hours later, the unit was aboard a U.S. Navy destroyer that was departing for operations in the Gulf of Tonkin. None of the Vietnamese had been aboard a warship or even a ship of any size. From the moment the ship pulled away from the pier under its own power, the Vietnamese hung over the rails, every one of them seasick. They were on the ship for only two hours, just long enough to disappear over the horizon. This class of destroyer had been constructed with a helicopter landing pad at the front of the ship. One at a time, two Navy Sea Knight helicopters landed, taking on CAP members. Most of the Vietnamese had never flown in a helicopter. So far, their mission has proven to be the most frightening event of their lives.

The flight of helicopters was joined by a sleek Cobra gunship. They turned to the west and were soon "feet dry" and flying over Quang Tri City and Thach Hanh. The helicopters landed at Hill 10, the most remote section of Quang Tri Combat Base, the ammunition dump, which held a ten-day reserve supply of ammunition for the Third Marine Division.

A general-purpose tent the same size as Steve's had been erected for the squad. A Marine corporal pointed out the locations of their bunker and fighting holes in case of an attack during their brief residence. As a unit, they ate in the division mess hall, delighted by the hamburgers, French fries, and soda pops being served.

Early the next morning, Steve briefed the unit again, using a sand table model and explaining the mission fully.

"This is Xa Hai Truong. It is three hundred meters from the Thach Hanh River. The village backs up to a tree line. In that tree line covering the village and river approaches is a mounded machine gun bunker.

"Our first objective is to neutralize that bunker silently, without warning the enemy squad in the village. That part of the operation will be carried out by a team of U.S. Navy SEALs. Our only support will be from our sixty mortars. Steve pointed to a spot on the map. "We will make our way to this location. We will drop our vests there. Lan and Roger will set up the mortar and prepare to fire in support of our assault. The assault team will move forward to locations about three hundred meters from the target. Our machine gun, Jay and Gary, will be located right here.

"The SEAL team, the machine gunners, the mortar crew and the assault squad will all have radios." Steve noted the frequencies and code words. "This is a SEAL operation. Scott is the overall commander. After they have secured the bunker, they will turn their own weapons against the North Vietnamese. We will commence our attack upon their order to do so or when they commence firing upon the village.

"The mortars will open up at the same time. The effectiveness of the weapons' assault will determine when we move in on foot." Steve explained his contingency plan. On a course laid out by the SEALs, the squad walked through their attack plan. Then they ran through a live fire exercise. Relative locations and distances based upon Saah's observations and counted steps were fixed in their minds after repeatedly practicing the assault.

The squad was encouraged to sleep in on the morning the operation was to begin. At mid-morning, Steve held a weapons inspection. He made sure every member of the force knew the radio frequencies, codes, and rendezvous point in case the squad got scattered or someone got separated. No matter how little they might have been used, all radio batteries were replaced with new ones.

The team members ate a light lunch. They napped, talked nervously, wiped their weapons repeatedly, and ate a dinner meal of beef stew and cornbread. Almost unnoticed, the SEALs left. Steve assembled his squad with their weapons and equipment at dusk. Le Kinh and the Americans went down the line, applying grease paint in black, yellow, and green to all exposed flesh. A transport truck arrived. The squad climbed over the tailgate. A half-hour ride later, the truck pulled off to the shoulder of a crushed gravel road. The squad was discharged 12,000 meters short of their target. They would have a long march to get into place.

The SEALs were delivered by helicopter. They dropped into the river two miles upstream from the target. They did not use diving gear. They were dressed and equipped as infantry. Spending most of their time swimming underwater close to the bank, the SEAL team made its way down river for another mile.

The Seals slithered silently ashore. Progress was as slow as a patient cat stalking a nervous bird. The grass and brush hardly seemed to move as the four-man team moved inland six hundred meters to get behind and west of the bunker. They moved, stopped, looked, and listened. They sniffed the air. They moved forward again. Repeating this approach, it took them almost two hours to move six hundred meters. Closing in on their objective, they turned to the south. They moved south in the same stealthy manner for another hour. If their intelligence was good and their sense of direction and movement were accurate, they should be closing in on the bunker. Instead of moving toward the target, they were now searching for that bunker. The success of the operation depended upon their locating and securing that position.

There was no fire or smell of burning wood to give the bunker's location away. There was no movement or conversation. No cigarettes had been lit. No glowing tips were seen. During one of the periods of Stop! Look! Listen! A fortuitous sound alerted the SEALs to the enemy presence. It wasn't a slap at a mosquito, a cough, or a sneeze, but rather a rumbling fart that revealed the enemy's location.

The team made a slight change in direction as they closed in on the bunker. It was well concealed, even from the back. The Americans came upon it suddenly. A space had been cleared for about thirty meters in diameter around what would be the peripheral vision of the gunner inside the bunker. Tree stumps had been left in place. The timber had undoubtedly been used in the construction of the bunker. The experienced combat veterans had seen this kind of construction before. A large hole had been dug several feet deep. Trunks and branches had been woven into a roof with double, almost laminated layers. Dirt from the excavation had been used to form a mound over the gun pit. A carpet of dead, dry leaves and twigs had been spread over the mound and in the clearing. The bunker had been constructed of native materials, not concrete and steel. Still, it was a hardened position. The aperture for the machine gun was a horizontal slot four feet long by three inches wide.

The bunker gave off a faint, pleasant scent like cinnamon. From this, Scott knew the material used in the bunker's construction to be Vietnamese mahogany, also known as iron redwood. Growing unbranched to a height of fifty feet, the 200-foot tall tree could have a diameter of over eight feet. Excellent for quick and strong construction.

The bunker had a single entry. That was guarded by an alert soldier facing outboard. This changed the entire plan of attack. The SEALs, however, were flexible.

While the SEALs were in their lengthy approach, the infantry force hit the ground running, getting away from the truck as quickly as possible. The driver turned his vehicle around and hurried back to the combat base. The squad was swallowed by the night. With Le Kinh on point and Steve bringing up the rear, the squad formed two columns separated by ten meters. They forcefully marched over sparsely covered dry ground for nine thousand meters without being detected.

The squad reached the point where Lan and Roger would set up the mortar. The squad thankfully dropped their heavy ammunition vests at that location. Steve helped Lan struggle out of hers. "Good luck, sweetheart," he said as he moved the infantrymen forward.

"I no say for you," she hissed in a whisper.

Crouching, the patrol moved forward in fire team rushes. They covered the last three hundred meters on their knees and bellies. Le Kinh positioned his riflemen on a line about ten feet apart. The squad settled in to wait, watching the quiet village to their south.

Lan and Roger began unloading and stacking mortar shells. Roger set the range by adjusting the elevation of the tube. Lan established the aiming point. They waited.

The SEAL team was in position. Each member of the team knew what he had to do. On signal, they rushed from the shadows. There were no whoops or hollers, only four shadows rushing toward the enemy soldiers. The drowsy guard heard a sound. His head snapped up to look. He spotted the yellow twinkling of gunshots. Simultaneously, he heard four rifles firing on automatic. He felt bullets rip into his neck, his chest, and his stomach. The impact tossed him backwards into the bunker entrance. Neither of the machine gunners could see past him to fire on the SEALs.

Scott dropped his rifle while continuing his rush forward. Using the guard's body as a shield, he forced his way into the confined bunker, surprising the NVA. He had his pistol in one hand and found the fighting knife strapped to his leg with the other. He fired his pistol with the barrel jammed against a soldier's ear. The shot sounded like an explosion inside the bunker. A bloody mass of brains was blown against the opposite wall.

The remaining guard was paralyzed by shock and fear. He never recovered from the surprise of seeing his companions killed swiftly and violently. From behind, a knife tore through his kidney, and at the same moment another skewered his heart. Quickly, knowing they had only seconds before coming under fire from the village, the SEALs took up positions at the machine gun , one of them firing, another loading. One of the other two grabbed a shoulder-fired B-7 tube and half a dozen rocket-propelled grenades. He would fire the weapon while the fourth member of the team reloaded. After that form of mini-artillery was exhausted, they would immediately become riflemen.

Lan had heard the commencement of the battle. Using both hands to drop the mortar down the tube, she turned away with her fingers in her ears, her mouth open as she had been taught. Thunk! The mortar shot out of the tube. She didn't see or hear it explode. The soldier had not passed her another round. He seemed to be listening to the radio. Then she understood.

He gave her a thumbs up sign of approval. He shouted, "Up twenty, right fifty!"

Lan made the adjustments, thinking their first round had been very close. She was pleased and proud. Roger handed her a mortar shell, which she fed into the tube. She moved the tube one click either up or down and always one click to the right, twenty rounds in ten minutes. They were then ordered to move the gun to the left one click at a time, using the same sustained rate of fire.

Afterwards, while waiting for additional firing instructions, Lan wondered how the attack had progressed and how Steve was doing. While she denied it to everyone, Lan knew her heart was out there with a man who had a rifle in his hands.

The ambush squad had expected to hear a machine gun open up. Rifles had joined in immediately. With only a moment's hesitation, Steve was up hollering "Fire!" His M-16 was in his shoulder. He was aiming his fire in three round bursts through windows and doors. For the most part, the squad members were firing their weapons on full automatic, simply pointing them in the direction of their targets, most of their marksmanship lessons forgotten in the heat of the moment. Steve had noted the failure and would address it with more training.

Le Kinh, however, was not in a mood to wait. He moved from person to person, teaching them to exercise fire discipline and to aim their shots. He slowly gained control with the squad, maintaining a rate of fire to his satisfaction. The machine gun opened up from the right of the line and swept through the village to the left and then back again at a slightly different elevation. Most of the CAP members were unaware that they were being fired upon. They did not have the experience to know the puffs of dirt being kicked up around them were impacting bullets until one of the boys was hit. The bullet entered the base of his neck, traveled through soft tissue, and blew a fist-sized chunk of meat out as it traveled through his torso and exited through his rump.

Some of the NVA attempted to bug out from the rear of the huts into the nearby jungle. The SEALs in the bunker mowed them down. A hut took a direct hit from a mortar round, completely destroying it while killing six enemy soldiers. Coincidentally, the machine gun fire from both guns came together against one hut, shredding roof and walls. The heat of the glowing tracer rounds set the hut's roof on fire. Bullets killed four men inside. Smoke inhalation killed another. With the left side of the defense crushed, Steve led a four-man fire team forward to a position on an angle connecting the bunker to the west with the rifle squad to the south. It provided additional angles of fire and problems for the defenders.

Le Kinh saw and understood the tactic. He had a fire team holding down the right flank. He shifted the mortar fire in that direction, slightly beyond the village. Then, using a fire and adjust method, he directed the mortar until an almost direct hit was scored. The hut burned. The NVA soldiers exited front and rear. The SEALs cut down those exiting from the rear. The rifle squad decimated those trying to escape through the front door.

The remainder of the enemy, somewhat shielded by burning huts on both flanks, having nowhere to go, fought with desperation. The fire teams crept closer. The mortar fire was adjusted to impact just behind the hut, spraying those inside with deadly shrapnel and preventing their escape through the back.

The SEAL machine gun team, no longer needed to seal off the rear, repositioned themselves to anchor the west flank. Covering one another, one of the machine gun teams and the rifle fire team moved forward. Enemy defenses were weakening as the CAP unit soldiers advanced, continuing to fire their weapons as they moved. The radio operator fell with a surprised grunt. Her leg had collapsed beneath her. Bright red blood colored a trouser leg. Steve grabbed the girl and shielded her with his body. The fighting was at close quarters now. The strong-armed Americans administered the coup de gras with a hail of hand-thrown grenades. Le Kinh bandaged the wounded girl's painful but not serious wound.

The battle had lasted for thirty-nine minutes. The squad searched the area and lined up 31 NVA soldiers who had been killed. One of them was a young woman who had worn a pink blouse, sandals, and black trousers. She had died with a rifle in her hands. Steve was rather certain no one escaped the assault. The SEALs bagged up all the documents and tagged the weapons, which included SKS and AK-47 rifles, a machine gun , two pistols, a recaptured M-14, and several RPGs. There were bills, journals, letters, a photograph, and documents to be translated.

The Navy turned the follow-up actions over to the Army, as they had specialists who would sift through the ruins for anything of intelligence value. They would bring dogs and tunnel rats to search the surrounding countryside. The Navy didn't take prisoners, but the CAP unit did. While searching for bodies in the nearby woods, they had discovered a goat, two pigs, and seven chickens. In the huts they had not burned were approximately 500 pounds of rice. Steve heard and understood the words, "victory celebration". He radioed the major to advise him of the results and to invite him to attend the celebration.

A very pleased Major Hamlin came out in the helicopters sent to pick up the squad, three of them this time. One was loaded down with ammunition to replace what had been expended during the operation, a pallet of C-rations, and another pallet of beer. "My contribution to the party," the major offered.

Back at Thach Hanh, animals were slaughtered, chopped, and grilled. Onions, garlic, and other seasonings were added to pots of cooking rice. The C-ration meals provided a pot of spaghetti and another of beans and wieners, lima beans, spiced beef and potatoes, ham and eggs, and chicken and noodles. Pound cakes were chopped and added to a variety of fruit, peaches, apricots, and fruit cocktail, along with sugar and cinnamon to make a very tasty bread pudding. There were cigarettes and coffee for the adults, packs of Chicklets, cookies, jams, peanut butter crackers, and hot cocoa for the children.

The villagers contributed as well.

The wounded radio operator refused to stay in bed. She was a hero by all accounts, but not quite to the same degree as Steve. Over and over she told how he had shielded her from further injury with his own body. She claimed him as her personal hero, a man to whom she owed a life. When someone or something took Steve away from the adoring young woman, she hobbled her way to his side, ignoring the pain brought about by the movement.

Across a long, wide table set up for serving, Steve's searching eyes found Lan. There was a twinkle of amusement in those big brown eyes. With a nod toward the hobbling radio operator, Lan said, "She says for you." There was a giggle behind the hand that covered her mouth. Steve got up, chasing a mouth full of hot, spicy chicken with a half-can gulp of ice-cold Budweiser.

The legend of the Warlord of Thach Hanh, a name first applied to him by the radio operator who was constantly at Steve's side, was born. It seemed to grow by the minute. He and the village with its active CAP unit became a real concern for the local Viet Cong.

CHAPTER TWELVE
QUANG TRI COMBAT BASE

A week passed before Steve reported in person to the S-6 officer. After a full briefing on the ambush, he presented his case for another operation.

"Major," he said, "I know it's a little unorthodox, but I would like to conduct a training operation for my self-defense force."

"Toward what end, Corporal?"

"They need some seasoning under real combat conditions, sir."

"Are you proposing a combat operation, corporal?" The major seemed surprised.

"More of a light-running confidence builder, sir, a long patrol."

The major thought about that moment. "You do realize, of course, that an armed patrol could become engaged and suffer losses."

"Yes, sir. I'll only take volunteers."

"And if you encounter resistance?"

"Hold our ground if possible. Call for artillery support and whatever reaction force is required."

"Good in theory, but your experiences should tell you that theory only goes so far in combat."

"Yes, sir. I have to find out how these people will react under stress if we do nothing but carry rifles through rice paddies for a couple of hours."

"Do you have a military objective?"

"Yes, sir." Steve unfolded a map and spread it across the major's desk. "Xa Hai Phu, about six thousand meters south, southwest of Thach Hanh."

"Why Xa Hai Phu? It's hardly a dot on the map, half a dozen hootches at most."

"My intelligence says there is an NVA squad located there."

"Are they reinforced?"

"I've had a man watching them. For the past two weeks all he's seen is eleven soldiers, the same eleven all the time."

"They'll have tunnels and fighting holes, possibly a mortar and machine gun."

"Affirmative, sir. We've located their positions."

"They would be formidable for a squad of Marines. What makes you think two squads of misfits can handle them?"

"Pride, training and surprise, major."

"What's your plan of action?"

"About three a.m., under cover of darkness, when their guard will be at its lowest, we infiltrate the village. No one will know of our plans or actions except those of us who are going on the patrol. Quietly, we slip down the river beyond the target."

"Show me."

Steve pointed on the map. "You see this rounded arc of trees?"

"It looks artificial."

"Used to be a plantation, so it was cut that way."

"And this clearing cut into it like a wedge of pie?"

"That's where the village is located, so it has a broad view of rice paddies and the river to the front."

"Everywhere except through that thick growth of trees to the rear."

"Yes, sir."

"How do you propose to get through there undetected?"

"I've had a wood gatherer in there scouting, marking a trail for us."

"A brave man."

"Woman. Little old stooped thing, about 120 years old."

"Innocuous as anyone could possibly be."

"On my command, we attack with our weapons on full automatic, moving forward at a brisk pace."

"What if they bug out?"

"A green pop flare will be my signal to commence the attack...and for my mortar teams to be ready to fire if the NVA moves across that rice paddy."

"You think your people are disciplined enough to hold their fire until the enemy comes into range?"

"That's one of the questions I need answered, major."

"Well, then, you've got your operation, with one condition."

"What's that, major?"

"You bring in the SEAL team for support and leadership."

Steve smiled at that excellent idea. He had not included them. He had not mentioned his plan to them. He hadn't wanted a hint of it to get out until he was prepared to seek approval to conduct the operation.

There was one person in Thach Hanh Steve had trusted with his life. He'd earned that trust in the crucible of combat. That man was the former Viet Cong soldier Le Kinh. Steve would have to brief him into the plan and not only trust him but give him responsibility for selecting personnel and bringing them to an operational status.

The NVA and V.C. habitually used sand tables to make models of bases, towns, and facilities they planned to attack. The elaborate models were accurate to scale, challenging the finest works of professional architects and engineers. Steve had been trained to make models that were accurate but considerably less artistic and elaborate. Using a contour map where each irregular shape represented a difference of twenty meters In elevation, Steve used thick cardboard to form his map model. Their target was in the lower right quadrant of the sand table. Most of the model was devoted to the terrain approaching the target village.

The table was in Steve's tent. When not working on it, he kept it out of sight, covered by a poncho. Late at night, after the peasants who had labored hard in the rice paddles all day were asleep, Steve and Le Kinh worked on the model. Using clay from the river, the Kit Carson Scout smoothed out the rough edges of the cardboard. Colored clay formed the rivers and channels, complete with sand bars. Roads and footpaths were clearly defined. Using aerial photographs supplied by the major, terraced rice paddles were accurately depicted. Foam, twigs, and natural materials formed brush lines and thickets, even individual trees.

Paper, sand, clay, grass clippings, glue, and various coloring agents were all used. Whittled sticks depicted structures. Making the model took a week of concentrated effort until Le Kinh and Steve were both satisfied with the results. The planning of the attack did not take form until after the model was completed. At that point, Major Hamlin brought the Marines and SEALs together in Steve's tent.

Steve was quite impressed with the SEAL team's leader. It was easy to see how Rocco Bartinell had gotten his nickname. Brick wall also fit. Large-framed and heavily-muscled, the SEAL might have been only a few chromosomal alleles from a Neanderthal. Bull-necked and iron-jawed, the SEAL was an expert with small arms, explosives, and all aspects of combat.

When informed of the mission, Rocco reacted with candid doubts. "Well, that's quite an undertaking for a CAP unit. Do any of them have real combat experience?"

"Myself, Le Kinh, a disabled Viet Army sergeant."

"What about your support?"

"On standby without knowledge of our operation. We'll have machine gun and mortar teams on call in the village."

"The best use of my team would seem to be in cutting off the river traffic moving south from north of the bridge. We can get the Brown Water Navy to do the same south of your target. That leaves me and three others to get your troops down river and fit in with your assault plan."

"That's good," Steve said. "I'd love to keep you all together in one team, but on this operation I have a different role in mind for you."

The SEAL and the major both displayed poses questioning this action. Steve addressed the SEAL.

"These people are inexperienced and roughly trained. If the four of you will take up the roles of fire team leaders with three locals assigned to each of you, we'll have a squad with good leadership and experienced leadership. You can help serve as examples of what and how to do things properly. In essence, perform as instructors on a training mission, but a real mission at the same time. Le Kinh and Bui will each have a fire team. I'll be in overall charge."

"So," the major questioned, "four SEALS, one Marine, and twenty Vietnamese irregulars are going to take on an experienced NVA squad?"

"I'm sure the SEAL team could handle this by themselves. Major, but that's not the point or the mission."

"This could make your village a priority target for the local cadre."

"Not if they don't know who carried out the attack," Steve told them with a smile spreading across his face.

"What have you got up your sleeve, Kowalski?" the Major asked.

"No enemy survivors. We torch the village. We leave a trail to follow as we exfiltrate. Upon extraction, we leave one of their bodies and his weapon near the bank of the river. We put a few rounds into a SEAL raft, one that's been seen running up and down the river frequently and will be recognized."

The major sat back, exhaling in a rush at the audacity of the plan.

Rocco roared with laughter. "And so we become the target of the enemy's vengeance instead of your village?"

"You guys are just like us. I'd love for the dinks to come after me if I had a squad of Recon Marines at my back rather than a village full of women and children."

"You could almost be a SEAL with that kind of thinking, Kowalski."

"You could almost be a Marine with a little more work, Rocco."

The major enjoyed the exchange, knowing that the respect among the men flowed both ways but did not eliminate interservice rivalries. He stood before the exchange went further. "The operation is approved, gentlemen. The CAP unit has overall command, with Rocco as second. How much time do you need before conducting this operation?"

Rocco looked to Steve, who asked, "Can you be ready in four?"

"Five would be better. We'll have to get a couple more rubber boats in order to transfer all your people as well as one to replace the one we will sacrifice. We don't want to paddle and we don't want to run outboards. We'll need the time to pull the engines and replace them with less powerful, quieter ones."

"Like those on little flat bottom bass boats?"

"Exactly, like a trolling motor."

"Pushing heavy loads upstream, how much will that slow us down?"

"An hour, tops. We aren't going that far."

With the parties in agreement on the time, command decisions, and make-up of the operation, the men returned to their daily routines at their own locations. Held at Steve's tent, a planning session was agreed to the following day under the guise of a poker game. The major contributed a case of cold beer. Steve bought rice and vegetables, which Lan, although she continued to maintain her distance and a cool resolve toward the Marine, had cooked for him. Rocco went fishing from a rubber raft, flying along the river, tossing a quarter-pound block of C-4 explosive over his shoulder every fifteen seconds.

With the fuses burning, the blocks of military explosive sank, exploding on or near the bottom of the river, throwing up a depth charge type of geyser. Villagers netted the fish that floated to the surface. Rocco provided fish not only for the poker game but for the entire village, at the same time demonstrating how loud and powerful the raft engines were.

The poker game was intentionally boisterous. Lan served the meal, assuring the villagers that the barbarians were indeed enjoying themselves. The village was quiet by ten. The party broke up at midnight with the Americans falling asleep on cots. They were awakened at 4 a.m. by Le Kinh. The sand table model was uncovered. Options were discussed. Details were ironed out. Every issue was brain stormed and considered without regard to the person's rank who put the idea forward. Decisions were quickly made.

The assault force would wear no helmets. They would each wear a white bandana as an identity. A SEAL sniper was to be stationed at a point overlooking the moon-lighted rice paddles. Five fire teams would work their way through the thick forest at the rear of the four hootch hamlets. When Steve popped a green flare, four men armed with LAAWs would fire up the assigned structures.

Although they would not have the distance to come close to the hamlet, the mortar crews at Thach Hanh would fire barrages at maximum range, creating noise and the illusion of a much larger force, leading to confusion and possibly fear. For Steve, it would also provide them with a sense of having participated in the mission for his villagers, a positive moral factor.

"Machine guns on both flanks will fire up the huts obliquely for thirty seconds. The squad will then attack from south to north," Steve instructed.

"What about the civilians?" the Major asked, concerned over the political aspect of collateral damage.

"There are no civilians in that village, Major," Steve answered resolutely, ending that line of discussion.

The operational phase for the assault began. While keeping one raft on the river the SEALS quietly changed out their engines. Steve gathered the necessary weapons and coordinated the logistical aspects of the assault. Le Kinh put the CAP unit through a brief but rigorous training program, including short night patrols. He watched keenly, teaching, correcting, evaluating, and selecting his assault team. He announced his choices to Steve who was in complete agreement with him on each selection. It would not have mattered who he selected, Steve would have agreed with his scout.

Steve had insisted upon two women being in the assault group, saying "It will be good for moral of the village and the CAP unit. All the women of the village will bask in the honors of the women on the operation. Their pride and resolve will be stiffened should the village ever come under attack. Two women, two crippled former soldiers, fourteen boys not yet of military age, Le Kinh, the sergeant, myself and the SEALS will make up the reinforced squad."

The guard around the village was doubled for the night of the attack. All fifty-two members of the self-defense force were on duty. At two o'clock Le Kinh quietly walked the perimeter, stopping to instruct the chosen members of the assault force to silently make their way to Steve's tent. Once all were present the Marine conducted a final briefing on the operation, utilizing the sand table.

Equipment was inspected. Hands and faces were camouflaged with black, brown and dark green grease paint sticks. White bandanas were issued. They would be worn once the fire teams were in place.

It was a short walk down to the river in the shadow of the bridge. Two teams, eight persons, were assigned to each raft. The SEAL team boat commanders pushed of, drifting until in deep enough water to turn on the quiet electric engines. Like elephants on nose to tail parade, the boats were linked by nylon ropes. But for its pilot the last empty raft, with its gasoline engine intact, was being towed. The raft was to be sacrificed and left behind. The driver was a highly trained, quite deadly sniper who would remain with the boats.

The SEALS had effectively closed a two-mile stretch of the river. The patrol had the river to themselves. Nerves were as taut as stretched rubber bands. Hearts beat faster. Breaths became shallow. Fingers itched to touch triggers. The commanders had repeatedly cautioned the patrol members about the consequences of movement and noise. For most of the patrol members, this would be their first real combat action. Sneezes were stifled and coughs suppressed.

Within forty-five minutes, the sniper's raft was cut loose. He quickly made his way to the bank of the river. He took up a concealed location. At that moment, the patrol became real to them all. Fifteen minutes later, the remaining rafts nosed into the bank where branches grew out over the water, providing concealment. Quietly, the rafts were driven into the shadows and cover of leafy branches. Saah had marked the location with a freshly cut green branch that showed up as a white round dot against the black and green background.

Rocco was out of the rafts first, followed closely by Le Kinh and the sergeant. They fanned out, listening, allowing their eyes to adjust to darker surrounding than the moon shining on the river. Moving inland, the trio searched for Saah's marks. Once found, and rather quickly at that, Le Kinh returned to lead the squad to the rally point.

Flashing his hands with fingers extended four times, Steve reminded the teams they had forty minutes to get into their assault positions. He'd estimated it would take twenty-five minutes for the flankers with the longest distance to cover to get into place. There was no margin of error. The Vietnamese moved through the thicket like cats stalking prey. Silently, with no more disturbance than a breeze off the river, the teams moved inland. The three teams that took up positions at the base of the ambush had a wait that seemed much longer than it actually was. The smell of urine came to Steve's nostrils. Someone had urinated in place. Without embarrassing them, Steve intended to find out who had that much discipline.

Steve could not help but glance frequently at his watch. And then, with two minutes to go, he dug a cigar-sized silver canister from his pocket. At ten seconds, he began counting down. "One thousand one...one thousand two..."

At ten, the Marine slammed the base of the pencil flare into the palm of his right hand. The flare spat sparks as it jetted into the sky. Like an octopus spreading its tentacles, the flare burst into eight sparkling green streamers. A LAWW fired, flying through the window of one of the huts. Another LAWW knocked down a door. A third exploded on the roof, setting the dry thatch on fire. The last LAWW punched through a thin wall, exploding inside the hut, setting it on fire as well.

The machine guns opened up from the flanks simultaneously, orange tracers glowing against the dark background. A gun with green tracers answered. Bullets chopped through the tree branches overhead, smacking into trunks, a real baptism of fire for the CAP unit. Most responded well. One boy of about fourteen dropped his weapon and covered his ears with both hands. Steve noted it but had no time to deal with it immediately. This was one of the things he had to find out about the members of his defense force.

Steve gave the signal to advance, hoping the enemy machine gunner would continue to fire high. Firing a 40mm grenade launcher as fast as he could eject a shell by opening it like a shotgun to reload and fire again, Steve fired rounds into all the flimsy structures that could barely be called buildings. The teams were firing their weapons, a few with remarkable results. One gun was firing almost straight into the air. Another was extremely wide of the target. Steve needed to know who was behind those weapons.

A uniformed NVA enemy soldier burst from one of the burning huts. Almost immediately, he stumbled and fell, struck by a bullet that could only have come from the sniper. The return fire was silenced. The excited CAP members continued firing their weapons as fast as they could pull the triggers. Le Kinh was moving from person to person with orders for them to "Cease fire!"

The houses were burning fiercely. Explosives and ammunition inside them were cooking off. There would be nothing left to salvage, no intelligence documents or captured weapons. The team leaders reported in. There had been no friendly casualties. There was no reason to wait and go through the buildings once the ashes had cooled. There were good reasons to get away from the scene as quickly as possible. In extracting themselves from the ambush zone, the squad collected the enemy soldier who had been killed by the sniper. He was carried to the river and laid out as if he'd been shot there. The raft with an old engine was sunk by firing a burst from the soldier's AK-47 rifle into it as well as into the motor in order to destroy it beyond use.

As they climbed into the rafts, Steve noticed one girl he called Flower step into the water up to her waist. She stood there a moment, allowing the river water to wash away the urine from her trouser uniform. The squad rode back to the village in silence, each person remembering his or her part in the action. The victorious soldiers returned to Thach Hanh just after seven o'clock. The village was quickly abuzz with the news of the operation.

"Good job," the beaming major said after being briefed. He departed, and Steve, now seen as something of a heroic warrior, was again in sole charge of Thach Hanh and its bridge. For days following the attack on Xa Hai Phu, the participants told and retold their personal and collective accounts of the ambush. When asked to do so, Steve spoke of what the squad had accomplished, studiously avoiding mentions of his own rank or even of individuals, not wanting to plant a seed of jealousy or the idea of favoritism in anyone's mind. He spoke only of their accomplishments as a unit. He did, however, quietly dismiss the young man who had covered his ears and promote Flower to fire team leader.

His village returned to its mundane daily routine of barely surviving and doing the best they could with what they had. Skinny cocks crowed at the rising sun. Dogs howled at the moon. Fat pigs wallowed in the mud. Villagers labored in the rice paddles. Steve walked the streets of the village, watching and planning. He made new friends. He ate with various families. He passed out cigarettes and candy, always giving the village more than he was given. He pushed for completion of the school. He continued to train his defense force, sometimes in one-on-one sessions but generally in small groups, shoring up any weakness he ascertained in them.

Abundantly well-supplied in part due to numerous invitations to take meals with village families, Steve delivered a welcome case of C-ratlons to the nuns at the Catholic Church. He found the French architecture of the church fascinating. The Mother Superior invited him to stay and pray but did not invite conversation. The French novitiate was nowhere in sight during Steve's visits. The Marine didn't feel it prudent to ask for her or to send her a personal gift, which he was inclined to do.

After a brief visit with the Mother Superior, Steve patrolled the village much as a police officer on his beat would do, noticing people, thinking of security issues, and always looking for ways to make the village more defensible. He stopped to chat with the children and passed out lemon drops and jelly beans and with the adults, who all appreciated his gifts of American cigarettes. Steve watched for new faces coming into the village. Any furtive appearing movement captured his attention. He made notes of comings and goings, of routines and exceptions to those routines. He saw nothing that troubled or puzzled him. The village appeared quiet and secure in the shadow of Quang Tri City. It pleased him, but it didn't satisfy him. He knew there were things he wasn't seeing and hearing, important things he was missing.

Steve knew there was V.C. cadre in nearby Quang Tri City, if not still in the village itself. There were V.C. and NVA soldiers in their hidden tunnels and bunkers nearby, as well as some living openly in the city and its nearby villages. He knew he would never fully understand the many levels of currents in the political and governmental channels of Vietnam.

Steve knew he was considered a barbarian in spite of the Vietnamese customs he attempted to honor. He did the best he could without giving it much thought. It was a balancing act of remaining true to his mission and orders, even discipline, of being a Marine and "going native" in order to be truly accepted and trusted by the villagers. On the one hand, there was respect, and on the other, acceptance. He wondered if they should be balanced.

Those were just passing thoughts, shallow wonderings, actually. Steve was a Marine. His orientation was in action, preferably aggressive, offensive actions. The CAP unit was a part of civil affairs. Psy-ops and pacification programs were all new and foreign to Steve. They were a bit too passive to suit his nature as a hard-charging Marine, Steve needed action. He needed something positive to report. He began considering available options. He decided there was one with merit.

Steve met with Le Kinh to lay out his immediate plans. The tall Vietnamese soldier was more than an acquaintance or even a casual friend. He was a right arm with a good military mind, especially when it came to small unit tactics. The Marine tossed the Vietnamese a cold Budweiser from his cooler. Le Kinh popped it open with an explosion of foam. The tall man's Adams apple bobbed as the scout guzzled half the beer in one breath.

"I'm sure all the V.C. and NVA in I Corp know all about our part in the operation against Xa Hai Phu," Steve began.

"They will be planning their reaction, to punish us."

"And to make us an example."

"Yes, that too."

"Do you think I was wrong to take the offensive like that?"

"No." There was no lapse of time for Le Kinh to think before he answered emphatically,

"Well, with QuangTri at our back and the First ARVN Division Headquarters at Ai Tu to our north and the large American base to the west, I'm pretty sure they'll hit us from the south, "the Marine concluded.

"Not Likely, Ha Shi."

"Oh, why not?"

"They know that is what we will expect. They will come from the north."

"Past Ai Tu?"

Le Kinh laughed. "The entire Second NVA Division is already between us and Ai Tu."

"With their headquarters at Gio Linh?" Gio Linh was a village that had seen heavy combat on numerous occasions. Steve remembered Gio Linh. He had been in and out of the village so many times he could recall a map of the place in his head and the faces of the villagers who lived there.

Halfway between Quang Tri City and the DMZ, Gio Linh was one of the villages that resisted every pacification effort. The area surrounding the village had been the scene of numerous bloody battles. In one incident deep in the dry season, Steve was walking point for a platoon as it approached Gio Linh through a huge valley of drying out rice paddles. The stalks of grain had changed from green to brown. The mature rice stalks were curved over with heavy heads of purple streaked grain. Steve was worried by the fact that there were no women working the seemingly abandoned field at a time when they should be busy harvesting their crop.

The harvesting had begun. Rows of stiff stalks like Nebraska corn dotted the full length of the rice paddies all the way to the edge of the village. Like the wheat fields in Oklahoma, rice had been planted all the way to the tree lines on both flanks. The trees as well as the thick growth of rice could be hiding a large number of enemy soldiers waiting to spring an ambush. Was that why the women had disappeared?

Under normal circumstances, when the Marine passed along the nearby road or flew over it, lines of women laborers in their conical straw hats would be industriously working in those rice fields. They usually seemed to pay little attention to the passing Marines. Their absence caused Steve to grow suspicious and cautious. He checked his weapons while on the move. The magazine in his rifle was full.

He could feel the bayonet strapped to his leg and the weight of grenades in each of the pouch-like pockets of his camouflaged jungle trousers. He flicked the selector switch on his M-16 from semiautomatic to automatic. If the patrol was ambushed, they would need to gain fire superiority immediately. He gave the silent signal for Look! And Listen!, alerting the patrol to his concern. Steve knew without a doubt the platoon was walking into a battle. But that was his job as a Marine. Find the enemy and destroy them, even if you had to risk exposing yourself and giving them the first shots in doing so.

The scout walked on, leading the patrol another fifty meters until he imagined he could almost hear the NVA soldiers in hiding breathing. He signaled for the patrol to spread out and hit the deck, disappearing among the rice stalks, perhaps drawing the enemy's fire by doing so. If the enemy was in the rice field, they were being very quiet and very still. Hovering dragonflies shimmered in the sunlight as they fed on the seed heads. The Java sparrows so damaging to rice crops gripped swaying stalks and consumed the grain in surprising quantities. An invasive pink bellied cage bird from China, the birds calling "Chop! Chip!" seemed undisturbed.

But absent was another habituate of the rice fields, the long-necked yellow egret with its beautiful, luxurious crest. They stalked crabs, fish, snakes, and frogs in the wet paddies. What did their absence mean?

It wasn't just the rice field but a deep green tree line on the near horizon that bothered the scout. Those deep shadows could be concealing any number of NVA soldiers who had their weapons aimed at him right now. Tree lines often concealed bunkers, machine gun teams, and mortar crews.

Nearer, more like a part of the village, the green crowns of tall palms rustled in a slight breeze sixty feet above his head. The coconut palms grew close together, tall and slender, branchless like an undressed tree that sprouts a head of green feathers eighty feet up there. It would provide an enemy spotter with a grand view of the relatively flat terrain around Gio Linh. Steve scanned the treetops for snipers. Just because he had never spotted any in a palm tree didn't mean they weren't there. Maybe I've watched too many war movies, Steve thought. And I'm living in one. Shoulda watched space adventures or something. The only thing Steve didn't worry about was enemy airplanes dropping bombs or soldiers dropping from them. Not in this war.

The platoon commander stood, pointing. He was using hand and arm signals to control his squads. He spread them out even further as he prepared to approach the village. The Marines knew from training and experience that he wanted them to approach at 10-yard intervals. The riflemen crouched and moved to their new locations, prepared to approach the generally hostile village on a broad front. That accomplished, the lieutenant signaled for his platoon to move forward in a wedge with the scout on point. This formation allowed the riflemen on the outside edges of the wedge to fire their weapons to the front and outward to their near flank without worrying about hitting another Marine.

The command group moved up into a relatively secure position in the center of the wedge with a fire team designated to provide rear security. It was an excellent formation for the terrain being crossed. From the center location, the lieutenant could move his machine gunners, mortars, reserve forces, and grenadiers quickly to wherever they were most needed.

The nervous Marines were hot and sweating. They were weighted down with flak jackets. Their shoulders were draped with lengths of linked heavy machine gun ammunition and bandoliers of bullets for their rifles. Their faces reflected anticipation, concentration, and expectation, with their fears most often hidden beneath those masks.

As the platoon renewed its advance, Steve recalled early lessons learned in Vietnam. "Don't walk on the dikes. They might be mined. Walk slower through the mid-calf deep dung and mud of the rice paddy. Die in a shit-fertilized field instead of on the dry dike."

Gun barrels spit orange flashes from the dark shadows of the tree line, like twinkling fireflies on a dark Dallas night, only deadly. Two Marines went down with growing red blossoms on their chests. The lieutenant, map on his knee, head down, radio handset to his ear, had reacted slowly. Fucking desk jockey punching his combat career ticket, Steve thought, trying to figure out where we are.

Down in the rice paddies, under fire, I can't see shit, only a mass of branches and leaves. Give me the radio, lieutenant. I'll fire a Willie Peter spotting round where I know we aren't and figure out where we are from that. But I'm just a dumbass enlisted man. I couldn't possibly know what I'm doing. If we were in the Army, I'd give odds this new lieutenant would be fragged before he could get his whole platoon killed.

I'm going to write a book about this one day, not necessarily about the things I've done or seen, but what goes on in the mind of a Marine during all these experiences. The things you think and say to yourself or wish you could say out loud. I think I'd call it "Under My Helmet."

And then a stupid fucking new guy revealed his inexperience. In a field of brown rice stalks only three feet tall, he stood, extending a LAAW like he was on a firing range back at Camp Pendleton.

"Get down!" Steve hollered.

Bullets slammed into the newbie, propelling him backwards with the force of their impact. The tube was pointed toward the sky as he fell. The missile fired skyward. Reflexes, Steve thought. Or perhaps he wanted to clear off a cloud before he got to heaven.

An increasingly heavy volume of gunfire was being exchanged as the Marines fought back.

Steve realized some of the incoming originated from the left flank. He rolled that way. A crazy-assed corpsman ran past the scout. A moment later the corpsman came scrambling back, helping a wounded Marine, blood running down his leg. I never met a corpsman who wasn't a hero, Steve thought.

The platoon was exposed behind very small dikes. They were under heavy fire from two directions, unable to move, able only to die. The Marines had no counterpunch. They had not achieved fire superiority. Steve noticed a radioman hugging the foul earth of the rice paddy. His head was turned sideways, cheek to ground, as he desperately called for artillery support now that the lieutenant had finally figured out their position.

One of the men with his face in the dirt had cocked his head enough to dribble water from a canteen into his mouth, until an enemy sharpshooter hit him in the hand. Still another in virtually the same pose was smoking a cigarette. So much for priorities, Steve thought.

Fuck this, the scout thought. I'm not going to lay here and be a target for these dinks. He began an infantry crawl forward through a foot of moist buffalo crap and human turds. Someone had seen him and was covering him with machine gun fire. Thank you, brother, the scout thought.

Enemy bullets sought tender young American flesh. Puffs of dirt exploded all around the Marine. Steve realized that the enemy was not just firing in his direction. They were firing at him since he seemed to be the only thing moving at the moment. He rolled to the lowest point in the rice paddy, perhaps a spot where a buffalo had wallowed. A fire team followed. They got their rifles to their shoulders and engaged the enemy.

Encouraged by the four-man fire team that finally showed some fighting spirit, an entire squad began moving with the fire team providing them covering fire. Their weapons joined in seeking out the enemy. Behind their position, one of the machine gunners brought his weapon forward and began sweeping the tree line with damaging gunfire, moving the weapon from left to right and back again. Steve knew the weapon was chewing the shit out of trees and leaves but wondered if it was hitting anything else as it had not suppressed the enemy fire.

At least those guys are firing toward the enemy, Steve thought. Give them credit for that. The machine gunner's face was set with determination. God, Steve thought, I can read a whole book of experiences and feelings in that kid's determined face. He was scared. Steve was scared as well. But he knew both of them were more fearful of letting their fellow Marines down than anything else. Steve wondered who that gunner was trying to prove something to, besides himself. Was constantly trying to prove yourself worthy of being a Marine? What made Marines so different?, he wondered. There was firm resolve in the set of that young warrior's jaw. He was ready and willing to take the fight to an enemy he didn't know, had never met, and had to learn to hate and demonize as gooks, dinks, and slopes.

The enemy had their own experienced leaders and heroes. They met the squad's rifle fire with an increased volume from their own weapons. They obviously understood the concept of fire superiority. The NVA opened up on the Marines as they rose from behind the dikes to press their attack. Two Marines were killed right away. Seeing their comrades cut down, the rest of the

Marines dropped to the ground. Where is our fire support? Steve wondered. Good Marines were dying because there was no artillery or air strikes to suppress the enemy fire.

Again, the Marines attempted to gain fire superiority with their light infantry weapons. They didn't aim their rifles. They simply pointed them in the general direction of the enemy and fired them on full automatic. The enemy mounted an assault in spite of the volume of fire from the Marine positions.

Steve burned through a twenty-round magazine in one breath, but the Marines stopped the advance of the numerically superior enemy force. Steve reloaded his magazines from the bandolier of boxed ball ammunition the Marines had all carried into this battle. That meant he had used half the ammunition available for his rifle. Soon, Marines would be scrounging for ammunition from their own dead. In spite of the heavy volume of enemy fire, the Marines pulled themselves out of the mud that clung to their boots by grasping at rice stalks. Sometimes they got a hand from above or a shove from behind. They were now more visible to the enemy, who was shooting right straight into them from no more than two hundred yards away. Steve felt as if he had a hot gun barrel right in his face.

Then the enemy mortars began firing. The Marines were exposed enough for those weapons to inflict serious damage among their ranks. After each explosion, rocks and filthy mud rained back down on the Marines. The mortars were on target. Steve's ears rang painfully. His nose was bleeding as a result of the blasts. One of the Marine snipers moved up past him to take up a position among some rice stalks. He wore a soft cloth cover rather than a helmet. A silver peace symbol was hung from his neck. The medallion of a skull with darkened eye sockets hung from the shorter chain of a second necklace.

The sniper had seen something. Now he was stalking it. He searched for it through his high-power scope, but his vision through the device was too narrow. He turned his head to call for his spotter who was already searching through his high-power binoculars.

"Your two o'clock. Six hundred meters," the spotter called.

The sniper turned back. He looked through his scope but did not seem to be able to find his target. He lowered his rifle for a moment. He picked it up and looked again. The rifle barrel moved with his search. The rifle stopped moving. Steve could see the sniper going through his motions: breathe, relax, aim, slack, squeeze. The special high-powered weapon with a heavy-duty barrel bucked slightly as it was fired. The sniper seemed pleased. Steve was in no position to evaluate the results.

The dinks were still firing their weapons at the Marines. Behind Steve, the platoon's radioman went down. He wasn't moving or moaning. He wasn't being treated by a corpsman. The radio appeared to be operable. The lieutenant was down on the ground, raised up on one elbow, calling into the handset for artillery support.

The target was from two hundred meters out on up to six hundred meters at the edge of the tree line. The Marines would advance behind the artillery barrage and pray there would be no short rounds falling among their own ranks. The flanking enemy fire had been coming from a slight rise, which was the highest ground for miles around. The lieutenant indicated this was to be the direction of the platoon's attack. The supporting fire finally arrived with heat and anti-personnel shells being fired to the flank while heat and smoke were aimed at the tree line.

The billowing smoke obscured the vision of the enemy to the front. The Marines moved into the assault. In spite of the artillery exploding all around them, the enemy was still offering up stiff resistance. A Marine close to Steve was shot in the elbow. Steve could see the shock and pain in the man's face as he was hit. As the Marines closed in on the hill, they became packed closer together. The NVA gunners and riflemen seemed to be giving the Marines everything they had in a desperate attempt to stop their spirited assault.

The hard-pressed enemy fell back. The Marines leapt over a trench line and continued their assault. Their momentum, however, had been slowed as not all the Marines could leap over the deep and wide trenches. They fell or leaped down into them and had to scramble up and out on the other side. Although the NVA soldiers fell back, they stopped the Marines' advance at another freshly dug trench line. Panting and trying to keep his head down, Steve was surprised to drink the last of his water.

The artillery fire was lifted. The Marines were too close to the enemy for it to be safe. The Marines knew what was coming. They were all looking at the top of the small hill as a flight of F-4 Phantoms streaked low overhead. The top one hundred yards of the ridge was engulfed in multiple balls of fire. The cauldron boiled orange and black.

"Follow me!" the platoon commander shouted, waving his.45 pistol in the air. Somehow, the exhausted Marines found the strength to get their legs under them and to propel their bodies upward and forward.

Napalm burns fast and furious. By the time the Marines had fought their way to the top of the hill, every tree for 500 yards in all directions was completely denuded of leaves. Ground cover, including a thick carpet of dead leaves, was nothing now but smoking piles of ash. Tree branches that had not been blown off by the artillery had burned off, leaving only the main trunks and, in some cases, the stumps of trees. Many of them were still burning. A little bit of hell had reached out and licked the hilltop.

Steve hid behind a large tree that had crashed to the ground. It was still burning and smoking in places. The scout's eyes stung. They were as red with irritation as if salt had been rubbed into them.

His throat and lungs felt like they were burning. The knees of both his trouser legs were ripped. One knee was bleeding from a deep gash where he'd hit a sharp rock when going to ground under heavy enemy fire.

In spite of the artillery, the napalm, and the furious infantry assault, the enemy was still in this fight. Steve rose up to look for targets. He felt a hammer blow to his left bicep that turned him around. A corpsman came out of nowhere and began providing first aid: a shot of morphine and a pressure bandage. He filed out a wound tag and put it around Steve's neck. The scout just had to read it. As many as he had seen, he had never read one before, and in spite of being wounded, had never had one attached to him. The tag indicated the time and the amount of morphine he'd been given. The morphine was the reason he had been tagged, to prevent another corpsman from giving him an accidental overdose in case he passed out. He'd only been given half a dose. Steve had been wounded and drugged, but like the NVA, he was still in the fighting.

But there were no targets. There was no incoming rifle fire. Enemy resistance had been overcome. Men were walking up the hill, lighted cigarettes dangling from their mouths. Steve was a non-smoker and did not understand why anyone would want a cigarette at this time. The hill was shrouded in smoke. How many years of jungle growth have we destroyed, Steve wondered. His drugged thoughts were disconnected.

Objective taken.

Light casualties. Tell their mothers we suffered "acceptable" casualties.

Christ, I wish it would rain.

The fighting, however, was not over. The enemy was still in that tree line. But the Marines had cleared the flank and now held the high ground. The platoon established a perimeter on the hill and began to dig in around it. Steve started a hole right in front of a scrawny bush that did nothing to conceal him. It was not by choice. A dumbass sergeant had pointed to the spot and told the scout to dig. He, of course, was back in the brush that was withered but still green and able to provide some cover.

The enemy didn't give the Marines long to dig in or recover. Steve was not nearly deep enough when they launched their counterattack. In spite of his wound, he had been trying to dig his way to Dallas on the other side of the world. The NVA had regrouped and come back in the attack, opening fire from only one hundred yards away, consistent with their doctrine of negating the superior might of supporting arms by closing with the enemy.

The Marines responded vigorously. They used everything at their disposal: rifles, machine guns, light mortars, you name it, the whole arsenal of light infantry weapons. In spite of the enemy being on top of them, they called for air strikes. The aircraft still on location zoomed in, being effective with strafing runs as close to the Marines as they dared.

As soon as the aircraft pulled out of their gun runs, the Marines were up and charging the now disorganized enemy line. Half an hour later, they were past the tree line and were digging new holes on another minor ridge line. Training me to be a ditch digger or gardener, Steve thought.

The remaining enemy force seemed to melt away, most likely into their secret tunnels all around Gio Linh. Bodies littered the battlefield. Steve knew he could easily have been one of them. It was only a matter of inches from his arm to his chest. A six hundred-yard-long path of destruction told the tale of the battle.

Reinforcements arrived to "police" the battlefield. They retrieved the bodies and weapons of Marines who had been killed. They carried them in ponchos to waiting helicopters. The enemy bodies were searched for documents that might be of intelligence value. Weapons were collected. Many of them disappeared and were later claimed as trophy weapons by men who had not participated in the hard-fought battle.

Steve was transported to the Naval Support Activity Hospital at Da Nang. A local deadener rather than morphine was injected into his arm near the wound. A few scalpel strokes he did not feel as more than a tug on his skin opened the wound further. A probe disappeared into his arm. A chunk of metal was retrieved. He heard a metallic clink in a pan. Not a bullet, but shrapnel. Sharp. Jagged. A twisted scrap of steel. Steve spent three days in the hospital more to guard against infection than to recover and got a ticket back to combat duty.

Steve knew he would see Gio Linh again. That place is going to be the death of me, he thought. Steve was brought back to the present when Le Kinh agreed that Gio Linh was most likely an enemy headquarters.

"No," Steve told Le Kinh. "Gio Linh is not the enemy headquarters. Every time we get close to that village, the NVA reinforces it heavily through the tunnel system to make us think it is their headquarters. They defend it with such spirit that the Americans think it must be their headquarters."

"Smart."

"When the time is right, they will come out of the tunnels like bats out of a cave to suck the blood right out of Quang Tri."

"In the meantime, we've got to get ready for them."

"Many of the villagers are anxious to participate in the next action."

"I plan on giving them a chance. For now, though, I need for you to be especially vigilant with the night watch. Train them all the same. In rotation. Run patrols out to 1,000 meters so they all know the terrain in every direction and the distances are easy to identify landmarks. Stress ambushes, again at obvious locations within 1,000 meters. Prepare them to conduct any kind of ambush called for."

"You mean like Ls and Xs and straight lines?"

"Yes, exactly, but don't go beyond those for now."

"And only on major intersections?"

"Yes. Just keep it very obvious. But teach tactics and ambush discipline."

"That will be most important in a real situation."

"You know what to do, but don't initiate any contact at this point. Avoid it, but your people have to be armed, just in case."

Within days Steve returned to duty to oversee the training schedule he had proposed for the CAP unit.

CHAPTER THIRTEEN
QUNGTRI COMBAT BASE

Major Hamlin, who had grown quite comfortable in his relationship with Corporal Kowalski, sent his driver out with orders to bring the corporal to his headquarters for a personal briefing. The officer had ordered a hot lunch, steak, mashed potatoes, salad, which would be a rare treat for the young Marine. Before the meal was served, the major revealed a large map of Quang Tri Province. It depicted the city, the Thach Hanh Bridge, with Route 9 running east to west and Route 1 running south to north roughly along the Thach Hanh River. Red and blue push pins designated the military-political orientation of each named village within the province. Quang Tri and Thach Hahn were blue. Almost every other village was red, including Gio Linh, the only village of any size between Quang Tri City and the DMZ to the north.

There was no pin in Xa Hai Phu. It had been wiped out. "To the south, a village of comparable size to Gio Linh is Xa Hai Thien, which is located at the junction of Highway 1 and Route 8, which branches off to the coast," the major said, pointing with a swagger stick. The pin in the village was blue, but all around it were dozens of smaller villages with red pins stuck in them.

"We have a CAP unit at Xa Hai Thien. Before you leave today, we will supply you with codes and radio frequencies to facilitate direct communications between the two of you."

The men sat for lunch as a PFC waiter brought in trays of steaming food. The major continued his briefing during lunch. "That CAP unit is a light squad, eleven Marines with no backup like you have at Thach Hanh. The village doesn't have the size to support a self-defense force like yours. They have been training a dozen locals to aid in defense if they are attacked.

"You and your indigenous force are going to serve as the immediate reaction force in that case."

"I would have to split my command in order to go to their relief, leaving about half behind and throwing a reinforced squad into the rescue effort," Steve noted.

"That would double their defense force. All they'll have to do is hold on until you get there."

"The NVA could roll over them and be on their way to Thach Hahn before we could get to them. That could leave us vulnerable."

"In that case, dig in wherever you are and defend Thach Hanh from that location."

"Yes, sir. I can see the value in that, in not fighting within the village if we don't have to."

"In that scenario, Thach Hanh will be reinforced quickly. Once that bridge is secure, we'll send a force to your relief."

"Do you have intelligence indicating an imminent threat to the CAP Unit?"

"Look at the map. The threat has always been imminent. But after your recent action, we have been expecting retribution against local friendly forces. We've been hearing more about Xa Hai Thien lately. Let's say we have some concerns."

"I do have the security clearance to know, Major."

"Well, yes, you do." The major thought about that moment. "We have received several slightly varying but similar reports of a planned assault on Xa Hai Thieu."

"Slightly varying being more credible than duplicate accounts?"

"Exactly."

"What level is the intelligence, sir?"

"Everything from C-3 to A-1."

"Then I'd say they are going to get hit. Any idea when?"

"Sooner rather than later."

"I might be able to spare a couple of really good people to help them prepare their defenses and bolster their numbers."

"No, I don't think that's a good idea. You are going to need your people if you get hit in a rescue effort."

"I've got one man, major, a retired ARVN sergeant major. Lost his left leg in an artillery exchange. He gets around, but not well on a march. He's a really staunch fighter from a fixed position, a bunker or fighting hole. He speaks English fairly well. That could be a plus for your boys. And a Vietnamese sergeant major might help the morale of the village and stiffen their resolve. He could also be useful if he has a couple of weeks to further train the locals they do have."

The major thought about that moment as he chewed a cut of his mushroom gravy-covered steak. He raised his fork as he spoke. "One man like that will help them more than losing him will hurt you. Send him in quietly. In the meantime, keep your force fully geared and ready to move."

"You sound pretty sure about this, major."

"It's not a matter of if they are going to get hit, but when."

"Can you give them a squad of Marines?"

"We could. But that would be counterproductive. The NVA will just delay their attack, hit somewhere else, and when we move our squad out, they move in. We have to let them hit the CAP Marines while we are prepared for them. The villagers need to see us putting up stiff resistance on a small unit local level, defending their village."

"That could have positive results in Thach Hanh as well."

"Thach Hanh is a success story. You've got to keep it that way." The major gestured toward the map, using his fork like a swagger stick pointer. "We've got to work on changing all those red pins to blue."

Realistically, Steve knew that was not going to happen. He knew the major was aware of it as well. The career officer had to perpetuate the myth of the politicians and superior officers who had established the official positions no matter how ill-advised they may be.

The major caught the flash of cynicism expressed on Steve's face. It was gone before he had to address the issue. "Okay, we both know we are trying to build a dam with loose grains of sand. And we both know it can be done if you dump enough sand quickly in the right location."

"Even then a lot of sand is going to get washed away in the process, major."

"Unfortunately so."

"Our is not to reason why..."

The major raised his glass in a toast to the Marine Corps saying, which Steve matched as they chorused the remainder of the phrase, "Ours is but to do and die."

The major pushed his chair back, indicating the end of the briefing. "Anything you need out there, Kowalski, just say the word."

"I can't think of anything realistic at the moment, sir."

"How about a reconnaissance flight?"

Steve hadn't thought of that. In the Marine Corps, even battalion commanding lieutenant colonels rarely had the weight to pull a personal reconnaissance flight. "You've taken on a full-time job at Thach Hanh, Corporal. Fortunately, we have an E-6 staff sergeant on the way in with the proper clearance, MOS, and rank to take over as our chief scout. You are hereby relieved of that duty with my congratulations on a job well done."

Steve had known this was coming. It simply meant he would no longer attend the Citadel briefings or report to Captain Maxwell. The tradeoff was that he would have even more time to devote to the civil affairs operation in Thach Hanh, a brief respite from the real war being fought out in the jungle. After the reconnaissance flight, Steve returned to the village with thoughts of the briefing on his mind.

He wrote his mother about the flight.

Sometimes, In the midst of war, among all the destruction and misery, even madness, you see a scene so beautiful it stays with you forever. Imagine flying through puffy scattered cotton balls of clouds, the sky graying with dusk. A city spreads out below you, surrounded by verdant green fields in a fertile valley.

There is a banana plantation with breezy rows and columns of trees like soldiers on parade.

Dark green hedgerow 'fences', dirt streets with light traffic. Lights

There were few moments in Vietnam like the one Steve had described for his mother. He simply couldn't tell her some of the realities of the war. Memories of Gio Linh were among those he did not relate to her. He recalled one incident as he fell asleep.

Jones Creek and the Battle for Dong Ha were bigger than Steve knew at the time of his participation in them. The Jones Creek Battle, largely an Army operation, was just a part of the summer-long NVA offensive that raged throughout I Corp.

The squad was on patrol in a field of rice stalks just after harvest. There was a small village ahead. It consisted of half a dozen thatch roof structures. The homes were surrounded by brown-packed earth. It appeared to be a poor hand-to-mouth village with the residents barely scraping a living from the soil. The houses were built on stilts. Steve thought that indicated the monsoon flooded this plain, bringing rich nutrients for the crops. He thought of the Nile and its contribution in a similar manner, a useless fact learned in school.

There was a mental ping in his mind, something like a distant radar return. Where are the people? Where are their animals? The scout sensed trouble. The NVA could be waiting for the Marines up ahead, accounting for the absence of normal activity in and around the village. He could imagine thatch window coverings being raised, revealing machine guns. They began firing.

With that image strong in his mind, Steve wondered what he should do. The village was one of the patrol check points. They had to go in there. He knew the patrol couldn't march in naked like this. He was in Vietnam to fight, to die if he must, but not recklessly or needlessly. He had a heavy responsibility to the Marines in the squad. He couldn't spend their lives like they were pennies of little value. He couldn't lead them into an ambush. The squad leader, a corporal, was either weak or inexperienced. He had let the scout know he was in charge of the squad during the patrol.

Steve knew he had a responsibility to the civilians as well. They could be hostages in their own homes. He couldn't just start firing up the village the way he could if they were in a free fire zone.

There would be no recon by fire. No preemptive air or artillery strikes. No mortar fire. He had no choice but to put some mother's son at risk. Some good young Marines may die here, he thought.

Steve was well versed in the small unit tactics he would employ. He used hand and arm signals to communicate with the squad. Spread out! Like playing an organ. Wider! First Team, far left. Second team, far right. Third team and attached personnel up the middle with me. Watch! Look! Listen!

Everyone seemed to understand and be responding well. The squad was soon in place. They began their advance in random fire team rushes. Ten yards, twenty; rush forward in a crouch, hit the ground and roll to the left the first time, then to the right two times in a row. Roll once and be ready to fire the first time, twice the second time. Do not be predictable. Spread out so you don't roll into one another.

Guns were suddenly firing at the Marines from every window and doorway, even from a trench line beyond the village. Steve's prediction had been correct. As the bullets snapped past his head, the Marine imagined every one of them screaming, "Die Marine !" The bullets were kicking up gritty dirt close enough to blow into and sting his eyes. He wondered about the rest of the squad as well as the civilians. Combat is a voracious monster that feeds on chaos and suffering.

Combat is also hectic and chaotic. Sometimes you are working through being shocked or dazed when the bullets begin flying, driven by adrenaline and reaction, fueled by a survival instinct and training or experience. The squad was doing well. They were low to the ground, M-16s smoking, spitting hot spent shell casings out to the right side. A beaded band around his helmet, various medallions, and a silver peace symbol around his neck, a Marine had taken cover behind a large rock, probably the only one between the squad and the village. His weapon was raised, spitting bullets on full automatic. He was shouting over his shoulder. His words were lost in memory, perhaps never heard, but he was providing covering fire so other men could move forward.

The machine gunner had been hit. A Marine raced to his side. He knew that gun couldn't be left silent. Steve didn't know who had stepped up. All he could see was his back. He was heavily loaded down with four canteens, a dozen magazines for his M-16, two hundred rounds of linked machine gun ammunition, anti-personnel grenades, smoke grenades, and a LAAW. And he was wearing a heavy pack. Steve was similarly encamped.

If I can see backs, I need to move forward, Steve thought. You lead from the front. Some memories were sharper and more focused than others. Steve wondered if that was because they were more meaningful or if it was just the way you saw things at the time. Square-jawed, tough-looking, his helmet cover ripped, perhaps by a bullet, a "blooker" man carefully aimed his M-79 40mm grenade launcher. Steve loved that weapon. He was pretty good with it himself.

He observed another man, leaning back, torso slightly twisted, left arm fully extended, right arm cocked to throw a grenade, similar to a quarterback throwing a football. That should have been our Heisman Trophy pose for soldiers, Steve thought. In the midst of the intense battle with enemy guns firing their way, Marine riflemen all around him rose, exposing themselves while firing their weapons. They dove back down, reloaded, rose, and repeated the process. The scout saw a man, wounded, with a bandage around his left arm. But more seriously, his head was wrapped in a bandage that covered his eyes. Dripping blood had made three paths down the left side of his face. He had either passed out or died. Helmetless, the radioman sat beside him, calmly speaking into the radio. Was he calling for a medevac or for fire support?

Another wounded Marine was exposed still to enemy fire. And another, in a more concealed, protected position, extended his M-16. The wounded man's face was contorted in pain as he was pulled to safety. And then the squad was up and advancing even as others were bleeding and dying around them. A brave young man stood, aiming a LAAW. He fired the weapon and hit the ground. One of the hootches exploded with his direct hit. An enemy machine gun was silenced. Encouraged, the squad rushed forward, close enough now to throw their hand grenades. One of the hootches caught fire.

Marines rushed into the enemy-held hootches, clearing them of the NVA and using them as cover to fire on the enemy in the trench lines. Grenades exploded among those defenders. By themselves, they did not create the huge ball of fire and smoke depicted in the movies. Their damage was done by deadly shrapnel.

Given covering fire by the machine gun and the riflemen inside the hootches, a fire team, a man short due to his being killed or wounded, charged forward and took the trench line. Resistance seemed to melt like a cube of ice on a desert rock. The enemy guns had grown silent. The dinks had disappeared. Where did they go? Steve wondered. Bunkers and tunnels, I'll bet, he thought, looking around.

Two wounded Marines were comforting one another. One of the men who had been shot in the face had a bandage around his forehead with another "toothache" style bandage under his jaw and chin. He was leaning against a small tree. In his lap, a man with similar wounds, bandages around his forehead and left eye, peeked up from the edge of his bandage as he was given a cigarette. Steve knew those men would become friends forever.

After any battle, a reorganization process always has to take place. Priority is given to protecting against an enemy counterattack. A fire team in the trenches provided that security. The wounded needed to be treated, and the more serious cases evacuated with the dead. Weapons and ammunition were gathered and redistributed evenly. Inside the hootches were seventeen dead enemy soldiers. A part of Steve's job was to search their bloody bodies for documents and anything of intelligence value. The souvenir hunters were already taking anything they wanted to keep or use for trade.

Steve knew they had killed more than seventeen of the enemy, although the Marines had not collected the bodies. He spotted drag marks and heavy blood trails leading away from the trench where more NVA soldiers had died. As the intelligence scout, one of Steve's responsibilities was to fill out an official report after each patrol. This report provided the division intelligence office with such data as time and size of the patrol; the patrol route; and any contacts and results, both friendly and enemy.

At the end of that form, the scout is asked to provide observations, recommendations, and suggestions for other actions required.

Observations were critical to building an overall picture of the enemy. Reporting "engaged by an estimated enemy squad armed with SKS and AK-47 rifles, grenades, and RPGs. Results 3 NVA KIA, 1 USMC KIA, 2 USMC WIA, captured 1 SKS rifle, 2 AK-47, various gear, ammunition, and documents," is a bare bones report that does little to add to the intelligence about the enemy. Still, it's the type of report most scouts file.

Adding the condition of the weapons, for example, is part of the important observation process. Are they shiny and new? Are they worn with split wooden stocks taped or wired together? Is there anything new you've not seen on the battlefield before? What do the enemy soldiers look like?

Do they appear healthy or sickly? What about the equipment they are carrying? What is the state of their uniforms? Are they wearing distinctive unit patches? How about the cut of their hair? Rations or cigarettes they may be carrying could reveal the state of their supply and morale.

Steve reported that the unit had engaged a numerically superior enemy force that put up stiff resistance. They appeared to be well trained and were equipped with standard NVA light infantry weapons that were in good condition. He took documents from the bodies, including journals, letters, and photographs. He cut shoulder tabs from uniforms. It all went into a plastic bag with his patrol report.

Medevac and resupply choppers had been called for. With all of this accomplished, it was time for the Marines to go looking for those bunkers and tunnels. They began by following the blood trails. They followed them until they suddenly disappeared. After a brief search, the Marines uncovered a tunnel entryway that appeared to be a small well hole. It could have been easier if they'd had a dog on the patrol with them. The tunnels in Vietnam were scary places. Not many men wanted to go into them. Those who relished that sort of combat were called "tunnel rats." They didn't have one in this squad. That meant the role would fall to the scout, to Steve.

The NVA are superb pick and shovel engineers. They built hundreds of miles of roadway with little else. Using those instruments, they built complex bunkers and tunnel systems. Steve dropped all the gear he could so he could maneuver in the cramped tunnels. "You guys keep a sharp eye out for their bunkers and for anyone coming out of holes in the ground," Steve cautioned the squad.

NVA tunnels are not just an underground hallway leading to a larger room. They were most often multi-level mazes with numerous branches. Steve had a bit of unsettling experience in fighting his way past and through the NVA tunnel system. He tied a knotted nylon rope to a tree and threw the weighted end down the hole. He waited a moment. There was no response. He had been expecting gunfire. Leaving the rifle with the pistol in hand, the scout began descending the knotted rope. The hole was so small his shoulders were scraping both sides of the hole, sending loosened dirt to the bottom, announcing his presence.

The darkness enveloped him. He couldn't see anything. He began feeling a bit claustrophobic. He forced himself to continue traveling deeper into the tunnel. His foot finally touched bottom. Steve was certain he was about to be attacked, perhaps feeling a knife in his back or slitting his throat. He crouched and quickly moved away from the entry into deeper darkness. He held his breath, listening.

All he could hear was the loud, fast hammering of his own heart.

He wondered if it was safe to use his pencil flashlight with its red lens. He really had no other choice. It held it backwards, as far away from his body as he could. He rolled it across the floor of the tunnel. There were no shouts and no sounds. He appeared to be alone in this part of the tunnel. The base was less than three feet wide. The top formed an arch about four feet from the floor. Even the Vietnamese had to crouch to move through it. The bare tunnel was surprisingly clean. Steve took that to mean it was being used frequently. This could be a major find.

Steve knew he had to crawl through what he was sure to be a certain death trap. He turned his flashlight off and groped his way along in absolute darkness. It seemed like he crawled for hours. He expected the knees of his trousers to be threadbare before he got out of that tunnel.

The Marine bumped his head- hard on a rocky surface. The tunnel had narrowed as well as gotten smaller in height. With his hand in front of him, he could feel that the tunnel had been reduced in size by approximately one half. The Vietnamese must have to belly crawl through this portion of the tunnel in order to reach the next, he thought. I could use some fucking grease. He honestly tried to squeeze into the tunnel; however, with his broad shoulders and size, there was no way he could go any further in that tunnel, which was something of a relief.

There wasn't room for him to turn around. He had to back out of the tunnel. It was a much more difficult process than moving forward. He could feel his knees bleeding. His muscles were aching. He wanted to stand and relieve the cramps that were now coming in waves. After what seemed to be an eternity, he emerged into the daylight, sweating and sore but glad to be alive. He was determined to pay the little gook bastards back for his discomfort at their expense. All around the tunnel entrance and at varying distances from it, he rigged booby traps, using everything he had learned in two combat tours and schools to change them up and disguise them. "I hope I get a lot of those smart little bastards," he told his buddy.

"So, how did you end up spending most of the summer in the jungle along the border with Laos?" a new man asked.

"Well, that battle was a microcosm of what was going on throughout the flat lands and backwater marshes of northern and eastern I Corp. With the exception of one fairly large battle fought by the 4th Marines, the Battle for Dong Ha was a constant series of small unit running gun battles with elements of the 2nd NVA Division.

"During a battle, your focus is very narrow, usually on that particular gook or groups of gooks that are currently trying to kill you. But those guys in headquarters see a bigger picture. They knew the Dinks were suffering heavy losses but were being resupplied and reinforced with fresh troops infiltrating into South Vietnam and the battlefield from the Ho Chi Minh Trail inside Laos. They were ending in massive amounts of men and supplies with impunity along that trail network."

"So they sent the battalion in to block them."

"An entire division couldn't block them. We were sent in to locate them, to destroy as much of that network as possible, and to slow down that rushing tide of incoming men and materials we couldn't possibly match.

"They sent us in by helicopter. I was relieved to be out of that damned desert, to get back to Quang Tri, to hot meals and a shower. That didn't last long. They rushed us through a pre-op prep. New clothing, boots, and the whole dog and pony show. An armorer went over our weapons, individual as well as crew-served. They cut the usual four-day procedure down to two. Then the whole battalion loaded down with field marching packs minus the blanket roll, of course, and lined up at the LZ. So, we knew this was going to be one of the biggest heliborne assaults the Marine Corps had ever undertaken.

"The helicopters, which were primarily used to haul wounded troops and cargo in their early days in Korea, came into their own as weapons platforms during the Vietnam War. Seen as a force multiplier due to the mobility they provided, helicopters became jet-propelled and were armed with machine guns and missiles. Attack helicopters for use against ground forces as well as armor and artillery changed the battlefield, all since I joined the Corps.

"We trained in helicopter exit and entry from the ground. Most of the scouts learned to rappel from a helicopter and be picked up on a rope ladder dragged past them on the ground, at over 100 miles per hour! That was pretty exciting stuff for a nineteen-year-old kid until bullets started punching holes in the thin skin of the helicopters and blood began to cover the deck.

"The most common helicopter seen in Vietnam is the UHIE, the Huey. They are primarily Army helicopters. They must have thousands of them. Their flights often fill the skies like the stories of passenger pigeons. You hear the unmistakable eggbeater sound of their whirling rotors. Looking up into an early morning sky, you see dozens of HUEYs flying in formation, all banking perfectly the same, a virtual parade of helicopters. If you see more than six of the birds at one time, you know they aren't Marine Corps choppers. Many of those Army choppers are flown by warrant officers who are my own age and with less education. They are essentially the equivalent of World War Two's flying sergeants.

"A routine Army experience you will never experience as a Marine goes like this. There are eighteen HUEYs lined up on the ground, engines howling, and rotors whipping the air. Overhead are nineteen more. It's an awesome display of power as thirty-seven Army helicopters filled with Sky Troopers take off for an operation. That's a reinforced company going out in one lift.

"Imagine loading an entire battalion of airborne soldiers and transporting them at high speed, flying low to avoid visual detection and most anti-aircraft weapons. Your landing zone is twenty minutes away on the other side of a mountain ridge. A long line of helicopters, dozens of them, jump up over the ridge in a convoy of aircraft. Door gunners open up, hosing down any movement and tree lines where enemy forces might be overlooking the landing zone.

"I've never seen the Marine Corps do that. We might not have that many HUEYs in the whole air wing."

"Just think of the firepower of thirty-seven door guns alone. You know, the Army allows a certain amount of 'paint' decorations on their helicopters. There's always the unimaginative white shark's tooth against a blood-red mouth."

"On the nose of one, I saw a caricature of a nigger with a bone in his nose and the words, 'Witch Doctor'."

"Bikini Babe on the nose of another. I wonder what squadron flies HUEYs decorated with a big yellow dot in the middle of which is a hunched hissing black cat."

"Who was in Dak To in '67 with shark's teeth plus the words, 'Easy Rider' on the fuselage?"

"Who was 'Head Hunter' over 39?"

"Or a huge white spider with a black Ace of Spades painted on its back?"

"And the Air Cav, yellow crossed swords with a white lion in the top right corner and in white, 'Gang Busters' above?"

"I wonder who flew 'Big Gun'?"

"A cocktail glass and a pair of dice on each door with the words 'Chicago Transit!'"

While the HUEYs' were sleek and glamourous, the Chinook the Marines called a "shithook" was the Marine Corps' workhorse helicopter. She was wide-bodied and sturdy. She could carry heavy payloads internally or externally. There were four open portholes on each side of the fuselage. She squatted down on four wheels more than she landed. Her forward rotor blades were right above the cockpit. The tail rotor mounting was elevated above the ramp.

Troops entered and excited the helicopter from the rear ramp. The first man on was the last man off, meaning a commander had to know the order he wanted his troops on the ground. The net seats strung over pipe frames could be pulled out and fastened to the sides, sort of like a Murphy bed, for hauling cargo or for loading Marines like sausages in a casing. With so few helicopters available, seats were seldom folded down.

"A dozen 'shithooks' came in to deliver the first lift, an entire company with its attachments. The sun was high, creeping past noon. As crowded as we were, the cooler air at altitude was refreshing. The Chinook didn't have the speed or maneuvering capabilities of the smaller, faster HUEY. We crossed over the mountains at the performance level of the aircraft. We took a long but steep approach to the landing zone, a large valley, more of a bowl actually, closely pressed on all sides by triple canopy jungle growth.

"The hydraulic ramp was lowered while we were still in the air. That was the last time we would be cool for days. A fire team of riflemen were the first men off the chopper. They peeled to the left. A second fire team followed, peeling to the right. The squad leader had chosen to send his third fire team up the middle with a machine gun team following them. Within thirty seconds, a reinforced thirteen-man squad of twenty-five with an added four-man machine gun team, four-man mortar team, corpsman, scout, and radio operator were out of the helicopter and in the field of battle.

"The Chinook lifted off, heading out to bring in another lift, another company. We were not under fire, not yet, but there was no doubt that we were being observed and reports of our presence were being made. Perhaps we had caught the enemy by surprise and they had not had time to mount a defense.

"I knew they were out there, watching as we established a small perimeter. They would not fire on us now. They would leave us for later. They wanted the aircraft. 1 knew they'd be set up for the next incoming flight. Anti-aircraft guns, rifles, machine guns, shoulder-fired weapons, all would be brought to bear against the helicopters, maybe even mortars as they came slowly in for a landing.

"I was holding my breath in anticipation as the six Chinooks loaded with Marines flared for landing in the valley. A shoulder-fired missile slammed into the left engine of one of the Chinooks. Trailing smoke, the helicopter moved across my position so close I could feel the heat of its burning engine. I imagined I knew how the men who were only passengers inside the aircraft felt. The pilot was searching for the first available place outside of the designated landing zone, which was now enveloped in explosions from enemy mortars to set her down. The crew fought the fire with on-board extinguishers. They put down safely. The riflemen exited quickly and established a perimeter around the aircraft. They prepared to defend the helicopter and themselves.

"On the line, we suppressed the enemy fire. Our mortars were set up to go into action as soon as the aircraft had departed. The remaining Chinooks braved the enemy fire to land, hopefully to safely discharge the squads aboard them. As it neared the ground, an RPG round flew into one of the helicopters' bodies through its open ramp. The warhead exploded on impact inside the aircraft. A ball of flame was contained for a moment inside the aircraft, burning men alive. Others died after breathing fire that seared their lungs. The ball of fire fed off fuel and lubricants, expanding and shooting like a dragon's fart out the open back of the dying Chinook. Thick smoke poured from the cockpit. The fuel and ammunition exploded. The aircraft came apart in small and major pieces. The aircraft, her crew, passengers, and cargo were lost. One of the men on the ground who had landed safely was decapitated by the whirling blades.

"I'm not really a religious person, but I prayed for those men as my soul cried for them. I didn't know yet who was aboard that flight. They were all Marines, and therefore all of them were my brothers regardless of rank, color, creed, or any other defining factor. The combat loss was heavy on our hearts, but it was not demoralizing in spite of being somewhat numbing. The gooks fired their mortars, machine guns, and rifles at us. Determined, we fought back savagely. They came at us again and again throughout the day, stopping while still in the shadows of the tree line. We fired at muzzle flashes and shadows."

The memories are painful. My weapon was hot in my hands. The sun was drying me from the outside in. Every sweat pore seemed to be working overtime. My throat was raw. My eyes burned. I heard moans and grown tough men crying for God and their mothers. I smelled the gunfire and even the blood. Is that my own fear I smell as well?

"This is combat. It is dirty. It is often inhumane. It is almost always cruel. Blood. Anguish. Maimed bodies. Death. Loosed bowels. Resolute courage and, in rare cases, abject cowardice. The enemy broke contact as night fell. We had found the enemy. Maybe he has found us would be a more accurate statement. That part of our mission had been accomplished. Another day of survival was the secondary mission for each of us. I'd mark one off the short timer's calendar if I were in my tent back at the rear. We'll need replacements for our combat losses and resupplies. The gooks will be waiting for that, eager to knock down some more of our helicopters.

"'Day is done' comes to me from some memory. Thank God. I smell like a fucking goat. I need a bath and a shave. I need to brush my teeth. I have patches of heat rash in several sensitive areas and painful inflamed saw grass cuts on my hands and arms. We'll be getting replacements with the supplies. More meat for the fucking grinder. I hope it is not a load of Fanugies. Some second-tour men who wouldn't crap their drawers when the gooks hit us again would be a blessing.

"I am so weary I can hardly stand. I could use a cold, cold Budweiser in a frosted glass. And I'm is not really much of a drinker. Hell, what kind of Marine am I? I wondered. I'm only one fisted drinker. Jesus, I'm even choosy about pussy. I miss my red-haired goddess. I hope she is happy. I wonder if she knows how hard it was to leave her. I hear her voice again as we made love for the first time."

"Think beautiful, Steve. Think beautiful."

"With her, I always have and always will whenever I think of her, no matter what the future holds for us. I smile at my inner thoughts, which are interrupted by shouting lieutenants. Sergeants are scowling and bellowing. My thoughts turn to matters at hand, to standing a watch throughout half the night, to improving what will become our fire support base, to moving out on patrol into the jungle tomorrow, to being worn down a little bit more in every way possible by this war."

CHAPTER FOURTEEN
THACH HANH

While Le Kinh worked with one squad of the self-defense force, Steve worked with another, concentrating on patrolling. They rotated the squads daily. They drove their part-time soldiers hard. After the recent attack, the squad members accepted the rigorous training well and even looked forward to the variety of training and information they were being given. Steve began his new lessons with a lecture. Lan served as his translator.

"Patrolling is a large part of a soldier's life in Vietnam, more than major operations, more even than perimeter duty or any other activity. For me, a patrol is an armed unit of men sent out by a higher headquarters to cover some ground and take a look at what's out there. It's basically the same thing the police do.

"I take every patrol seriously, even these short training exercises. I feel a heavy responsibility to get my patrol members home safely while taking them into the face of danger. There are other kinds of patrols. The terrain of Vietnam is as varied as any country on earth. It is patrolled by boats, airplanes, and soldiers on foot. We patrol swamps, deserts, mountains, jungles, and everything between and beyond. The Navy flies a CAP, a Combat Air Patrol. They go up there, fly around the fleet, keep their eyes open, and provide early warnings to defend the fleet. That's one form of defensive patrolling.

"Defensive patrols are run to protect an installation and offensive patrols to locate and destroy the enemy. Some combat patrols are designed to lure the enemy out of hiding and force an engagement by a larger force on standby. Probably the most well-known of all patrols are the search and destroy missions.

"Patrols can be of any size. The number of soldiers on a patrol is a factor of your intent and the expectation or knowledge of the target area, and, of course, your mission. As a scout, I've led everything from squad-sized patrols to a battalion in a harrowing night march and four-man reconnaissance patrols. No patrol is ever the same as another. No patrol should ever be considered safe. The route you covered safely yesterday may have been mined during the night. A growth of trees that provided shade for your patrol's noon break yesterday may be crawling with enemy soldiers today. They may have dug fighting holes and trenches among the trees. They may have set up mortars and machine guns, even clearing fields of fire.

"You don't use the same route back as the one you used to reach your consecutive check points. The enemy will often watch you depart and set up an ambush, waiting for you to return with your guard down, waiting to surprise you, to kill you. On a patrol, you have to remember that every step you take might be your last."

During the training exercises, the commanders drilled the squads on proper reactions, on formations, and on every item and issue that could present a danger to the friendly forces. It is usually given that a unit that trains well will perform well, but there is no way to train for the real thing when bullets are being fired at you with the intent to kill you. Steve believed his defense force needed some sort of action to keep them sharp and focused. What he wanted was a soft target.

Steve requested the major coordinate with the S-2 officer to locate such a target. While that was being decided, classes in Thach Hanh continued. These included language lessons in English, French, and Vietnamese. Weapons training continued. Scouting, patrolling, ambushes, and building defensive positions were all stressed. As important as the training, bonds were being formed. The unit was coming together as a small but capable fighting force. With half his defense force, roughly representing a reinforced squad-sized combat patrol, in attendance, Steve covered every aspect of receiving an order for the patrol he was about to conduct. Even Marines did not receive training to this extent.

A patrol routinely begins like an operation or movement to action with a warning order, such as be prepared to conduct a squad-sized (reinforced) combat patrol from CAP 123 at Thach Hahn to Hill 17 position 982076, 21 May, 1969. Check points will be six locations with map coordinates, with code names, radio frequencies, supporting units, and times indicated.

Sending out a patrol may seem to be a small, routine thing. Generally, it's quite the opposite. The intelligence department and the unit commander, usually a captain commanding a company, review the order simultaneously. The intelligence officer assigns a scout to the patrol. The captain assigns the patrol to one of his platoons via the platoon commander, a lieutenant. The lieutenant assigns the patrol to one of his squads. The squad leader, usually a sergeant, and the assigned scout meet. Sometimes a platoon commander will accompany the patrol in order to evaluate his personnel. In the case of a platoon-sized patrol, he will, of course, be the patrol commander.

Decisions have to be made. A map is laid out. The leaders study the map. Questions are asked, such as "Has anyone been here before?" The scout provides his knowledge and observations. It is important that he describe anything not evident on the map. Questions such as "What do we watch for are asked. What areas do we need to avoid?"

The check points are plotted. The route to each is left up to the patrol leader with input from the scout or others with knowledge of the terrain. Times to check points have to be realistic, as your patrol must physically be at the designated checkpoint when it is called in to your headquarters so your progress and current location can be noted. That prevents friendly units from firing on your position.

You have to brief the patrol members as a group, asking questions to make certain everyone is fully informed about the mission. Does everyone know the codes to be used on this patrol? They do change frequently. Does everyone know the radio frequencies we will be using on the company and battalion networks? What about artillery and air support? Who are we taking along for support? Mortars? Machine guns? Radiomen, the grenadier, and scout? That is twelve men to add to a full strength squad of thirteen men. Do you expect to encounter native personnel? In that case, you may need to add a translator. In an area where no one has been before, a Vietnamese Kit Carson scout may be assigned to accompany the patrol. A scout dog and a handler might be assigned to the patrol. A sniper and his spotter could also accompany the patrol. If the patrol route is to be along a well-used road or path, an engineering team with mine detectors might be out on the point. The larger the patrolling unit becomes, the more support staff are required. A squad could swell to three times It numbers with those added personnel, which complicates all forms of logistics.

What weapons do we need? How much ammunition will everyone carry? Water? How long is the patrol? Will we need to carry rations? Have we covered everything? The unit leader tells his men all they need to know in case they become separated or the leaders become casualties.

The lessons were provided to each thirteen-person squad. The lessons were repeated a week later. Steve knew some would grasp the information quickly while others would not. He hoped the Vietnamese would talk and ask questions among themselves so the knowledge could be absorbed in a manner that could be utilized effectively. At the end of one such lesson, Steve announced that the unit was going to conduct a patrol.

"Although this is a training exercise, we may encounter the enemy. Once a patrol steps outside of its guarded unit perimeter, you are truly at war, not just taking up space in a war zone or on watch, which is important and holds an element of danger. We may be fired upon by ambushers, snipers, mortars, or artillery. Be constantly vigilant.

"Clean your weapon. Fill your canteens. Change your socks. Bring 100 rounds of ammunition. Inspection will be in ten minutes." The Marine watched as the patrol members scurried about and assembled in the street. He began his inspection. Once satisfied that all his charges were properly outfitted, he signaled to his Vietnamese scout that all was ready.

Steve's sleeves were rolled up. He wore a soft cover rather than a helmet. The civil defense force had not been issued flak jackets or helmets. Accordingly, Steve did not wear his. There was no minefield or barbed wire perimeter to work through. The patrol was formed on the bridge in two columns with rifles pointed outboard. Walking through the squad to take his place at the front of the patrol, Steve stopped when he spotted Lan and her mortar team.

"You ready to go, sweetheart?" he asked.

"You say for me. I no say for you," she said with a touch of anger, some embarrassment, and some resignation in her reply.

Smiling at the girl, Steve left and took his place with the scout element about 100 meters out front of the main body of his patrol before contacting his battalion headquarters.

"Candy Tuft, Candy Tuft, this is Candy Tuft CAP123 Viking Six, over."

"Candy Tuft. Send your traffic. Over."

"Supper guard slugger at bat. Over."

"Affirmative. Slugger at bat, 0752 hours. Good luck. Over."

The Marine signaled the patrol to move out. He set a quick pace to start as he wanted his personnel off the exposed road as quickly as possible. The scouts were acutely aware of every sound around them. The patrol members swallowed dust kicked up by a quickly passing convoy rumbling toward Quang Tri Combat Base. The patrol remained on the road until they had passed the rice paddies dotted by water buffalo and peasants working the fields. They stepped off northwest toward Cam Pha, a hamlet known to be sympathetic to and supportive of the V.C. and NVA. This was to be a real patrol with real danger attached.

The scout element's job was to clear an area before moving the main body into it. It had to be done largely on the move. The scouts fanned out into the green thickets, searching and listening. Steve signaled the patrol to move forward. On the double, they moved off the road and disappeared among the covering brush, taking up firing positions as they had been taught to do. A few deep breaths, a drumming of heartbeats, and a tingling of nerves. No incoming fire. The patrol moved on.

Out in front of the main body of the patrol, the scouts moved forward cautiously, stopping at irregular intervals to look and listen, glancing back to assure they had not lost contact with the rifle squad. With the movement and the stop, look, and listen actions of the scout element, the patrol accordioned, bunching up and then spreading out. Steve made a note to work on maintaining proper distance in future training sessions. He would mention it to Le Kinh during a break.

Moving into the thickening brush, the patrol became restricted to a single file marching order. They were traveling light on this short patrol. No helmets, no flak jackets, no packs. Plenty of extra machine gun rounds. As much as they might be needed, no one minded carrying extra belts of 100 rounds for the automatic weapon. The M-60 simply devoured rounds at a rate of over 600 per minute. Steve made another note for machine gun training to stress firing. In short, well-aimed bursts.

The man on point moved forward, scanning all around, a mouse in a barn full of hungry owls. The patrol was alert. Rifles were at the ready, locked and loaded. Thick stands of bamboo closed in around them, limiting visibility. But up ahead, Steve knew the patrol would be exposed crossing a creek, an obvious ambush point.

Steve signaled for the machine gun team. He wanted them up forward to cover the crossing. A lean, dark man with a broad smile full of yellow teeth moved forward with his team. One of them was a schoolgirl. The bipod near the front end of the weapon was extended. A long belt of linked ammunition hung from the weapon. A round had been chambered. The gun team was ready. In his youth, the gunner had been a soldier. Green leaves had been woven into his cloth hat. The gunner saw what Steve had seen. He knew what the Marine wanted. Looking to the left and then to the right, the experienced veteran selected a site for his weapon. It was under the spread branches of a broad leaf tree, among shadows but with a covering view of the fording point. Steve gave his approval with a thumbs up gesture. The machine gun would punish any enemy force that was revealed.

There were several options available to Steve. He could order the machine gunner to sweep the opposite tree line in a reconnaissance by fire intended to draw enemy fire in return and get them to reveal themselves and their locations. He decided against that action. He could move the squad forward and cross in a rush all at once, but he didn't think the civilians had the training or the discipline for that. If they came under fire, he knew they would have difficulty reorganizing. That was something else he would have to work on in training. Would the enemy give them time to learn all these things? With defense as their major role, would they really need to know that type of thing?

Steve signaled for Le Kinh to come up. He pointed down toward the creek. "I'm going to cross first with the scout element. The sniper stays behind, ten feet or so from the machine gun. The dog handler and his German Shepherd will accompany me as I cross the opening."

Steve looked out at the crossing. It was so exposed, leaving his squad vulnerable. There was so much potential danger here. Steve's armpits were wet. Beads of sweat had formed on his forehead. Sweat gathered across his shoulders and ran down his back. He was burning adrenaline which he might need later. What's with adrenaline anyway? he wondered. Where in the body is it produced? What controls its release? How much of the stuff does your body produce? Can you ever run out of adrenaline? What happens then? God, there's so much I don't know. It was one of those odd moments when a thought or a string of thoughts hits you from out of nowhere at a time when you would hope to be more focused on the immediate task facing you.

Behind Steve, the patrol members had crouched down, sensing imminent action with the call-up of the machine gun . They had not yet gone to ground or melded into the jungle as more experienced troops would have done. "Take a break," Steve instructed Le Kinh. "No fires."

The sniper's spotter was searching through his powerful binoculars for possible threats and targets. During the five-minute break, Steve did the same, noting reference points as he did so. He pointed those out to Le Kinh. The Marine selected a landmark that would serve as a rendezvous point in case the patrol became scattered. Steve pointed out where he planned to cross the creek.

"When the scouts reach the tree line, we'll spread out and see if we can spot any sign of the enemy. Give us about five minutes on the other side. Shooting or not, you'll need to get the patrol across the creek in one movement. Then, if unopposed, you'll turn and cover the machine gunner and sniper team as they cross the clearing. If we run into opposition, they'll be in an excellent position to cover us, especially if we have to fall back."

Behind the scouts, half the patrol was on watch while others sipped from their canteens. A young man who wore thick glasses poured water over his face. Another was writing in a journal. His rifle was jammed into the ground by its bayonet. He was resting his back against a tree. A machete was close by. A girl rested her head in the lap of another.

One man seemed to have sprouted a bush from his cloth hat. He had scooted into the underbrush and was alertly watching. Good man, Steve thought, perhaps someone worth promoting. Another man was almost invisible in the brush. He too watched intently. They might make good one-on-one instructors. Although still within a mile of Thach Hanh, the patrol was in Indian Country. The enemy could come at them from any direction at any moment.

A pudgy teenager intently watched his sector; however, he had not camouflaged or hidden himself. Not doing so endangered the entire patrol. His rifle was aimed down the back trail. Steve would have to provide him some of that individual training. Steve stood. The scout team followed him as he began making his way down to the creek, weaving his way around thick stands of brush. He paused at the last bit of cover. The Marine took a deep breath. He motioned the scouts forward and charged across the creek, splashing through the water loudly. Any watchers would have their full attention focused on the scouts and be unaware of the squad hidden in the cover on the other side of the creek.

The scouts threw themselves down in the foliage on the north side of the creek. The ground was wet and slippery. They had not drawn enemy fire. Now there were other concerns. Putrid marsh odors surrounded them as it was disturbed by their passing. A nasty odor rose from the disturbed muck. It was a terrific environment for snakes. And for leeches. Steve hated those slimy little blood suckers. They would attach themselves to your body and keep sucking, bloating on his blood like the rest of Vietnam. There was no time to stop and check for them.

Steve knew there were snakes in the immediate vicinity. Some of them were as deadly as bullets. He knew giant boa constrictors love marshy, wet grasslands. They can slither about in that environment relatively unseen, taking prey that came down to drink. A twenty-foot snake does not fear men. There were others, small and poisonous, that didn't fear men either. They were designed to blend into the surroundings. But Steve could not watch for them. His eyes were probing the entire area for signs of the enemy.

It was like fidgeting, waiting on an opposing center to snap the ball so you can brush off his hard block and go after his quarterback. Better if they aren't there, Steve thought, but we are a combat patrol. We are looking for a firefight, for an opportunity to test my people, and to punch the enemy in the mouth to bloody him.

The scout moved forward. The thick muck slowed him down, coating his boots and forming a big ball of mud around each foot. The scouts moved slowly through the marsh, stench, and slimy mud. A branch from a thick bush would have allowed them to scrape some of that off and move faster, but there was no time even for that. On dry land again, the mud would dry and fall off. Their feet, though, would stay cold and wet. He could feel the grit between his toes. They moved into the tree line, continuing to search for the elusive enemy.

Where are they? Steve wondered. The NVA has watchers. They have to have seen us to know approximately where we are, if not exactly. Why have they let us get across the creek and the clearing without opposition? Have they set up an ambush for us? The scouts moved deeper into the jungle, fanning out and searching. Nothing. The squad would be crossing the creek now. The scouts continued to move forward and seek out the enemy.

The scouts reached checkpoint four, a small mound that was the high ground for miles around. They were joined there by the squad. After a short break, the long hot patrol continued, taking another route now in returning to Thach Hanh. Although they had not found the enemy, the patrol had produced value. Corrections would be made. Lessons would be prepared and taught. Staff evaluations would be made. Individual counseling would be offered.

No enemy had been spotted on this patrol. No shots had been exchanged. This was more usual than not. But you never know. You just...never...know.

Steve was out of bed early. He turned his boots upside down and banged them sharply together to dislodge any spiders, scorpions, or even snakes that had crawled into them during the night. He shook his trousers and uniform blouse out for similar reasons. It was a routine he had established, a good habit. Many of Vietnam's insects and snakes were poisonous, some deadly so. They liked to crawl into dark, warm places.

Reaching into a bucket of water, the Marine splashed his face, neck, and arms with the aromatic liquid supplied by Lan. The camphor tree is a native mountain timber. Its waxy leaves were often boiled, producing an effective insect repellant. Lan had taught him to identify the tree and prepare the native remedy for the mosquito bites he suffered.

Steve had spent a restless night. It wasn't due to the rather uncomfortable cot, the mosquitoes buzzing in his ears, or to the tropical heat. He'd grown used to both of them. It wasn't nerves, stress, or combat memories that had kept the young man awake. The major had called Kowalski with orders for him to report to the headquarters. Steve had expected to be briefed on a new operation. Instead, he was ordered to "stand down from all but pure CAP unit activities. He was ordered to "concentrate on civil affairs matters and self-defense issues."

No reasons were given for these instructions. Kowalski was curtly dismissed without further discussion. The major's attitude toward him seemed to have changed, to have become strained. Perhaps, Steve thought, I have overstepped my bounds on that last action. Maybe it was getting someone wounded, a woman at that. Steve knew the inactivity was going to drive him crazy. He was tempted to request a return to a combat unit. He was, however, on what amounted to an extended vacation "fishing and swimming in the river, watching the girls, and eating in the restaurant or private homes. It should have been a no-brainer. Steve was not a coffee drinker or a smoker. He didn't need any stimulants to kickstart his day.

He used the radio to routinely check in with the SEALs and the Army detachments. All was quiet. The Marine kept his rifle locked and loaded during the night, ready for instant use. He did not generally walk around the village that way during the day. With so many children around, there was just too much potential for disaster. He removed the magazine and jacked a round out of the chamber. The bullet went back into the magazine he would carry in his pocket.

He picked up five packs of C-rate cigarettes. Each held four cigarettes. The first twenty adults Steve encountered during his morning walk would each get one. The others would hear, "Hoot het roi!" which was "Smokes all gone." He emptied a bag of 100 butterscotch candies into the large button-down pocket of his trousers. A smaller bag of peppermint candies went unopened into his right breast pocket.

Using the flash suppressor of his rifle, he caught the wire around a case of C-rations and twisted until the wire broke. He looked through the box of twelve meals until he found the particular one he wanted. Breakfast was ham and eggs eaten without warming. The heat was provided through a liberal splash of Tabasco Sauce. The meal was eaten quickly. The can was tossed into a box. Hanh, who now cleaned the tent and did Steve's laundry, collected the tin cans for her father, who was lining the exterior of their hut in fish scale fashion with them.

Steve shouldered his rifle. He stepped out of his tent into the village as a new day began. Breakfast was being cooked. Rice in every case, but with numerous variations in its preparation. Glutinous rice is rolled into small balls with fingers and eaten salted. Rice with soy sauce. With nguoc mam. With milk. Seasoned with fish oil. A sprit of greens. With fiery peppers. With citrus acid. Rice soup for the ill and elderly. Mashed rice for young children.

Steve wondered what the day would bring. Would it be a day of peace, of children's laughter, or of tears? Would it be mundane or memorable? Things were slow at the moment. Maybe he should take some time to write some letters. It was more of a small duty than anything else. The family wasn't particularly close. When the right time came, Steve had left the nest with a sense of looking forward more than anything else. He hadn't been shoved out, but he knew he was expected to be on his own at eighteen after high school graduation. He knew he would be welcomed back, at least just for a short period of time. But Steve was a grown man and independent.

He wrote Mary, who had grown somewhat distant, a brief letter as well. Steve really didn't know what to tell her. She had responded with something of disinterest in what he was doing in Vietnam, with his descriptions of the people and places he saw. Something he never wrote about to anyone was the combat and everything related to it. There was one exception.

Steve had respected his journalism teacher and admired his ability to convey ideas and thoughts. He could never seem to master all the skills required to become a professional writer. In his letters to John Boyce, whom Steve wrote often, he described in a disjointed manner everything he did and saw or thought about in an unmasked, frank way, revealing himself to a man he trusted.

After completing his letters, Steve continued his daily routine. The first person he met on his morning patrol was Saah. The stooped woman smiled and greeted the Marine with a cackle like a hen that was announcing the arrival of a new egg. She was on her way out to the forest to gather wood. There were many wood gatherers in Vietnam. Every village had to have one. That provided her a meager living but was a perfect cover for her more profitable intelligence-gathering activities.

The primitive Bru and Montagnard continued to practice slash and burn farming, depending upon the resulting nitrogen to fertilize the poor jungle soils. The Vietnamese did not cut trees to provide fuel for their cooking fires. They only gathered fallen branches and other dead wood. The gatherers had to go further and further afield to collect the wood needed to support their villages. They often gathered smaller branches the tribesmen did not burn in their fields. In order to protect her cover, Saah had to continue her daily work activities.

"Chao Ba," Steve greeted the elderly woman. She made a slight bow to him in the Vietnamese tradition. Her lips and teeth were stained purple and black from the betel nut and leaves she chewed. Steve knew the betel nut was a mild stimulant. It was in wide use throughout Vietnam. Like most Americans, he wouldn't know a betel nut if he stumbled across a tree full of them. Betel nut is somewhat like an overgrown, misshaped acorn.

Steve had known Saah would be one of the first people he encountered each morning. He reached into one of his pockets. He presented a mini-pack of four cigarettes to the elderly woman. The pack was green; Kools, a brand he knew the elderly woman favored. She secreted them away quickly and shuffled on up toward the bridge to begin her route west.

Steve continued south. The smells of the village had become common, comfortable, and welcoming to him, like those of a barn to a cowboy. Wood cook fires were burning. He walked down to the river. The wooden fishing boats had absorbed the blood, oils, and odors of fish caught over many years. They contributed a distinct odor to the village mix. Human night soils and livestock excrement used to fertilize the rice fields had strong smells in the mixture. The river also contributed to the general odor that enveloped a village like a thin fog. After operating for weeks in the jungle, where the air was less polluted and the odors were more natural and pure, the Marines could often smell a village before they saw it.

The fishermen were drifting down to their flimsy craft, nets draped over their shoulders. Thin boys who would have been in the sixth grade or above in developed countries were scattered among them. Steve had learned from them how to cast a twelve-foot net. He looked forward to fishing that way at home. Babies and young children, many of them still sleeping, were being delivered to their elderly babysitters, women who, for one reason or another, could no longer labor in the fields. Men who had reached that point in their lives didn't seem to do anything but bask in the sun and remember the past.

In any human endeavor, it seemed to Steve the real story was always about the people. The real stories behind the magnificent photos sent back to earth from the moon and beyond were the people involved, and not just the astronauts who became so famous. It is the dreamers, the visionaries, the scientists and engineers, even the dedicated workers in a manufacturing facility who assembled a rocket or a satellite.

In Vietnam, the people were where Steve saw the stories he would tell if he could. He wanted to ask them all, How has the war affected you individually? How has it changed your life? Will you share your story with me so I can tell others?

In a relocation camp as part of the pacification program, families had been forced from their homes and relocated to "pacified" areas supposedly firmly controlled by the South Vietnamese government. After removal, the families were sent to processing centers, barbed wire compounds, where they were interrogated, had their identities checked, and were assigned to a small plot of land that would never be their own. Entire villages were not relocated together. Resentment and distrust of the government grew into resistance and hostility. The effort to win the hearts and minds of the people was a colossal failure.

Steve and his squad had marched past a relocation camp with its wire enclosure in four inch squares. He couldn't help but think of the American Japanese who had been placed into camps during World War Two. Four boys, maybe six years old, their brown eyes shining and wide smiles on their faces, hung on the fence begging for cigarettes. Failing In that effort, they asked for cau, candy. A snaggle-toothed boy reminded Steve of himself at six. Steve stopped and handed him a chocolate bar. The fence sprouted little hands outstretched to the Marines. Shrill voices cried, "You souvenir me cau."

The marching Marines didn't stop. Steve wondered why there was too often so little time for compassion in a place and situation where it was so desperately needed. The squad was on the move, on a mission. The voices followed them, shrill now, and loud. "G.I.! You numbah fuckin' ten!"

Number one to one boy and number ten to a hundred others, Steve supposed. The corpsman did stop. He kneeled down in front of two naked boys, younger than six. The head of each had been swallowed by a steel G.I. helmet. The corpsman handed each of them a cookie and moved on to catch up. It was an act of diplomacy on a grass-roots level, or maybe a touch of humanity among the madness of war.

Steve saw many people in passing. He tried to read their stories in their faces, but reading faces is like judging a book by its cover. What is inside that person? he often wondered. What is going on behind the smile or the scowl? Who is the real person behind the mask that changes with the environment and situation the way a chameleon changes colors? How many smiling faces and cordial greetings camouflage their real feelings? Steve knew Americans did the same thing and thought perhaps all people do it more than is realized.

At a memorial ceremony after the battle for Dai Do, Steve stood at attention, facing a long row of rifles with fixed bayonets jammed into the hard ground. A pair of worn boots was at the base of each rifle. A helmet was atop each weapon. Damn, he thought, how many did we lose? After a speech by the regimental commander, eight senior officers, colonels, and even generals bowed their heads in prayer. What are they really feeling? Steve wondered cynically. Are they in a hurry to get away from here? Do they have a meeting to attend that they consider more important than paying respect to the men they sent out to die? Do they have air-conditioned quarters to go back to? A beer cooling in the refrigerator? A hot Vietnamese mistress in their bed? Is this really for those fallen men, or is it for us and our morale? Maybe it is nothing more than a photo op for the brass.

After being dismissed from the formation, Steve made his way back to the S-2 tent. He passed six black soldiers, shirtless, sitting on cots in their tents. A look was exchanged. The anger on their faces did not appear posed and defiant. Their posture and attitude appeared to be natural. You see what they feel not in their faces alone but more so in their eyes. Do they hate me because I am white? Steve wondered.

The following morning Steve flew out to join the squad at Leatherneck Square during the heat of summer. There was no shade in this bare strip of land called The Trace. The enemy had not been completely quelled. Stragglers were still attempting to reorganize into fighting units as they retreated into the DMZ, fighting every step of the way. NVA artillery firing from North Vietnam sought the Marines. Enemy bullets hunted for their flesh. There was no return counter battery, no air strikes. Where is our support, our suppressing fire? Steve wondered. He felt exposed, like a huge red zit on a gorgeous photo model's nose. His face pressed to the earth, his breathing creating puffs of dust and dirt, he wished he was an armadillo that could dig a hole faster than a man with a shovel. He breathed in grit with every breath. He was sweating like a fat broiling chicken. God, I need to pee, he thought.

My throat is parched. Next to him, the kid from Missouri snaked his canteen from the holder on his hip. With the left side of his face pressed hard to the ground, he dribbled water into his mouth. Good idea, kid. Stay low to the ground.

The black lieutenant, big enough to be a wall all by himself, stood tall in spite of the enemy contact. Big enough to have been a college or even pro football player, he cradled his rifle in his left arm while referring to a map in that hand. The radio handset is in his right hand. He raised it.

"Fire mission!" He is talking to Whiskey Battery, calling for artillery support. A smaller man, pale white, with a large radio pack on his back, stood close, nervous, attached to the officer by the coiled umbilical cord of the radio handset. It was a scene seen daily all over Vietnam.

Even after they return from the operation, Steve paid close attention to people, making memories, perhaps for something he will write later. In the S-2 tent, the Vietnamese Kit Carson scouts are seated on the ground around a low table of a type seen all over Vietnam. They are eating balled sticky rice with chopsticks. They dip the rice balls in Nguoc Mam, the common pungent fish sauce, and deftly deliver the dripping ball of rice to their mouths. They smile at Steve and flash him a peace sign. Are they all what they seem to be? Steve wondered. Can they all be trusted? He didn't think so. Can any of them, he wondered. What will come of them after the war?

Steve exits the tent to give the scouts some privacy among one another. He visits the club where he nurses a beer he only wants because it is cool. He begins to watch the people around him, characters perhaps for the writing he may one day undertake. Who is this guy? He asks himself. "I've seen him in movies. Plays a bad man most of the time. Lee Van something or the other. Not him, of course, but a near look alike. Unshaven for a day or two, just like in a movie I can't quite recall. He is intent on a card game being played at a nearby table. Not the movie star, Steve knows, but sure looks a lot like him. Do I have one of those out there? John Wayne, I was told years ago. I freaking wish. Pilgrim. Friends Meyers and Swift pose in front of a bunker. Steve liked the way this one is reinforced. Two layers of sand-filled 55-gallon drums, one standing on the other with runway matting across the top supporting four layers of sandbags. He thought he would see if he could trade a captured rifle or something to the Seabees or engineers for a double crisscrossed layer of steel matting and more sandbags. Steve's nose had been broken in a bunker when the roof came crashing down during an artillery attack. Maybe it makes me look meaner, tougher, like a fighter you don't want to mess with or meet in a dark alley, he thought. It is now a part of my mask. I wonder what my mother and Mary will think of it canted to one side and humped.

Steve made his way to the field operations center. A young Marine was sitting next to an eighteen-inch tall bush he was decorating like a Christmas tree. Where did he get the bell and the red balls? A truce, a hot traditional meal, and back to the killing and the dying.

Steve spotted friend Leerch. His back is to the scout. Leerch was the tallest Marine Steve had ever seen. His M-16 is slung like a toy he had outgrown on his right shoulder. He was playing his guitar. "Where have all the soldiers gone?" Steve knew where too many of them had gone.

Monsoon. Water everywhere, in everything. In the field, your feet are growing webs between your toes. Quack. Weather only a duck could love. I expect to see Noah's ark floating by any minute.

A young Marine looking up the hill where the enemy has a bunker we have to take. Waiting for the platoon leader's whistle to charge up that hill in the face of enemy machine gun fire. Daily courage. Facing daily fears. To my right, the scout/dog handler crouches. The look on his face is intense. Beside him, his German shepherd lies at rest, panting. His long tongue hangs from his mouth. Beautiful dog. I love to have them on my patrols.

The Bob Hope Show. Les Brown. Beautiful girls, including Susan McIver, one of Dean Martin's Golddiggers, the all-girl dance troop. Susan and Jimmie are my favorites.

I watch the traffic on the Thach Hanh River Bridge keenly. The narrow bridge was a choke point on a major artery leading to the interior, to Cua Viet, Cam Lo, Quang Tri Combat Base, The Rock Pile, Khe Sahn, and the deep mountain jungles along the Laotian border.

A convoy of vehicles, obviously not American, caught Steve's eye. Aussies, he thought. Where did those guys come from? No helmets. They all wore bush hats with the left brim pinned to the crown with some type of Aussie badge.

Different gear. Oversized boxy ammo pouches. Belts of ammunition strung from left shoulder to right hip and right shoulder to left hip. Odd-looking, distinctive rifles. Something of a cross between an

M-14 and an M-16. Fires a thirty-caliber round. More breakdown parts than the 14 or 16 or AK-47. May have a problem with jams, Steve concluded.

Must have a real kick. They have all taped extra padding to their rifle butts. An older man with a forehead in full retreat seemed to be in charge. His cheeks were sunken, his eyes hollow. The five men in the vehicle with him all wore their chin straps. That would be a bit of a distraction, Steve thought. Two of the men wore single colorful ribbons denoting some type of award sewn above their breast pocket.

The Aussies are well-disciplined troopers. They do not toss cigarettes or tins of rations to the begging children. They don't whistle at or call out to the schoolgirls selling cold sodas.

I'd like to have that bunch close by, Steve thought as they exited the bridge toward a destiny Steve would never know.

One morning waiting to cross the bridge coming out of Quang Tri City was a truck that must have been twice Steve's age. It sagged like Saah under her load of chopped wood. Its tires were bald. The cab was green under a thick film of orange dirt. The sides of the body were a faded blue, with the top being white but polka dotted with large rust spots. The truck was full of people. A small boy sat on top of the cab, guarding straw baskets of goods that had been tied there.

Those boys were fearless. When the truck stopped, they would dart in and out of traffic, snatching a purse and stealing what they could. They rode on the backs of those giant, fierce-looking water buffalo. Behind the truck was a tired old bus. Yellow like a school bus, right under the open windows, nine of them on each side, were three four-inch strips of freshly painted red, white, and blue. Baskets and luggage were stacked and tied the full length of the top of the bus.

Behind the bus were two military vehicles, U.S. trucks with South Vietnamese markings. The drivers appeared to be South Vietnamese soldiers. The passengers were women and children. The beds were loaded with household goods. Our tax dollars are hard at work.

Coming into the city from the west was a slightly smaller bus bearing orange and white colors. Like the yellow bus, its colors were fading, and its roof was covered with baskets, ducks in cages, and luggage. Behind it was a rare blue Citroen of an early '40's vintage. It was followed by a small green panel truck and a convoy of American military traffic that held no interest for me. These guys weren't going to blow up my bridge or shoot at me.

In his sunglasses, helmet, and flak jacket, the driver of the convoy's lead Jeep posed for photos with eleven children. The oldest four boys posed with a degree of flippancy. A girl sucked her thumb. A very young boy smoked a cigarette "souvenired" by the driver. The children were dirty, ragged, and generally unkempt. They disappeared when the one-way traffic began moving east. They had gone to the other side so they could talk to drivers there.

A short time later, the driver who had posed with the children realized his Jeep was missing a side mirror. Also missing were his watch, his bolstered pistol, a box of C-rations, and two grenades. Another day in the Nam.

A toolmaker's stone sharpening wheel was turned by a converted bicycle. On their way to the fields, women stopped at his place to have their knives sharpened. Sparks flew and bounced off the ground, and the metal tools ground down the wheel. It was primitive but efficient.

Children gathered eggs and fed livestock. Boys with shovels and wheelbarrows gathered droppings to spread in the fields. The daily parade of schoolgirls began. It was like watching the migration of pastel butterflies. Steve greeted each of them by name as they passed, now knowing everyone in the village. Typically, a couple of soldiers would be waiting at the bridge for no other reason than to watch that parade and catch an eye if they could. What started routinely became a day of surprises.

The parade began with a girl who rode her moped across the bridge every morning. A book bag hung from the handlebars. This was a girl who would be noticed in any crowd. She was always perfect in every way. Typically, she wore a bleached white au-dai with white pantaloons. Even the straw hat she wore at a cocky angle had been bleached or painted white. Her sandals appeared quite fashionable and a little out of place.

Her long black hair fell to the small of her back. The wind pressed her blouse to generously rounded breasts on a slender frame. Steve knew he could encircle her small waist with his thumbs and middle fingers without squeezing. The thin fabric of her pantaloons revealed a high-cut panty line. No one knew the girl's name or where she lived, only that it was somewhere to the west of the river. She never stopped, never spoke to, or acknowledged anyone. She didn't wave. She did not make eye contact with the Americans. She ignored whistles and comments completely. The aloofness and mystery added to her allure.

Another girl, dressed similarly, carried a sun-shielding parasol rather than wearing a straw hat. This was Linh Hoang, a sixteen-year-old who was one of Steve's fire team leaders. The passing Marines who blew her kisses and asked her to go "short time" with them had no idea that she was a soldier as proficient with an M-16 as most of them.

A pair of women came walking out of Quang Tri to catch the bus at the bridge. It was the gray military bus that delivered civilian workers to the combat base. These women obviously did not fill sandbags. They wore low-cut white blouses and pegged black jeans. Their hair was cut short in a western fashion. They wore sunglasses with large oval lenses and pink frames. They were not nearly as appealing as the schoolgirls. They were, however, much more approachable. They carried on a lively banter with the passing soldiers. Steve did his best to ignore them.

From the south end of the village, Specialist Jay Thomas, a handsome brown-haired young man from Ardmore, Oklahoma, escorted Thu Duc to the bridge. The little beauty didn't even come up to the Americans's shoulders. The girl wore no makeup. She didn't need it to be beautiful. She styled her mane of dark hair long and parted over her left eye. A jade Buddha set in a gold frame hung from a delicate gold chain around her slender neck. The seventeen-year-old looked to be no more than twelve to Steve. Quick to laugh and tease, the very proper young lady was quite attached to the soldier. Steve wondered what the future might hold for them individually and possibly as a couple. Were people wondering the same about him and Lan?

A group of five girls passed Steve on their way up to the bridge and school. They had all cut their hair short since he had last seen them the day before. Their neck-high blouses were olive, pink, orange, and dappled with greens and blues. They greeted him in chorus. "Chao Ong, Ha Shi Caul"

Hello, Corporal Candy.

"Chao Co,"he responded. The next passing pair surprised the Marine. Rose Kym, a very attractive, slim-figured girl, had tinted or bleached her hair. It was faintly red. She wore a bright summer dress, something you might see in Hawaii. The stunner though was Lan. Once he spotted her, Steve couldn't keep his eyes off the doctor's daughter. Lan's hair seemed to be a shade lighter. Her brows had been shaped by plucking. Her eyes had been emphasized with dark eyeliner and lash thickeners. Those brown eyes were shining as she boldly approached the Marine. Steve could smell an intoxicating floral perfume. Her long hair, worn loose, was parted down the middle. Her inviting lips had been glossed with a hot pink lipstick. More unusually, she had somehow framed those lips with a thin black border.

Suddenly, it came to Steve. He had seen the girls chattering on about a French fashion magazine someone had brought to the restaurant a week or so back. But his attention was still riveted on Lan. She wore large gold hoop earrings and a gold watch. Around her neck, hanging from a twisted gold chain and nestling in her cleavage was a gold heart with two small diamonds in the center. Steve had to tear his eyes from the exposed swells of those proud young breasts, revealed by a low-cut strapless black blouse that hugged her tiny waist and flared with large ruffles at her hips. A tight black skirt was also revealing, short at mid-thigh. High-white boots with a polyester shine reached to just below her knees, revealing an enticing stretch of slender but not thin legs. If his mouth hadn't gone suddenly dry, Steve would have whistled.

Lan stepped close. Steve's eyes were drawn down the front of her blouse as if magnetized by her breasts. The girl allowed the Marine to look as she fumbled in his thigh pocket. Lan extracted a butterscotch candy, which she presented to one of one of her friends. Her hand went back into the pocket, burning a path along Steve's leg. He gasped as the girl gripped his thigh. It wasn't an accidental thing. She released him and then squeezed his leg again, before extracting another bit of candy. She still had not stepping back. Steve found his voice.

"Is there some kind of special event today?"

"Graduation. Today I woke up a child. Tonight, I will be a woman."

And some kind of woman, Steve thought, an orchid among skunkweed.

"Tomorrow I will begin work in the rice field."

An image flashed in Steve's mind. Lan under a straw hat, gray hair curled in a bun, lips purple and wrinkled by the sun, loose, sagging, her energy and vitality sapped by hard work, the heat and years of life lived on the same page every day with no hope for anything better.

"My mother will search for a husband. The nun says if I go to the convent in Saigon, the church will teach me to become a nurse."

"Lan, you are so beautiful you will have no problem finding a husband."

"I no say for you," she said, but the teasing that had always been there in the past had been replaced by sadness.

Steve was at a loss. What could he say? What could he do? Lan submitted to her fate while Steve performed his duty. He watched daily as Lan went with a crowd of women to the rice paddies where she labored a minimum of twelve hours each day for a meager wage while growing old early. She no longer had time to loiter and socialize at the restaurant. Steve rarely spoke to her except when she joined the CAP unit for training or duty.

Steve went more often to watch the workers in the rice field from a distance. It was all he could do. The fields were flooded. The Asian plows, dark slate grey water buffalo, plodded in the mud, plowing the field, mixing the fertilizer into the soil. Women gathered bundles of thin green stalks and set them in the rice fields. The well-fertilized and carefully cared-for shoots would grow quickly. Steve thought of onion sets. It was pure back-breaking stoop labor, but it was a routine way of life in Vietnam. It saddened Steve to think of Lan's spirit being broken by this way of life. Had her family been less prosperous, Lan might have resigned herself to becoming a bar girl or prostitute in the city.

Steve had begun to have flashbacks of other operations during the night. He slept fitfully or laid there for hours, remembering. In one of them, the company was operating in the Que Son Valley. It was a routine combat patrol, but with so many new men coming into the unit at the time, it had really been more of a training patrol. The squad-sized patrol had been reinforced, almost doubling the size of the thirteen-man squad Steve was leading as the scout. The patrol route had reached its third objective and turnaround point with no reports of contacts or sightings of the enemy. Still, Steve knew he could not let his guard down for a moment.

The Marines were not in "Indian Country" where they could fire at anything that moved. Fortunately, the orders to only fire after being fired upon had been rescinded. Still, they had to be careful of potential collateral damage in an area scattered with populated villages and hamlets. It wasn't a free-fire zone at all.

Steve led the patrol to a stream. He didn't know what else to call it. Too small to be called a river, certainly. Too shallow to be called a channel. The fast-moving water was a bit cloudy, like an old man's eye filmed with an early cataract. Where the scout chose to cross the channel, water spilled over a walkway of rocks about two feet higher than the next level.

In crossing, the cool water only wet his trousers to mid-calf. Still, it had an overall cooling effect, which was quite welcome. The stream was about eight feet wide. There were brush-covered banks about five feet tall on each side for some twenty feet to the north and south. The patrol was exposed during the crossing. For that reason, Steve had the men rush to the other side all at once. On the north bank, they followed the stream. They came upon a village. The locals were minding the store, so to speak, appearing to be going about their daily tasks. This was a poor farming village. The monsoon rains flushing out of the jungle-covered mountains to the west had undoubtedly created those banks over a long period during the annual flood.

Those monsoonal waters delivered an abundance of nutrients to the alluvial valley. The villagers there did not have to depend upon slash-and-burn techniques which required frequent moves. They were permanent residents. They had no need for a well. Their hamlet was not large enough to support any type of public buildings or commerce. There was no central plaza or streets, only a few dirt foot paths.

Because of their permanency, their homes were something of an improvement over the poor thatch huts the Marines so often saw in Vietnam. Concrete slabs took the place of packed earth where rice was thrashed and meat and vegetables were chopped. A dozen or so women and children were squatting along the banks of the stream, pounding clothing with a rock. The naked children splashed in the stream. The scene was like a photo right out of a travel magazine or a National Geographic.

A woman stood, shading her eyes to look the Marines over. Steve wondered if she was counting. Was she noting their weapons and direction of travel? Once the patrol was out of sight, would she alert the V.C.? You just never knew what was behind the mask the Vietnamese wore when they encountered American troops.

Steve knew they weren't going to be ambushed right there because the women and children didn't disappear. Still, they hadn't approached, begging for candy or cigarettes. What was the reason for their not doing so? It was out of the norm. Steve concluded they were being watched by the enemy, and the villagers knew it. He kept an eye on them in passing.

Before he fell asleep, Steve wondered what his experiences in Vietnam were doing to him. How had they changed him? Had they made him more of a man? Had they made him less human with the killing and his callousness toward all the things he had seen and done? How long would he remember Vietnam? He knew there were things he would never forget. What was that going to cost him in the future? The Marine spent a fitful night remembering things he would write John about:

"While on routine patrol in thick jungle cover, we came upon an enemy camp. We went to the ground prepared to attack. We prepped our assault with a generally ineffective mortar barrage. The enemy had dug in hard. Our route was going to be restricted. We attacked a series of mutually supporting machine-gun bunkers. It was like a bowling alley where they were shooting the pins all lined up close together.

A gun in a well-concealed bunker on our left flank took out the only man ahead of me in that assault, one of my Vietnamese Kit Carson Scouts. I wheeled and hit the ground. My vision was suddenly like a movie close-up shot. The bunker on the flank was covered with a mound of dirt, leaves, and growing foliage. I knew how they had constructed those bunkers. We all did. The NVA soldiers were the best pick and shovel engineers in the world.

I had been carrying a LAAW. Many times during the long, hot march through the jungle, I had wanted to throw that thing away. I was glad I hadn't. I pulled it out of the canister and extended it for firing. Looking through the sites, I thought I was too damn close to miss that bunker, but I didn't want to just bounce off the reinforcing. That would not have accomplished a thing except I wouldn't have to carry the LAAW anymore. Fat lot of good that would do me if I got shot by someone in that bunker.

I could see the slot that allowed the machine gun to traverse as it was fired. I was close enough to throw a grenade, but I could toss grenades all day and not put one in that four-inch slit. The bunker was too well supported for someone to pull a John Wayne and flank the position so they could virtually push the grenade through the small aperture. This had to be done the real way, not the movie hero way.

It was going to require a straight shot. I didn't have to account for windage or adjust to fire uphill or downhill. Shouldn't be too hard for a man who had begun his Marine Corps career as an antitank assault man with a bazooka-like rocket launcher firing at moving tanks. I simply aimed the thing and squeezed the trigger. The round went right into that opening like a bullet hitting the bull's eye dead center. I expected it but was still a little surprised. There was a muffled explosion. The bunker didn't blow up or blow apart. There was a flash of light and the rolling echo of a small explosion. The brush and leaves on top of the bunker shook. Doesn't make for good movie effects, not that I give a crap about that anymore.

I pulled the pin on a grenade and rushed forward, hoping I wouldn't stumble or fall with the live thing in my hand. I shoved the grenade in the bunker and rolled away with bullets from the supporting bunkers impacting all around me. I don't know how they all missed. Someone had said a prayer for me. Thank you. Mom.

1 waited through four seconds of eternity for that grenade to explode. My ears rang painfully when it did. I lay there a moment, stunned and a little afraid to move because of the machine guns firing at me from two directions. But I was on my feet almost automatically, rushing that bunker. The company moved in through the gap and spread out again. We eliminated the bunkers one by one.

There were seven of them. I held up to catch my breath. I must have been holding it for the last twenty minutes during the attack.

The captain commanding the company stopped next to me for a moment while I guzzled my way through half a canteen of water. "Good shot," he said, handing me another LAAW. Shit, I almost uttered. I picked up my weapons and moved into the gap where the rest of the rear-end platoon was moving forward. Someone had dragged five bloody bodies out of the bunker I'd taken out. Confined in that bunker, they had been chewed up like hamburger by the LAAW and my grenade. My stomach lurched. I could taste the sourness of it, like biting into a rotten orange.

The company was taking a break in an old, deteriorated trench line. The enemy had been here for a long time. Sweating men who had just survived a vicious battle drank too much of their water too fast. Others had that dazed-after-action look, although we were only a bit more than two hours into our combat patrol. There was more to come.

A tearful, tough-looking guy who had just lost a friend was among those who had that shell-shock look on their faces, or really, in their eyes. On his helmet, using a black marker, he had written, "I'm not a tourist. I live here." I knew exactly how he felt.

I wondered what this place was doing to me. Who and what was I becoming when this type of thing, killing the enemy and seeing your comrades die without feeling the loss, was normal? I had personally killed five men. The sight of their mutilated bodies had made my stomach a little queasy. Emotionally, I was unaffected. It had become too common. I couldn't let it eat at me, at least not now. Would it come later? Would Mary or my mother see a monster or a killing machine in my eyes? Would I adopt a mask to hide behind? If so, how long would I have to wear it?

Steve woke from his troubled dream of remembrance. His bladder was full. It had been a hot day, and he'd drunk three canteens of water. His bladder was telling him it was closer to three gallons. He gathered his rifle and strolled down to the river to piss. He didn't consider the danger that might be all around him at all. Returning to his tent, he sat on the edge of his cot, his head in his hands. If he'd been a smoker, it would have been a good time for a cigarette. He lay down and closed his eyes. His mind returned him to combat.

The wounded is a face of war combat veterans cannot forget. Even if you believe you have become numb to it after seeing so much of it, the bloody, shattered bodies, the moans and cries, the loss of friends and comrades, all have a deep and lasting effect that might not manifest itself overtly for years. The memories are in your brain ticking away like a time bomb waiting for a fuse to be lit.

Five white Marines deep in the thick jungle assist a wounded Negro. He has passed out. A corpsman holds an IV bottle high over the wounded man's body. One of the Marines holds the wounded man's head. Two men have his body. Another his leg. The trouser of his other leg hangs bloody and empty from the knee. There is only one color in my Marine Corps, and that color is Marine Corps green.

An arm around the shoulders of his squad mates, one black, the other white, a wounded Marine is assisted to the medevac point. Fatigue is etched in all their faces.

"There are no niggers, spicks, wops, kikes, rug heads, or greasers in my Marine Corps. There are no blacks, browns, whites, or yellows in my Marine Corps. Every Marine is one color, and that color is Marine Corps green."

"Sir, yes, sir!" we all shouted back to the drill instructor. "Thank you, sergeant. Thank you, drill instructor."

A black Marine with a bandaged head reaches out in anguish, not due to his painful wounds but to the muddy, bloody body of a white squadmate who is being covered with a poncho, a hurt deeper than his wounds.

A "white boy" evacuates a wounded black Marine in a fireman's carry. A four-man Marine rifle team. Three African Americans and a wounded white boy, a "cracker" from Georgia. One of the black Marines carries the wounded team member on his back. Steve is immeasurably proud to be a Marine at this moment.

CHAPTER SEVENTEEN
MEMORIES OF A VILLAGE

The objective was a government-friendly village just off Dong Han Creek. A marshy area full of snakes and leeches, Steve didn't relish a thousand-yard trek through wet smelly rice paddies, an act sure to infuriate the villagers before he would ever have a chance to talk to them. The scout decided a narrow, hard-packed road would be their route of approach.

About twelve feet wide, the road was primarily a foot and cart path with some scooter traffic from time to time. He would have to be vigilant for mines. He was certain any recent digging would be evident. Because of that danger, maintaining a proper distance was stressed. He kept the patrol well spread out. The squad approached in two columns with personnel staggered like the teeth of a zipper.

It was a lengthy approach, not the kind infantrymen are comfortable making. They were exposed every step of the way. They moved quickly down a straight portion of the road. The sky was streaked with thin layers of gray clouds. Mountains to the west rose in a blue haze on the horizon. Nearer, but still in the background, was a long line of green too uniformly even in height, to be a natural growth. A plantation of some type, Steve thought. The trees had obviously all been planted at the same time.

Rice grew lushly in wet fields on both sides of the road. The Marine knew the fields had been liberally fertilized with cow, buffalo, and pig dung as well as human night soil. He could smell it with every breath. It seemed to settle on his teeth and clog his nostrils. Rice wasn't all that grew lushly along the patrol route. There were stands of a short, thick palm crowned with verdant sprays of leaves. They were obviously being grown as some kind of commercial crop, but Steve didn't know enough about agriculture to know what it might be.

Pines grew tall and thin, reminding Steve of new growth stands of East Texas yellow southern pines. Three of them growing closely together leaned out slightly over the road at the point where the dirt path made a slight curve. Whatever was around the bend in the road was hidden by a wall of thick vegetation. Steve signaled the patrol to a halt. The squad members went to the ground, rifles pointing outboard.

Staying close to the base of the pines, Steve scouted forward around the curve. The patrol was quite near the village. In spite of it being known as a friendly village, there was always a chance that the NVA had moved in to punish the villagers for their alliance and to force their cooperation with the local V.C. cadre. Seeing nothing to alarm him, Steve stood and waved the patrol forward. He could see a cluster of trees up ahead. The path appeared to disappear into it. A house, more substantial than the straw hootches he saw so much of, was visible ahead. It appeared to be a concrete block structure coated with yellow stucco. There was a wide covered porch. The roof was of red tile.

The patrol came upon a barefoot, wide-eyed boy. He was carrying a toddler on his hip, most likely his brother. The child wore a shirt but was bare-bottomed, a typical Vietnamese rural village scene. The boy did not run back to his village shouting an alarm. He did not beg for cigarettes or candy. He stopped, watched the patrol for a moment, and then, hitching the child a bit higher on his hip, went on his way.

A moment later, the patrol was in the bowels of a beautiful terrarium. It was hot, humid, and green, with the brown scar of the path cutting through it. All types of plants grew up to overhang the dirt road. There were yellow-green shoulder-high ferns and a stand of a dozen or more slender pines with scattered hardwoods and scrub brushes of every description. Palms dominated.

Five women, apparently heading to a market, walked into the path between the squad's columns. They were middle-aged women who appeared beaten down by the lifestyle of a Vietnamese peasant. The women shared an aged-before-time look. Dressed alike, they were all barefoot. Their feet were ugly, heavily calloused pads.

Each of them wore black pantaloons, sun-bleached light purple blouses, and straw hats tied with a ribbon under her chin. The first two women bore long chogi sticks over their right shoulders. At each end of the pole was suspended a large square woven basket filled with rice. Steve estimated that the total load of each set of baskets weighed more than the woman carrying them. In many ways, the Vietnamese were an amazing, resilient people.

In her baskets, the third woman carried a load of packages wrapped in white paper. Each package contained fish or meat of some kind. Another woman came behind them carrying baskets loaded with fruits, longans, pineapples, jackfruit, and darien. The last woman carried her hat in her hand. Atop her head was a huge basket. Because it was covered, Steve did not see what she was carrying to market. After the women had passed through the patrol, Steve signaled for the radioman.

"Keep an eye on them," he instructed. The patrol moved on. The village they came upon was actually on a lower level than the dirt road. Steve had seen this type of construction before. The path down to the village had been hewn with shovels and picks digging out an unusual stairway. The risers were about nine inches in height. The treads, however, were about a meter square. Stones had been pounded into all the exposed surfaces to prevent the clay soil surroundings from being washed away by the heavy monsoon rains.

The homes were built of slender concrete columns and beams. The walls were of sun-dried clay and straw blocks. They looked as if they were in the late peeling stage of a bad sunburn. Here and there, one could see a streak or splotch of the paint the houses had once worn when they were young. Large but shallow pockets of concrete had weathered away. In one place, Steve could see exposed too small reinforcing bars that had rusted and turned black.

The patrol entered the village. The residents appeared happy to see them, especially when the Marines began passing out cigarettes. A crowd of smiling people gathered around each of them. They ran their hands up and down the exposed arms of the Americans, feeling their hair.

"Like a monkey," one who didn't know Steve spoke Vietnamese said. They gathered around a Marine nicknamed Leerch, who, at six and a half feet tall, was a giant to the Vietnamese. He passed out Luden's cherry-flavored cough drops to the children. The villagers were soon tugging at the Marines, each wanting one of the money machines to make their home his temporary residence. Perhaps Steve's first thoughts about the village and its people were wrong.

Ong Phung, the man whose home became Steve's for a brief period, was a hard-working rice farmer. He owned a water buffalo which he rented out to his neighbors for a small fee. There was a calf his son cared for. "In three years," he told Steve, "I will have another calf. The older calf will have been broken to the plow. A man in a nearby village is saving his money in order to purchase the aging cow."

Phung's wife smiled and chattered constantly. She prepared their meals on the floor in a space that served as their kitchen. Rice was the staple of every meal. If you were sick, she served rice soup with medicine that included jungle herbs and home remedies the Vietnamese all knew well. For breakfast, there was rice with buffalo milk or honey from the jungle when they could find it. For lunch and dinner, the rice was mixed with slivers of fish or chicken, even pork. At dinner, however, greens were added along with a desert, usually fresh fruit from the nearby trees. Steve turned his rations over to Yahn at every meal. She incorporated them into the meal. Not being a coffee drinker, Steve didn't miss that packet, which was much appreciated by Mr. Phung. That and the sugar and creamer packets were a real treat for the man. Yahn jabbered considerably over the salt and pepper packets. Their teenagers, both good-looking kids, a son and a daughter, enjoyed the packets of Chicklets gum that came in each meal.

They all enjoyed the hot chocolate powder Steve mixed with the strong buffalo milk. Cookies, jams, and peanut butter were all wondrous new treats for the Vietnamese, as were the main meals.

Steve saved the chocolate bars for the baby. Not even starving Ethiopians would eat the John Wayne crackers, and the Vietnamese in this village were not starving.

For all it lacked, the village was something of a godsend for the patrol members. The village chief had been expecting them. The squad was to stay in the village throughout the harvest to protect it from the NVA tax collectors who habitually confiscated a large portion of every crop. In spite of everything Steve had seen and thought, this was a small but comparatively prosperous rural village.

Each home and its plot of land were defined by a border of thick, thorny evergreens. Everyone seemed to have a dog and at least one pig. The homes had concrete floors. Steve had witnessed these being built as well.

He had grown up in a two-story brick home. The foundation was surrounded by a thick, deep perimeter. The floors were on compacted sand, crushed gravel, and four to six inches of concrete.

In Vietnam, the reinforced perimeters were roughly dug and quite small in comparison. Sand was delivered and spread by hand. It was sprinkled with water and compounded by pounding. A thin layer of cement was troweled smooth over the sand. Most of the foundations lasted for many years. It would not have passed the most liberal building code anywhere in the United States but lasted in Vietnam for a century or more.

The homes were open and airy. They were shaded by tall trees that spread their branches and broad leaves over the tiled roofs. The wide porches also helped keep the houses cool. At one end of the village was a concrete well. The base was shaped like an octagon. It had a four-inch curb on the edges. The well was about two feet tall and three feet in diameter. It was surrounded by trees, primarily slender palms. The corpsman pulled up the first bucket of cool water.

"There's all kinds of things you can see in this water," he announced. "No telling what in there you can't see. Boil it and use your halizone tablets."

The squad members all found a place to call their own for the next two weeks. Not having to sleep in a hole in the ground was a blessing. Still, Steve required all of the squad members to dig fighting holes outside the village for defensive purposes. The adults and older children had a full day of chores to complete each day. There was always work to do, from the labor-intensive rice farming to caring for a variety of animals or gathering dead wood in the jungle for the cooking fires. The old women and young girls babysat. The boys of their age fished, picked nut and fruit trees, and worked the vegetable plots of each family.

The corpsman ran an unofficial MEDCAP, administering to the medical needs of the Vietnamese as best he could with the limited supplies available. The Marines wanted a quiet presence. Aggressive patrolling might prevent the tax collectors from coming into the village while they were there; however, they would return with a vengeance after the Americans left. The Marines did not hide. They always had at least eight men on watch, twelve during the nighttime hours. They set Claymore mines out each evening and retrieved them at first light. Wherever they went and whatever they did, their weapons were right at hand. While they maintained a military bearing and discipline, there was time to fish with the boys, write letters home, take a bath at the well, or adopt a puppy.

The women would not allow the Marines to cook or wash their own clothing. Steve took his boots off and aired his feet at every opportunity. The Americans often participated in the village activities. They carried water and other loads. They helped patch houses when and where they could. Every American had his own camp follower. The boys were anxious to run errands. After they had boiled the well water and added halizone tablets to their canteens, the Marines returned them to the canvas pouches which were soaked in water and hung from a tree branch or rafter. The evaporation process actually worked to cool the water. The girls kept the pouches wet. Minh, Phung's daughter, was one of Steve's camp followers. The vibrant young lady was one of the few young Vietnamese girls Steve had seen who curled their hair. She then swept it back and held it off her ears with silver berets on each side. There was no way to "dress up" or appear provocative in the black pantaloons and grape blouses the women in this village wore. Minh, however, did pay special attention to herself and to her personal hygiene.

She caught Steve looking at her as he picked up a sweet smell from her hair. She cast her eyes to the ground as if she had been caught doing something wrong. Steve reached out and took a lock of her hair in his hand, gently bringing it to his nose.

"Tot lam," he told her. "Very good."

Minh took his hand. She led him to the edge of town he had yet to explore. Very large hardwood trees grew on both sides of the trail there. Clusters of large, bright red flowers were in full bloom from vines that grew up the tree trunks. With the agility of a monkey, Minh climbed one of the trees. She began picking flowers, passing them down to Steve. Those flowers had a fragrance that was not unlike what he had smelled in the girl's hair. They walked silently back to her home after she had gathered a small load of blossoms. Steve watched as Minh gently plucked the petals, discarding everything else. She gently washed the petals in cold water and spread them on a woven mat. She set them out in the sun to dry. In a small screw press, Minh worked hard but got nothing from the crushed petals, which she immediately rubbed into her hair. She left them there a few moments before combing them out. That gave Steve an idea.

Here was a girl who had lived in the jungle all her life. She'd never been to school. She'd never read a book. She'd never ridden in a car or attended a concert, dance, or sporting event. The only bed she'd ever known was a straw mat over a hard frame. She'd never been to a mall or a supermarket. She didn't know what a refrigerator, freezer, or air conditioner was. There were so many things and places she would never experience. Working all day in the rice fields would have her looking twice her age in another six or seven years. At twenty-five, she would look sixty. Her lips and gums would be stained black by betel nut. Her hair would be gray and without luster. Her unattended teeth would be rotten. Hard work in the fields would leave her stooped. The sun would sap the youth from her skin.

Steve wondered if she dreamed of something better, if she could even imagine something better. How can you dream of something you don't know about? He wondered. How can you aspire to go places you have never heard of? This was the true reality of Vietnam and other parts of the world Steve would like to show people at home. Minh seemed happy enough, perhaps because she didn't have enough information to compare her life to that of others. Steve was tempted for a moment to draw a picture of the two-story brick home he'd grown up in. He decided not to do that.

He was getting short. He knew he would be gone from this place within sixty days. The village and the people would soon forget him and his Marines. Likewise, he expected to forget this particular village and give little or no thought to them upon his return to the United States. But what of Lan and Thach Hanh? He would never forget them. How much a part of him had those people become? How could he just abandon them, go home, and forget them as if they no longer mattered or existed?

CHAPTER EIGHTEEN
QUANG TRI PROVINCE, REPUBLIC OF SOUTH VIETNAM

Xa Hai Li wasn't much of a village. It was comprised of seven bamboo and straw structures built on rough wood platforms raised about four feet off the ground by perhaps twenty irregularly spaced rough wooden piles. It had once been a stand of trees cut for burning and to provide the foundation for the houses. Each pile was about six inches in diameter, indicating a relatively young growth of trees.

The sides of the hootches were built of straw mats laboriously braided together with jungle vines. The roofs were of straw panels and dry palm fronds. Both ends of the structures were open, most likely for what little ventilation could be achieved in the oppressive heat.

Dogs, children, pigs, and even chicks and a goat had sought shelter from the sun in the shade under the hootches. Villagers scrambled from the fields and ran to their homes, dragging howling children with them upon spotting the patrol as they emerged from a nearby tree line.

A lone brown cow took a few challenging steps toward the Marines. It was tethered to a lone tree among the houses. Surprisingly, the tree looked to Steve like some kind of pine. It didn't offer much shade. The ground was dry and cracked. What vegetation there was grew in parched patches. There were no fences or growths of shrubs defining borders. These people didn't expect to be here for more than a few years before they moved on to another location where they could practice their primitive slash and burn style of farming.

An old man who was no doubt the leader of this community hobbled out of one of the hootches. Dried, withered, and weathered by age and life in the tropics, the man wore the traditional wraparound and head scarf of the Montagnard tribesmen. "Toi Ha Shi Steve," the scout introduced himself. The old man uttered a mouthful Steve did not understand. The old man seemed to realize that at once and changed from the local dialect to Vietnamese.

"Saht Cong?" he asked, pointing to Steve's rifle.

"Toi kackydau beacoup V.C." Steve explained that he had killed many V.C. Being a non-smoker, the Marine kept the packets of four cigarettes that came with each C-ration meal for just such encounters. Steve fished out a pack of Kools and presented them to the old man. The man bowed slightly, grinning through a mouth full of teeth that would have given a dentist nightmares. They must have been a constant source of pain to the old man.

Seeing their headsman engaged in conversation and accepting a cigarette, the villagers had come to their porches. They had quickly determined that the Americans were not an immediate threat to them. The villagers rushed forward to beg for cigarettes and whatever else the Marines might be willing to give up.

Steve was faced by two young women. They could have been twins. The Montagnard are a small race of typically unhandsome people. Those girls reminded Steve somewhat of the Yanomamo Indians of Brazil he had studied during an anthropology class. They were wrapped in colorful cotton blankets from the waist to their ankles. They were bare from the waist up, a scene straight out of National Geographic Magazine, a thirteen-year-old's Playboy magazine in the late 50s and early 60s.

Their course dark hair was parted in the middle and tightly wound into a bun. They wore woven beads about two inches into the hairline. Dark eyes. No make-up. Broad but flat noses. Their mouths were flat lines. They neither frowned nor smiled. They wore necklaces of brown and green jade above their collarbones. Another longer strand of jade beads hung between their breasts. Breasts firm and round, surprisingly full. Dark, small aureoles.

"I'd do her," one man said.

"Yeah, if it was real fucking dark," his buddy retorted.

Through Le Kinh, the Marines announced their intention to help Xa Mai Li and villages in the immediate area to be safe from the V.C. tax collectors. The Montagnard village was a good choice for establishing a base camp. They were all armed with old rifles which they kept in good shape and knew how to use. They were the sworn enemy of the V.C., and they knew the terrain.

The squad dug fighting holes around the village and settled in to cement the relationship. That includes eating and drinking with the men and providing medical services for all in need. The children gravitated toward the Americans who liberally shared the cigarettes, candy, gum, and cookies from their rations. The beautiful children with their laughter and smiles created rare moments of pleasure for the soldiers. Their mothers let the Marines care for the children while they hawked various goods to other Americans. One fetching young lady went to the Marines every day with her basket full of freshly picked fruit. Her pineapples made the canned C-ration pork paddies something the Marines could really enjoy. In the days to come, Steve wondered about the fate of that young lady and her village.

A call came in from headquarters ordering Steve to return to the Combat Base. A helicopter was sent to bring him in so he knew something important was taking place and he would be a part of it.

Flying over Hue after the Tet offensive, Steve saw the city as a rabbit warren of ugly, too-close homes. The destruction wrought by mortars and artillery, grenades, and missiles was horrendous. He could follow the path of the fighting by the level of destruction. Parts of the city had the look of a devastating Oklahoma tornado or of a German city that had been pulverized by Allied bombs.

Vietnam was said to enjoy some wonderful architecture, but Steve never saw any, and he looked. There may have been a beautiful Vietnamese city, but Steve never saw it. The cities he saw were all crowded with refugees. The cities had been poorly maintained. They were full of trash, rats, and disease. There was little in the way of modern sanitation or general services.

The most beautiful place Steve saw in Vietnam was a small clearing under a triple canopy mountain jungle. It was like nature's cathedral with the sun beams broken up as they filtered through the leafy canopies. Soft ferns grew underfoot. An uncountable variety of orchids with a rainbow of colors and kaleidoscope patterns grew from fallen trees that were covered with mushrooms and moss.

Steve hoped the war spared that place. Wounded, Steve really thought he was going to die there. He wouldn't have minded having it for his final resting place at some point in the future. The setting was one he would remember often.

The headquarters meeting was brief and pointed. The command was responding to an intelligence report of nearby tax collectors and V.C. death squads targeting locals who supported the government. The CAP unit was to continue conducting combat operations to interdict the tax collectors and recruiters and to deny this resource, which enabled the enemy units to operate locally rather than depend upon a supply chain that was hundreds of miles long.

The CAP unit's first new target was Trieu Phong, a hamlet north of Quang Tri City. Steve returned to the base camp at Xa Hal Li to prepare for the operation. They bid farewell to the friends they had made among the Montagnards and returned to Thach Hanh to plan and launch the operation. The SEALS were again tasked with transporting the CAP combat team to its final destination. Most of the CAP unit was to be involved. After a period of inactivity, they seemed excited by the possibility of being engaged in a combat action. The Army detachment provided six men.

The team loaded up in the SEALs' shallow draft boats. Ten boats carried the reinforced company to the village. Those boats were a first and only for Steve, one of the things that made the event memorable. From time to time, the Marines operated in villages rather than thatched-hut hamlets. Generally, the villages were a little more affluent than hamlets. Not rich by any means, but better off with a larger population and a more diversified economic base. Such was Thieu Phiap, a village near Gio Linh along Jones Creek.

The houses were largely of rustic French style. There was no doubt their construction dated back to the colonial period. Each of them had probably belonged to a French citizen at one time or another. Built on concrete foundations, the walls and columns appeared to be of reinforced concrete. The roofs were of red clay-colored slate tiles. The windows were louvered. Everything was flaking and deteriorating due to a lack of maintenance. The village was eerily silent. The patrol approached with caution.

The most solid-looking, best-kept house was that of the village chief. The front of the house was bullet and blood spattered. The chief and ten members of his family were laid out on the porch in front of the house. They had been wrapped in thin, bloody blankets. Their heads were covered, but their bare feet were exposed. These people had been lined up and executed in front of their house in full view of their neighbors. A message was sent. Several men were assigned to carry the bodies to the boats for delivery to Quang Tri.

The Marines toured the village. There was a concrete building with a sheet metal roof that would become one of the platoons' barracks. The sign across the front read Ve Vo Cua in blue letters. Slender trees grew in the middle of a paved street, a boulevard, actually. On that road was a private residence with a high stone fence topped with four feet of barbed wire. A Marine who climbed the fence reported seeing a Yamaha motorcycle. "It looks shiny and new," he reported, as if he were ready to take it for a drive.

The chiefs house became the Marine Company's headquarters for two weeks. The intelligence section to which Steve was assigned was given a bedroom which he shared with his radioman as they were required to man a 24/7 radio watch, which included maintaining the ever-changing situation map depicting reported friendly and enemy locations with symbols indicating the identity and size of the units. They marked movements and contacts. They were ready to brief the company commander or visitors of any rank at any time.

Steve climbed to the roof of the headquarters building to watch over squads on patrol. Beyond the village, terraced plots were laid out irregularly. A series of six rectangles oriented with the ends outboard. At the top were eight running in the other direction. In the center is a mishmash of variously oriented rectangles, L shapes, and square plots. All of them were barren and brown. Immediately to the left of the rice paddies was a series of rich green plots. Steve wondered what was growing there.

The plots, both green and barren, stretched for half a mile in every direction. Four large plots had been flooded. Several thick tree lines outlined the plots from there out. Finger ridges rising to the left and to the right with a high crossing very green main ridge line revealed to Steve that the village was perfectly situated at the base of a broad, deep alluvial valley. The NVA would be in those mountains, watching.

Two of the scouts assigned to the company operated with the squads in the field. A CAP translator accompanied each of them. The experience should prove valuable when they were on their own. In spite of the disappointment at finding the village chief had been killed, the situation was one of the most desirable Steve had experienced in Vietnam. Rations were cooked in a real kitchen. Fruits, vegetables, spices, and a variety of fish and meat were purchased cheaply from the villagers. The village was not large enough to have an ice house. It did have a central well. It was blue with concrete benches in a circle around it. The citizens surrounded it several times a day like cattle at a water trough. The Marines suspended their canteens on ropes down in the well, cooling their drinking water.

A squad of riflemen took Steve upstream in a rubber boat. The boat sat low in the water. It appeared to be perilously overloaded. The Marines poled themselves away quietly. Several hundred feet from the bank, an outboard motor was started. They pushed upstream against the current until the river broadened. They rode past the never-ending scenes of bamboo hootches and rice fields.

The Marines were vulnerable from both banks of the river. Again, Steve felt as if he were a moving target that could not be missed. The jungle growth had crept down to the river until a solid wall of thick vegetation lined the banks like a herd of leafy trees that had come down out of the mountain to drink. Branches like long necks hung over the water's edge. Thirty meters beyond, as if they were pushing the growth of twenty-foot-tall trees into the water, were more trees with thicker trunks and less foliage but with twice the height. Among them was a scattering of sixty-foot giants. Teaks and mahogany trees.

Steve heard monkeys in the trees chattering their shrill alarms. They were difficult to see in the tangle of grass, but he spotted one as it leaped from limb to limb in the tops of the trees where they felt safest. Thinking that watching monkeys could get him killed, Steve turned his attention back to searching the river bank for signs of the V.C. He felt guilty over the momentary lapse, like when Mrs. Lee, his algebra teacher, had caught him watching Janice Jose's tight-skirted wiggly ass instead of the problem she was solving at the blackboard.

The river curved, running north and south for a short time before making its inevitable way east to the gulf. The driver turned the boat in sharply as the promontory of the curve would help shield their landing from watchers. The Marines waded ashore on the south side of the river. They pushed quickly inland through snarled jungle growth that seemed to have fangs rather than thorns. The scout was searching for paths or any approach to the village. He had to know where they were. The squad fanned out as they moved inland.

A click of a noisemaker, a paratroop trick from World War Two, announced that someone had located a path. The squad converged on the sound. Steve gave the kid who had located it a thumbs up. Quickly assembled, the squad moved in single file without flankers in the thick jungle near the path. Steve took the lead.

The footpath was hidden from aerial observation by a thick canopy of interwoven branches and leaves. In places, they had been tied together with coconut hemp to form that protective covering. The path seemed to wind in and out in the manner of an old river. At a point where the path turned back toward the river, the Marines came upon a flimsy structure of typical bamboo and thatch. It was raised from the ground about four feet by thick bamboo stilts. It was only about the size of Steve's bedroom at home. There were no animals about, no nearby cultivated fields. The structure was old and ill-kept. There was no furniture or furnishings. There were no decorations. "What is this place? What is it used for?" one of the Marines asked.

"Just an abandoned farm hut. Five minutes," Steve ordered, giving the men a break. The squad took up positions around the hootch while Steve plotted its position on his map overlay, noting the path as well. The men took a drink from their canteens but did not light cigarettes or open cans. They were soon on the move again. The path they continued to follow led them to a branch of the river. The creek that fed the river was broad and shallow. The bottom was of golf ball-sized rocks that had broken off as boulders from the mountains to the west. Broken apart as the monsoon floods moved them ever toward the sea, the rough rocks were broken down and smoothed by hundreds of years of tumbling downstream.

The banks of the river were sandy and broad. A village built on stilts had been established on the nearby plains. Stepping out into the open cautiously, the Marines spread out. Three nearly naked boys playing at the water's edge spotted them first. They stood, their eyes big, mouths open. The trio recovered from their surprise quickly and ran toward the Marines, their hands out. "We aren't the first Americans they've ever seen," Steve said as he took in the village and its surroundings.

Coconut palms grew along the banks of the broad creek. Coconut palms seem to always grow at a slant. Steve noted, wondering why. Did God make them that way so men could more easily climb the tall, branchless trunk to reach the nuts?

There were only five poor huts in this isolated hamlet. The adults paid the Marines little attention as they entered the village with an entourage of children following. The Marines spread out, moving between the structures, peering into but not entering or searching the homes with more than their eyes.

Steve saw clay pots and straw storage containers full of rice. The hamlet was almost hidden among the surrounding jungle growth. Leaving it behind, the Marines followed a footpath that took them through a small cultivated area, not more than ten acres. This was a temporary community of slash and burn farmers. The crops to their left were just coming up, nice thick rows of something with light green growth, only a foot tall at this point.

To their right, the crops were something darker, already more than two feet tall. It wasn't rice, wheat, or corn. Steve didn't know what it was. He knew the farming techniques would deplete the soil in two or three seasons. Then these people would move on. The Jungle would quickly repair itself and reclaim its own.

There was no threat here. While there was no threat, there had been intelligence to gather, not the hard kind of war-changing intelligence coup you always hope to achieve, but soft intelligence. The more you learn about the terrain, hamlet locations, the people, and their political alignments, the better you are able to understand the entire scope of the region and what you face. With the paths noted on his overlay map, Steve moved the patrol forward, stepping into an area that was like being swallowed by the jungle. The jungle presented a multitude of dangers.

Nerves were on edge. Fingers moved toward rifle triggers. Aware that they could be ambushed at any moment, every man was studying the totality of the environment, hoping he would be able to spot a camouflaged bunker or see signs of the enemy before they were seen themselves. The jungle captured and magnified the heat. The men were soon wet with sweat. On a C-ration diet, it didn't take a soldier long to become lean if he marched routinely on long daily patrols in the jungle, which was as good for losing weight as a sweatbox. The experienced Marines knew that vigilance could not be maintained at a peak level for extended periods of time. Most patrol leaders took a brief rest at checkpoints or hourly. Steve rested his patrols for ten minutes every half hour in the deep jungle environment and rotated his point units frequently.

Death sometimes gets very close and personal for soldiers, but especially for a scout walking point. Steve Kowalski was specially trained for that job rather than being appointed to the dangerous position because he was the new guy no one had formed attachments to. He was proud of the fact that he had never led any unit into an ambush. He wasn't sure if it was due to his training and experience or just blind dumb luck, but he was grateful no matter the cause or reason.

Steve held the patrol up after spotting an irregularity in the foliage ahead. He crept forward alone. He had spotted something that was more than a game trail and less than a dirt road. It was a footpath used by villagers and their livestock. The scout waited a moment, listening and watching. He waved the patrol forward. A four-man fire team faced down the trail while the remainder followed closely behind the scout as he followed the path.

The path curved slightly to the right and then curved back to the left around a vegetable plot surrounded by a border of tall, mature bamboo. The bamboo was more than a fence or a border. It provided shoots for eating and wood for burning and building. Steve crept forward again. To his right were mature rice fields ready for harvesting. The grain was tall and thick, with heavy heads curved downward.

Up ahead, maybe 150 yards away, Steve spotted movement. A black pajamaed figure, crouched, ran from left to right. A civilian? V.C? From that point of view, they could fire on the patrol right over the vegetable field and through the bamboo. Steve motioned for the squad to watch their flanks.

Something moved in the rice paddy at his two o'clock. Steve whirled, firing his M-16 on full automatic, a combat instinct telling him it was a threat and not a civilian. The squad behind him flung themselves to the ground.

A V.C. soldier fell, his chest sprouting blood. There was a surprised, maybe puzzled, look on his face. He rose, ran, and staggered forward, falling finally at the edge of the footpath. He struggled to bring his rifle up. Steve fired another long burst from his rifle into the man. The bullets chewed the V.C. up.

Guns opened up on the Marines from about ten o'clock to two o'clock across their front. It seemed like the Marines might be outnumbered. Steve called, "Grenadier up!" The "blooker" man low-crawled to the scout's side. Steve pointed out where he thought the enemy was thickest. The grenadier fired volleys of 40mm grenades from his M-79 grenade launcher.

It was critical for the squad to gain fire superiority as quickly as possible. The short, stubby weapon with a maximum range of 900 yards was just what Steve needed to accomplish that goal. The grenadier began pumping the rounds out as fast as he could fire, breaking the weapon down like a shotgun, extracting a shell and loading another one, then snapping the weapon closed to aim and fire again. The 40mm rifle grenade was deadlier than hand grenades. The long range made them a formidable weapon for a lightly armed squad.

Steve had enough clear space to fire a LAAW through the bamboo. Two fire teams of gutsy riflemen moved forward through the vegetable plot right up the barrels of the enemy guns. Their weapons weren't silent as they advanced. One fire team charged up the footpath that curled to the left, flanking the enemy position.

Rifles were blazing all around. Ears were ringing with the sounds of battle. Everyone on both sides had gone to the ground. You really couldn't see if you had hit anyone. The Marines would have to close with the enemy in order to force them out of the village. There was no choice for the Scout. Steve took a deep breath, turned to yell over his shoulder, and charged forward, his rifle firing on full automatic. His example and cry of "Follow me!" emboldened and energized the squad members who came to their feet and rushed across the exposed farm plot.

Up and running, breathing hard. Heart beating rapidly. Adrenaline pumping. Nerves tingling. Almost as one Steve heard a shot and the smack of a bullet hitting flesh. The radioman went down. Blood spread from a wound between his navel and hip bone. He rolled on his back, his face full of shock and pain.

The Marines went to the ground again to change magazines. The enemy seized the opportunity to move and increase their rate of fire. A line of NVA soldiers sprang up to assault the Marines from the right flank. One of the enemy soldiers stopped to raise an RPG to his shoulder. Steve's eyes focused on that extremely effective weapon. The grenade had a long-shaped nose cone attached to what appeared to be a standard number ten can fused with a slope down to its long base which holds the dry propellant. It was more effective than the grenade launcher.

The rocket fired. Fortunately, it sailed beyond the Marines, exploding harmlessly on their left flank. In a nanosecond, Steve had a thought. Our sophisticated LAAWs are no match on the battlefield for this rather crude and cheaply produced weapon. Why don't we just copy it and turn them out in tremendous numbers the way they do? Is it stupidity or arrogance on the part of our leaders? Maybe It is an ethnocentric thing, a desk jockey's irrational belief that the piece of junk LAAW they provide is superior because it is American-made. That kind of thinking is getting a bunch of us killed over here, he thought.

The firefight was brief and savage. Marine rifles responded to the threat with an angry stream of lead. Their superior marksmanship training was evident. The enemy had taken up good firing positions in the village. A soldier seemed to be firing from every window. A well-trained squad, the Marines were now firing in three and four-round bursts.

A house on the edge of the village exploded after being targeted by the grenadier. A fire team reacted quickly and moved to flank the enemy. With grenades and rifle fire, the main body pressed this advantage as the flankers drew the enemy fire. They rushed to the wall of the closest house. One of the Marines tossed a grenade through a window. His fire team rushed into the house on the heels of the explosion.

The NVA began to bug out, the fierceness and resolve of the Marines being no match for the superior numbers with less heart. They cleared the village of enemy soldiers room by room, house by house. The Marines found blood trails and drag marks leading back into the jungle. A fire team took up a position to prevent a counterattack. Steve held everyone else in place for a moment while he called in a sit rep and to give nerves a chance to settle down.

While the men smoked a cigarette and took a drink from their canteens, Steve went back to the first soldier he had killed. A part of his job was to search the bloody bodies for any form of intelligence documents. There were none in this case. In one of the fields close to the village, Steve came upon a scene that stabbed him in the heart. A boy, no more than six or seven, lay face down in a rice paddy. Dried blood was caked on his leg, back, and neck.

Next to him, clad in black, hair trimmed close, a V.C. soldier had died. Steve saw a foot, then the leg, and a body mostly hidden among tall stalks of rice. A farmer? Had he killed the soldier? Was the

Boy his son? Steve would never know the story of the tragedy, a small story, a single piece in the vast mosaic of the war.

The bodies were collected and lined up all in a row, combatants and civilians lined up like curbside trash for pickup. The Marine had been covered with a poncho. A family had retrieved the body of a young woman. Her body was laid out on a woven mat. Her head rested on a thin pillow. She wore the clothing in which she had died, a white blouse and pantaloons. The white blouse was pink and red with blood. Her bare feet were bloody. Her face was smeared with more blood which matted her hair. She was not a combatant but collateral damage. Her grieving brother watched over her. Fear, tears, grief, shock. All the quintessential faces of war.

CHAPTER TWENTY
THE CITADEL
QUANG TRI CITY, SOUTH VIETNAM

Major General Lemuel Smith, newly appointed commander of Marine forces in I Corp, strode to the podium from which he had been introduced and would make his opening remarks. He was trailed by his aide and selected colonels of staff. By Marine Corps standards of physicality, the general appeared to be a "feather merchant." At five foot six inches tall and 165 pounds, the general was as hard and tough as any of the thousands of Marines he commanded. He made sure of that with regular, rigorous workouts and runs. Still, he could not escape being called "Little" Smith.

In every other way, Lem Smith was recognized as a military heavyweight. He was a problem solver, a fixer. His commands were often units that needed "straightening out." Smith was also brilliant as a tactician and strategist. Several of the papers he had written as a student in various war colleges over a decade ago were still being used as teaching tools. His recommendations had often been implemented as Corps-wide policy. Above all, the general was a fighting Marine who spent more time in the field among his troops than behind a desk. He recognized that the political aspect of having stars on your shoulder was his weakness. That awareness had been a prime factor in selecting an assistant with a degree in political science.

The assembled briefing officers of the joint commands who met daily at the Citadel to exchange intelligence data and to plan and coordinate operations stood and politely applauded as the new commander stood before the podium. Outside of the senior Marines present, few of the military men knew the general by more than his excellent reputation. They had all learned about him and his past within days of his appointment.

The general stood behind the podium, looking out over the assemblage. He did not lean on the podium or use it as a prop. He did not use notes. He knew exactly what he wanted to say. General Smith had chosen the venue in order to evaluate not only the quality of the intelligence being exchanged but the personnel as well. He had been well-schooled by previous commanders on the problems brought about by the convoluted chain of command, which only made sense in the political realm, evolving due to interservice rivalries and national jealousies, to say nothing of wide-spread corruption, not all of which was limited to the Vietnamese. Many of these men knew their careers were at stake with the change in command.

The general patiently waited for the applause to die down before speaking. He had taken public speaking courses and instructions and even joined Toastmasters when it became evident that he would rise to a rank requiring him to give briefings to senior military and political officials and to give speeches such as this. It was a bit of an unorthodox approach, but one that had brought him positive results. The general was constantly aware of his hand gestures and body language, of making eye contact, of the use of voice deflection, and such things as eliminating "uhs" from his speeches and his personal communications.

"Thank you for that warm welcome," he began. "Be seated, please."

The general was not in his dress uniform. He wore the green combat utility uniform his Marines in the field wore, with a difference. His uniform was new, clean, starched, and ironed. His combat boots had been spit-shined. The general was not wearing the stars he'd earned in part while serving as a battalion commander during the Korean conflict.

For his actions while commanding an infantry battalion at the Kwanzu Bridge near the Chosin Reservoir, then Lieutenant Colonel Smith had been awarded the Medal of Honor. Few in the room were aware of that. The men had taken their seats. The general could see everyone's face now. They were looking to him with a wide variety of expectations. He looked them over, making eye contact with the men he knew, and more he did not. Not much escaped the keen scrutiny of this extremely intelligent man, a man who had an IQ of over 150.

General Smith noted such things as the state of uniforms, haircuts, and other signs that betrayed or revealed the discipline or lack of the same in a command and therefore his unit. He wondered why one battalion had sent a junior lieutenant. While his eyes examined those present, the general began his speech.

"With the drawing down of American forces and what is being called the 'Vietnamization' of the war, U.S. Marine forces remaining in I Corp will continue in our combat role with emphasis on protection of American forces and installations. We will stress and reinforce the use of helicopter mobility as a force multiplier. A significant number of Vietnamese have been trained in the United States as helicopter pilots. We will utilize this asset in joint operations."

This put the Vietnamese on notice. The war was really being handed over to them. "Supporting forces will be drawn down at a slower rate than rifle companies to ensure that our technological and firepower advantages are maintained.

"U.S. Marine Corps forces in I Corp will assume an expanded role as advisors and teachers. Personnel being transferred as a unit to the United States will not be replaced; however, personnel in those units with more than six months left to serve in the country will be transferred in order to bring remaining units up to their full authorized strength.

"The designated Marine Division of the past will no longer have a presence in I Corp. Tomorrow the Commanding General, Third Marine Division, will be reassigned to a higher post he has so well earned. I will assume command of the 7th Provisional Marine Division, made up of forces and assets remaining in country as well as Vietnamese units and officers selected for training purposes. This will provide the senior command authority for all forces within I Corp. The assistant division commander will be a Vietnamese general officer yet to be appointed.

"I will be visiting individual units with specific orders on how the new command structure will become a part of the Vietnamization program. I fully expect some U.S. Air Force, Navy, and Army units to become integrated into the division's structure."

That was a rather shocking announcement. It was not well received by senior officers of the other service branches.

"I look forward to working with all of you. Thank you."

Not given to answering questions at such a forum, the general ignored the raised hands and voices and stepped down from the podium. The tall, dark-haired aide, what the Army called a general's dog robber, cleared the way for General Smith through a pressing crowd of junior officers who wanted to rub shoulders with and greet the general. Using the same blocking-out skills he had learned on the basketball court at Notre Dame, Major Jim Hartshorn led the 52-year-old graying general to the Jeep they'd ridden in from the division headquarters at Dong Ha.

Nothing the general had seen came as a surprise to him. The division headquarters was lean but not too thin on staff. Tents were spread out and well camouflaged. No truck parks or clusters of assets provided a large target for nearby enemy gunners. Outposts from squad to company in size held key terrain around Dong Ha. A white crushed gravel road had been built by the engineers to support heavy, high-speed military traffic such as armor. Roads ran north to the Vietnamese Frontier Division Headquarters at Ai Tu Combat Base, west to Quang Tri Combat Base, Cam Lo, and Khe Sahn, and south to Quang Tri City.

The old citadel was a relatively small enclave, little suited for modern defense of a city. It was crowded with structures and vehicles. The stone walls were low and thick with circular openings where 15th-century cannons had once been posted. A shanty town had been established along the east wall. Typically, the families of Vietnamese soldiers went to war with them. It was a long-established history of the Vietnamese culture. The general was giving much thought to how to handle that aspect of combining Vietnamese units into his command structure.

General Smith was visiting front-line commands, seeing them firsthand, assessing their strengths and import, making notes on improvements and units he wanted moved, locations that could be reduced or that needed reinforcing. In only a week, the little general with the temperament of a bulldog had already fired two staff colonels, sending them home for new postings. Although he would not write their fitness reports as he had not officially taken command, the general's actions effectively ended the careers of those officers.

This was not a move to replace staff with personnel of his choosing. The general was more than pleased to keep effective, top-notch leaders in key positions. He would request three candidates for each vacant posting from the office of manpower management. He knew others would hear of the openings and lobby in their own way for those appointments. How they went about competing for the assignments would tell him something about the applicants. He was not partial to those who played a game of military politics, although there was an element of that in any command position that could not be ignored. Since politics was an increasingly important part of military life at his rank, the general was no more of a political animal than he had to be. He was unconventional in many ways. The key to obtaining General Smith's approval for the postings would be being the most qualified, proven officer for the job.

The major had strongly advised against the Jeep tour. A general officer had every type of aircraft in the air wing at his disposal. Flying seemed safer. "No road in I Corp is safe from snipers, mines, or ambushes, general," the aide had reminded him. "The snipers will certainly target a man with stars on his collar."

"My troops are on those roads daily in Jeeps, trucks, and other vehicles, as well as on foot patrols," the general countered as he reached to touch the stars that were so important to him that validated his career choice made so long ago, the sacrifices he and his family had made, and the hardships they had endured. "I will not ask those men to go where I won't go, and by the same means. Now let's do it."

The general was a fighting Marine, not a paper pusher who let others do for him or asked of others what he would not do or had not done. In spite of professional jealousies over the medal that sometimes actually worked to hold the hero back, the fiery, intelligent, and factually politically astute lieutenant colonel had risen to his current rank and would surely go beyond that, possibly even to the office of the Commandant and a seat on the Joint Chiefs of Staff.

Commanding this new alignment of a provisional division in combat would either end or further his career. The general's adult life had been spent in the Marine Corps. He was not ready to see his career or that way of life end.

"At least remove the shiny stars, general," the aide suggested. "Please."

The general nodded and removed the insignia of his rank, two silver stars on each collar. The major removed the gold oak leaves from his collars. The men took their seats in the Jeep and began their trip to the largest Marine Corps base in I Corp, Quang Tri Combat Base, which was six miles to the east of the city. In spite of being so close to the DMZ, the city they drove through on their departure appeared charming and relatively unchanged by the war that had been waged nearly on its doorstep for almost a quarter of a century.

When they'd departed Dong Ha it had not escaped the general's attention that the major had brought along rifles for both of them, including a supply of loaded magazines and a box of ball-shell bandoliers. An M-79 grenade launcher and a bag of 40mm rifle grenades were on the back floor, along with a case of C-rations. The Jeep was a command vehicle with its telltale long-range communications antennae. There was also a PRC-25 field radio strapped to a backpack. The general had refused an escort. He appreciated the offer but hoped they would not need the escort or have to use any of the weapons.

The half-hour ride from Dong Ha had taken them through miles of flat terraced wet rice paddies twinkling in the sun-like mirrored mosaics. The rice had been planted by hand in even rows and columns, as it had been done throughout Asia for centuries. Women with their lips and gums stained crimson and black by the betel nut opiate they habitually chewed worked the fields. Conical straw hats were tied with colorful ribbons under their chins. Although they seemed to pay little attention to the passing Jeep, the general could almost feel their eyes on his back as the Jeep passed.

How many of them are V.C. or at least sympathizers? He wondered. Would they have recognized the vehicle of an American general? Do they have a way of communicating with NVA units ahead of us? Will they establish an ambush to hit us somewhere up ahead? Where might that be?

The general had known the terrain would appear different in the Jeep from what he had observed flying in. From the air, he had noted every overlook, water crossing, and possible choke point. He would pay the same degree of attention to the city as they passed through it on their way to the Quang Tri Combat Base.

"I wasn't impressed by the briefing, Jim."

"No, sir."

"No one truly seemed to be on the mark where intelligence is concerned."

"No, sir."

"Not one briefer or intelligence officer mentioned the fuel lines the NVA have slowly installed within their own borders but only one day away from the DMZ for most heavy vehicles."

"You're right, sir," the aide responded, knowing that by mentioning heavy vehicles, the general meant tanks.

"None of them seemed to know or be concerned with the nearness of SAM units along the northern and western borders," the general said, wondering how soon he would be able to talk the Vietnamese Air Force into bombing those locations.

They were soon on the outskirts of Quang Tri City. Although it was South Vietnam's third largest city, Quang Tri only had a population of roughly one quarter million, and even that number counted a large influx of refugees. Unlike Saigon with its teen and even preteen prostitutes, G.I. bars, con men of all types, and G.I.s looking for a good time, Quang Tri remained relatively pure in its charming Vietnamese culture.

That was due largely to the fact that the U.S. military had no headquarters or other significant presence within the city. Few American forces were allowed liberty or freedom to roam the streets at leisure. Quang Tri was more purely Vietnamese in that it had also been less influenced by the French colonial period than Saigon. And Quang Tri lacked the cultural, political, and religious history of Saigon and Hue.

Signs of the war were obvious, of course: refugees, military traffic, uniforms, and weapons. That would mean inflated prices, a thriving black market, and swirling levels of intelligence and counterintelligence activities. The Jeep came to a halt as they were leaving town at the approach to the Thach Hanh bridge. They pulled over to make room for the one-way traffic entering Quang Tri City.

Choke point! the general thought. Emphasizing his thoughts like exclamation points were explosions that suddenly rocked the city. The general felt a wave of concussion with each explosion. An Army MP with his white gloves and silver helmet whistled and waved. At the other end of the long bridge, a second MP had halted westbound traffic.

As soon as the last truck had passed going into the city, the MP waved those leaving the city forward onto the bridge which had a speed limit of fifteen miles per hour. They passed a Marine in a diving suit who was standing in the middle of the bridge, apparently rubbernecking like some kind of tourist. Who is that and what is he doing? the general wondered.

As the Jeep neared the west end of the bridge, a truck that had pulled over to allow traffic to pass blew up, struck by artillery, as was the truck directly in front of the Jeep. Arms of flames reached out to embrace them. Shrapnel and truck parts whistled past their heads. The Marine they had passed in the middle of the bridge only seconds ago came running up to them.

"What do you fellas do?" he asked.

CHAPTER TWENTY ONE
THACH HANH, SOUTH VIETNAM

Thach Hanh was prepared for war. The opening salvos of the battle had already impacted. The storm was still to come. The machine guns and mortars were quickly in place. An aid station had been established. The kitchen was already cooking. Ammunition was being staged. Sandbags were being filled. All the smoothness of these preparations was the result of numerous practices and classes.

Steve was moving from one location to another, checking every detail and calming nerves, including his own. He was on the radio, talking to other Marine Corps units, trying to piece the puzzle together to give him a larger picture of what was going on in I Corp. His command post was at the center of the bridge, a sandbagged U facing north. Sandbags were being filled and delivered to each end of the village. The crew-served weapons were ringed with sandbagged walls.

The pink restaurant was reinforced with bags. The windows were covered with bamboo screens. It would serve as the kitchen throughout the battle. The cooks mixed a combination of C-rations and local produce, including duck, chicken, fish, and native rice, to provide meals.

Steve's tent was sandbagged six feet high. Doctor Quoc was laying it out as the first aid center. Lan was at her mortar. In her absence, the doctor was assisted by several untrained local women who had previously served as midwives.

Steve looked for weaknesses in his preparations. Although they should have been safe from the east adjacent to Quang Tri, he was uncomfortable with the exposure there. "Le Kinh," he suggested, "we need some eyeballs on the east flank. They don't need rifles. They just need to be able to warn us if something is coming our way from Quang Tri City."

The Vietnamese scout sent two trios of pre-teen boys, all of whom had volunteered, to watch that exposed flank.

"Send all the people with old rifles who want to volunteer to the west flank. Spread them out along the river."

Satisfied that the rear and flanks were as secure as he could make them without weakening his main line of defense, Steve returned to the bridge. A squad from his Vietnamese self-defense force had taken up positions at each end of the bridge, placing themselves at the command of the Americans in charge there. Two more local squads had spread themselves out along the length of the bridge. They were all facing north.

Steve walked the bridge, making personnel adjustments. Unlike a Marine platoon commander who had to accept the soldiers assigned to him, the scout could move the Vietnamese at will. From the training they'd received and their conduct on patrols and under fire, Steve knew who remained calmest under stress. He knew who among them had the most heart and who performed best with each weapon. He pulled three boys and one girl from the hot zone at the west end of the bridge. He replaced them with two girls and a boy from the east end. He noticed the raised eyebrows of the clerks, but they did not question his decision.

Women were still filling sandbags, filling a truck bed for delivery to the bridge. The Army specialists who had been sent out to lay what mines they had returned. Steve met them at the east end of the bridge. "Good job, guys. Maybe that'll slow them down long enough for us to get in a few good shots at them."

"Maybe more for the first few," Gary added.

"That's the edge I need. Get on down to your compound. Reinforce everything. Put up stiff resistance, but don't sacrifice yourselves. Be ready to bug out. Pop a red and then a green pencil flare so we'll know you're coming in. We'll fight the battle from the bridge."

The SEALS had returned in the meantime and were standing there listening. "How bad are things?" Steve asked them.

"Real bad, or real good, depending upon how much fight these people have in them. There's a full-scale battle going on around Ai Tu."

"How large?"

"Division at least, maybe even corps-sized."

"Damn, I hope those ARVN troops find their nuts."

"Or their hearts."

"Did you guys get a few shots in? Give 'em something else to think about."

"Yeah, we took out a track, disabled an artillery piece, and scattered some of the infantry troops."

"You all okay?"

"Yeah, no casualties."

"Okay. You can't defend your camp. Rig it for command detonation. Load up your boats. Send us everything you can spare. Head up north until you run into an enemy force. Play a hit and run game. Shoot up everything within your range and then fall back. Keep us advised on what's coming at us and where they are. Direct Naval gunfire and air strikes if you can get them. That's your role. Throw everything you've got at them; no need to conserve ammunition."

"You got it. Ski."

"Fight your way back to the bridge. But once you reach here, you're out of the fight."

"No way, man!"

"The river is too restricted here. You'll be sitting ducks. We'll need you to evacuate our wounded and to get as many women and children evacuated as you can. Most who can will flee to Quang Tri City before you can begin the evacuations. We've already sent the smallest children there with the oldest adults."

"Do you intend to give up the northern sector of the city?" The short gray-haired clerk interrupted.

"Unfortunately, that's close to the plan. A retrograde action is dangerous even for veteran troops and even with a short distance. It's better for us and for morale for us to pick a place and make a stand. The SEALS and the Army unit will hold out as long as they can, making those bastards pay for the ground they do take."

The administrators seemed to accept the young man's plan. Actually, they were quite impressed with the entire scope of his defensive scheme. Steve left, being needed elsewhere.

"I don't know of anyone who could have planned this better," the taller clerk said. The older Marine and his companion observed as the villagers responded to Steve's instructions. There was a fever to the hectic activities of the villagers, yet instead of chaos in the face of a major enemy attack, there was an obvious level of organization to the frenzy. There was no sense of panic or doom.

"Mortars and machine guns are in place and on standby. They have been well-positioned. The crews appear to know what they are doing. They have to be nervous, yet they have exhibited no fear," the tall Marine noted.

"They appear to be well-disciplined and trained, but they aren't regular Army. I can't help but wonder how they're going to hold up under fire," the older clerk commented.

The MP had overheard the remarks. "These people might surprise you," he responded. "They've conducted more combat operations than most infantry companies."

"How did that come about?"

The MP told the pair everything he knew and had heard about the CAP unit from its beginning to the present. The Marines listened without interrupting. They began to understand completely the reasons for the confidence the young man was exhibiting.

"They call him 'The Warlord'," the MP said in conclusion.

That surprised both Marines. "Why?" the tall man asked.

"Well, generally, a warlord takes over a territory. He recruits and trains an army to defend it. He is the sole authority within that territory. It is something like a feudal kingdom."

"He doesn't seem to rule with an iron fist."

"That's just it. His castle is a tent. His army is made up solely of people who can't qualify to be in any regular army. He took these people, drove, and challenged them. He called upon the best Marines available to train them. They trained in small groups with individual instruction where it was needed. I believe every one of these boys and girls and crippled old men would qualify on a Marine Corps rifle range."

"Training is one thing, but combat is another experience entirely," the dark-featured man offered. "What about those experiences?"

"Patrols, night patrols, ambushes, assaults on an enemy village. They've done it all, and quite successfully."

"Casualties?"

"One KIA, several wounded, including one of the girls."

"And how did that affect morale?"

"There was some keening and wailing, of course, but the kid had put himself between the enemy gun and the wounded girl. Made him a hero to the whole village. There must have been twenty people trying to fill that one open spot in the unit afterwards. Mostly women."

"What about civil affairs?"

"The Marines ran a country fair operation, ferreted out a couple of V.C. With those patrols and ambushes, the V.C. tax collectors don't come to Thach Hanh anymore. He had the SEAL unit relocated and brought in the Army outpost. They contribute to security and the village commerce. The Marines run a med cap in the village once a month or so and are building a school on the south end of the village. He got his church to donate school books and supplies for the kids."

"You make him sound like some sort of superman."

"No," the sergeant laughed. "The kid can't fly, He doesn't wear a cape. He does know how to get things done."

"Like a dog robber."

The MP knew a dog robber was a general's aide who used his position to get things done, often through unofficial channels.

"Something like that, but he's got personality rather than weight of command." The MP pled other needs to end the conversation. "Stay alert," he told them as he moved away.

The Marines watched as Thach Hanh continued to prepare for war. Girls with rifles on their shoulders were manning every class of weapon. The village was ready. There was nothing left to do but wait. Waiting. Anticipating an imminent attack you know is coming is often the most difficult phase of combat action. Tension builds. Commanders on all levels question their readiness and their decisions. Men pray. They think of home and wonder if they will ever see it again. Some bite their nails. Weapons are cleaned and checked repeatedly. Combat knives are sharpened.

Eyes were fixed on the far horizon. Men wondered when the enemy would come over the slight hill. How many of them would there be? How will I perform? Will I survive? Will the village? The questions were soon answered. The NVA had learned a hard lesson and adapted quickly. A Marine reacted to a sound he had heard before: the shrieking of artillery. "Incoming!" he shouted.

The soldiers ducked behind their sandbags, feeling safer than they actually were. The puzzled civilians did not seek that refuge. A trio of artillery shells passed over the bridge, splashing into the river. The explosions created depth charge-like geysers. The waves washed small, flimsy fishing boats to the shore. Stunned fish rose to the surface and were washed downstream.

Steve was on the radio, shouting, "Sea Dragon, Sea Dragon, this is CAP one, two, three, six over."

The admin clerks listened as the scout called for smoke rounds to be placed five thousand meters out across the northwest, where the tanks had come from. The older man smiled. "That'll take away the advantage of a spotter," he said.

The spotter, though, had seen the impacting rounds and was able to adjust fire once before his view was obstructed by the thick, oily clouds of smoke. Three heavy artillery shells fell short of the bridge. Unfortunately, they impacted among the homes in the north end of the village. One round blew a gaping hole in a wall, killing an entire family that had chosen not to evacuate. Another slammed into the roof of an abandoned home. The third blew a large crater in a dirt street.

Although blinded by the smoke, the artillery commander used the last coordinates as his base. He adjusted his fire from left to right, destroying more houses and ruining the street. Civilians, some of them bleeding from shrapnel wounds, were making their way to the east end of the bridge. Many of them had to be carried. It was a hard decision to make, but Steve ordered his personnel to "stand fast!" He radioed for the medical staff to meet the refugees at the intersection of the village road at the east end of the bridge.

The artillery impacted on a line moving to the west, exploding harmlessly among fields. Steve called for more smoke. The enemy adjusted their aim again. The next volley of shells impacted in the north end of the village again and moved to the east into Quang Tri City. A secondary explosion created a ball of fire and a plume of black smoke, an aiming beacon that rose above the ground-hugging smoke screen.

Obviously believing they were on target, the NVA gunners began firing everything they had with that black plume as the center of their impact grid zone. They were doing some damage in the city, but nothing that could be considered militarily significant. The smoke was obscuring the bridge. The battle was engaged. It was just a matter now of reacting to events and to what the enemy would throw at them.

It was a surprise. The SEALS came racing back south through the smoke that had drifted across the river. They were firing into the smoke as they came. And they were under fire. Machine gun bullets were ricocheting off their armor plates. Something was chasing them on the river, and Steve knew that was not a good thing. He could see a body slumping over one of the gun mounts. The boat had been hit by something that had exploded, punching a hole above the water line and blackening the surrounding steel. The boat, however, was under power and steerage and was fighting back.

Wondering if there had been a fire aboard, Steve directed his machine gun team to his left to be ready. He extended the tube of a LAAW and sighted it at the center front edge of the smoke screen. He waited on whatever was out there. Still, he was surprised when a reinforced barge full of enemy troops appeared through the smoke. A small naval gun had been mounted forward of the bridge. Atop the wheelhouse, a fifty-caliber machine gun was firing on the SEALs. At least fifty enemy riflemen were firing their weapons at the retreating naval vessel.

The Army outpost south of the village took the barge under fire from the flank. Its machine gun decimated the packed enemy soldiers. The machine gun on the bridge opened up, punching holes through the steering house window. Steve's LAAW impacted at the base of the heavier gun. Mortars whistled out of the sky, splashing and exploding all around the barge. One finally punched through the deck plates. The barge exploded from within spectacularly. It caught fire and began sinking, drifting to the east side of the river.

NVA soldiers who had survived the defensive fires jumped into the water. Riflemen on the bridge began picking them off one by one. No mercy was shone. The villagers were protecting their own. There were no wounded yet for the SEALS to evacuate.

"We're down to one engine," Scott reported. "But we've got guns and ammunition. I'll tie up to the pier in the middle of the river under the bridge. We'll take on anything else that comes down the river."

"Did you see more barges or other boats?" Steve asked.

"A gunboat did most of the damage to us. They've got at least four more barges full of troops coming down the river."

"Damn, they can be landing them anywhere behind that smoke screen."

"Or bring them straight down the river."

Steve made another quick decision. He called the Army outpost. "Sammy, are you guys rigged to blow?" he asked.

"Affirmative."

"Get out of there. Bring all the weapons, ammunition, and explosives you can carry. Work your way back to us, but booby trap every house you can along the way, and chase any civilians still there out of their houses."

"Roger that."

Steve prepared his response to the new threat. Using a building near the river as his reference point, he plotted the grid coordinates across the river thirty-five hundred meters from the bridge. He relayed those numbers to Sea Dragon as on-call fire. He established another on-call impact zone for his mortars at twenty-five hundred meters. He would have liked to have provided some flanking fire, but the risks outweighed the advantage.

The gunboat came through the smoke screen first. The boat was spotted five hundred meters beyond his kill zone. It was firing as it came. Heavy caliber machine gun bullets were punching into the sandbags along the bridge. Sand bled from the bags. After taking cover behind his own sandbags, Steve keyed his radio, alerting Sea Dragon to stand by for his imminent fire order.

Steve looked up to see where the boat was. He chanced a quick peek over the sandbag wall, quickly estimating speed and distance. He dove back and counted down. "Seven...six.."

Steve pressed the button down on his hand set and sent a brief message. "Sea Dragon, On call, register one, fire!"

Six ships of the Sea Dragon Task Force had the range to respond. Their gunnery officer had laid out a deadly impact zone for each ship and each of its guns. All of them fired on his order.

"Shot out!" the Navy radioed. The distance was too far for shrapnel to be a factor. Although he still had to worry about the enemy guns, Steve had to observe the incoming naval bombardment. He had to be able to adjust fire.

The river seemed to explode all at once with geyser impacts. At least three heavy shells from the Navy's shotgun pattern hit the NVA gunship. It was raised up out of the water, its back broken.

Steel cracked and buckled. Rivets and bolts popped. Fuel and ammunition exploded. Steam burned flesh. Fire ate at everything it could consume. Skin blistered and burned. Lungs were destroyed by fire and smoke. Bones were broken and bodies were crushed. They were trapped in the wreckage as the gunboat sank quickly.

A handful of weaponless men struggled ashore on the far side of the river. They were no longer a serious threat. During this action, the smoke screen had thinned, as emphasized by artillery rounds now landing in the southwest corner of the village. Although the NVA artillery now had the range, Steve called for more smoke rounds.

Unfortunately, the smoke worked both ways, hiding an approaching tank column. The enemy commander wisely spread out on a wide front behind the smoke screen. The first indicator of their presence was impacting shells from their main guns that struck the south end of the village. Civilians were wounded and killed. Thatch huts burned. The fighters maintained the integrity of their positions.

The villagers went into action. One group designated to assist the wounded delivered them to the medical tent where Doctor Quoc was suddenly very busy. After treatment, the injured were carried to the schoolhouse to await evacuation to a better equipped hospital. Their numbers grew swiftly, yet the civilians had not panicked.

The fighters had yet to be tested, but they knew it was coming soon. Steve crawled to the west end of the bridge, keeping his head below the level of the sandbags. This was where he expected to see tanks and troops with an array of weapons, possibly artillery and most certainly heavy mortars.

"I could sure use an Ontos down here," he commented.

The Ontos is a tracked platform with a low silhouette. Unlike tanks and self-propelled howitzers, the Ontos has no turret or main gun. It is not heavily armored. They have a short turning radius, almost like a riding lawnmower. But the Ontos was armed to the teeth with six long barrel 105mm guns in two clusters of three on each side. A fifty-caliber spotting gun was attached to each barrel. The Ontos was a pure tank killer. She didn't haul trash or troops. Marine riflemen loved the Ontos. But Steve had to fight the battle with what he had rather than what he wished he had. He signaled for the SEAL commander to come up. While waiting for him, he talked to the Marine administrators.

"You have any luck with that artillery support?"

"The NVA are pouring across the DMZ on a wide front. Every gun they've got is firing in support of units trying to stem that flow."

"How about air?"

"Sorry, nothing available."

Steve accepted the situation stoically. Scott had joined the Marines. The scout turned to him.

"Scott, those NVA tanks are going to come clanking through that smoke screen any minute," Steve said, pointing. "They are most vulnerable from the flanks, but I don't have anything that will reach them or stop them."

"Except my guns."

"Exactly. I can't order you to go, but if you could head upstream and stop short of the fog where we can still see you and they can't, you could wait for an opportunity to hit them hard and then scoot back here before they can react."

"We can do that."

"Be aware of what might be coming through that fog on the river. If you hear a gunboat, bug out. We'll cover you with mortar fire."

"That it?"

"No. When you see them coming, I'll call for naval gunfire. I'll move the barrages behind the leaders, hopefully catching troops and support vehicles bringing up the rear."

The tactic surprised everyone who heard the plan, as the tanks were the most obvious threat. Steve explained himself.

"They'll think they've come through the barrage. They'll rush to get here and run right into our mine field. That should stop them in their tracks briefly. Take the best shots you can at the nearest targets. Before they can recover from that, you haul back here. Get down to the schoolhouse and complete your mission of delivering our wounded to the hospital ship."

"We sure don't like the idea of leaving in the middle of a battle."

"Scott, this is the best use of your SEALs as an asset."

"Understood. Well then. I'll be off." The SEAL extended his right hand. "Good luck, Marine." The men shook hands. Scott departed.

"It's hard to send men like that out to face death," Steve commented.

The clerks exchanged that look. Steve scooted down under the bridge to make his rounds of troops down in the village. He spoke brief words of encouragement to everyone he encountered.

"How's it going, sweetheart?" he asked Lan.

"I no say for you," she said in a teasing but insistent tone.

"You know you love me," he teased back.

The girl blushed brightly, casting her eyes down.

"You are all very brave. Keep up the good work," Steve told them as he departed. One of the other girls on the gun crew patted Lan on the shoulder, smiling with understanding. He stopped a moment to encourage Cpl. Obasi's squad. He didn't know what to say. "You guys know the score. Don't chew through your ammunition. Fire short, three-round well-aimed bursts. Make every shot count. Fight and die like Marines."

"Ooorah!"

"You've got a good squad, Holt. Let's try to get these babies home to their mommas."

"Will do, sir."

Steve left the squad with a feeling of confidence. He made his way on foot down to the village. Steve stopped by the medical tent. Doctor Quoc's smock was smeared with blood. There were not enough supplies for him to change after each procedure. He didn't change gloves. There was no autoclave to sterilize instruments. They were simply rinsed in boiling water, wiped with an alcohol pad, and put back into service.

Barrels were filled with bloody bandages and wrappings. Steve thought there were most likely some body parts in there too. Supplies were being depleted quickly. At the school, Steve walked among the wounded, offering words of encouragement. Along the way, he had passed a collection point for the dead. There were nine bodies there already. A family was gathered around one of the wounded. One of the women was slowly fanning a handful of incense sticks. They were all praying. "Saah, one who knows," was dying. A Buddhist, she clearly knew that having died, we are born again; having been born, we die again. This birth and death from one moment to the next is the endless spinning wheel of Samsara. "May she return to us as one of the Noble Ones," a friend of the old woman prayed.

Steve approached. There was a tug at his soul. Saah lay on a cot, rasping her last breath. The Marine took her bird's frail hand in his own. He kneeled beside her, folding her hand in his and silently praying for her. Steve stayed only a moment after Saah's passing. He knew there would be more deaths. He would do his best to limit them, even if it cost him his own. He had a quick gulp of hot green tea with a machine gun team before making his way back to the east end of the bridge. Artillery was still pounding away north of them. Steve was grateful and hoped the shelling was not costing lives elsewhere, although he knew it must be.

Back at his command post in the center of the bridge, Steve was informed that the Navy Task Force was firing the last of their smoke shells. He passed the information to everyone by radio and by word of mouth. "Be ready! They'll be coming through in about ten minutes!"

The defenders steeled their nerves any way they could, a kiss to a religious medal, a prayer, deep breaths. Some of the girls hugged one another. Adrenaline is pumped through veins. Throats grew dry. The SEALs bobbed in their boat in the middle of the river, the good engine idling quietly. They too were experiencing pre-combat jitters. They were hard men, tough men, but they were flesh and bone and nerves, not steel.

The enemy tanks advanced through the thinning smoke veil on a broad front. It was a frightening sight for soldiers so lightly armed and with no air support. Steve noted the alignment of the advancing tanks, made the necessary adjustments, and called for Naval gunfire. Within seconds, the terrain around the tanks shook with explosions. Two tanks in the center of the line were destroyed in that first salvo.

The surviving tanks kept on coming. The Navy fired another salvo. The tanks were four thousand meters out. Another was burning and stopped in its tracks with the surviving crewmen abandoning the vehicle. As planned, Steve, although he could not see the targets, adjusted the Naval shelling to the rear of the tanks. He called for air bursts, the most devastating form of artillery for use against ground troops in the open. He asked for sustained fire with broad coverage.

As predicted, the tanks raced into the open. Steve became worried at 3,500 meters. At the range of 3,000 meters, he would call for mortars. Where are the mines? He wondered. A single explosion answered his question. A tank that hit one of the mines was disabled but not destroyed. The tanks ground to a halt; it could not be more fortuitous for the defenders. Steve called out the range to his mortar crews.

Both mortar crews went into action. The fuses had been set for armor. The rounds were high explosive anti-tank. Not currently under fire, the mortar crews worked smoothly and with confidence. Lan dropped a round down a tube and turned away, hoping she would not experience a dangerous hangfire. After each shot, one of the crew members splashed the tube with water to keep it cool. The crew would have to fire the weapon as quickly as possible, beyond its safe sustained rate without the aid of cooling water.

The mortar barrage further unnerved the enemy tankers. The mortar crew had been instructed not to predictably fire their mortar in a general "walking" pattern with a fire, click, fire, click pattern of adjustments, the click moving the tube slightly to the left or right. With two mortars firing in random patterns, the tank drivers could not guess which way to maneuver so as to escape the incoming explosive rounds. One unfortunate driver drove his tank directly under a mortar that struck the top of the turret where the armor was thinnest. The hot core of the shaped charge burned a quarter-sized hole through the tank's plate. Shattered pieces of hot steel like shrapnel killed crewmen, started fires, and exploded ammunition. The tank was quickly engulfed in flames.

The tankers were confused. They could not see the Navy ships and did not know that they had been struck by Naval gunfire and not artillery. They could not spot the mortars that had taken them under fire. They were looking for targets when fire from a flanking force barely missed one of the tanks. The second shot from that source scored a perfect hit at the bottom seam of the turret.

The resulting explosion blew the turret off the tank. The interior was a cauldron of fire that melted metal and set off the stores of ammunition. The tankers now had a target. They focused on the brown water Navy boat. Too many guns and too many rounds fired at her doomed the American boat. Disabled, burning, her guns out of action, and holed below the water line, the boat was dead in the water. The enemy took their vengeance out on her. The boat sank slowly but fortuitously in the middle of the river, blocking everything but shallow draft vessels from approaching the village along that waterway.

In spite of their success against the boat, the enemy tank unit was still in trouble. They were being slaughtered by the combination of naval gunfire, mortars, and land mines. Their supporting infantry forces were facing a similar fate. To their east, the river blocked their escape. Naval gunfire was impacting to their north. A mine field lay to the south toward the bridge, which was their primary objective. They fled west, hoping to skirt the minefield and find the road that would take them to the bridge and open the way for their army to capture Quang Tri City.

It might have worked, but the older administrator had seen the entire battlefield in his mind. He had radioed for help, explaining the situation to the commander at the Quang Tri Combat Base. The Army's Fifth Mechanized Infantry sent twenty of its tanks to counter the threat, knowing if Quang Tri fell the entire country might follow.

Unsupported by ground troops and supporting arms, which would have slowed them down, the tanks raced eastward in column, staying out of sight. They reached a grid location selected by the man on the radio at the bridge. On signal from the tank unit's commander, the armor wheeled north in a row, facing the highway, the road to Quang Tri the enemy column was searching for. There was no time for them to dig berms. The tanks found the best location possible to provide both cover and fields of fire flanking the enemy once they reached the highway. The tankers would remain silent until they initiated a tank ambush against the enemy forces. The American tankers established a killing zone about a thousand meters in length. They camouflaged their vehicles, prepared their weapons, and waited.

Steve ordered the mortars to cease firing as the surviving tanks outran the range of the light weapons. Fires in the village had burned out. Smoke fouled the air. The wounded had been evacuated to Quang Tri City's civilian hospital. The response allowed the villagers to replace sandbags, to resupply ammunition of every type, and to pass out a hot meal of spiced pork from C-rations, rice from the village stores, and pineapple from the village plots. Coffee and tea were brewed. The meal was delivered to the men and women in place on line. The clerks noticed that while a group of women served the meals from a common pot, going from man to man, one woman served only one man. That woman was Lan. The man was Steve.

The female soldier crouched down in the command post to eat her meal with Steve. After a few moments, the clerk approached the open end of the command post. The girl was seated, leaning against one wall, the Marine opposite her. In the small space, their legs were like zippers, his, hers, his, hers. They were eating the same rations as everyone else. There was one exception.

"What's that?" the clerk asked, pointing. Steve held up a glass.

"Pink lemonade, Vietnamese style. Would you care for some?"

"I don't think so. I think you'll be pleased with the support we've been able to get from Quang Tri Combat Base. The Fifth Mechanized has sent us twenty tanks. They are setting up a flanking position on Highway Nine. You've fought a good battle, son. I think you've won."

"That remains to be seen. If the NVA has thrown a Corp at us, this is just the leading element. There'll be many more. They'll be bringing up towed and self-propelled artillery and masses of troops. We are still in a position to stiffly defend the bridge but not hold out for long against those odds."

"I think you're right, son. Enjoy your meal. I'll be getting back to my post."

The man turned.

"Pop!" Steve called. "Good work. Thanks. Keep a sharp eye out."

"Will do, son," the clerk answered over his shoulder.

Once again, the defenders of Thach Hanh waited nervously yet resolutely. They waited at their mortar tubes and other weapons. They waited in the medical tent and the school. The nuns waited on their knees, praying. Women chewed betel nuts to calm their nerves. Men smoked or chewed gum. Weapons were broken down and cleaned. Canteens were refilled. Ammunition was redistributed.

"Here they come!" shouted a sharp-eyed guard at the west end of the bridge. Heads swivelled. Sure enough, the tanks were there, advancing toward Quang Tri along Highway Nine. The men on the bridge could hear a faint creaking and clanking associated with armor on the move. They were there, just at the edge of the 60mm mortar range. The defenders were scared but held fast.

The Fifth Mechanized Infantry Tank Commander watched with held breath as the first of the enemy tanks entered his killing zone, his tank ambush. He whispered into his headset. It was an instinct, not a necessity. "Patience, gentlemen. Do not allow that lead tank to escape the kill zone. We have seventeen tanks approaching in column. From the right flank, one...two...three...four...seventeen, he said, assigning each of his gunners an enemy tank in the column as a target. Wanting the lead tanks stopped for certain, he called its number twice. He did the same for the last tank in the column.

These men had practiced their craft under a variety of conditions at Fort Hood, Texas, and again at Fort Still, Oklahoma, for six months prior to their overseas deployment. It was not going to be a fair fight. The Fifth Mechanized Tanks were on line flanking a slow-moving tank column that had no scout element, no air support, or ground troop support. They were solely focused on the bridge, turrets, and guns facing toward that objective. Due to their earlier experiences with air bursts, hatches were closed, limiting visibility.

"Tail's clear," announced the tank commander on the far left of the line, noting that the last tank had entered the killing zone.

"On your command, one," the overall commander announced.

"Steady."

The enemy tanks stopped. They were in the kill zone. Gun barrels raised as the enemy targeted the bridge. The same thing was seen by the MP Sergeant at the west end of the bridge. Although the tanks were far beyond its range, he stood and aimed a LAWW. The MP fired his missile. It exploded in the road short of the tanks. The lead enemy tank fired. The 105mm round passed through two of the burned-out trucks at the end of the bridge. It exploded when it impacted the third. The MP's left leg was sheared off just above the knee. His body was peppered with shrapnel. The clerks retrieved him, dragging him to the relative safety of their position. The taller man took off his belt and used it as a tourniquet to stop the heavy flow of blood. The leg had been partially cauterized by the heat of the steel that had sliced through it.

The American tankers fired as one, reloading and firing again independently. Each tank had hit its target. Unfortunately, due to a miscount, tank number twelve was struck twice while number eleven escaped the initial shots. The turret turned. While they were reloading, an American tank was destroyed by the single enemy shot the NVA column fired at their attackers. The revenge-filled American tankers fired their third and even fourth rounds into the enemy tank before their commander called out.

"Cease fire! Cease fire! Mission accomplished. Return to base."

The tank battle had lasted for less than five minutes. The burning tank column created a gray column of smoke rising toward the clouds. The bridge and Thach Hanh had been saved, but the defenders knew the battle was not over yet. The afternoon passed. The enemy made no more offensive moves. Both sides seemed content to settle in for the night.

Steve ordered his forces to remain on fifty percent alert. The cooks sent a meal of fish and rice flavored with a fiery sauce to every post. The clerks noticed that once again Lan personally delivered Steve's meal. She was joined at his position by Doctor Quoc and his wife who stayed the night even though their daughter slept for only four hours before reporting to her post at the mortar to stand her watch. The night passed quickly. Requests for resupply and evacuation of the wounded were not approved. The radio reports listened to throughout the night were not encouraging. The First ARVN Division had simply disappeared primarily via desertion, opening the way for a full-scale invasion of South Vietnam.

The South Vietnamese Air Force finally flew real combat missions. Ammunition, tanks, and troops were rushed north. Quang Tri City was under siege. Enemy tanks and troops were on the outskirts of the city. The ARVN forces at The Citadel were putting up stiff resistance. Ships in port had been put to sea.

The bridge defenders were back at one hundred percent alert before dawn. Sweet rice and tea were served for breakfast. There was only one thing the defenders could do. They waited. They listened to the sounds of a major battle for Quang Tri City taking place to the near east. They knew their time was coming, and now it could be coming from multiple directions. They waited for it.

The next attack came at them from the river: five armored barges full of NVA infantry. Their guns were firing as they floated toward the bridge. A shell hit one of the bridge's piers. Concrete shattered and cracked. The entire bridge shook but held. Other shells impacted the north and south ends of the village. Still, the defenders waited. The barges were not within the effective range of their weapons. They were taking hits and rolling with the punches. When the first barge came even with a building that had a large red three painted on it, Steve read an azimuth and called for mortars.

The mortar crews, short on ammunition, fired as fast as they could, putting the rounds at 2700 meters in front of the barges, daring them to run through that curtain of destruction. The mortars contributed; however, what stopped the river assault was the lead barge slamming into the sunken SEAL boat. Four barges backed away quickly, but the crash had hung the lead barge up. "Guns up!" Steve called without hesitation. The automatic weapons teams quickly took up positions. They began firing up the barge which was not totally defenseless. Its mounted gun took out one of the sandbagged positions on the bridge itself. Glowing orange tracer rounds allowed the gunners to quickly bring their weapons on target. It was a slaughter. The barge was beyond rifle range. Steve used all his leadership skills to maintain fire discipline and prevent the villagers from wasting their ammunition.

The burning machine gun bullets started a fire on the barge, which quickly spread. The NVA soldiers who could do so leapt overboard. The machine gunners continued to target them. Streaks of red appeared on the surface of the river. Bodies floated face up, face down, swept with the current to the sea. A reinforced infantry platoon was virtually annihilated. There would never be any remorse regarding those battlefield deaths on the part of the defenders.

The NVA commander had been surprised by the stiff resistance encountered at Thach Hanh. He was frustrated and then angered. He vowed to burn the village to the ground. The defenders had run out of mortar shells. Of course, the enemy commander did not realize that. Out of sight of the defenders, the barges beached themselves on the east bank of the river north of the village. Two full infantry companies came ashore and assembled for a quick march on Thach Hanh. In the meantime, at the bridge, Steve was trying to figure out what was coming next. He worried about naval sappers more than anything else.

There was an abundance of explosives available. Steve called for a case of C-4 with cord and detonators. He cut each of the twelve one-pound blocks of the plastic explosive into quarters. Using a plier-like crimping tool, he pushed one of the handles in to a depth marked by a red line in each block. He cut and tested the timing of the det cord that would burn underwater. He wanted an underwater explosion that would kill or disable underwater swimmers.

He split the end of the cord he inserted into the detonator. He fit the tip of the fuse into his engineer's tool. Holding it low behind his back, he applied slow pressure and crimped the cap. He gave the cord a light tug. By themselves, the detonators were dangerous, but less so once he slipped them into the cavity he had created with the tool. He molded the plastic explosive around the detonator and a quarter inch of the det cord.

Steve laid four dozen quarter-pound blocks to the side. He could not trust this to a villager who did not have the proper training. "Listen up, people!" he shouted. "I need a show of hands. If you've had demolition training such as Land Mine, Demolitions, and Warfare School, raise your hand."

Steve was surprised. The only one raised hand was the tall clerk who had been driving the communications Jeep. "Alright then, you're it," Steve said, pointing to the explosive charges. "This is our defense against sappers, our only defense against them attacking the bridge from underwater. Every thirty to forty-five minutes you pull the cord and drop one of these babies about ten feet to one side or the other of one of the piers. Make it completely random on timing and which pier."

That problem resolved, and Steve addressed the next perceived weakness in the village defense. During every lull in the fighting, Steve would be looking for problems to solve, evaluating the strengths and weaknesses of his defenses. He called for more sandbags, in part to keep his people busy and in a positive frame of mind. He had the mortar crews, which were now out of ammunition, pick up their rifles and reinforce the troops on the bridge. Lan took up a position in Steve's command center. No one questioned her actions.

With the threat now also possibly coming from Quang Tri City, the Marine thinned his guarding forces to the rear and west flank, transferring them to the eastern flank with orders to engage any enemy soldiers spotted within three hundred meters. He returned to his post, picked up his binoculars, and searched the terrain, watching and waiting.

Lan was nervous. She needed to be doing something. She made her way down to the café, not to socialize with her friends but with a mission in mind. She had the girls open every box of C-ratlons and take out the condiments, salt, pepper, chewing gum, a pack of four cigarettes, sugar, creamer, and coffee. She had the girls make a large pot of hot drink using the packs of instant coffee. She delivered the coffee and cigarettes to the Marines. She had been instructed to treat everyone equally. She sent the other girls to the defensive lines with coffee and cigarettes for the Vietnamese.

"Thank you, sweetheart," Steve told Lan as she passed his sandbagged location. The girl stamped her foot and, with hands on her hips, leaned forward.

"You say for me. I no say for you." She flounced off to deliver coffee and cigarettes to the clerks who were laughing at the exchange.

"I think the lady does protest too much," the older man said. The defenders sipped their coffee, smoked their cigarettes, and waited. They didn't have to wait much longer. They hadn't seen the NVA soldiers infiltrate the north end of the village. They first became aware of their presence when the booby-trapped Army compound exploded with a thunderous roar. A lot of C-4 had been used. NVA soldiers had been killed. They would now be more cautious moving through the village.

Steve didn't need to issue orders. The enemy opened up with rifle fire. He could spot flashes as enemy soldiers worked their way through the village toward the bridge, firing as they came. "Make every shot count!" Steve ordered as his riflemen engaged the enemy infantry. A machine gunner firing from a window traversed his weapon from left to right. Two defenders went down. Two heroic young women who were not part of the CAP unit and self-defense force ran forward to check on the wounded men. One of them was already dead. They dragged the other seriously wounded soldier down the bridge to Doctor Quoc.

Obasi Holt aimed a LAAW and fired. The little missile sailed through a window, impacting against the back wall. The shrapnel killed the machine gun crew. Heartened, the defenders picked up LAAWs and began searching for targets. Machine guns chattered. Rifles banged, but not wildly. Shots were fired at movement, at real targets. Marine discipline was proving itself when it was needed most, in the heat of battle.

Using the concrete houses to cover their movements, the enemy infantry closed in on the bridge. From the height of the bridge, Steve realized he could throw a grenade a significant distance. He gripped a smooth, round fragmentation grenade in the same manner as he would grip a baseball for pitching a fork-finger fast ball. He pulled the pin, stood, and threw the grenade like a center fielder trying to throw a runner out at home plate without relaying it. The grenade landed and exploded beyond the closest of the enemy ground troops.

The NVA were firing up everything they could spot, but with little effect. With grenades and rifles, the defenders would hold them at bay due to their superior terrain advantage, the bridge. The enemy commander called for his grenadiers. RPGs swooshed through the air. The bridge was a narrow target. Most of the rounds flew overhead and exploded in the village beyond, creating casualties among the civilian volunteers.

One of the rocket-propelled grenades knocked out another sandbagged position on the bridge. Another struck the center of the bridge from the bottom, holing the wood cross planks and wounding two men with large wood splinters. One of them was Corporal Holmes. Both returned to action after being treated and bandaged. The NVA grenadiers had to stand and expose themselves in order to aim and fire their weapons. Three of them went down, struck by the defending marksmen. It didn't take an expert rifleman or a trained sniper to hit a human target at such close range.

The enemy commander called for his mortars. Those shells also flew mostly over the bridge, doing little damage. However, one of them hit a support column of the Catholic Church. The nuns were burled in the rubble as the corner of the building collapsed. The novitiate, who had been on her hands and knees scrubbing the wooden kitchen floor, escaped injury. The nuns at prayer did not. Released from certain bonds now, the French woman made her way to the medical tent where she assisted Doctor Quoc.

Another mortar fired at an extreme elevation landed on the bridge, blowing another hole in the planking. Steve knew they had to knock that mortar out. With the weapons at hand, there was only one way to do it. In combat, Marines are used to hearing calls such as "Corpsman up!" when a man was wounded or "Guns up!" when a machine gun was needed. Steve issued a call probably never previously heard on the battlefield.

"Baseball players up!"

The clerks looked at one another quizzedly, as did others who might have thought the Marine had gone off the deep end. When no one responded, Steve repeated his call. Two G.I.s and Cpl. Holt crouched low and made their way to the center of the bridge.

"Pop," Steve called. "Spot that mortar!"

To the trio who had answered his call, Steve asked what position they had played.

"Left field."

"Short stop."

"Catcher."

He would have preferred pitchers, but these hard chunkers would do. Steve explained his plan. Each man retrieved a case of fifty grenades and spread out along the bridge. The defenders hunkered down while searchers with binoculars tried to locate the mortar tube. While the search was continuing, a mortar shell punched through the thin sheet metal roof of the schoolhouse, killing six wounded defenders, four of whom were female. They had all been waiting to be evacuated. Two elderly civilian women who had volunteered to tend them were also killed. It was a hard blow to the village.

The damaging mortar position was finally discovered. "Behind the blue house with the black French shutters!" one of the men called out. The baseballers rose simultaneously, cocked their arms, and hurled their grenades. Each man threw three grenades. One went down with a bullet in his shoulder, but the NVA weapon was silenced. The conflict ground to a standoff. Both sides strategized on how to gain an advantage. Steve pulled two men from the now less threatened west end of the bridge to replace the casualties on the bridge. He had no report on the number of casualties they had taken, but he knew the number of defenders was thinning.

Steve theorized that it would be highly unlikely for the NVA to attempt a flanking maneuver to the west. The only access to the bridge other than the highway was up the dirt road leading down to the village that intersected Highway Nine at the east end of the bridge. That route was heavily guarded. The only way those infantry troops could take the bridge would be to assault in overwhelming numbers and be willing to accept heavy losses in doing so. The NVA had a history of making such sacrifices.

Steve walked his lines, trying to bolster morale, providing encouragement and consolation. The CAP unit had suffered one in three casualties. The Americans had taken forty percent casualties. Steve had been so focused on leadership he had not realized the extent of his losses. Civilian losses more than matched the total of that suffered by the defenders. Old women and preteens who had never fired a rifle were picking up weapons and silently taking places on the lines with the surviving defenders. Steve replaced his much-needed rear guard and flank guards with those people, thinking all they needed to do was fire warning shots.

The stalemate continued throughout the night. Lan slept with her head on Steve's shoulder. Flares lit up the night sky to the east as Quang Tri was slowly cut off by surrounding forces. Pounding artillery was destroying the city. As he fell asleep, Steve wondered if Thach Hanh would be crushed between two enemy forces. The Marine was shaken awake by one of the drivers in the early morning hours. "Sarge needs you," the driver implored. "We've got a situation down at the east end."

Lan stirred. Steve laid her gently down on the rough and dirty surface of the bridge. He made his way to the end of the bridge. The problem was obvious right away. The Americans at the east end of the bridge were holding rifles on a ragtag bunch of Vietnamese soldiers. From their shoulder patches Steve was rather certain they were deserters from the 1st ARVN Division. Many of them had discarded their weapons. It was going to be a touchy situation.

Steve issued his first instruction when faced with the dilemma. "Sergeant, have your men form a line, rifles at the ready. Guard the bridge and the road down to the south end of the village. Leave the road to the north open."

Lan, thinking she might be needed as an interpreter, walked up to stand close to Steve.

"Watch them. There could be enemy infiltrators among them. Let one man through." Steve looked at the faces of scared men. He chose one. "That guy, the tall officer.

"Lan," he said, "interpret for me. Be firm but accurate in what I say." Steve turned and walked down the entire length of the bridge to the west end with the ARVN, Lan, and American soldier following. He stopped short of where the trucks had been hit by artillery early in the battle. With Lan translating, he made his point.

"Down this road you can see seventeen enemy tanks, all destroyed, along with their crews, that tried to take this bridge." He turned slightly, pointing again. "Out there are at least a dozen more destroyed tanks and many men who will never rise again." He pointed down the river where the bridge of the sunken barge could be seen. "They came at us in barges. That is what we did to them. Over one hundred men died in that vessel alone."

The Marine turned and pointed south. "This village will survive. We have food. We have weapons and ammunition. We have fierce determination. There's no place for cowards in this village," he said, remembering the stinging accusation from Lan of a few months in the past when he did not initiate action against an enemy force.

The ARVN officer cut loose with a venomous tirade. Lan responded in kind, speaking much too quickly for Steve to understand. Steve stepped forward until he was nose to nose with the officer, leaning over to achieve that position. "Tell him this, Lan," he said with bitterness hanging on every word. "We Americans came ten thousand miles to defend people like those in this village. Every one of them is Liet Si." He used the Vietnamese term for hero.

"We would not cross the street for cowards and deserters. If you try to pass on this bridge, you will die like those tanks. Return to Quang Tri and fight with honor or take that road to the north as your escape route."

Another shrill heated exchange followed. It continued as Steve and Lan escorted the soldiers all the way back to the end of the bridge. Steve ordered the ARVN soldiers not be allowed to pass through the perimeter lines. Lan was happy to translate his orders.

"No one passes this line," he instructed. If they try, shoot to kill. And shoot anyone who raises a weapon. They can return to Quang Tri, or they can take the road to the north. They have five minutes to clear that road before we start shooting anyone on it."

"Why don't we disarm them now? You know they may join the NVA and turn their guns on us," the MP said.

"I'd rather have them out there than inside our lines shooting us in the back."

"You don't trust them?"

"Of course not. I have no trust in or sympathy for cowards and deserters."

Steve and Lan returned to his post, but they could not sleep. She fixed canteen cups of C-ration hot chocolate and shared a tin of crème-filled cookies. Afterwards, Lan nestled against Steve again. It was where she felt most comfortable and safe. Although tempted, Steve kept his hands to himself. Before Lan could fall asleep, the still night was shattered by rifle fire. A fierce gun battle had been engaged between the South Vietnamese deserters and the North Vietnamese. Steve sprung to his feet, rifle in his hands, shouting, "Support them!"

Muzzle flashes gave away one's position in the dark. The Marines fired at those flashes. The engaged enemy forces were too busy countering the nearest threat to fully engage the bridge defenders. At Steve's orders, the machine guns remained silent, conserving ammunition. The firefight lasted for half an hour. During that time Steve had called for his baseball team to hurl grenades at any revealed target their arms could reach.

The third day of the bridge defense began before dawn with an attack the defenders had anticipated and prepared for. Staying in the cover at each side, a platoon of NVA soldiers stepped into the dirt road and charged uphill, firing their AK-47s as they came. If they took the east end of the bridge and could hold the crossroads, the defenders on the bridge would have to retreat to the west or die defending the bridge.

A machine gun and a dozen M-16 rifles firing on full automatic cut the attackers down. They never had a real chance. Their mass was compressed to a choke point. Those in the middle and rear of their ranks could not bring their weapons to bear on the defenders. As soon as those in front of them went down, they were exposed to the murderous gunfire.

In warfare, there is seldom a shutout in such exchanges. A commander has to learn to accept losses and hopes for a favorable report of light casualties versus high casualties among the enemy forces. That is the type of report Steve got. Seventy enemy KIA and three friendly, two Americans and a Vietnamese woman. "Take that, you bastards," Steve murmured.

The North Vietnamese took the day to reinforce, perhaps to rearm and certainly to reorganize and rethink their strategy. Steve drew out a map of the village with every house noted. Lan and the clerks helped him, pointing out features and proportions. Intermittently, shots rang out as a sniper spotted movement in the hamlet or on the bridge. The only result known was that a Marine was shot in the left arm. Lan treated his wound, and the man remained at his post. Lan and Steve returned to his command post.

"I wonder what he's up to now," the tall clerk told his companion. He found out shortly when he was selected to join a small group at the sandbagged command center. When he arrived Steve was packing explosives into a shoulder bag. He made a surprising announcement, starting with the map he had drawn. Using a red ink pen, he had added color to the map since anyone else had last seen it.

"These structures I've marked in red are known locations of the enemy forces. They seem to have pulled back just beyond our ability to throw grenades at them."

The map was passed around. Everyone took a hard look at it. "I'm going down there tonight."

Lan gasped.

"I need a couple of volunteers who can help me lay mines and booby traps right under their noses. I need a couple of sharp-eyed marksmen to protect us while we go about our business."

"Four men?" the clerk asked.

"Six would be better."

"What have you got in mind?"

"We are going to sneak down there, plant as many of our explosives as possible, and get back while it's still dark."

"How will you get in?"

"Not on the road, that's for sure. And not by swimming."

"What choices does that leave?"

"We go under the bridge along the escarpment to the south side. We infiltrate close and start laying our mines a block away from the red line where the enemy is known to be. We can't rig our mines for command detonation, so we rig them for pressure, for trip wires, using any ingenious thing we can think of."

"What have we got?"

"Plenty of Claymores, some bouncing Bettys, grenades, and C-4."

"What's your plan?"

"We use the simplest devices closest to the enemy."

"Trip wire and Claymores."

"Right! Quick and easy to set. You can place them in trees or doorways, at various heights, all virtually soundlessly."

"After the first one goes off, they'll be looking for our mines."

"That's why we do the simplest ones first. We work back toward our line, laying the more complicated mines as we move back. That way, if we are discovered or it gets late before we finish, we will have laid the maximum number of mines possible in that time period."

"How do we get them to run into the mines?"

"We don't throw any more grenades. I want them to think we are out. They know by now that we have no mortar shells."

Steve drew three red lines through the village. They all converged back at the west end of the bridge. "We work in two-man teams. One lays mines. The other covers him. Be prepared to get out of there if things go all to hell."

"I'm in," the tall man volunteered.

"Good. You lay mines."

Another mine layer volunteered. Each of the men chose a rifleman to act as his security.

"I go with Steve," Lan said.

"No, Lan. Not this time. Your people need you here." That, of course, was not his reason for not including her in his plans. The mission was simply too hazardous to expose the girl.

"Reassemble here at 2400 hours," Steve instructed. The raiders departed, leaving Steve alone with Lan. The girl reached behind her head and unclasped a gold necklace she always wore. A jade Buddhist pendant hung from the middle of it.

"You wear," Lan instructed. "It brings you much luck and many prayers."

Lan fastened the necklace around Steve's thick neck. It fit him like a choke collar, but he left it on. "I'll bring it back to you," he promised.

"Please. I love it very much."

Steve knew that was a double entendre he was not prepared to address. What has my lighthearted flirting brought about? He wondered.

"You sleep now," Lan told him. "I guard."

Midnight came too soon. Steve wiped the sleep from his eyes and went through his patrol protocol. No steel helmets for this mission. Grease paint covers faces, necks, and hands. Dog tags taped together. The explosives were carried in canvas shoulder bags usually used by the grenadier to carry his supply of rifle grenades.

From the west end, the Marine patrol went under the bridge along the small concrete escarpment and came up on a narrow strip of land on the north side of the village. Taking pre-selected routes that would limit their exposure to the enemy, the teams split up. Independently, they moved silently 100 meters deep into the hamlet. Steve's progress was slower. The NVA had a guard at the river. Steve spotted him when he became silhouetted against the skylight.

The Marines could not shoot the guard. They could not pass him and leave him in place. He would have to be taken out silently in hand-to-hand combat, meaning a combat knife attack. Steve began pulling the canvas bag carefully off his shoulder. A hand stayed him. The clerk pointed to himself. He laid down his rifle and pulled one of the famous leather-hilted K-bar fighting knives from a leg sheath.

Steve knew there had to be more to this clerk than he had let people know. Steve crouched down to cover his teammate. The man moved like a jungle cat on the hunt. As quietly as a creeping shadow, he closed to within six feet of his prey. This was the edge of the danger zone when some inexplicable sixth sense was most likely to thwart such attacks.

It is also the point of no return, the point where you launch your attack swiftly with deadly results. The K-bar was violently slammed into the Vietnamese soldier's kidney as a hand over his mouth stifled his startled cry. Borne to the ground face down, the stricken soldier could not see his attacker. The K-bar ripped through the kidney and stabbed down at the base of the man's neck, scrapping the collarbone. The next stab cut through the carotid artery. It took the soldier ten long seconds to die.

The team moved on, needing to make up for lost time. Fifty feet from the enemy red line, Steve laid his first Claymore. The mine was set to fire down the long axis of a dirt street. It was rigged with a thin, sand-colored trip wire pulled across the street at a height of three inches. It was quick and simple to set. Steve backed away, looking for a likely spot for his next mine.

He sacrificed his rifle. What enemy soldier wouldn't pick it up when he saw it laying there? The rifle was attached by a thin wire to a Claymore mine hidden in the fork of a tree branch. When pulled only half an inch the booby trapped rifle would set off the deadly mine. Another mine was rigged as a pressure plate device.

Further away, Steve dug into the road in an irregular pattern, planting Bouncing Betty mines. When stepped on, the mines would shoot three feet into the air before exploding. The mines were concussion-sensitive. One mine exploding in a field could set off most or all of them. Accordingly, Steve planted an alternating string of mines at the edge of the path where they were least likely to be stepped on. He went back to the center of the road, where he planted three mines in a bowling pin pattern forward of the mines to the flanks. If one of them was stepped on, all the mines would detonate, killing those who had passed by without stepping on the mines as well as the men all around the man who had stepped on the mine.

Steve laid surprise firing devices at an intersecting east-west road and south down the next intersection. There he laid mines back to the west and then another block south until he ran out of explosive devices. The team did not wait to meet up with the other mine-laying teams. Their job was to sneak in, lay their mines, and sneak back out undetected. That part of the plan was successful.

Steve could not remember breathing at all during the somewhat terrifying three-hour mission. Lan had fallen asleep. Steve needed to unwind to release pent-up energy. The scout, who was not a smoker or a drinker, drank beer at the restaurant while he checked on staff and supplies. The young girls who had been cooking for everyone had taken their place with rifles on the line. They had been replaced by three snaggle-toothed elderly women. Steve drank a Ba Mui Ba. Beer the Marines called "Tiger Piss."

The Marine stopped by his tent to shave, take a sponge bath and change his clothing. He took a moment to talk to Doctor Quoc who was concerned about his daughter. Steve promised to be her personal protector without treating her in a significantly different manner than he did the other girls in his CAP unit. Steve retrieved his backup weapon from a wooden locker.

He cleaned the rifle as he talked to the doctor. The medical facility was dangerously low on bandages and medications. "When you don't have anything left to work with, doctor, get your family out of here. Send for Lan. Take her with you. Take a fishing boat, any boat, and hide out in one of those channels along the river. If things get too tough on the bridge, I'll send Lan down to you."

Lan's mother gratefully took Steve's hand in her own. "Thank you," she said in a bit of the English Lan had taught her.

Steve's next stop was along the village street where he observed people preparing to depart. They would all flee to the south. He worked his way back to the bridge while formulating his next move. Lan met him at the bridge.

"See, I bring you good fortune," she said.

"Yes, you did." Steve moved to unclasp the necklace.

"No, you keep," she insisted firmly.

Steve took the girl by the hand, looking into her brown eyes. "Lan, I want you to leave. I've talked to your mother and father about it."

"No!" she insisted. "I stay with you. Where you go, I go."

"Ah, so now you say for me," Steve teased.

"No," Lan insisted somewhat tiredly. "I no say for you."

"I'm staying until the end, Lan. I may die here."

"You die, I die."

"But you mustn't, Lan. Please go."

"No, I cannot. I stay. We fight."

With that settled, the couple returned to the bridge command post. Steve took the map showing the streets and paths that had been booby-trapped. His plan, as revealed to the clerks, was repeated up and down the line. "Use your rifle fire to force them to take these avenues."

He addressed all who could hear his steady, low voice. "The civilians are beginning to give up. They are packing to move out. I know we are being watched from somewhere. I just don't know where. When daylight comes, I want it to appear that we only have two defenders at each end of the bridge and four on the line, including me and Lan.

"I want everyone else to go down into the village, appearing to be leaving. Instead, you'll hide out in the hootches closest to the bridge. Wait there. No fires, no cigarettes, no noise.

"Look at the map. When the NVA come charging out of those houses thinking they're going to overrun us, the six of us are going to force them into mine lanes with our firing patterns. When that general assault begins, our hidden soldiers will rush up to the bridge to add to the surprise and maybe break the back of this attack."

"I think that just might work," the older clerk affirmed.

"You two want to hold this end of the bridge? It could be dangerous. I can get you out of here; get you back to your typewriters."

The clerks laughed aloud. "We're just a couple of typewriter tigers," 'Pop' said, causing another peel of laughter from the taller Marine. "We'll stay."

The MP and the baseballers stayed as they would be needed to accurately throw the last of the grenade supply. Lan was now the only Vietnamese remaining on the bridge.

There were only three sets of eyeballs watching from the bridge throughout the night. Fortunately, there was no action. The CAP unit soldiers had seen enough. They knew they couldn't hold out much longer. Many of them were fleeing south with their families. The defenders had no mortar support. They were out of grenades and probably low on bullets and rations. The NVA were making their assault plans. The bridge was theirs. The final assault would begin at dawn.

Machine gun fire crowed minutes before the roosters stirred. Green tracer rounds filled the air above the bridge. Sandbags sagged as they lost their contents. Bag walls crumbled.

"Deep right field!" the MP yelled, announcing the direction of NVA forces on the move, apparently attempting a flanking maneuver. Accurately hurled grenades cut them off. The NVA fled from the barrage of hand-thrown explosives, moving south, right into a landmine ambush. The survivors tried to escape to the west, directly into a Claymore trap. This scene was being played out throughout the village. NVA unit commanders hesitated to move down any path. A barrage of grenades chased them back to their pre-assault positions with far fewer numbers and lower morale.

The standoff didn't last long. "Brown water Navy, coming in hot from the south! They want us to fire the enemy up to cover their approach," Pop called.

"Bring our people on line! It's OK Corral time," Steve answered.

The defenders fully manned the bridge. Steve rose and fired a full magazine on automatic. All the defenders followed suit. Rifle and machine gun fire, LAAWs, and grenades all covered the sounds of the vessels approaching on the river.

The Brown Water Navy ships were heavily armored and ugly with awkward angles. Steve didn't associate them with sleek modern warships. They sat low in the water like the first ironclads. In spite of all that, they had speed and power. M-91-2 and M-91-3 resembled a landing craft with a ramp at the bow. There was a bridge amidships with a helicopter landing pad on the fantail.

A fully contained three-inch naval gun was mounted on the forward starboard deck. A fifty-caliber machine gun was mounted atop the bridge. An odd-looking nozzle type of weapon had been installed opposite the naval gun. The ships began firing all weapons as soon as they cleared the bridge.

The enemy shifted their fire to the boats. Their bullets only scratched the armor. The fifties opened up, ripping through concrete cinder block homes as if they were made of rice paper. The naval guns completely destroyed houses among the village structures. The boat's most awesome weapon was the nozzle. It spat a stream of liquid fire, napalm, one hundred feet.

The village was reduced to flames and rubble. The boats passed the village, turned out of sight, and came back for another run. That allowed the NVA to fire all their weapons at the bridge in a desperate attempt to break out. There were enough of them to do some serious damage among the defenders. One after another, they fell. There was no corpsman to come to their aid, no chaplain to give them last rites or words of comfort.

Those who rushed to the side of the fallen did so in order to retrieve their ammunition, which was now in a critically low stage. An RPG round, one of many fired at the bridge, struck Steve's forward sandbagged wall. Although it absorbed the explosion and the resulting shrapnel, the wall fell apart into the river leaving him and Lan exposed.

The enemy gunners concentrated their return fire on the exposed couple. A machine gun bullet slammed into Steve's left thigh. His leg collapsed. He fell on top of Lan, knocking her down, actually saving her life in the process. He rolled off of her. With bullets flying only inches above their heads, Lan made a supreme effort to drag the Marine, who was more than twice her size, to safety. She pulled him into the next sandbagged position. There were no bandages, no medication. Lan ripped off her white blouse, shredding it into strips. Trying to stop the bleeding, she stuffed a strip into the wound in spite of Steve's cries of agony. She bound the wound tightly.

The battle was in the mopping-up stage, but it was not over yet. Steve knew the bridge had been held, but at a horrendous cost. Steve rolled to his stomach. He rose to a kneeling position and began firing his rifle at the remaining enemy forces. Return fire slackened as the enemy soldiers tried to escape and chose their targets carefully.

The clerks dove down below the sandbags and joined Steve and Lan. "How bad are you hit?" Pops asked.

"A deep scratch," Steve responded through clenched teeth.

"You did it, son, but don't worry. I've got it from here."

The tall man reached into his pocket. He retrieved a pair of oak leaves, which he began pinning to his collar. Steve was surprised, but not nearly as surprised as when 'pop' pinned the twin stars of a major general to his own collar.

"General, I don't understand."

"What's your rank, son?"

"Corporal. Corporal Steve Kowalski, general."

"Well, Corporal Kowalski, I'm new in the country. Just been here a few days. I've always believed the commander on site needs to be given an opportunity to prove himself and grow in the process. You achieved that quite well. Not only that, as the on-scene commander, you had the respect and loyalty of the people. You knew them. You knew their strengths and weaknesses. You were able to use that knowledge to get maximum efficiency of your resources by assigning the right person to the right job every time. I couldn't have done that on my own."

"Thank you, general."

"Don't thank me, corporal. We owe you our thanks and our gratitude. With the medals you're going to get and orders to OCS, you'll go far in the Marine Corps."

"Thank you, general, but I don't think the Marine Corps is the career for me."

"This will help you with a political career as well. Voters love a war hero."

"I plan to study architecture at Oklahoma State, General, on the G.I. Bill, of course."

"The Marine Corps' loss. I'm sure you'll be a fine architect."

"And I'll always be a Marine."

A burst of rifle fire whistled close by overhead. Lan rose to return fire. Two AK-47 rounds punched through her chest and flung her on her back to the ground where she lay gasping for breath. Steve dragged himself over to the badly wounded girl. He pulled her upper body to his own. "Oh, Lan, oh, no," he whispered.

The girl trembled. Her eyes had lost their focus.

"Lan! Stay with me, Lan!" Steve cried.

The girl's body convulsed. She vomited a stream of dark, frothy blood. Her lips quivered as she tried to speak. Steve leaned closer so he could hear her small voice.

Painfully, she whispered. "I say for you, Ha Shi Cau. My liet si. I say for you, warlord."